THE GOOD, THE BAD, AND THE NOT-HORSE

The American West was not the most miserable land I had ever traveled, but it came quite near to it. It was the scenery, more than anything, that drove the spirit out of the body—endless, empty plains that did not so much roll as slump with varying degrees of hopelessness, with barely a proper tree to be seen. The late summer sun beat the ground into something like the bottom of an oven.

"I grow weary of Kansas," said my not-horse. "The rivers here are scarcely enough to keep me alive."

"Hush, Karl," I said to the *näcken*. "We are near to town, and to the warlock. I would prefer if we did not announce our presence."

The *näcken* sighed with a great, exaggerated motion that set the saddle to creaking, and stomped one hoof on the ground. With a pure white coat and standing at a lean and powerful seventeen hands, he made a magnificent mount—as fast as the swiftest mortal horse and far more tireless. "As you wish, Anastasia."

"Warden Luccio," I reprimanded him tartly. "And the sooner we catch this creature and his master, the sooner you will have served your probation, and the sooner you may return to your homeland."

The *näcken* flattened his ears at this reminder of his servitude.

"Do not you become angry with me," I told him. "You promised to serve as my loyal mount if I could ride you for the space of an hour without being thrown. It is hardly my fault if you assumed I could not survive such a ride under the surface of the water."

"Hmph," said the *näcken*, and he gave me an evil glare. "Wizards."

—From Jim Butcher's "A Fistful of Warlocks"

BAEN BOOKS
edited by DAVID BOOP

Straight Outta Tombstone

To purchase Baen Book titles in e-book format,
visit www.baen.com

STRAIGHT ★ OUTTA ★ TOMBSTONE

Edited By
DAVID BOOP

STRAIGHT OUTTA TOMBSTONE

This is a work of fiction. All the characters and events portrayed in this book are fictional, and any resemblance to real people or incidents is purely coincidental.

"To Tony Hillerman, the first person
I ever wrote a weird western for.
You and your words are missed."
DB 04/12/17

CONTENTS

FOREWORD

David Boop

Collected here are stories from my idols, my mentors, my peers and my friends. When I sent out invitations, I asked each author to give me their favorite and/or most famous characters in all-new stories set in the Old West. They did not disappoint.

From Warden Luccio to Bubba Shackleford, they came. We get a visit from Mad Amos, and Dan Shamble shambles by. A barmaid lives up to her name "Trouble," and a dragon named Pete wants to court the sacrificial girl, not kill her. Chance Corrigan, Hummingbird and Inazuma, Bose Roberds. Never before have these characters shared the stage like this. Cowboys and Dinosaurs. Adventurers and Aliens. Time-Traveling Samurai and Clockwork Gunslingers. Vampires. Zombies. They're all in here.

Why weird *Westerns*, though?

Well, because unbeknownst to many, the genre has a long, proud history these creators all wanted to be a part of.

Do you remember the *Wild, Wild West* TV series? Maybe you read *Jonah Hex*, the *Two-Gun Kid* or other cowboy comics. Did you, like me, watch old B-movies and serials such as *Valley of the Gwangi* and *The Phantom Empire* on Saturday afternoon TV? How many of you snuck to the living room once your parents were asleep to see *Billy the Kid Versus Dracula* during a late-night movie monster marathon on Halloween? I certainly did. Seriously, there are far more weird Westerns out there than you can imagine. So much so, somebody filled an entire encyclopedia of them.

The Encyclopedia of Weird Westerns by Paul Green [McFarland; 2nd ed. February 25, 2016] explores a whole cottage (*cabin?*) industry that stretches back to the earliest days of the American West. Did you know one of the first dime novels published in the U.S. would be considered steampunk by today's standards? *The Steam Man of the Prairies* is a fictional account of a man crossing the West in a carriage pulled by a thirty-foot steam-driven robot.

Researching the titles listed in Green's encyclopedia, I met many new characters cut from the same piece of rawhide as two of my favorite protagonists: Indiana Jones and Brisco County Jr.

And now, thanks to the authors represented here, you are about to meet a few of them yourself.

So, find a comfy chair, kick up your spur-heeled boots, and relax as we return to the dust-covered land of ancient magics, mysterious creatures and pioneers hell-bent on survival.

Welcome back to the Old West.

DB 12/16

STRAIGHT ★ OUTTA ★ TOMBSTONE

BUBBA SHACKLEFORD'S PROFESSIONAL MONSTER KILLERS

Larry Correia

Bubba Shackleford got off the train in Wyoming, eager to find some cannibals to shoot. He loved his job.

The town was bigger than he'd expected. With the hard scrabble frontier behind them, Cheyenne had turned into another bustling center of American commerce. The platform was crowded with folks coming and going, giving the place an industrious feel. It took a hardy people, tough as nails, to civilize this rugged a land, but they'd still be scared to death if they knew what manner of evil was breathing down their necks.

Then Bubba noticed the signs. Weary eyes from staying up all night keeping watch. Nervous glances sent in the direction of every stranger. No children running about. And an unusual number of cheap wooden coffins stacked in front of the undertaker's. Yes, sir, Cheyenne had itself a monster problem.

This was his company's first monster killing contract in the West, and the furthest he'd ever been from home.

1

He was a southern man, born and bred, so he didn't care for the way the air here was dry and sharp enough to make his nose bleed, or the way everything as far as the eye could see was so unrelentingly *brown*. It was March, and there was still dirty snow piled in the shade. Wyoming struck him as a harsh and unforgiving land, nothing like his blessed green home in Alabama. For the life of him he couldn't figure out why anyone would want to live in such a godforsaken waste.

"Wyoming sure is pretty!" Mortimer McKillington exclaimed as he lumbered down the train's metal steps.

"You say so, Skirmish." He'd hired the big Irish strongman because he'd figured anyone tough enough to be a New York bare-knuckle fighting champ *might* be hard enough to be a good monster hunter. He was, and then some. Over the last year Skirmish—as his friends called the freckled giant—had proven not only to be good with monster killing, but also an obnoxiously optimistic traveling companion.

"I do." Skirmish took a deep breath, expanding his barrel chest. "Ah, smell that fresh air."

It smelled like horseshit and coal smoke to him. "Have the boys unload the animals and wagons. I'll look for our client."

"Cheer up, boss. This is an adventure."

"I'll be cheery once we put these man-eating bastards in the ground."

"And we get paid."

"*And* we get paid." Because battling the forces of evil was rewarding and all, but on its own paid for shit. Now having a big company like the Union Pacific give them a sack full of gold coins to kill the monsters damaging their tracks? That was much nicer.

He didn't have to search for long, because his new clients immediately sought him out. They'd known which train he was on, and Bubba Shackleford did tend to stand out in a crowd. They must have been given his description, which was usually some variation of tall, broad shoulders, narrow waist, long mustache, probably looks like he's ready to shoot somebody. The words short-tempered and pragmatic often made it in there too, but Bubba didn't mind. Establishing a proper reputation went a long way in the monster killing business.

Two men were pushing through the crowd, heading his way, one fat, one thin, both in tailored suits remarkably free of grime. The round fellow in the bowler hat had the look of a businessman. He pegged the one that looked like a tubercular rat as a government man. They all tended to have that same disapproving air about them.

"Excuse me, sir. Are you the monster killer, Bubba Shackleford?" the plump one asked. Before Bubba could so much as nod, he was already getting his hand vigorously shaken. The businessman's hand was very soft. "I can't believe an actual monster killer, here!"

"Keep it down about the *monster* business, Reginald," the thin one hissed as he glanced around.

"I'm Reginald Landon of the Union Pacific. Welcome to Wyoming, Mr. Shackleford. We're so glad you made it on time! This is Mr. Percival from the governor's office."

Whenever a hunter got this warm of a welcome in civilized society, it meant things had gotten desperate. "From your harried demeanor, gentlemen, I assume there's been another event since our last telegram?"

The company man gave him a grave nod. "People have been disappearing after dark. They hit one of our depots west of town last night. Four men dead, ripped limb from limb and their flesh consumed by the ice-hearted beasts."

"Perhaps we should retire to someplace more private to discuss the matter," Mr. Percival stated, as he watched Bubba's men unloading crates of ammunition from the train. "Washington was very specific that this needs to be dealt with *discreetly*."

"Discretion is the general rule for this sort of affair," Bubba agreed.

The McKinley administration was adamant that monster problems be kept from the general public's knowledge. Good thing too, because otherwise the quiet handlers of said problems, such as himself, would be out of business.

"The Army sent a patrol from Fort Russell in reprisal, but the soldiers never returned." Landon looked around at the crowd, then leaned in conspiratorially, presumably so as to not cause a panic. "The Indians are saying the poison woman has come back from the dead to curse us. This is the handiwork of *Plague of Crows*."

He'd heard that name. A legendary evil back from the grave? Bubba pondered on that new fact for a moment. "Gentlemen, we may need to revisit the amount of my fee."

Whenever some foul abomination started eating folks the common response was to gather up a bunch of brave men to track the beast down. That often worked, but killing monsters was dangerous work and too many of those brave men didn't come home. A vigilante mob could usually get the job done, but often at a terrible cost. That was how Bubba Shackleford had first been exposed to the supernatural, and it was only through luck and pluck that it hadn't culminated in a massacre.

The more civilized a place was, the more likely monsters became the law's problem to deal with. Only there was a heap of difference between dispensing justice to some run of the mill murdering outlaw and something like a foul nosferatu, or a flying murderer bat, or a tentacle bear. There were a handful of sheriffs and marshals of his acquaintance who were worth a damn against the hell spawn forces of evil, but most were sadly lacking.

The Army? They had the bravery and the guns, but they were the most hidebound and hamstrung bunch of all. Every monster was different, and if you wanted to beat them, you needed to learn fast and adapt faster. Soldiers were always useful, but best when led by an officer with the wit to grasp the inconceivable, and the freedom to get the job done. Good luck with that!

The first time Bubba had killed a monster, he'd made a bit of a name for himself, and strangely enough job offers had begun to arrive. It turned out there was always some critter causing trouble somewhere. The work suited him, not to mention it was *far* better money than farming. It was a fine job, provided you didn't mind extreme violence, physical discomfort, and the constant looming threat of death. Those early years had been more miss than hit, but he'd survived while the things he was chasing usually didn't.

In time he had joined forces with other men uniquely suited to the monster killing arts. Bubba had never aspired to leadership, but they all looked to him for guidance. Until one day he'd found himself the official boss and owner of a real company.

It was purely by accident that Bubba Shackleford's Professional Monster Killers had become the most successful—albeit possibly only—company of its kind. His operation was above the rest because of knowledge, dedication, and preparation, but above all else, it was because they possessed an adaptability of the mind. The supernatural could neither surprise nor confound them. They could not be shaken.

Their attention was undivided.

Killing was their business.

Rooms had been provided at a hotel near the station, but most of his men were at the local saloons, and would probably drag themselves in sometime before dawn. There would be drinking, gambling, whoring, and possibly some fighting, but hopefully no hanging offenses committed because he couldn't spare the manpower.

Bubba Shackleford sat alone at the hotel bar, in front of the same glass of whiskey that had been sitting untouched for the last hour. In his hands were the telegrams that had been waiting for him at the Western Union office. They were all from his secret weapon, the Scholar.

He still didn't know the Scholar's identity, just where to send messages to reach him. Hell, the name Scholar had come about because the only signature on the letters he had received had been the letter S, and the name fit. The notes had arrived shortly after Bubba's reputation as a monster killer had spread among those in the know. Whoever S was, he wanted to keep his identity secret, and he seemed to know damn near everything there was to know about certain kinds of monsters. Bubba figured that S was probably an employee of the government who would be jailed if word got out he was telling secrets. One of McKinley's agents had confided in him that the reason they kept monsters secret was something about how the more folks believed, the stronger monsters got. Bubba didn't know about that. It sounded like horseshit to him, but as long as the government contracts paid on time, he didn't care.

Repeatedly he had tried to pay for the information provided, but Scholar would have none of it. His reasons for helping remained his own. Regardless of his mysterious motivations, Scholar was right more often than not, and some of his clues had proven vitally helpful in the past.

The first telegram had been sent a couple of days into their train ride.

DESCRIPTION MATCHES INDIAN LEGEND OF CHENOO ONCE HUMAN CURSED HEART SLOWLY TURNS TO ICE CAUSING MADNESS CANNIBALISM AND MUTATION WILL RESEARCH AND REPORT —S

Chenoo was a new term for him, but Bubba wasn't familiar with the legends of this region. He'd need to remedy that. There was nothing quite as unpleasant as coming across a new beastie and having it suddenly squirt flaming blood out its eyes at you, or discover that bullets just bounced off its hide. Though Scholar seemed to know a lot, many critters still remained complete unknowns.

The most recent telegram had arrived yesterday.

HAVE RETAINED SERVICES EXPERT REGIONAL FOLKLORE WILL CONTACT IN CHEYENNE CHENOO EXTREMELY DANGEROUS USE UTMOST CAUTION RAYMOND —S

Strangely enough, Scholar was about the only person around who still used Bubba's birth name. Even his sainted mother had given up on Raymond years ago. Bubba paused to drink his whiskey, which wasn't half bad since it had been imported all the way from Tennessee. The Union Pacific rep had made no mention of any knowledgeable types in town, so he could only assume the man hadn't arrived yet. Sometimes the so-called experts were right about monster vulnerabilities, and sometimes they were wrong, but it usually beat flipping a coin.

He heard boots on wood, and turned to see that one of his men had returned to the hotel. Balthazar Abrams had been one of the first of the professional killers, hired because he'd been quick enough with a knife to leave a ghoul in pieces in a New Orleans alley, and proven indispensable ever since.

"Telegrams? You heard from the Scholar, Boss?"

Bubba motioned for him to take the stool next to him.

"Things we're hunting are called Chenoo. Used to be men, but their hearts turn to ice. I doubt that's a metaphor."

"Things used to be men, they're the worst. So these Chenoo alive, dead, or atwixt the two?"

"I don't rightly know, but Scholar's sending us an expert." The proprietor had heard the conversation and come wandering back in from the kitchen. "Bartender, another whiskey, and one for my friend here."

The bartender paused when he saw Abrams, and a look of surprise came over his face. "This is an upscale establishment, Mr. Shackleford. We don't cater to his kind here."

Abrams had been born a slave, but he'd been a free man for over three decades, and was as good at killing monsters as his best white man—who happened to be Irish—and frankly Bubba didn't care what some pencil dick thought about any of his crew.

"Pour or I'll come over that bar and pistol whip you to within an inch of your life." He used the coldly casual tone he normally reserved for contract negotiations or ordering executions.

"What? I'll get the sheriff!"

"Tell him he'd best bring friends."

The way Bubba stated that must have made it abundantly clear that he meant every word. The bartender swallowed hard, fetched a bottle and another glass, poured them both a—very shaky—shot, and then fled to the back room.

Bubba took another drink. "I cannot abide a man lacking in hospitality."

"I swear, you're going to pick a fight that gets us killed one of these days," Abrams muttered.

"More than likely." He passed the telegrams over so that Abrams could read them. Every man in his crew was literate, and if they weren't when he hired them, they were expected to learn fast. Abrams was a sharp one and, since he was good at ciphering, even trusted to balance the company books. For the rest, he didn't care if they could read the Bible, but they'd at least be able to decipher the instruction manual for an unfamiliar explosive device and retain their fingers.

"When the Scholar is warning you to be careful, you know it's bad."

"The fat man from the railroad told me some stories about what happened to their workers. Something's been prying up track to derail trains. A work crew went out, got attacked. Only a few made it back alive, but the town doc never seen the like of what happened to those. The curse starts with a chill they just can't shake, then it crawled in them, deeper and deeper. Settles in the heart, they say. The afflicted act like they're freezing to death, always shivering, like they needed to get something warm in their belly. They tried hot soup, whiskey, but they only got crazier and meaner, insisting that the only thing would make them warm again was drinking hot blood, and then most couldn't talk at all. They became nothing but animals."

"Unfortunate," Abrams said as he unconsciously shifted his stool a little closer toward the fire.

"By the time they get the look of a man froze to death, they'd turned pure evil. Most of them lost their minds, killed some folks, and fled. They're still out there. One barely kept his mind, saw what he'd done, got down on his knees and begged for death. They put nearly forty bullets in him 'fore he expired."

"And that one asked for it. Imagine what the ones who don't want to die are like."

"From the way that whole Army patrol disappeared, I'd say they're stridently opposed to the idea. Locals think this is Plague of Crows' doing."

Abrams gave a low whistle at that name. Everybody in their field had heard of her. She'd raised unholy terror in this region when the railroad had first come through. It had taken a lot of blood and treasure to stop her the last time. "You renegotiated our pay, right?"

"Damn right I did."

A young lady walked into the room. It was a bit odd to see a girl of such an age, probably not even twenty, out at this late hour of the night, unescorted. However, from the way she was openly and brazenly wearing a gun belt and matching Colts over her skirts, she didn't seem the type inclined to be chaperoned.

She spotted Bubba, took a moment to compose herself, and walked toward them wearing a look of intense concentration. She was a dark haired, big boned, solid country girl. Bubba nodded politely. "Ma'am."

"Mr. Shackleford, sir." Apparently she had done her research. She stopped before them, cleared her throat and spoke loudly, as if she was giving a prepared presentation. "I'm Hannah Stone."

"Are you our regional folklore expert?" Abrams asked.

"Huh? No." That question seemed to throw her off of

her prepared remarks. "What?" The poor girl looked rather nervous. "I don't know what that is."

"Drink?" Bubba offered, because that seemed the gentlemanly thing to say, and Southerners had a reputation to keep up.

"No thanks. Makes the hands shake, can't shoot as good." She took a deep breath before blurting out, "I'm applying to join your gang."

Bubba shared a look with his perplexed associate. "*Gang* makes it sound like we're here to rob the bank."

"I know what you do! I've seen monsters. I know they're real."

He had entertained variations of this conversation a hundred times. Would-be monster hunters were constantly knocking on his door looking for work—he turned most of them away, probably doing them a favor—but he always kept an eye out for talent. Only this was his first ever employment petition from a lady.

It was inconceivable. It was one thing having a man's death on his conscience, but he couldn't imagine sending a girl to her doom. "I'm sorry. We ain't hiring now."

But she was a determined sort. "Word is that you're always looking for sharpshooters. I'm the best shot you'll find in this state and I need the work. I figure a man who'll hire Negroes, Mexicans, and Irish might hire a woman." She looked at Abrams. "No offense."

"None taken." Abrams seemed rather amused by the whole thing. "Our Irishman's not so bad."

"I've done men's work before. I used to work for Buffalo Bill Cody. Mr. Cody said if a woman could do the same work as a man, no reason she couldn't, and get paid for it too."

"Buffalo Bill? Wait . . . Hannah Stone. I've heard of you!" Abrams clapped his hands with glee. "We're in the presence of a celebrity, boss. Annie Oakley taught her to shoot."

"Mr. Cody made that up for the show. I already knew how to shoot when I got there and I was a much better shot than *her*." It was obvious Hannah was not fond of her supposed mentor. "But she was more famous and popular because she was better at the talking part . . . and show business . . . and generally liking people."

Well, she certainly wasn't a cup of sunshine. Bubba remembered her story now. It had been in the papers all over the place.

"Way I heard it told is you got fired from Buffalo Bill's Wild West show because there was an accident and your partner got hurt."

Hannah thought about how to phrase her response for a long moment. "The events which occurred could be described in such a manner."

"You were supposed to quick draw, shoot from the hip, and knock a cigarette from out of this fella's mouth at ten paces."

"Twenty. The crowd always loved that trick. We did it plenty of times. Last show there was some . . . extenuating complications."

"That's some mighty big words to say you blew his lips off."

"Well, in my defense, Mr. Shackleford, Bob was being awful shaky that day. I'd warned him not to skip breakfast."

Bubba didn't know what to say. Hannah remained standing there, awkwardly. She tried to smile. It looked painful. He felt bad for her. But not bad enough to give her a job that would just get her killed. "It was a pleasure to meet you, Ms. Stone, but truly, you've been misinformed as to my company's intentions. Good luck in your endeavors and good night."

Hannah's eyes narrowed to a determined squint. "Well fine then." She stomped away.

Abrams waited until the surly young woman was gone before he picked up his whiskey and chuckled. "Women hunting monsters? Imagine that. Next thing you know they'll want to vote!"

When Bubba finally retired to his hotel room, he nearly shot the Scholar's expert on regional folklore.

He'd used a key to open the door, walked into the darkened room, paused . . . and immediately drew his Colt and leveled it at the shadows in the corner. He thumbed back the hammer. He couldn't see her, but it was a woman's voice that came out of the darkness.

"How'd you sense I was here?"

Bubba never knew. It was just instinct, but it seldom led him astray. And right now his instinct was telling him whatever was in the shadows of his room was *very* dangerous. "Come out where I can see you."

"I don't belong in the light. You pull that trigger and you won't live long enough to regret it."

"Lady, if you think I'm the one who'll be regretting matters, you must be unfamiliar with how bullets operate."

"Do not test my patience, Raymond Shackleford. I have been asked to help guide you. I am not your enemy. The one you call Scholar and I have made a deal."

"Well, ain't that something?" Any monster hunter worth his salt learned not to make deals with voices in the dark. His eyes were adjusting, and now he could barely make out a narrow female shape, but his gut was telling him this wasn't no normal woman. Only Scholar hadn't let him down yet, so he held his fire. "Who are you?"

"Mohtahe Okohke. The white man calls me by a different name."

"Plague of Crows," Bubba muttered. Witch. Necromancer. She'd sacrificed the living, raised the dead, scourged the plains, and terrorized both settlers and Indians both. "Plague of Crows died."

"Briefly. Only do not fear. My war is over. I've made peace with your kind for now. The death that's upon this people is not my doing. Not too far from Granite Springs there is a new mine dug. Inside, a Stonecoat slept, until they blasted into his home. He made the ice hearts, and their curse will spread until his anger is spent."

He kept the Colt on her. "What's a Stonecoat?"

"A spirit of deep earth and cold streams, with skin like rock and slush for blood. Bad medicine, Raymond Shackleford."

"How do I kill him?"

"Even if you make it through his Chenoo, you can't kill a spirit. And you will probably die in the attempt."

"If it was easy, they wouldn't need someone like me."

"There have always been warriors like you, Raymond. The Stonecoat may no longer recognize this world, but he will recognize you, *if* you are brave enough. If he sees there is still worthy strength in this world, the spirit can return to his rest." Two glowing white orbs appeared in the shadows. Her eyes were too unblinking and round.

"That's all?"

"It is enough. Now my part of the bargain is done. I go to collect what is mine."

Suddenly there weren't just two lights, but dozens of glowing eyes from head to toe. A terrible screech filled his ears, a rush of air, and then he was surrounded in beating wings. Talons scratched him as the stream of thrashing birds poured past, through the open door, into the hall, and down the stairs. Bubba heard the proprietor scream incoherently as the flock of crows burst out the front door and into the night.

Damn it, Scholar. What have you gotten me into?

Bubba Shackleford lowered the hammer, holstered his gun, brushed the black feathers off his bed, and went to sleep.

The professional monster killers set out early the following morning.

It wasn't until Bubba got dressed that he realized Plague of Crows had scratched two words into the hotel room's wall for him. The proprietor was going to love that. The witch had also left him a present. It was a stick. It had been colorfully painted and had some beads and feathers on it, but it was still just a stick. He pondered on the short message for a bit, took up his fancy new stick, and went downstairs to get some coffee.

Outside the men prepared. Despite the governor's

admonition to keep things quiet, their two armored war wagons always attracted some attention. The odd-looking combinations of wood and sheet metal were far lighter than they looked, mostly because—to the contrary of what most bystanders assumed—they weren't designed for stopping bullets, but rather were to provide emergency shelter from tooth and claw. He had built a war wagon heavy enough to stop rifle bullets once, but it had been such a pain in his ass on the one hunt they'd tried it on—they'd spent so much time getting it stuck in the mud and exhausting horses—Bubba had abandoned it in a Mississippi field to rust.

Each wagon was pulled by a full hitch of sturdy Clydesdales. It appeared that they'd made the long trip just fine, and were eager to get to work. Bubba always used his own horses, and never counted on local stock. Most horses weren't worth spit when monsters started howling and blood started flying, so he stuck to animals of a proven calm nature. The rest of the men were on horseback, of various breeds, but all of sound temperament. Bubba hated losing animals almost as much as he hated losing men.

In addition to the small crowd who had gathered around to poke at the war wagons and ask questions his men weren't likely to answer truthfully, he spied the young sharpshooter, Hannah Stone. She was down the street, sitting on a horse and watching them. She was wearing a big hat, a duster, men's trousers—no awkward side saddle for her—and appeared outfitted for a long journey, which immediately gave Bubba a bad feeling. So he wandered over.

"Good morning, Ms. Stone."

"Mr. Shackleford."

She was wearing at least two revolvers he could see, there appeared to be a whippet gun hung from a rope beneath her coat, a Winchester repeater in a scabbard on one side, and a longer buffalo rifle in a scabbard on the other. There were shells poking out of every pocket. On the balance it was enough lead and steel that he felt bad for her horse.

"That's an awful lot of firearms upon your person this morning, Ms. Stone."

"Well, I wasn't sure which ones I'd be requiring today, Mr. Shackleford, so I brought an assortment. I'm going for a ride."

"To where?"

"Wherever the wind carries me."

More like wherever the Chenoo carried her off to eat her. The obstinate little girl intended to follow them looking for monsters. "There's dangerous things out there right now, Ms. Stone. I wouldn't advise such a course."

"I've killed a monster before."

"I don't doubt that, but did you go looking for it?"

"Well . . ." That gave her pause. "No. It was self-defense. But I'm still going out today."

"I ought to make you stay."

"And how do you think you're going to do that, Johnny Reb? I'm sure the good folks of Cheyenne would love to watch some stranger try and carry off a local girl on his back like some manner of barbarian. Or you going to have me arrested for riding my horse on a public street?"

She had him there. "You are remarkably stubborn."

"I prefer the term steadfast. Like a rock."

Like a pain in my ass. "Suit yourself." He went back to the wagons, wondering how guilty he was going to feel when she got herself eaten by Chenoo.

Garlick was driving the lead wagon, and Pangle was manning its potato digger. Hagberg and Abrams were on the second wagon and its gun respectively. Bubba, Skirmish McKillington, Hub Bryan, and Mexican George were on horseback. Two always ahead of the wagons, and two behind, taking turns eating trail dust. Four trained hunting dogs ranged about, chasing rabbits, happy to not be on a train. One sharp whistle would bring the dogs back and put them to work. They had spare horses, spare guns, enough ammunition to hold a small war, and every totem, trinket, and supposedly magical whatsit you could think of, from half a dozen faiths, some of which might even be helpful.

As the wagons rumbled along the dirt road, Bubba pondered on using his growing wealth to purchase one of those newfangled "automobiles" with a gasoline engine that he'd been reading about, just to see what kind of weapons and armor he could mount on one to see if it was any good for monster hunting. He was an innovative sort like that.

He had a map, the directions were clear, and there was easy road the whole way. Even with the lumbering war wagons, Granite Springs was a leisurely day's ride. They would arrive a few hours before sundown. Taking their time would ensure the horses were recovered from the train ride, and his men from their hangovers.

So they rode until the afternoon, found an abandoned homestead that made for a good defensible position, and parked the wagons in front of it. From the dried blood and scraps of clothing inside the cabin, the Chenoo had already taken the previous residents.

They mounted the potato diggers on the war wagons' roofs, rolled out their cannon, and made camp. Bubba set watches, then ordered the construction of a bonfire sufficient to be seen for miles. It would drive off the lingering chill and also hopefully attract some Chenoo. Plague of Crows had made the Stonecoat sound territorial, so maybe it would show itself. If that didn't work, they'd hit the mine early in the morning.

While his men worked, Bubba climbed atop a war wagon and scanned the horizon with his telescope. There was one rider in the tall grass behind them. Hannah Stone really had followed them. "Aw, damn it."

"What is it, boss?" Skirmish shouted at him. "We got Chenoo?"

"Worse. Job applicant." He'd been hoping she would get a little bit out of civilization and get cold feet, because it took guts to ride through the wilderness quiet and alone while you knew monsters were lurking about, but no. She was too hard headed for that. It would be dark soon. It was one thing to brave Chenoo in his fortified encampment, but one girl alone on the plains would be easy pickings.

"You want that I should scare her off?" Skirmish offered helpfully.

"She's likely to shoot you. I've got this." Bubba climbed off the wagon, whistled for a dog, and walked to where he'd tied his horse. "I leave her out there alone and she's gonna die."

"Well, that would certainly learn her," Skirmish shouted after him.

As he rode, there was an awful screech on the wind, a sound so angry and hungry that it caused all the hair on his arms to stand up. His hunting dog, Beaux, began to whimper. There were Chenoo near and hunting. If he sent Stone away, she'd never make it back to town before dark, and some of the nearer homesteads might not be much safer abodes. He reached her a few minutes later. Stone was riding, wary, with her repeating rifle in her hand. She'd heard the scream too.

As Bubba drew near, he loudly hailed her, so as to avoid ending up like poor lipless Bob. "Damn your obstinate hide, girl. I can't believe you're going through with this."

"Yep." She was scared—probably regretting her choice now that the Chenoo were making a bunch of racket nearby—but on the balance, mostly smug. "You want another gun hand yet?"

"Well, you ain't hired, that's for damn sure. But come on. You're at least staying close for safety."

Bubba Shackleford really couldn't abide a failure of hospitality.

The shrieks had increased in intensity, and they were much closer now. The sounds were blood curdling. Abrams and McKillington already had everyone in position and the bonfire was raging as Bubba and Hannah came tearing in at a full gallop.

Bubba pointed out the men for Hannah. "You've met Balthazar Abrams already. The big one with the freckles is Skirmish McKillington. The real ugly fella with one eye is Sid Hagberg, loves himself some dynamite. The scarecrow-looking one is Orson K. Pangle, esquire, solid with a gun. Harvey Garlick is the little one that used to be a preacher, pay him no mind if he gets spun up. Hub Bryan was a good cowboy but better monster killer. And Mexican George is over there on lookout, but he's our best rider and a crack shot."

"Why do you call him Mexican George?"

"Because nobody in Alabama would call him Whore Hay. We had two Georges at first, though White George got his hand bit off and quit, so I suppose it could be just George now, but it stuck."

Hannah took in the roaring bonfire, and the position of the wagons. "You want the monsters to see you. You're trying to draw them in."

Perceptive. "More I can draw off tonight, less I have to fight tomorrow inside a mineshaft. The dogs will warn us if they get close, and then we turn their ambush back on them."

"The doc told me they had to shoot that one cursed ice heart forty times," Hannah pointed out.

One of Scholar's telegrams told of an Indian legend where you had to shoot a Chenoo in the heart with seven arrows for it to die, but he was a man of the modern industrial age. Bubba gestured at the machine gun mounted atop the nearest war wagon. "That's what those are for."

Hanna looked at the Colt-Browning M1895

suspiciously. "Heard of these things. Seems wasteful, spraying all those bullets over the countryside."

Of course a sharpshooter would feel threatened by the idea of being replaced by volume. "Bullets are cheaper than men and I'd rather spend brass than blood. They'll probably attack in the middle of the night. We let the Chenoo come to us through a wall of hot lead, and then you can do your thing. Try to listen for once, and you might live 'til morning." He began to walk away.

It appeared that it was beginning to sink in that she'd gotten herself into some dire circumstances. He had to admit he was enjoying her discomfort. It was one thing to talk about hunting monsters, but it was entirely different when you could actually *hear* them.

"Wait, Mr. Shackleford, where are you going?"

"To eat supper and get some sleep before my watch."

A Chenoo screeched. She jumped. This one had to be less than a quarter mile away. The hunting dogs began barking in response. "You can sleep through that?"

"Well they ain't going to get this over with any faster if I'm tired with a growling stomach. Sleep well, Ms. Stone."

The Chenoo struck in the darkest hour.

The shrieking had stopped after midnight. Since the monster killers knew they were still out there watching, the quiet was worse than the noise. Only their dogs were well trained, so when the monsters tried to sneak up, rather than barking, they pointed. Hub Bryan and Orson Pangle were on watch, and they'd immediately gone to waking everyone else up.

The men got out of their bedrolls without a sound, guns already in hand. Bubba had slept in his boots and the thick leather coat that served as armor against claws and teeth. He signaled everyone to move into position. Low and slow, his killers got ready. The last person he woke up was Hannah, because he didn't want her startled and making enough noise to warn the Chenoo. Only by the time he crawled over, she was already sitting up, next to a wheel on a war wagon, eyes wide, watching the swaying underbrush and shadows cast by their huge fire.

"Couldn't sleep," she whispered.

Bubba was perfectly well rested, but he'd done this sort of thing a lot.

He spotted something white and glistening moving through the brown grass. The Chenoo may have lost their human reason, but they were still animal cunning. They were moving toward the homestead's corral, probably to slaughter their horses, so there could be no escape. But he'd been ready for such a move, and one of the machine guns was already pointed that direction.

It was his first look at the monsters. Some were still shaped like men, only with skin so white they near glowed, and their flesh pulled tight over pointed bones, lips drawn back to show their naked teeth, red eyes bulging from their sockets. Some of those were still wearing scraps of their Army uniforms. The ones who'd been cursed longer, they weren't men at all anymore, but all twisted up, hands like claws, stooped like apes, speckled with spurs of bone and blue pustules, and giving off so much cold that the dew had frozen to them in shimmering sheets of ice, that cracked and left sparkling dust as they stalked forward.

Shivering despite the bonfire, Bubba knocked on the side of the wagon. "You got company, Balt. Far end of the corral. Get to threshing." Then using hand signals he told the others to keep watching their appointed fields of fire. "Now!"

Abrams popped his head and shoulders out the hatch on the top of the wagon, and took up the potato digger's grip. The gun's nickname came from the reciprocating lever under the barrel, which would dig a hole in the dirt if you were shooting it prone. He'd had to repeatedly assure Skirmish that "potato digger" wasn't some Yankee insult toward the Irish. Fire blossomed out the end of the potato digger in a continuous roar. Pangle must have seen something on the other side of the homestead, because he opened up with his machine gun too, and now both of them were burning money into noise. Bullet after bullet slammed into Chenoo, ripping off chunks, and flinging them down, jerking and twitching. Their blood flowed like slush.

"Goodness gracious! That was magnificent!" Hannah shouted as both guns ran through their belts. Sharpshooter snobbery only went so far in the face of such magnificent destruction. "I need one of those!"

If only the Chenoo were so easily impressed, but the rest of the monsters sprang up from their hiding places and rushed the homestead. Bubba realized that this wasn't a raid. This *horde* was every missing person in the region. Their unearthly screams pierced the night as the spirit-haunted husks rushed across the fields. All of the Hunters started shooting, working levers and bolts as fast as they could.

The monsters were tough to kill, and for each one dropped, others gained ground. Most of his men were shooting new Krag-Jorgenson rifles, which were fast to load, but they couldn't keep up with this onslaught. Surprisingly, Hannah was as good as her show biz reputation suggested, and she was working her Winchester's lever as quick as a sewing machine's needle, methodically putting slugs through hearts and heads. Pangle and Abrams got their potato diggers reloaded, and their volume of fire increased dramatically again.

He saw where several Chenoo had bunched up to climb the fence, and shouted for Skirmish to fire the cannon. It was loaded with grape shot. The big man yanked the cord. There was a deafening boom and when the boiling cloud of smoke cleared out, there was nothing but a pile of splinters and frozen meat where they'd been standing.

Skirmish moved to reload the cannon, but before he could do so, a *boulder* fell out of the sky and smashed it flat. His man sprang back to his feet, astonished but in one piece. However, their cannon was a goner. Did these damned things have a *catapult* or something?

No. It was worse. Bubba spotted where the big rock had come from. And it hadn't been launched. It had been *thrown*. The being was a hundred yards away, vaguely shaped like a man, only ten feet tall and wide as a wagon.

"What is that?" Hannah Stone shouted.

"Stonecoat," he answered. And there was no path through the mass of rushing Chenoo to do what Plague of Crow's message had told him to. "It's an earth spirit who—"

Only Hannah Stone hadn't waited long enough to hear the answer, and had instead picked up her buffalo rifle and promptly dropped one heavy round, smack dab into the middle of the Stonecoat's forehead. Gravel chips flew off, but it didn't so much as flinch. Instead it began ponderously moving their way.

Bubba was watching and calculating all of this with a mind as cold as a Chenoo's heart, and he saw exactly how the battle was going to unfold. The monsters weren't dying easily, they were too numerous, and the swarm was nearly on top of them. "Into the wagons," Bubba ordered. He didn't like abandoning valuable horses, but didn't see much choice.

It was four men per wagon. They clambered through the doors and pulled them shut behind. The inside of his wagon was extra tight, because they had an extra body. It wasn't exactly lady-like, but Stone crawled over Bubba's legs so she could stick her sawed-off shotgun through the firing slit in the wall and promptly blew a hole through an old Chenoo's head. His killers stuck their rifles through the other firing slits and kept up the onslaught. The interior quickly filled with choking fumes. The wagon rocked as the Chenoo crashed against it, like a boat in heavy waves. They began to scratch and tear at the seams.

"Boss, the big one is coming this way!" Abrams shouted down through the hatch.

"Good," Bubba stated as he pulled the colorful, supposedly magic stick from out of his coat. Then he wouldn't have to run as far to reach it. He began climbing up. "Move aside, Balthazar, I'm coming up."

He squeezed past and onto the roof. It was worse than

he'd thought. Chenoo were strong, and they were sticking their claws through the slick sides and pulling themselves up. He turned just in time to witness the Stonecoat reach the other war wagon. The spirit stuck one great hand beneath, and effortlessly *flipped* the wagon on its side. It crushed a bunch of Chenoo in the process, but the Stonecoat didn't seem to mind.

It turned its attention toward their wagon, and approached, rumbling and flowing across the ground. Its body was made of millions of moving pieces, it was like watching a rockslide . . . *up*. The Chenoo on that side of the wagon were smart enough to get out of the way, leaving Bubba a clear path to follow some very questionable advice.

That witch had better be telling the truth.

Bubba stood atop the war wagon and shouted at the Stonecoat. "I'm Bubba Shackleford, professional monster killer!" He pointed Plague of Crow's stick at the spirit. He shook it and the beads rattled. "Go back to sleep, you old spirit! I protect this land now!"

"What the hell are you doing, boss?" Abrams shouted as he struggled to clear a jam from the potato digger.

"Establishing dominance." Bubba replied.

"It's big as a locomotive!"

"It's a warrior thing. *Yeeee haaaa!*" Then Bubba leapt over the side.

The message Plague of Crows had scratched on his hotel room wall had been simple.

Count Coup.

His boots hit the ground hard, and he rolled onto his shoulder, but nothing broke, and there wasn't time to dither with tons of living gravel coming to crush him. Bubba sprang to his feet. The plains warriors counted coup by touching their foe and getting away, only as it loomed over him, he realized just how suicidal that was. Every sensible man in the world would have turned and run for his life, but sensible men did not become monster hunters. Bubba charged the behemoth.

The Stonecoat ponderously lifted one huge arm overhead. Dirt and bits of rock rained down. It was prepared to deliver a blow that would smash an ox into paste, but Bubba ran right under that fist, still bellowing his war cry.

Reaching up, he whacked the gigantic monster square in the face with a decorative stick.

The spirit paused for just a moment. If it had eyes, it probably would have blinked.

He'd touched his enemy in the middle of battle. Which was good, but the second part of counting coup was getting away alive.

Bubba dived to the side as the fist came down. The impact shook Wyoming. It missed him by a cat's whisker, but the ground beneath erupted upward in protest, flinging him through the air. He crashed back down to earth, flat on his face, then scrambled on his hands and knees as the monster lifted one epic foot to stomp him like a mouse. But by the time that impact came, he was already sprinting away.

He ran toward the bonfire until he realized it wasn't following him, so he turned around. *Did it work?* The Stonecoat was just standing there. It probably didn't speak English, but Bubba taunted it anyway. "That's right,

Stonecoat. You got touched. So quit your bellyaching and take your ragged ass back to your hole."

Then he realized that his breath had come out as steam. Despite being twenty feet from a roaring blaze, it was freezing cold. Bubba looked around and realized he was now completely surrounded by ice-hearted Chenoo. They hissed at him through their exposed teeth. The circle was slowly closing in.

Maybe it was time to be diplomatic. Miners had blown up its house after all. He pointed the stick at the Stoneheart. "You leave us alone, and we'll leave you alone. Nobody will trouble your rest again."

It stood there for a glacially long time. It was obvious that the Chenoo were beholden to its will, because there was absolutely nothing stopping them from rending Bubba limb from limb. The hunters in his wagon had stopped shooting to watch, and the only noise was the crackling of flames, and the shouting coming from the hunters in the rolled over wagon who were now stuck.

There was a rumbling, like an earthquake. Bubba knew that was the spirit talking. There were no words, but pictures formed in his head. Courage was sufficient. It was going back to the depths. Cover it in water and sand, and trouble it no more. The pact is done.

"I'll inform the governor." This looked like a good spot to make a reservoir.

The Stonecoat slowly lifted one hand. When it dropped it, every Chenoo soundlessly collapsed, like puppets with their strings cut. Then the Stonecoat itself was gone, the spirit whisked back to its hole. The body remained, but it was no longer animated, and the rocks parted in a shuddering cloud. When the dust cleared all that remained was a tall pile of gravel.

Bubba tossed Plague of Crows' stick into the bonfire. He didn't know if it was actually magic or not, but it was best not to trifle with such things. They always came with an unexpected cost . . . Besides, he had a sneaky suspicion he would run into her again one of these days.

Other than some bumps and bruises, and Hub Bryan breaking an arm when the wagon flipped, they were unscathed. While they rode back toward Cheyenne, Abrams figured that even once they ate the cost of the ruined wagon and cannon, this was going to be by far their most lucrative job yet. Monster killers loved getting paid.

"Split eight ways, it's still the most gold any of us have ever seen," Abrams shouted. The men cheered.

Bubba was riding alongside Hannah Stone. The young woman hadn't said much since the battle. She'd conducted herself admirably in the fight, and a flexibility of mind need not be limited to the supernatural.

"Make that nine ways, Balthazar."

She looked over at him and grinned. This time the smile was real.

TROUBLE IN AN HOURGLASS

Jody Lynn Nye

They called her Trouble, because that suited her so much better than Kerrilynn, which was her real name. We all glanced over as she sashayed into her family's saloon that Tuesday morning wearing a black corset so tight that you could put your two hands around her waist and still have room to lace your fingertips together. She looked like an hourglass, with plenty of sand on the top and enough on the bottom to look interesting. Though you'd better not take an interest, unless you wanted to find out what kind of Trouble she was. No matter how long a man had been out working his claim outside of Center City and would have fallen in love with a half-pretty mule, let alone a truly lovely girl of nineteen with a peach-skin complexion, cascading golden hair and bright blue eyes, it wasn't worth it.

We stared down into our drinks on the battered wooden card table until she pouted and left the room again. I know I heaved a sigh of relief. I'd been the target many times when Trouble wanted to show off.

Her ma, Jo, ran the saloon, because her pa was no use at all, unless you count amusement value, that is. Denton Kuhn had a brain the size of the Rocky Mountains, and common sense so small you could fit it in a thimble. He was always spouting ideas that sounded like he was drunk off his ass, but if you sniffed his breath you never got a whiff of alcohol. No, his delusions were purely a function of his own mind. Nolan and Mick, their two sons, were nice, normal boys, interested in raising hell and chasing girls. Trouble took after her daddy. She had all the same pie-in-the-sky ideas he did, but less patience, so she was always jumping the gun when she ought to have waited a mite. We were less afraid of the shotgun Jo kept under the bar than we were of Trouble gettin' enthusiastic about something.

"Three dollars," I said, figuring the coast was clear. I had three sevens.

"Raise you two," Dustbowl Bob MacNair said, pushing two silver disks into the middle of the table.

"Uh-oh," Big Mike Simpson muttered, glancing up in alarm. "Save yourself, Duncan Wrayburn."

It was too late. Two hands plunked down on my shoulders, and a cascade of sweet-smelling red-gold hair poured down alongside my ear.

"How'd you think I look?" Trouble asked. She wriggled into view so I could take in the corset at eye level.

"Uh, kind of nice," I said. It was true, but as noncommittal as I could make it. Her touch was making my blood percolate.

"Got somethin' I want to show you, Duncan."

"Thanks, Kerrilynn, but maybe later." I gestured at my

cards. "We got this game goin' on, and I stand to win enough to reshoe my horse."

"Yeah," George Simon said, tryin' to save my bacon. "He's the big winner so far. We got to have a chance to get it all back, Tr— I mean, Miss Kerrilynn."

"Oh, you'll be able to take it off him later," Trouble said. She put her shoulder under my arm and heaved. It didn't matter that I was somewhat over six feet and muscled enough to break horses. She was strong for a girl. My chair groaned as it slid backward on the board floor. I had no choice but to go with it. I looked sadly at my three sevens as I laid them face down. Big Mike gathered them up without turning them up, which saved my feelings a little. I had no time to think any more about it. Trouble hauled me out the door and around the back of the saloon, down the short path to the little cabin that her daddy called his lab-or-a-tory.

"You gotta look at this, Duncan," Trouble said, pushing the door open and shoving me inside. "See what Daddy's been makin'?"

I looked. At first glance, it seemed to be an elaborate contraption for distilling whiskey, with its floor-to-ceiling coils of copper tubing and glass vats. Then I realized I couldn't smell no alcohol. The wood-fired boiler in the corner was set up to drive the gears in bronze and copper mechanisms fancier than the engine in Doc Mulligatawny's new auto-mo-beel. They clacked and turned around the centerpiece of the whole thing: a massive blown-glass bubble that looked like a gigantic timekeeper. A big varnished box with controls on it stood nearby.

There was no sense in me guessing its purpose. I wasn't no scientist.

"What is it?" I asked.

Trouble put an arm around the narrow center of the huge device and leaned on it as if it was her best girlfriend.

"Ain't it pretty? It's Daddy's time machine!"

"It's a clock? That why it looks like an hourglass?"

She came over and smacked me one in the chest with the back of her hand. It stung. Like I said, she was strong for a girl.

"No, silly. You use it to *travel* in time. Backwards and forwards."

"Why would anyone want to do that?" I asked.

Trouble's blue eyes brightened.

"Money! All the good silver stakes within forty miles have been found out, but if we go back maybe two years, we can rush in and file a claim on the good ones before the prospectors do. Then we'd be rich!"

I shook my head.

"That ain't ethical, Kerrilynn," I said. "Preacher Dryhew would tell you that on a Sunday. That'd be robbin' the people who did all the work findin' them in the first place."

"Oh." Her pretty brow wrinkled. "Guess it ain't ethical. It was a good idea, wasn't it?" She wasn't bad, but her mind ran too far ahead sometimes before her tiny lick of common sense rescued her.

"Kind of. It'd save a lot of trouble, but not our souls." I glanced around, hoping Denton Kuhn could put his firebrand daughter under control. "Where's your pa?"

She shrugged, making her bosom bound up and down

in a distracting fashion. "Don't know. When I found the gears turning like that, I thought he might have taken a little trip in time. He'll be back. He always is. Do you want to try out the machine? We can go back and move Richard McGreevey's gang's horses out from in front of the bank so when he robbed it last year, they wouldn't be there. That would be ethical."

"But they were there, Kerrilynn," I pointed out, trying to keep things reasonable. I looked around nervously. To mention McGreevey's name was like calling the devil. I half expected to see him there leering at us from the corner. Besides, I was nowhere near convinced that Denton Kuhn's invention would work. I didn't want to end up in the middle of Si-beeria or the Sahara desert in case it mistook time for distance. I had a herd to maintain and a blacksmith bill to pay.

"Well . . ."

I saw that look in her eye. "And don't you go messing with it neither, Kerrilynn!"

Trouble pouted, puffing up that pretty little lower lip of hers.

"Oh, all right, Duncan Wrayburn! I'll leave it be. For now."

Not completely convinced, I pulled her outside and shut the door. Out of sight, out of mind, like my grandpappy used to say.

I went back to the game. While I was gone, Big Mike lost five dollars to Dustbowl Bob, and he was sore about it. I was just in time to keep them from getting into it right in the middle of the floor. Behind me, Kerrilynn had taken her ma's place behind the bar. While she poured drinks, she chattered on about her pa's inventions. The stories were always good telling, because almost all of his creations had gone wrong somehow.

". . . That so, Miss Kerrilynn?" a gruff voice asked. I took a peek back over my shoulder. Vince Slocum had one elbow on the polished rail of the bar. Almost everyone in town was afraid of him but her. The sheriff suspected he was part of McGreevey's gang, but couldn't prove it, because all the men had dressed up like scarecrows to rob the bank. The horses they'd ridden were stolen, and found wandering around in Peter Hickock's meadow afterward. Kerrilynn's idea of moving them before the men could make their getaway was a good one, if only it had happened like that. Slocum had been in the corner talking quiet-like with Ned Pearson, the clerk from the telegraph office. Pearson had slipped out a little while ago. Slocum clapped down his shot glass. "I'll be going now."

"That's two dollars, Mr. Slocum," Kerrilynn said brightly.

To my surprise, I heard the clatter of coins. He *paid*. Probably he thought it was bad luck to cheat someone who had been touched by the fairies. All of us at the poker table listened to the thumping of his boots across the floor and the creak of the door hinges, not looking up from our cards. He'd once shot a man for staring at him.

After a few more rounds, George Simon put his hands on the table.

"I got to get back," he said, standing up and nodding toward the big clock on the wall. The hands said 11:30. "I promised my wife I'd get back before dinner." He gathered up his stakes. He had most of our money. The rest of us scooped what was left into our pokes. I had managed to win four dollars. Not enough for my purposes, but on the way there. I dropped a silver dollar on the bar for taking up a chair all morning long. Jo came over to smile at me. She pocketed the tip.

"Where'd Trouble go?" I asked.

"Probably out back," Jo said, with a rueful smile. She knew her daughter all too well.

"Then I'm goin' out the front," I said.

I shoved open the louvered double doors and strode out into the sunlight. I'd have to walk home because of my horse, but it was a nice day for a walk.

"Duncan?" Trouble's voice came to me from the left. I stiffened, worrying what she wanted. But for a change, it sounded kind of quavery and nervous, not at all like the girl with all the confidence in the world. Warily, I turned.

On the wooden sidewalk just at the edge of the saloon wall, Trouble stood with her hands in the air. An arm in a black leather sleeve encircled her tiny corseted waist. Trouble looked as if she had two heads. One of them was hers, golden hair, big scared eyes, and all. The other belonged to a man with a big, black moustache and crazy, cold green eyes. I knew that face. It was on wanted posters nailed up in the saloon and down on the front wall of the sheriff's department and the telegraph office. He had a gun pointed at Trouble's temple. My heart sank to my boots.

"Richard McGreevey," I whispered.

"You come here, Duncan Wrayburn," he said, real low and menacing-like. "I don't want to have to put a bullet through this girl's pretty head right here. Put your gun down on the bench, and come over slow and easy."

"Yes, sir. I mean, no, sir."

I eased the heavy Colt Peacemaker out of my holster and set it down, then edged toward him with my hands up. He gestured with his pistol.

"Walk ahead of me. Keep your hands in the air!"

I had no choice but to do what he said. I kept glancing back over my shoulder to make sure Trouble was all right. Her big, blue eyes were wide with fear.

"Where we going, sir?" I asked, through a dry throat.

"Denton Kuhn's shack. Just walk!"

We stepped off the sidewalk onto the dry dirt and sagebrush. As we came around the corner, Vince Slocum came alongside us, looking pleased with himself. I looked at the rear door of the saloon. I didn't know whether to hope Jo Kuhn would come out or not. She was a good aim with that shotgun she kept under the bar, but she wouldn't have it with her if she was just throwing out dishwater.

At the door to the shed, McGreevey waved us on in. We stood at the side of the room with our hands up while he looked over Trouble's pa's latest invention.

"Vince here said you told him it was a time machine," he snarled at Trouble.

She tossed her head. "I say a lot of things."

I groaned softly to myself. McGreevey was a dangerous man. Now was not the time for her to show some sass!

"He said you can make it work."

"Maybe so," Trouble allowed. "Maybe not. Daddy

does new things to it all the time. He might have it set up different than it was this morning. I ain't seen him since breakfast."

McGreevey cocked his gun and pointed it at her.

"Make it work, or I'll blow a hole in you."

"Now, look here, McGreevey," I said, starting forward, "leave the girl alone! She hasn't got no sense. You know that."

Slocum smacked me across the face with his pistol. It hurt, but I stood my ground.

"If you shoot me, I can't make it work," Trouble said.

McGreevey turned the black eye of the pistol toward me.

"Then I'll shoot *him*."

Trouble's mouth opened into a little O, but nothing came out. She bustled over to the box at the side of the hourglass and started fussing with the ivory and brass dials and levers embedded in it. Since none of us could figure out what she was doing, there was no way to know if she was doing it right.

"When do you want to go?" she asked. McGreevey pulled his fob watch out of his vest pocket.

"Nine this morning," he said. "Yeah, that ought to do it."

Trouble took hold of a big crank that was on the side of the box and wound it three times. The gears attached to the glass bubble let out a big moan, and the bubble itself opened up like a book. Trouble pointed at it.

"There you go," she said. "Step in, and the next thing you know, it'll be nine o'clock again."

"Oh, no," McGreevey said. "We ain't getting in there

so you can send me back to Bible times. You're coming with me! Move it!"

He gestured with the gun.

"But there ain't room enough in there for all of us!" I protested.

It didn't matter. Samuel Colt's cold steel did the persuadin' for him. Trouble twisted a dial on the box, then got in the glass bubble and pressed as tight against the rear of it as she could. We piled in after her. I had to hold one arm straight up in the air and the other down across my back as the two gunslingers pressed in and the hourglass closed. It was a real tight fit.

"Nothin's happenin'!" Slocum snarled.

Then, suddenly, the glass seemed to shrink around us, crushing us close together. The small enclosure stank of Slocum's body odor, McGreevey's expensive cologne, and my nervous sweat, tempered with the clean smell of lavender soap from Trouble. The room outside got real bright until I couldn't see nothing but pure white light. My guts felt like they were being crushed by Trouble's corset. I tried to yell, but I had no breath in my body. Just when I thought my stomach was going to come out past my spine, the squeezing stopped. The bubble grew back to its normal size, and split open.

Slocum jumped out and looked around.

"It's a fake!" he bellowed. "Nothin' changed!"

I pointed out the window.

"Look at the sky," I said. "The sun's back in the east."

"Well, God in His Heaven," McGreevey said, tilting his hat back with the barrel of his gun. "All right, you two. Move out!"

"You got what you wanted," I said. "Why don't you just let us go?"

"Because I *ain't* got what I wanted yet," McGreevey said, curling his lip. "Not another word!"

The men made us mount up on their horses ahead of them, and whipped them up with the end of their reins.

We rode all the way out of town, and into an arroyo choked with sagebrush several miles outside Center City. I kept my eyes wide open the whole time. Sheriff Ezekiel Parker had gathered us all as a posse at one time, thinking McGreevey's hideout had to be there somewhere, but we never found it. Now I saw why, but it wasn't going to do us no good.

A beaten-up, gray-walled cabin huddled against the side of the arroyo. A sunburnt man in dusty leather chaps and long johns open at the neck leaped up from a chair on the porch and ran to take the reins as we swung off the horses. Slocum pushed us both into the house.

Inside, it was as smoky as the inside of a chimney. Eight or nine men sat around a table, drinking from a shared jug and puffing on cigars while they played cards. When the boss stalked in, they all jumped to their feet.

Slocum pushed us toward a couple of the men.

"Tie 'em up," he said.

"You get your hands off me!" Trouble protested. I did my best to defend her. Both of us kicked and struggled, but we were outnumbered. They trussed us up like pigs for the spit with a couple of old ropes and then dropped us into a corner.

"Didn't you just leave, boss?" one of the men asked.

"You were gonna stake out the Wells-Fargo gold shipment."

"I been gone for hours," McGreevey said. "Gather around, boys. You got to hear this. Vince?"

"I been talking to Ned Pearson," Slocum said, eager to please McGreevey like a schoolboy. "The Wells Fargo gold is comin' in by the noon stagecoach."

"Why, that dirty dog!" Trouble exclaimed. "Those messages are confidential!"

McGreevey tipped his hat to her.

"That kind of language is unbecomin' to a lovely lady like you, Miss Kerrilynn. I'd be obliged if you would shut the heck *up*."

The air of menace in his voice was enough to silence even Trouble. She clapped her mouth closed, but she kept glarin' at him.

"The sheriff'll already know about that," a gap-toothed man with stringy red hair said. "He'll be waitin'."

"No, he won't, Carson," Slocum said, with a broad grin. "He won't hear it until ten o'clock, and then he'll be staying close to town, waiting to escort it through. Pearson said that the coach is comin' in by way of the north road past the Sioux village. It ought to be passing there in about"—he glanced at his pocket watch—"maybe an hour. We got time to get there and hide out in the valley at the bottom of the hill and rob the coach long before it ever gets to Center City."

"How can you be here when you were there?" Carson asked, frowning. "I don't see how that's possible."

"Ask Denton Kuhn—later!" McGreevey laughed. "Come on, boys! Let's ride out!"

The men scrambled for their hats and gun belts, and lit out, leaving us behind. I waited until the sound of hoofbeats receded in the distance, then struggled against my bonds.

"We got to get to town and warn everyone," I said. "Can you cut me loose?"

Trouble looked abashed. She glanced down at her tight bodice.

"Got none of my tools," she said. "Ma don't like it when I do experiments in the bar."

I wriggled until I had my back to her, roughing my face on the splintering boards of the wall.

"See if you can undo my bonds, and I'll untie yours," I said. My fingers poked and prodded at the knots around her slim wrists. Frustration made me impatient as I failed to undo even a single one. She didn't have much more luck.

But we didn't have to. Just at that moment, Denton Kuhn came barreling into the cavern and scooped up his daughter.

"You all right, honey?" he asked, cutting her free with a sweep of a wickedly sharp Bowie knife. He bent to sever my ropes, too. I stood up and rubbed my hands, marveling as Sheriff Parker and a dozen men, including George Simon and Dustbowl Bob, armed to the teeth, streamed into the little house and hid themselves behind the battered furniture. I hadn't even heard them arrive. Trouble gave her pa a kiss on the cheek.

"I'm fine, Daddy," she said, beaming, back to her bubbly self in a heartbeat. "You found us!"

Denton Kuhn looked at his own pocket watch, a confusing contraption cased in gold and blue glass.

"And right on time," he said. "Ten eighteen on the stump."

"You sure about all this, Denton?" the sheriff asked, glancing out the cracked window. He was a big man with graying temples in his slicked-back brown hair and the beginning of a pot belly. "Because I'm gonna look like a colossal fool if you're wrong."

"I'm not," Denton said. He looked a lot like his daughter, tall and slim, with big, blue eyes, a shock of graying blond hair and a faraway look in his eyes. "Not if Duncan and Kerrilynn are right."

I must have gawked at him like a gaffed fish.

"About what?" I asked.

"About the stagecoach robbery," the sheriff said, turning to peer at me like some mu-see-um exhibit. "You two said nobody was hurt, right?"

I had no idea what they were talking about, but Trouble grinned suddenly.

"We didn't see it yet," she said. "But we will. I'm sure nobody gets hurt. Because I just said so."

"Well, all right," Sheriff Parker allowed, still looking wary. "We'll wait until noon and not a minute more."

"You won't have to," Denton Kuhn said. "Kerrilynn's good about remembering the time. They're gonna rob the coach at eleven-fifteen. They'll be back here at twelve."

Nervously, we settled down to wait. Nobody said a word. I had a million questions rumbling around in my head like startled cattle, and it looked like the sheriff had the same. We all got a little thirsty. I eyed the jug on the table but didn't dare try the gang's moonshine.

It was by the tick of the sheriff's watch at the stroke of

noon that we heard the thud of hoofbeats and the jingle of saddle tack coming back into the narrow valley. Every one of us crouched down below the level of the windows, guns at the ready.

McGreevey's men rode up to the house and swung off their horses, cackling and laughing. Two of 'em held small wooden chests with the Wells Fargo insignia painted on them. The boxes looked pretty heavy. Sheriff Parker breathed out sharpish, and Denton Kuhn grinned.

"Bring those in here, and we'll break open the locks!" McGreevey shouted, his teeth bright under his thick black mustache. He pushed back his hat and opened the door.

We let them all get a foot inside before the sheriff stood up and pointed his twin Colts at them.

"You just drop your guns right this second, Richard McGreevey," the sheriff said. "We finally caught you. I been waiting a long time to get hard evidence against you and your gang. You're under arrest."

McGreevey's usual air of suave superiority deserted him, and he gawked at us like a shocked chicken.

"Boys!" he yelled, going for his gun.

"She told 'em!" Slocum said, pointing at Trouble. "She knew!" McGreevey turned his gun on her. The other men started firing at us. Denton Kuhn pulled his daughter down behind a table.

My hand went for my holster. Automatically, I drew my pistol and pulled the trigger before he could get off a shot. At the same time, I remembered that the gun in my hand was back on the bench outside the saloon. How could it be here, too? I thought I had felt it settle on my hip just a moment before I pulled it. How?

I didn't have time to puzzle it out then. My slug winged McGreevey's arm. His shot hit the wall over our heads, and the gun fell from his bleeding fingertips. The sheriff put a bullet in his leg. McGreevey went down. Vince Slocum raised his rifle to blast through the table where Trouble was hiding. Diving for cover behind a chair, I fanned the hammer and put a slug into his trigger hand. He bellowed in pain. The shot went wild.

The rest of the posse came out from around the back of the house, drawing a bead on the others who hadn't come in yet. The firefight was short. McGreevey's band was far outnumbered by the posse. The boss and his men held their hands up in the air. I emerged from my hiding place, cocking my pistol. Firing on an unarmed girl got my blood boiling!

"Don't kill any of 'em, Wrayburn," the sheriff said, waving me back. "Justice is waiting for these villains."

"Been waitin' for a chance to take this gang down," Parker told us with some satisfaction, as we rode back into town ahead of the wagon the posse had thoughtfully brought along with them to carry the McGreevey gang. People turned out from the general store, the barber shop and the telegraph office to watch the procession. "There's a reward waiting for the two of you. About enough to pay for that reshoeing you need, Duncan. And a bunch more."

"How'd you know about that?" I asked. The sheriff gave me another one of those real strange looks.

"You just told me, about half an hour before we rode out to McGreevey's cabin," he said. "Just one thing I can't figure: How'd you get tied up between then and now?"

"It wasn't between then and now," Trouble said, with a knowing look. She rode ahead of me on the saddle on McGreevey's own horse, with one of my arms around her little waist. "It's between now and then. You'll see. It's all scientific and stuff."

The sheriff shook his head. If he wasn't used to the Kuhns by now, he'd never be.

"Well, come on down to my office, and I'll give you the money, soon as I get these boys locked up. A hundred dollars in gold."

"Yahoo!" I yelled, overwhelmed with joy. I could have done cartwheels down the main street. "See, Tr—I mean, Kerrilynn. We struck gold, and we didn't have to sneak on nobody else's claim to do it. Let's go claim it."

"We can't do it right now," Trouble said, putting her hand on my arm. She smiled at Parker. "We'll be back, Sheriff."

She swung off and headed down toward the saloon.

"Why can't we go get it now?" I asked, trailing after her like a calf following its mother. "And where did my gun come from? I know I left it on the bench!"

"I put it there," she said. "I just came in and put it back in your holster." She preened, putting her hands on her waist and twisted this way and that in a fashion that made my nerves fizz like a gasogene. "You never told me how good I looked from behind in my new corset."

I shook my head to clear the distraction. "How could you bring me my gun? You were there in the shack *with* me!"

"I won't be later," she said. "I'll get it then."

"All this talk of thens and nows is getting me confused,

Kerrilynn," I said. I pulled away and headed for the saloon door. "I need to go get me a drink. It won't take but a moment."

"You can't do that," Trouble said. She took my hand and hauled me back to her pa's lab-or-a-tory. I kept forgetting how strong she was. "Your mind has to be clear, so you're a good witness. We got to go see the robbery and tell Daddy where the hideout is. We got to get to the pass below the Sioux village first so we have time to hide before McGreevey gets there."

She set the gears and pushed me into the time machine. After getting tied up and shot at, my stomach wasn't happy to have another go at being squeezed out of my ribs.

"I'm gonna lose my breakfast!" I shouted.

"I'll make you lunch," Trouble promised. "Hang on!"

The light was coming at an angle from the east when we squeezed out of the hourglass. I gasped for a moment with my hands on my knees, until Trouble grabbed my arm and pulled me toward the door.

"Hurry up!" she said. "It's about nine-thirty now. Daddy!"

Just as we were opening the door, Denton Kuhn was reaching for the handle to come in. His eyes widened.

"Have you been touching the time carrier, Kerrilynn? Honey, I told you not to play with that! It's serious."

Trouble was undeterred. "Got somethin' more serious, Daddy," she said.

She explained about the hideout and where it was, and all about the robbery that was going to come. It was real strange to me, since I saw him coming to our rescue only

a short time ago. But Denton Kuhn was one of the
smartest men I ever knew, and it took him a far shorter
time to put the facts straight in his mind than it was taking
me.

He looked at his pocket watch.

"Well, you've got things going on all over the place,
baby girl, but I think you're putting it in the right order,"
he said. "Half past nine. I'd better go back to about eight
o'clock and tell the sheriff. It'll take time to get a posse
together and put it in position." He shook his head.
"You're a bunch of trouble, Kerrilynn, but you're a good
girl. See you in a while, then." He set the controls, dove
into the hourglass and vanished.

I stood, staring at the machine in wonder. I'd never
seen anyone else use the time machine. The big glass
bubble kind of spun him into a beam of light, then
swallowed him up. No wonder I felt like I'd been ground
up and spat out. I was still convincing my innards to stay
where they belonged.

"Come on, Duncan Wrayburn," Kerrilynn said,
putting out her hand for mine. "Let's go watch us a
stagecoach robbery. I bet it'll be the most exciting thing
you *ever* see."

"Nothing compares with you, Trouble," I said, but I
gave her my hand.

THE BUFFALO HUNTERS

Sam Knight

Kansas
1867

"I got another one!"

The young Russian woman's accent thrilled Tommy as he watched black-powder smoke curl around her delicately arranged black hair.

The train they rode in, the Kansas Pacific Railroad out of Fort Hays headed for Denver, continued to slow as passengers fired out open windows at the racing buffalo herd. Tommy thought the lace finery Miss Veronika wore, and the extravagant red-velvet bench seat she knelt one bent knee upon, to be at stark odds with the rifle in her hands and the fierce grin on her face.

The contradiction excited him. He had never met a woman so exotic. She was so cultured, yet so . . . wild.

"Hoo-Ya!" Baron Avram Alexandrovich, Veronika's father, roared over the sound of the train, the volley of gunfire, and the thunder of the buffalo herd outside. He fired his own rifle repeatedly with the glee of a child on Christmas morning.

Expertly, Veronika levered open the trapdoor on the top of the rifle barrel and pulled out the spent black-powder cartridge with her fingertips. She sucked air in through her teeth as she dropped the hot metal casing and held her hand out to Tommy. He handed her a freshly opened box of .50 caliber cartridges and admired the smooth proficiency with which she reloaded the Springfield rifle, turned back to the window, and shot again.

The jostling on the train tracks made aiming difficult, but there were so many buffalo it was hard not to hit one. Although Tommy could see where Veronika was aiming, he couldn't tell which of the massive creatures she fired at.

Cheers rose from somewhere ahead of the baron's private railcar as three more buffalo dropped from the racing herd. Harsh guttural laughter filtered back with the powder smoke drifting through the windows, thicker than the smoke from the steam engine's fire box. The ten Russian soldiers the baron traveled with were apparently enjoying the sport, as well.

Baron Avram fired again. "Forty! I get forty. Was forty? I lose count!" His roaring laughter filled the car. Boisterous, hairy, and barrel chested, he was nearly the opposite of his daughter in every way.

"Forty-two," Marcus corrected. Marcus, Tommy's childhood companion turned business cohort, wore a boyish grin that matched the baron's as he handed a fifth box of ammunition to the big man.

Tommy knew Marcus would rather be shooting instead of just restocking others, but they had been hired as local advisors for the baron and his daughter, and the money was the best they'd earned since setting out on their own. Their fun would have to wait.

Another empty shell clinked to the wooden floorboards as Veronika loaded and fired again.

Shaking his head, a smile slid across Tommy's face as he watched her shoot. Actually, this was the most fun he'd had in a long time.

The roar of gunfire lessened and dropped to sporadic reports as the buffalo herd veered away and raced south. Brakes squealed and brought the train to a halt as a last few passengers wasted ammunition on targets now out of range.

"Good God! Never before I run out of rifles to shoot because all too hot!" Baron Avram's face was ruddy with excitement as he held his rifle out in front of himself, carefully touching only the wooden stock. Marcus still held one of the other two the baron had been using, having been ready to trade it out again just before the herd turned away.

Tommy took Veronika's rifle as she stepped off the seat she had been kneeling on.

"Now what?" she asked, eyes sparkling with enthusiasm.

"The train will stay here for about an hour while the buffalo runners collect skins and tongues," Tommy said.

A dozen men were already visible through the windows, walking through the prairie grass with knives out.

"Papa?" Veronika's soft brown eyes nearly melted Tommy, even though they weren't aimed at him.

"*Da da da*. We go too!" The baron nodded to Tommy

and Marcus before stopping and looking down at his resplendent military uniform. "Ah!" He stopped and pointed at Veronika. "Change clothes!"

Veronika looked down at her elaborate dress and pouted her lips but disappeared into her private room as Baron Avram hurried into his own.

Marcus and Tommy, in their worn ranch clothes, looked each other over.

"This is all I got to wear," Marcus said. "You?"

Tommy punched him in the arm.

Blood stained the baron's arms up to his rolled sleeves as he worked his knife around the carcass of the two-thousand-pound bull. Wearing simple pants and white shirt, the supple leather satchel on his hip, with an elaborately stylized emblem of a rearing bear, was the only indication of the uniform he had worn earlier. After a skinner named Riggs demonstrated how, the baron had been eager to help. His boisterous laugh and enthusiasm made quick friends of all the men as Marcus and Tommy held and turned carcasses for him to skin. The knife the baron used, easily twice the size of everyone else's, was the center of the afternoon's jokes.

Until Veronika arrived.

Separating from the crowd of idling passengers, Veronika strode confidently through the grass wearing knee-high boots and wash-leather riding pants. A satchel, matching her father's, rode low on one hip and was the only thing breaking up her womanly outline. She brought many of the men, including the baron's own, to a complete standstill as they watched her pass.

Tommy flushed at his own thoughts, and those he suspected were in the other men's minds. Unable to do anything about the other men, he tore his own eyes away from her figure and forced himself to look at the train instead.

Unmoving, it sat on the tracks as waves of the golden sea of grass splashed around it in the light breeze. A wispy white puff escaped the smokestack at the front while the baron's private car, lacquered black with polished brass trim, was at the opposite end of the train. A dust devil kicked up and swirled chaff around, following the path the buffalo herd had cut through the plains.

"Do you have a knife I could borrow?"

Veronika's unexpected voice at his side made Tommy jump. Her brown eyes, meeting his, looking only at him, stole any possible words from his mouth.

"Everyone else seems to be using theirs." The corner of her mouth pulled up as Tommy looked to see most of the men still standing dumbstruck, watching her.

Swallowing hard, Tommy glanced to Baron Avram.

"Give her knife," the baron grunted, still pulling at the bull's hide. "She can use."

Drawing his knife from its sheath, Tommy handed it to Veronika.

"Do you know how to skin a buffalo?" she asked.

"Yeah." He nodded. "I mean, yes, Miss Veronika."

"Good. Let's start on that one." She pointed with the knife. "Show me how."

"None of the meats?" Baron Avram's voice boomed off the side of the train.

Marcus shook his head, taken aback by the Russian's intensity.

"What is it, Papa?" Veronika asked as she and Tommy approached, both bloody to their elbows.

Avram waved his arms expansively. "They leave all this meats to waste! All!"

"Too much to eat before it would all go bad anyway," Riggs, carrying a bucket full of tongues, said as he passed by on his way to the train.

"There's a bounty on the hides and the tongues," Tommy said. "A lot of men make a good livin' off the buffalo."

The train whistle drowned out the baron's response, but the expression on his face was more than enough for Tommy to decide not to ask him to repeat his words.

"Train leaves in five minutes!" the conductor, walking the length of the train, called out while ringing a hand bell. "All aboard!"

Avram snorted and stalked off toward his men, who had gathered in a small group beside the private car. He waved his arms and shouted in Russian. The harsh guttural language made it impossible for Tommy to guess the baron's temperament, let alone the meaning of the words.

"Don't mind Papa," Veronika assured Marcus and Tommy. "You two are doing a wonderful job." She rubbed her nose with the back of her hand but left a bloody smear on her face anyway.

"Oh, here." Tommy pulled out his handkerchief and offered it. When he saw how gray and dingy it was, he regretted the decision, but it was too late to take it back.

She probably had beautifully white lace ones in her satchel.

Veronika took it, wiped at her nose, and gave it back. "You are sweet," she said. "Thank you."

The train whistle blew again.

"We should board now," Veronika said and headed for the train.

"You are sweet," Marcus whispered in Tommy's ear, imitating Veronika's accent.

Tommy punched him in the arm and followed Veronika.

"Grab your bags, boys!" Baron Avram's bellow startled them both. He strutted back from the front of the train with a big grin on his face and his men in tow. "We stay and feast!"

At least twenty men more than the baron's contingent chose to stay and make camp, which surprised Tommy. It would be nearly five days before the train would return to pick them up, and most, like Tommy and Marcus, had little more than the clothes on their backs. Fortunately, Baron Avram had enough supplies to go around.

His men unloaded horses, supplies, rifles, and ammunition with the thought the baron would hunt a buffalo from horseback and take the trophy back to be mounted. Riggs unloaded a stack of wooden crates to be broken down into firewood, while others cleared away grass to make camp and prevent a prairie fire.

While Avram and a couple of men began quartering a large cow, his soldiers set up their tents in neat rows, and Veronika directed Tommy and Marcus in setting up a large, round tent she called a *yurta*.

"Buffalo cider?" Baron Avram's voice carried across the makeshift camp. "Ha! Is joke!"

"What is cider?" Veronika asked as she fastened ties to a pole Marcus and Tommy held overhead.

"Fermented apple juice," Tommy answered.

"Apples?" Veronika wrinkled her nose. "Buffalo apples? Like horse apples?"

Tommy realized she thought buffalo cider was liquid from buffalo droppings and laughed. "No. Almost as bad, but no. It's water in a buffalo's stomach."

"It can save your life out here where there's no other water," Marcus added.

"If you can stomach it." Tommy's face mirrored the disgust on Veronika's as she nearly came nose to nose with him while tying the next cord.

She stopped, arms overhead with fingers lightly touching his hand as he held the pole up, and met his gaze.

Tommy's gut tightened and his breath caught. Looking into her brown eyes, inches from his own, he felt a need to protect her, care for her, unlike anything he had ever experienced before. He wanted to sweep her up into his arms and—

A sputtering, choking sound, followed by raucous laughter, filled the camp.

"I think the baron must have tried the cider," Marcus said.

Veronika smiled, her face wavering close to Tommy's, then she pulled away and began working the next tie. "That would be Papa."

★ ★ ★

The grassland took on a fuzzy amber halo as the sun neared the horizon. The rich smell of meat cooked with sage filled the air. Baron Avram supplied vodka. Men, stuffed with meat and heady with liquor, laughed and broke into groups around smaller campfires. Some took up singing while others started a shooting contest, aiming for a distant mound of prairie dogs.

Tommy was careful not to drink enough vodka to cloud his head. He tried to warn Marcus to do the same, but Riggs egged Marcus on until he had to run off and make friends with a sagebrush, which the baron's men found exceptionally funny.

Surveying the camp, Tommy made sure he knew who Veronika was talking to. Satisfied she was all right, he walked behind the *yurta* to relieve himself.

"You are good boy." Avram startled Tommy as he approached from the other side of the round structure. "I have been watching. You are good boy. You keeping good eye on my daughter. I thank you." The baron stood next to him and began to make water.

Tommy nodded awkwardly and looked out at the plains until he finished. Buttoning up, he turned back to camp.

"Wait," Avram said.

Hesitating, Tommy looked back to the horizon and waited.

"I see way my daughter looks at you." The baron buttoned up and faced Tommy. "Is good, but is bad at same time. I always want to see her happy, but she is . . . "—he waved his hand as he stumbled over the word— "betrothed."

Avram took in a deep breath through his nose and

sighed. "I want you take this." He held out a small leather coin purse.

Tommy reached out and took it. It was deceptively heavy.

"Hide it. Show no one. Is gold. Is payment. You watch my daughter, protect her like I see you want to, but protect her from you, too, eh?" Avram winked. "You are good boy. Many men here. Many maybe not so good as you." He patted Tommy on the shoulder and walked back around the *yurta* to the camp.

The smell of burnt coffee roused Tommy. Next to him, curled up like a pill bug, Marcus snored lightly.

Tommy punched him in the arm.

"What?" Marcus sat up, looking around wild-eyed.

"Thought you was going to stay awake."

Rubbing the sleep out of his eyes, Marcus winced. "Yeah. Me too."

Commotion at the edge of the camp caught their attention, and they both rose to see. Men were gathering and pointing south, their voices growing louder with excitement. Stepping around the *yurta*, Tommy and Marcus peered out into the grasslands gilded by the morning light.

Distant shapes moved on the horizon.

"Indians." The word floated over from the crowd of gawkers just as Tommy realized he was looking at five men on horseback.

The watching men chattered nervously.

"That's the Smokey Hill Trail, ain't it?" one of them asked.

"I heard they attacked a stage out there. Killed all the menfolk in the middle of the night," a thin man with bloodshot eyes said. Tommy thought he looked to still be drunk.

"Reckon they on the warpath again?" someone else asked.

"I say we go give 'em a what-for!" the thin man hollered, stepping up to the front of the group, rifle in hand.

A couple began fidgeting with their rifles. The Russian soldiers, curious about the Indians, joined the group.

"Settle down, Martin!" Riggs shooed the drunken man back with his hat. "They ain't no threat. I recognize the tribe. Them's Shawnee. They just followin' the buffaler."

"Oughtta goddamned get back on their reservation!" Martin said, waving a fist at the distant silhouettes.

There were grunts of agreement, but as the dark shapes disappeared behind the slope of the prairie, the grumbling men broke up. After the night's revelries, no one but Martin seemed to feel much like a fight anyway.

"What is all the excitement?" Veronika came out of the *yurta* wearing the same clothes as the day before, but somehow looking as though she had just bathed and had handmaidens put up her hair.

"Indians," Marcus answered while Tommy gawked at her.

"The native peoples?" She stepped forward to see, but there was no one left in sight.

Marcus shrugged.

Veronika turned and met Tommy's gaze. He realized

he was staring and swallowed hard. Feeling the heat on his cheeks, the gold Baron Avram had given him suddenly weighed heavily in his pocket.

"Good morning." Veronika smiled warmly at him.

"Ma'am." Tommy awkwardly half-bowed as he tried to tip his hat.

The distant popping of gunfire reached their ears and the whole encampment turned to look in the direction the Indians had been spotted.

"They are hunting, no?" Baron Avram, coming out of the *yurta*, called out to Riggs. "We go before they chase buffalo away, yes?"

Tommy had never seen anything quite as tangled and wild as the baron's raised questioning eyebrows.

A breeze with the scent of greenery and fresh water from the nearby Smoky Hill River momentarily pushed the oppressive stench of death away, and Tommy took advantage of it, breathing deeply before the smell came back. The bloody scene they had ridden up on was unlike anything Tommy had ever heard of. Bodies, and parts of bodies, Indian and horse alike, were strewn everywhere. Shredded and ripped to pieces. The carnage was obviously not the work of men.

Looking down from the saddles of their horses, not a single one of the fifteen riders said a word. Only circling flies and nervous horses disturbed the silence.

Veronika coughed into a white-gloved hand, choking on the thick reek that seemed to pool around them.

"I should take you back to camp," Tommy said, but she waved him off. He looked to Avram for guidance, but the baron was already dismounting and looking at the ground.

"*Ya'kwahe* . . ." a pained, breathy voice called out, startling everyone.

"Here!" Riggs hopped down from his saddle and rushed to an Indian lying crushed under the corpse of a horse with its head torn off.

"*Ya'kwahe*." The Indian grabbed Riggs's wrist, then mumbled words Tommy couldn't hear.

"Throw me a canteen," Riggs said looking up to the men on horseback around him. Marcus was the first to respond.

Tommy dismounted as Riggs dribbled water into the dying man's mouth. "Let's get the horse off him," Tommy said, trying to decide how to reach around the stump of a neck.

"Don't bother." Riggs reached out his fingers and closed the dead Indian's eyes.

"Many men ask for water when dying," Avram said looking down at the man. "Apparently is thirsty work."

"He weren't askin' for water." Martin, who had come along to "see what the Injuns was up to," turned his horse sideways so he could watch the nearby tree line. "He was warnin' us about somethin'. You speak his language, Riggs. What's that thing he was talkin' about?"

Riggs stood and brushed off his knees. "An old legend. A giant stiff-legged bear. A fiercely territorial man-eater."

"Bears ain't territorial . . ." Tommy frowned at Riggs.

"Grizzly done this?" Martin interrupted, laughing nervously and spinning his horse to see behind himself again. "Goddamn big griz. . . ."

One of the Russian soldiers said something and pointed to the ground. Baron Avram hurried over and whistled low.

"This not bear. I know bear, and this not bear. More like . . . elephant. With claws."

Tommy hurried over to see a round track in the dirt, big enough to put both hands and feet inside.

"Elephant?" Martin cursed. "I didn't head out here with no expectation of seein' the elephant! I'm heading back!" He turned back toward camp and flicked the reins of his horse.

"There are elephants in America?" Veronika asked.

"No," Tommy stepped away from the giant track. "That's just an expression. It means getting into trouble."

A horse scream made them all turn.

At the tree line, Martin was on the ground, rolling away from a furred monster the size of a house.

Bear-like, the creature reared up on hind legs big as tree trunks, but leaned back on a tail just as thick. It scooped the horse up into the air with scythe-like claws then fumbled the equine, like a toddling child dropping a doll.

The horse's scream cut short as six-inch claws shredded it from throat to belly, spilling viscera everywhere.

Tommy's riderless horse bolted, followed by the baron's. Everyone started shouting at once. Avram barked orders at his soldiers in Russian, and Riggs remounted, following after the other men spurring their horses to flee.

"Get the baron out of here!" Tommy shouted at Marcus while running to Veronika's horse.

The giant beast dropped to all fours and, despite a strange, stilted gait, moved with amazing speed to capture the fleeing Martin. With a swipe of a paw bigger than Martin's chest, the creature sent the man flying toward Tommy, covering twenty yards in the air before landing and rolling floppily.

Tommy climbed up behind Veronika as the Russian soldiers fired at the charging behemoth. "Go!" he shouted. The other men were already far ahead, racing back to camp.

"Not without Papa!" Veronika fought him for control of the horse, turning back toward the beast.

The volley of fire didn't slow the creature as it charged the group of mounted men that, all together, barely matched its size.

Marcus reined his horse next to Avram and offered a hand. The baron took it just as the soldiers' horses, wild with fear, scattered, tossing men to the ground as the monster arrived.

"Go now!" Avram yelled, dropping back to the ground. He ripped off his shirt and began pulling off his pants. "Go!" He slapped the horse, giving it all the excuse it needed to run away despite Marcus's best efforts.

"Papa, no!" Veronika cried out as she tried to force the horse to her father.

Tommy, forgetting he was trying to take control of Veronika's horse, gaped as Baron Avram pulled a long furry belt from his satchel and wrapped it around his naked waist.

In a heartbeat, the largest brown bear Tommy had ever seen stood in his stead. With a mighty roar, the bear dropped to all fours and charged the giant beast, attacking from the side, distracting it from the men on the ground.

Veronika shoved backward at Tommy, forcing him to give her room, and then she was off the horse and running toward the battle.

"Veronika!" Tommy tried to go after her, but the horse had had enough and fought to follow all the other fleeing animals. In desperation, Tommy jumped off and, stumbling over part of one of the dead Indians, chased after her on foot.

Peeling her clothes off as her father had, Veronika tripped pulling her pants around her ankles and fell just long enough for Tommy to catch up.

Grabbing her naked arm, he pulled her to her feet. "What the hell are you—?"

"Run away!" Veronika yelled at him as she wrapped a fur belt similar to her father's around her naked body. "Run now!"

Under his hand, her muscles bulged and fur grew. In an instant, Tommy was pushed backward by her bulk and found himself staring up into the eyes of another bear. It roared in his face, teeth grazing his nose, and then it was gone to join the fray.

Stunned, Tommy watched the second, smaller, lighter-colored bear run past two Russian soldiers trying to reload their guns while dodging giant swipes of the monster's claws. The other three soldiers were nowhere to be seen. The two bears bit and slashed at the massive beast, pulling back out of reach and then attacking again, worrying at it like hounds.

Then one giant paw caught the smaller bear and sent it rolling through the grass.

"No!" Tommy drew his gun and was running to get to the bear's side before he could think what he was doing. The six shots he fired from his pistol went quick as he tried to distract the monster, but they had no effect. It turned its attention back to the larger bear. Tommy's heart leaped as he saw the smaller bear get back up. He grimaced when it ran back to the fight instead of fleeing.

Knowing it would take too long to reload and prime his black-powder pistol, he dropped it and scooped up one of the soldier's rifles. Searching for cartridges, he found two and looked up again just in time to see the tip of an enormous claw gut the last soldier.

Tommy loaded the rifle, fired blindly at the beast, reloaded and fired again. Neither shot seemed to do any damage, but the two bears had managed to carve long, bloody rents in the monster's fur. Frantically searching for more unspent cartridges, he began turning over mutilated soldiers and checking pockets.

Something giant and heavy landed next to him. It was the larger brown bear, apparently thrown. It began changing back to the unmistakable pink of a human form.

And the behemoth, now only dealing with one adversary, had its full attention on the smaller bear.

The baron was unconscious, or dead. The furred belt, unbound, lay under him. A squeal of pain from the smaller bear made up Tommy's mind.

Pulling off his shirt, Tommy rolled the baron off the belt and tied it around himself. Instantly, excruciating pain wracked his body. His legs wouldn't work and he fell to the ground in a terrible agony. Then a tearing, a ripping, and he was free. Powerful. Strong.

He roared with a pure pleasure of strength. Smells overwhelmed him. Blood. Horse. Man. Fear. And Other.

The beast.

Veronika.

He turned to look for her, tripping over the shredded pants clinging to his furred legs. He bit them off easily and charged the monster as it turned in circles to swipe at the light brown bear.

Tommy felt his claws dig into the dirt, giving him traction as he ran. The smell of blood threatened to overwhelm his senses. This combined with his fear for Veronika's safety, sending him into a rage unlike any he had ever known. He was on the beast's back, using his claws to climb the massive monster.

It swatted at him, but Tommy grabbed a mouthful of fur with his powerful jaws and held on like a dog. He caught a good grip and pulled himself higher, nearly reaching the giant neck, and bit again, deeper this time. Blood flowed into his mouth, hot and salty, and with a shake of his powerful head, Tommy tore a giant chunk out.

The monster roared and twisted, trying to dislodge him, but Veronika kept it off balance, attacked its legs, biting at hamstrings. It stumbled, falling to the ground with an earthshaking thump and a thunderous bellow of pain.

Tommy let go and raced away on all fours to avoid being crushed as the beast rolled over to right itself.

With an anguished roar, the creature turned its back to them and ran toward the tree line.

Veronika, racing back to the still form of her father, seemed content to let it go. Knowing he couldn't finish the beast himself, Tommy exhaustedly dropped into a sitting position on his wide haunches and watched it go.

"You are good boy. Very good boy. I like very much." Baron Avram slapped Tommy on the back.

Tommy winced at the sturdy blow that would have hurt even had he not been covered in contusions. He went back to wrapping a clean bandage around the baron's leg. Veronika had helped Tommy scrounge supplies from the saddle bags scattered around, and was currently sewing together a pair of replacement pants for him.

"That was not a bear," she said without looking up.

"You think I do not know this?" the baron chuckled.

"Do you remember, in Madrid, the giant skeleton at the Museo Nacional de Ciencias Naturales? That was a giant sloth." Veronika used her teeth to break a thread.

The baron nodded. "I think you are correct."

Tommy stood up with a groan. Holding a hand to the purple blotch spreading across his ribs, he said, "Whatever it was, I never want to see it again."

"You know, maybe my daughter is not so . . . betrothed after all." The baron winked at Tommy. "She would be bear of wife though, *da*?"

"Papa!" Veronika chided her father as she worked, but her smile was all for Tommy.

The sound of horses made them look up. The remaining Russian soldiers, led by Marcus, came into view, rifles at ready.

"I thought you was dead for sure!" Marcus called out

as they approached. He jumped down and ran over to hug Tommy.

Exhausted, Tommy just grinned and hugged him back.

"Where's your pants?" Marcus stepped back and looked Tommy up and down. "Or is that how you chased that thing off?"

Tommy punched Marcus in the shoulder.

THE SIXTH WORLD

Robert E. Vardeman

"Professor, please. We'll die!"

William McConnell ignored his assistant's plea. Dunlap needed to learn proportion and not complain when the goal was so close. McConnell swiped cold rain from his eyes as he fought to hold down the frayed map scratched onto a piece of lambskin. The faint berry-ink stains had faded since he had bought the map from the scout in a Taos saloon. McConnell twisted about to get a better look as lightning lashed across the sky.

"Here. We're almost here. See?"

Dunlap cowered by a rock, as if his life was threatened.

"Are you afraid of a little water? Grow a spine, sir! We are on the adventure of a lifetime, and we will advance science because of what we discover!"

New lightning filled the sky, turning the New Mexico Territory surreal. Shadows leaped to life and died almost instantly. What was illuminated came to him with incredible clarity. The rest remained hidden in afterglow and darkness. His research assistant was frightened, while he had never felt more alive.

"It'll fry us for sure, Professor."

As if God Almighty agreed, lightning struck a tree near the summit of the hill they climbed. The juniper exploded and sent down a rain of fragrant, molten sap. McConnell ignored the burning on his forearm. He hastily pressed his hand down on the map to smother a tiny blaze threatening to steal away the map to repairing his reputation. The faculty at Harvard had ridiculed him, even after long and detailed analysis of volumes found in the Warren Anatomical Museum. More than mock him, they had driven him from the academy, forcing him to take a petty job with the government. He would show them. Being assistant curator of the Army Medical Museum would lead him to greater recognition.

The map to that notoriety fluttered and flapped as a gust of wind rushed downslope from the lightning-struck tree, hot and wet and promising only new discomfort.

"The burial site is at the top, Dunlap. Press on. Show some gumption."

"The tallest spires get struck by lightning, Professor. That's why they put lightning rods there. I don't want to become a lightning rod."

"What do you know of such things?"

"My pa was a lightning rod salesman. He got himself struck putting up one on a barn in Virginia when I was nine. He got hit out of a clear sky. This isn't a clear sky." Dunlap curled up into an even tighter fetal ball as the wind began blowing harder.

McConnell shook his head. When they had embarked

on this expedition from Washington, D.C., he had high hopes for the youth. Dunlap had shown great skill piecing together skull fragments brought in for examination. Nimble fingers and sharp eyes had allowed his work to come to McConnell's attention, but the laboratory provided the true venue for the young man's talents, not the field where real discoveries were made. Worse, during their travel here, Dunlap scoffed at many basic theories of phrenology that McConnell took as gospel. Solid work by the field's great pioneers, Gall and Spurzheim and Binton, showed the way. His assistant refused to acknowledge their insights.

He instinctively reached back to touch the knapsack carrying the enticing piece of skull that had brought him into this wilderness. The outline beneath the canvas reassured him he was doing the right thing. The strange fragment had been found by an Army survey party two years ago in 1877, though where the artifact had been found was something of a mystery since the scout who had delivered it to the head surveyor had not noted the location nor had the surveyor considered it important until later examination. McConnell was happy the man had given it to the Army Medical Museum, even if he had done so hoping to have his name attached to a display.

Even luckier had been hearing of the old timer in Taos who had a map made after that expedition showing the location where the peculiar skull had been found.

He knelt with the map between his knees, got his bearings when another lightning bolt filled the sky, and then rolled up the map. McConnell tucked it into a coat pocket.

"This has to be the place where the scout found the skull. It has to be. Come along, Dunlap. We might have to dig to find other fragments for you to piece together." He faced uphill, glanced at his assistant and knew he would complete the trek alone. He began the steep climb.

Sharp rocks cut at his legs. More than once he fell forward and caught himself. Hands lacerated and lungs burning from the lack of air at this elevation, he fought forward to the crest and looked around. The blasted, smoldering juniper gave stark reminder of the danger he faced. He sucked in a lungful of air and choked. The mixture of fragrance and ash was intolerable for a city dweller. He took a step forward, then saw the dark rim. His excitement betrayed him. The frantic rush to the edge of the pit prevented him from noticing the crumbling lip.

McConnell tumbled downward and crashed into the mud twenty feet below. He moaned, rolled onto his side and looked up. A cry escaped his lips. The slick walls afforded no hand or footholds.

"Dunlap! Help! I've fallen into a shaft." He propped himself up and realized how true that was. This wasn't a naturally occurring hole. The sides were too smooth, bored down into the earth with cruel force. "Help!"

Two more bolts crossed the sky before a head timidly thrust out to look down. He caught his breath. His assistant had summoned the courage to answer his cry for help.

"Can you climb out, sir? I don't have a rope or any way of pulling you up."

"The sides are as slippery as if they have been

polished." McConnell poked about in the soft dirt but found nothing useful to aid in his escape. "You'll have to figure out some way to get me out."

"We saw those cavalry troopers earlier. They can't be far off."

"No, don't leave me. Find a way to—"

He spoke to a stormy sky. Dunlap had left without even dropping him spare food or water.

McConnell slept fitfully at the bottom of the pit. When the sun poked over the lip of the pit, he sneezed, stirred and then sat up. The sky was pure blue, cloudless from his narrow perspective and absent of the violent storms that had torn away at the mountain the night before. He propped himself up and ran his fingers through the mud around him. Water so close, yet he would choke if he shoved the mud into his mouth. Then an idea came to him. He took out the lambskin map and held it up. Sunlight showed it to be thin. He scooped a double handful of mud onto his precious map, then caught it in a pocket before squeezing. Filtering the mud to get water proved more difficult than he thought, but a few drops made their way through and across his lips, revitalizing him enough to begin pawing deeper in the muck.

He was sure this was the spot marked on the map where he would find an intact skull made entirely of an iridescent material like mother of pearl. When more than an hour of sloshing around revealed nothing but the bones of small animals, he gave up. He lay back and stared at the tiny portion of sky. The sun had arced past the zenith. The narrow rock shaft cut out the afternoon light and turned the day to night. Stars accustomed to appearing when the sun set now peered down at him.

"My tombstone of stars," he muttered through cracked lips. He wanted to scream and shout for Dunlap to return, but he feared his assistant had abandoned him to die.

What would his assistant tell the others at the Army Medical Museum? Would Dunlap even return to Washington or would he hightail it to points unknown, avoiding such annoying questions?

McConnell idly ran his fingers into the damp dirt and let chunks fall. The soft sounds masked those above, but the appearance of a silhouette against the sky caused him to start. He struggled to his feet, craned back and called with all his might.

"Dunlap! You came back!"

"Who is Dunlap?"

He squinted and got a better look at the man above him. An Indian. Probably a Navajo, considering he had invaded their holy lands to seek out the rest of the iridescent skull.

"Get me out. Please, I beg you."

A snort of disgust echoed down. For a long minute he thought he was being abandoned again. Then a horsehair rope snaked down and banged softly against the smooth wall. He wasted no time slipping it around his waist and tying it securely. A tug signaled his savior he was ready to leave his prison.

The rope cut into his middle. He ignored the abrasion as he tried to find footholds on the way up. There were none. Giving up on this, he let the Indian do all the work of getting him free. He popped over the rim and flopped belly down on the ground, sobbing in gratitude.

"You are filthy."

McConnell looked up. His guess had been right. The Navajo wore a headband made from an old neckerchief. Two slashes of red paint on his right cheek might be war paint. The man's wrinkled face spoke of age, but he moved with the litheness of a young brave. Strong hands slid under McConnell's armpits and lifted him as if he were a small child. Once he got his feet under him, he saw that he towered over the man. Deerskin britches and shirt hid much of the man's stocky body. What McConnell could see of the chest spoke of hardship. Scars crisscrossed the flesh. Incongruously, he wore a bowler tipped far back on his head.

He stared into dark eyes and felt as if he was being pulled away from his own body. He blinked and looked down.

"I apologize for my dishabille. It is quite dirty down there." He started to introduce himself, then stared, mouth clamped shut when he realized where he had seen the bowler before.

"The one you called to. Did he wear this?" The Navajo touched the bowler's brim when he saw McConnell's interest. He took it off and pointed to a bullet hole through the crown. "He had no more use for it."

"You killed him?" McConnell fought conflicting emotions. The Indian had killed his assistant and yet had rescued him. That made no sense.

"Those who would kill me shot him." The Navajo looked stern. "They are my people."

"Your own people want you dead?"

"I am Red Horse, a powerful medicine man. My seeking of knowledge has angered clan elders."

The Indian held out the bowler for him. McConnell couldn't bear the idea of wearing Dunlap's hat, not after he had been killed while wearing it. Blood smeared the inside sweat band. Dunlap had died a messy death. He handed it back. Red Horse settled it on his head at a jaunty angle.

"They scalped him?"

The Navajo looked surprised, then smiled and shook his head.

"Waste of time. No, we take horses, not scalps. They are more valuable. They are like your money, only we ride until they collapse, then we eat them. You cannot do that with paper money or gold coins."

McConnell again pushed away confusing emotions and tried to think logically.

"They took our horses?" He touched the bag where he kept the piece of skull that had led him here. This much had been saved. "How far to this place?" He fumbled out the map and held it up. The berry juice had smeared and the skin had torn in places, making its use as a map problematic.

Red Horse shrugged. McConnell refused to give up. The world had turned more dangerous around him, and on foot, his death seemed more likely than not. He could only press onward. He held out the skull fragment.

Red Horse recoiled at the sight and began a low chant that might have been a curse.

"I want an intact skull. It is for a museum in Washington."

The medicine man stopped chanting. "Where they have Cap'n Jack's skull?"

The question shocked him.

"How do you know that? Have you been there?"

"I learned English at a Pennsylvania school. I have seen the collection gathered after the Modoc War." Red Horse spat. "Cap'n Jack should never have believed Wovoka and his false Ghost Dance." The Navajo spat again. "Diné magic is stronger."

"Science is strongest of all." He held out the skull fragment and ran his fingers over it. "If I get an entire skull, I can determine the characteristics of the creature by the bumps and depressions." He stroked over the piece using only his fingertips. "There are twenty-seven organs represented in a human skull and only nineteen in an animal's. I need to find a complete skull to learn what—"

"Why not study the monster while it is alive?"

McConnell kept speaking, telling of the details he could find until what Red Horse said penetrated. He faced the Indian and stared. Red Horse averted his eyes.

"What do you mean?"

"On that mountain." Red Horse lifted his chin to direct McConnell's gaze to a nearby hill.

"I don't understand. You mean there are complete skulls there?"

"Complete." The Navajo nodded solemnly. "Complete living monsters, too."

"This is astounding. I can compare the skulls with the actual animal, alive, in its native habitat. But what kind of animal is it? I have no idea from this small piece."

"Monsters," Red Horse said. He held out his hand to

waist high. "Like us." He cast a quick look at McConnell. "Gray skin, not white or copper."

"Like us?"

"Arms, legs. Not enough fingers. Head." He drew a curious shape in the dirt with his toe.

McConnell dropped to his knees and lightly traced his finger around the drawing. He looked up.

"I must examine this skull. I have a craniometer to take precise measurements, but if needed, I can use my fingers. I am quite good at interpreting—"

Red Horse clamped a leathery hand over his mouth. He tried to pull away, but the Navajo clamped his other hand over the back of his head. McConnell struggled, then settled down.

"That one," Red Horse said, looking at a tall peak. "Close to holy peak, White Shell Mountain. I seek them out, too, but not for their heads. The monsters come from the Fourth World there into this, the Fifth. They follow the reed that First Man climbed."

McConnell had no idea what the medicine man meant.

It took all his breath to keep up with the pace the shaman set toward the mountain. As they circled the hill with the curious pit bored into it, McConnell summoned the courage to ask Red Horse why his own people had exiled him.

"I was banished because I seek to find the opening to the Fourth World. Our most powerful ancestors came up from the seas to this world. The gray monsters lead the way."

"Why? The ones with shiny skulls? Are they part of your mythology?"

"Religion," Red Horse said coldly. "It is my religion."

"Sorry. Mine is different. I—"

"I learned your ways in boarding school. The Hero Twins killed the monsters in this world."

"The Fifth World."

The Indian nodded curtly. His stride lengthened, forcing McConnell to trot to keep up. This might have been a ploy to prevent more questions from being asked, but McConnell was a scientist and always curious. In spite of the pace, he gasped out, "You think the gray people are coming to this world from the Fourth?"

"They are not people. They might be monsters. They fly about." He put his hands together and made flapping motions. "Only they do not fly like a bird. They hide inside metal skins and soar about the mountain."

"Why are we going there? Do they have a camp there?"

Red Horse took a long minute before he answered.

"They come from the Yellow World to the White world. They are monsters of the Fourth World coming to this one."

"You've seen them come out of the ground?"

"They go into the ground on that mountain. Never have I seen them come out."

"But you have seen the colored skulls?"

"We each want what we want." Red Horse snorted. "When a gray monster dies, the flesh goes away like snow in sunlight, leaving behind only the shining skeleton. Its spirit returns to the Yellow World."

When McConnell began stumbling and fell for the second time because of the frantic pace, Red Horse halted for a rest. They collapsed to the ground, but Red Horse remained upright and alert, head cocked as he listened to the world around them. McConnell tried but heard only the dull thudding of his pulse in his ears.

He propped himself up and asked, "Could I examine your skull?"

"You would find the animal parts in my soul?"

McConnell laughed. The medicine man listened more carefully than he had thought to his description of phrenology.

"You're quite human. I want to determine your character."

"If you cannot see my character through what I do and believe, bumps on my head will tell you nothing."

"That's not so. We all have a face we show the world. Our inner self is hidden but can be revealed through phrenology. Your personality and character traits become obvious because of the way they force themselves up from your brain. See?" He pulled out the skull fragment and held it up to catch the sun's setting rays. "These depressions show intelligence, great intelligence. That's all I can learn because of this being so small."

"Gray monsters are small. No more than this high." Red Horse held out his hand at about three feet.

"Stature isn't important. The reflection of your essence in your skull is. Even a small child shows its character, though often undeveloped." He launched into a description of how a baby's skull formed and how this was guided by personality. Red Horse listened, but

McConnell knew it wasn't to his lecture. He had given this so many times while at Harvard that it came easily to his lips. Dunlap had often praised his skill at delivering this very lecture.

He sagged as he wondered how to report the stalwart's death when he returned to Washington. Perhaps naming a region on a whole cranium for his assistant would be fitting tribute. There had to be new organs to find in such a strangely alien creature.

Gray monsters, Red Horse called them.

"You are sad because you mourn your friend?"

"What? Oh, why, yes, I was thinking about him. Dunlap was a good and loyal man. If only he had been able to get me out of that pit." He rolled over and looked at the Indian. "What dug that pit? The one you rescued me from?"

"The metal skins the gray monsters fly inside spit out sparks and fire and bad smoke when they come to ground. The tower of fire coming from below burned into the ground one night. I hid because it caused the ground to shake and bring down raindrops of hot rock."

"How long ago was that? The bottom was wet. That much hot gas should have fused it, not turned dirt to mud." McConnell had not dug down more than a few inches, and the storms could easily have blown in dirt and water.

Red Horse fell silent, then said, "It was after I conducted an Enemy Way sing. The chief's two sons were killed in a raid." He made marks in the dirt. "Twenty days ago, before the rains."

McConnell started to ask more, but his attention

diverted as a glowing verdant ball settled down on the top of the mountain. Then it disappeared. Words jumbled in his throat. He was so close to finding an intact skull. The gray men!

"They return to the Fourth World." Red Horse looked solemn.

"Like hell. They bored another hole into the ground and are hiding that round green *thing* in it. Let's go." All tiredness vanished with such a mystery to be solved. He doubted there were monsters such as Red Horse claimed, but whatever flew in the green-glowing *thing* might be the source of the skulls.

The darkness almost defeated his desire to see what went on atop the mountain. McConnell lost his footing frequently, but he persevered. After an hour of ascent, he stopped to rest. He coughed at the rancid odor coming down from above him.

"What's that smell? It's worse than a corpse flower."

"What is corpse flower?"

"It's a flower on a plant that a friend grows in the National Arboretum. The bloom smells like a decaying corpse. Are there dead bodies up there?" Visions of the skulls to be had danced in front of him.

"The monsters' flesh does not smell. It melts away quickly, leaving only the skeleton."

"An intact skull," McConnell reminded himself. That opened the door to real knowledge. He held his nose for a few feet, then breathed through his mouth to keep from gagging.

Another hour brought them to the lip of a crater. McConnell stared at the activity at the bottom of the pit.

From the way the rock had been melted, this might have been a volcano. The only fact that stuck in his mind was how fresh the walls looked. Intense heat had burned through the mountain, creating a hole a hundred yards across and half that deep. The vessel he had seen airborne earlier glowed in the center of the crater. It was almost spherical, being slightly elongated. He saw no windows or doors through the emerald shimmer surrounding it, but when he forced himself to look beyond the craft, he saw small creatures bustling about on the far side of the crater.

"Monsters from the Fourth World," Red Horse said solemnly.

"How do we get down to the crater floor?" McConnell looked around frantically. The sheer walls defeated any descent other than stepping off into space and falling. No human would survive such a fall.

"Where is the road leading to the Fourth World?" Red Horse shouldered past McConnell and put his hand over his eyes to shield the glare. "I would descend."

"These aren't monsters. They're ... pygmies." McConnell fixed on a rock fall a quarter of the way around the crater. "There. We can use that to join them."

"You will go with me into the Yellow World?"

"If you stand with me to get an intact skull." The question startled McConnell, and he hoped his reply was adequate. Somehow, it felt lacking, as if more should be done. He hesitated, then spit on his palm and held out his hand. Red Horse frowned, then spat on his own and shook hands. "That makes it binding."

The Navajo wiped his hand on his buckskins, but McConnell paid no attention. The pact had been sealed.

He made his way through the rocks on the rim to reach what he hoped would give a ladder. The crumbled rock afforded a way down, but the climb back would be too steep using the dislodged rocks. Not waiting to see if the Navajo followed, he twisted around, grabbed at prominent rocks and found they were not secure. He began sliding down, faster and faster. He grasped for other rocks and successfully slowed his descent. He still hit the crater floor with enough force to cause his legs to buckle. He flopped backward, staring up into the night sky.

McConnell's arrival had not gone unnoticed.

The little people circled him and stared, unblinking. Their skin was a dull, pebbly gray, their heads shaped exactly as Red Horse had sketched. Teardrop shaped eyes of pure coal black dominated their faces. Small slits took the place of nostrils. He wondered how they kept from drowning in a rainstorm. Whatever would Darwin say about that? No ears and only a tiny mouth completed the simple face.

High-pitched squeaks that might be communication sent tiny daggers into his ears. He rolled to his side, then came to his knees so he was almost face to face with them. Hesitantly, he thrust out a hand. The gray people did not respond.

"I come in the name of science."

No response. They continued to squeak, but he failed to catch any syntax, rhythm or sounds that might be individual words.

"Do you understand them, Red Horse?"

The Indian stood tall, proud, shoulders back and eyes

uplifted. He chanted in his own language. The gray people ignored him, too.

McConnell reached out slowly, not wanting to frighten them with a sudden move. When they held their ground, he put his hand on the nearest one's head, intending to examine the bumps and depressions to gain insight into the creature's character. Pain blasted through his body, tightening his muscles and freezing him to the spot. His hand curled around the dome of the gray skull—and he heard.

He *heard*. Voices rushed in from all directions, confusing and frightening him.

"Can you help?"

McConnell tried to speak, but his throat convulsed so powerfully he knew what it was like to be hanged. Words formed in his head but not on his lips. And he *said*, "How?"

"Two of the supplicants are ill."

"Supplicants?"

"We are on a holy pilgrimage to—"

McConnell almost screamed. The destination drilled fiery holes in his head. He yanked his hand away and sat heavily, staring at the gray man who had spoken to him mind to mind. Hand shaking, he stared at it, then looked back to the gray. Phrenology had just been taken to an entirely new realm. By touch of hand to head, he had communicated.

"Red Horse, they are religious people on their way to . . . somewhere. Put your hand on this one's head. You are a holy man. What they say might make more sense to you."

McConnell hated himself for such cowardice. The communication had been potent, searing. He should exchange as much scientific information as possible, especially now that a new field of phrenology was opening before him. He should, but the slippery, impure feeling of another's thoughts slipping through his brain left him weak and frightened.

Red Horse showed no hesitation as he placed his hand on the head of the nearest creature. He stiffened, closed his eyes and resumed chanting. When he began weaving about, as if he would fall over, McConnell went to steady him. To his surprise as he touched the Navajo, he found himself included in the silent exchange. It was as if a vista opened and clouds blew away. He meshed mentally not only with Red Horse, but with all the gray creatures.

He yanked back, shaken at such communication. Sweat beaded his forehead and his legs turned to water. Turning away, he sought something else to fix on. The vessel the gray creatures rode in hovered fifty feet away. The glowing emerald fog surrounding it brushed the ground. How it balanced on nothing but mist confused him, but everything he had *heard* added to it. The pilgrims had been to Earth before. When their ship had been damaged, they came here to repair it.

"The others who have been here," he said in a choked voice. "They think we are nothing but animals."

"They are from World of Spirits of Living Things," Red Horse said. Awe touched his voice. "They are not monsters. They are gods."

"Not gods, no, not that." McConnell forced himself to calm. "They've repaired their ship. Let them go."

"Two are sick. I can heal them. One is their healer. The other is a . . ." Words failed the Indian.

"Pilot. One is their doctor, the other is their pilot." McConnell knew the words that Red Horse didn't. "We should leave."

"I can sing a Blessing Way. This will heal them." Red Horse thrust out his hand to lay on the nearest creature's head. From the immediate flurry among the other gray people, they became excited. The keening he had heard before now threatened to deafen him. McConnell clamped his hands over his ears.

McConnell staggered away from the tight knot of creatures, now circling Red Horse. Together they herded Red Horse to the hovering vessel. Somehow, a doorway opened in an otherwise solid side, and they went inside. Red Horse had begun chanting.

McConnell hunted for a way out of the crater, to no avail. The rock slide they had followed down gave nothing in the way of footholds to regain the rim. After three circuits of the crater, he sank to the ground and stared at the vessel. A faint warmth radiated from it. He still shivered. The odor of garlic made his nose twitch and reminded him how hungry he was. He fumbled about in his pouch and found what remained of the food.

A dull whirring made him look up. A gray creature came from within the ship, looked around, then came to him. He touched its head. The sudden connection caused him to spin and whir at dizzying speed before he fought back to keep his own personality intact rather than merge with the creature.

"Our pilot is healthy again. Red Horse is a miracle worker."

"So quickly? A Blessing Way sing takes a week or longer. Or so he told me."

"Two weeks have passed."

McConnell almost lost his slight meal as explanations flooded him. Mathematics and visions of space and holes in empty space lashed his mind. Through it came a dim acceptance that time within the spaceship flowed at a different rate. Somehow this allowed the gray men to travel impossible distances between stars.

He broke down and cried tears of joy as it hammered into his head. He could not understand the concepts, but what few facts he clung to were good.

"I am glad your pilot is well. I sense that your healer . . . died."

"We must tend his remains." Confusion swirled and then the gray creature *asked*, "Will you see to the ceremony?"

McConnell stared into the black teardrop-shaped eyes and saw no hint of emotion, but through his contact of hand with head, he almost drowned in the flood of sorrow.

"I will, but don't you have rituals of your own?"

"We cannot take the body with us. It decays rapidly on this world."

McConnell ran his hand over the alien skull, feeling the bumps and trying to discover what he could of the physiognomy. His exploration ended when Red Horse came from the spaceship carrying a lifeless body in his arms.

"You could not save him?" McConnell's throat

tightened as he spoke the words aloud. He removed his hand from the gray creature's smooth head to keep from becoming addled due to so much emotion crashing against his mind.

"He was their medicine man. Now, I am."

McConnell accepted the body. He sagged as he took it in his arms. The corpse was heavier than he expected. Did life persist? A quick touch on the skull gave no hint of life or thought. Truly, this one was dead.

"You are also a holy man. Should we burn the body as your people do?"

"We must leave now." Red Horse straightened. "I have told them you will take this one's skull and display it in a place of honor."

"They want that?"

Red Horse turned toward the ship and stood straighter. "I travel with them to the Place of Melting Into One. It is the Sixth World."

"You aren't trying to return to the Yellow World?"

"I am First Man to the Sixth World." He turned back and put his hand on McConnell's shoulder. For a moment they shared a promise, a future, hopes realized as the gray people must every time they talked mind to mind. Then the Navajo singer strode off, head high, bowler set squarely on his head, the gray man who had come to McConnell trailing like an afterthought.

McConnell held the body, then realized he was trapped at the bottom of the crater. He called to Red Horse, but the Indian had disappeared into the ship. The vessel began glowing with a verdant light and rose slightly. McConnell was almost blinded as a beam lashed out to bathe the rock fall behind him. He shied away, then saw that a ramp had been melted in the rock that lead upward to the top of the mountain. Carrying his burden, he climbed, barely getting free when the ship exploded straight upward on a turbulent column of noisome gases that washed over him, burning him. He dropped to his knees and faced away. When he looked back, the ship carrying Red Horse to his Sixth World was only one of a constellation of stars overhead.

Gently he laid out the gray healer, then shrank back as the flesh evaporated, slowly at first, then with increasing speed until only the mother of pearl skeleton remained. The skull sparkled with reflected starlight as McConnell pried it loose from the neck and held it aloft.

The body meant nothing to him, but the secrets of the gray aliens lay in this intact skull. He ran his fingers over the bumps and depressions, already mapping the organs and unearthing the secrets of the soul to share.

EASY MONEY

Phil Foglio

Big Zack was tired. Bone tired. You could tell. Man was like a locomotive, huge and dark and when he was running, you'd believe he could lift a plow horse up over his head. Sledgehammer said he'd seen him do it, to win a bet over in Leadville.

But he weren't lifting anything now. He looked like the weight of his leather apron alone was gonna drag him down. Fair enough, the damn thing was made outta buffalo hide and easily weighed forty pounds, and that was when it was clean and dry, which it weren't. He shambled over to the fire, and slowly sat down on one of the logs.

Crackerbox, the cook, poured out a tin mug of trail coffee and set it down onto a rock in front of him. Zack stared at it blankly for almost half a minute before he realized what it was. He stripped off the great blood-soaked leather gauntlets and lifted the mug in both hands, which were so deeply sheathed in hornlike calluses that he held the burning hot mug without any sign of discomfort. Or maybe, the cook considered, maybe it burned like hell, and the man was just too tired to care.

Zack took a sip, and a gleam of life came to his weather-lined face. His sigh was the one given by a simple man enjoying a simple pleasure. "Much obliged, Crackerbox."

But the cook was already pouring out more coffee. The rest of the boys wouldn't've dared to knock off until Zack had, even though none of 'em was as tough as he was. But now that he had, they'd be dragging themselves to the fire just as soon as they'd finished stowing their tools.

First up was Joe Silverfoot. Crackerbox didn't know a lot of Injuns who took a cotton to coffee, but Joe gave a genuine groan of pleasure as that first hot mouthful went down.

Joe was the one who'd known 'bout the valley in the first place. Apparently it had been some sort of holy place to his tribe, but since they'd all been wiped out by the railroad company thirty years ago, he'd figgered its supposed holiness weren't doin' anybody any good a'tall, and he'd tried to sell it to Zack back when the big man'd been thinking about homesteading.

But Zack'd been discouraged by the near impossibility of gettin' in or outta the place. The only way they'd done it was with a mess of dynamite. But he'd remembered it, all right.

Next to arrive was Gunther and Helmut, the Boom brothers. They didn't talk much, least not that most people could understand, but they worked steady, and were some of the best damn drovers Crackerbox'd ever seen. It was claimed that each of 'em could drive a team of eight straight up a canyon wall, and when they were ready to leave the valley, they'd get a chance to prove it. Dynamite could only do so much.

The other half-dozen men staggered up at their own speed. Crackerbox had actually been ladling the last one his second helping of stew when Doc finally made his appearance.

It was obvious that the little man was unused to this kind of work, but he never complained, which earned him a heap of respect that smoothed over any irritation at the amount of it he actually got done.

It also helped that he had taken charge of the bone boiling, which had quickly been acknowledged as a worse job than even the butchering.

But it had to be done, certainly. Crackerbox had been dealing with dead animals all his life, he reckoned, and he'd never seen anything like the way these critters rotted away.

When they'd first arrived, there'd been the idea of tanning their hides. Zack'd brought in an old Québécois trapper, Two Knives Eugene, who swore he could tan skeeters. Watchin' the man's face the first time he'd seen what they was dealin' with had proved itself a treat, but he'd then roared out something about acceptin' the challenge and had set to, singin'.

But it hadn't worked out. Oh, he knew his business, and no mistake. He'd set up racks and pans and mixed up slurries of powders and dog shit that had people's eye's waterin'. He'd wielded a skinnin' knife like a stage magician, and even Crackerbox had learned a thing or two about removing hides, but instead of drying and curing, the skins had turned into sheets of stinkin' slime, even when they was buried in salt or smeared with whatever concoction Two Knives slathered 'em with.

Their meat was just as bad. It spoiled instantly. Crackerbox had even tried to pop it into a pot while Big Axe Chow carved it off a still quivering carcass, but even then it was like eatin' bad fish soaked with lamp oil. He'd had to throw out one of his best kettles, as even after scouring it down to the shine with sand, anything cooked in it tasted rancid.

Everybody agreed that these were the most useless critters they'd ever seen.

Their bones lasted, once you boiled 'em with borax, which was a durn good thing, since that was the whole point of this circus. Crackerbox sighed. The job was starting to get to him. Gettin' to all of them, really. They were so ready for it to be over and done with.

He was chopping out a slice of johnny cake for Doc when they all heard the steady clop of hooves and realized that Fancy Man was making one of his rare appearances at camp. The man was one of the best scouts anyone had ever worked with, but there was no denying that the man was like a ghost, and was hardly ever seen. This was doubly strange because when he was in town, Fancy Man was one of the most sociable and talkative men on the frontier. His way with the ladies was the stuff of legend, and it was even said that he once won an impromptu argument with a Copperhead senator from Washington, D.C., that had made a whistle stop in Laramie, scrounging for votes.

And now, sure enough, his white horse could be seen against the gloom and in less than a minute, the man himself, his famous blue feather flashing in the firelight from its place in his leather plug hat, entered the circle of men.

He rolled from his saddle, landed silently on his feet, and gave a small jerk of his head. His horse nodded once, turned, and headed off toward the paddock. Everybody tried not to show how impressed they were, but there was no denying that that there was a mighty fine horse.

Crackerbox dished out a bowl and Fancy Man took it with a low "much obliged, suh." He then walked, with those delicate, mincing steps that had caused men to fatally underestimate him from Dawson to Dodge, over to the fire and hunkered down to eat.

Everybody waited. Fancy Man never showed up unless he had something important to say. He polished off his stew, delicately wiped his mouth with a lace handkerchief he'd been given by the Jersey Lily herself (Big Zack swore he'd seen it happen), and looked up. "We're done," he announced. "Been up, down and sideways, and there ain't no more of them critters left." Having delivered his news, he settled down cross-legged, pulled his hat over his eyes, and dropped off to sleep on the spot.

This was welcome news indeed. They had been working every day for close to six weeks, and even with Doc's nightly recitation, tempers had begun to fray.

But now the end was in sight. Crackerbox considered the great corrals with their gigantic residents. Two, maybe three days of hard work, and they'd be packing up and hitting the trail.

Everyone else was doing the same calculation and a guffaw from Sledgehammer was confirmation of the wave of good feeling that was sweeping over the whole camp.

"Read it agin, Doc!"

Crackerbox nodded. This nightly ritual had kept them going, even when things had been at their grimmest. It would feel even better to hear it now.

Doc pulled the folded handkerchief from his waistcoat. From within that, he extracted the tattered scrap of newsprint. As always, he made a show of polishing and adjusting his spectacles, and, in a clear, firm voice, read:

JUNE 17, 1902. CHICAGO: Today representatives from the American Museum of Natural History in New York City, presented to bone hunter Barnum Brown, a check for fifty dollars to be drawn on the First National Bank, for delivering the perfectly preserved skeleton of an immense, unknown creature that scientists have declared to be thousands of years old.

Although there are those who contest this seemingly farfetched assessment of the "dinosaur's" age, there is no denying that the remains are ancient enough that they have turned to stone!

"We are always looking for more fossils," (which is what scientists call these ancient animal remains) said Professor Felix Cahill, "and can assure your readers that our museum is willing to pay top dollar for exemplary specimens."

Doc finished, and as always, passed the scrap around so that they could compare the newspaper's fanciful line drawing with the animals they'd been rounding up. As always, there were smiles and nods all around, even though it was pretty obvious that the artist had never actually seen one of the great lizards in the flesh. But as Sledgehammer had sensibly pointed out, "Them city boys can't even draw up a good lookin' mountain lion!" There was no arguing with that. No, things looked good.

Fifty dollars for bones thousands of years old!

They couldn't wait to see what them city slickers would pay for fresh ones.

THE WICKED WILD

Nicole Givens Kurtz

"A wind can move the branches of trees,
but it will never move the head of a man."
—African Proverb

1901
New Mexico Territory

"Who there?" Zara Gibson whirled toward the sound.
"Come on out here now!"

The gods grew up in the foothills of this place. In the gods' shadows, hills, mesas, and arroyos remained, or so the Navajo believed. The gusts of wind swept through the valley between the natural monuments.

The wind didn't silence the crunch of footsteps.

She waited.

One breath.

Two breaths.

Three breaths.

The wind died as if listening too. Nothing. She resumed her walk along the untamed path toward home. A body couldn't be too careful.

Out here, the West wasn't just wild.

It was wicked.

Zara suspected the wickedness had found Chad Wilkins. A prick of anger fed by the heavy loss of the Civil War. She'd spied him fooling around in some arroyo consumed by thick billowing smoke, but no fire. She'd smelled the odor of spoiled eggs, thick like the smoke, and took off. With her heart pounding, she prayed he hadn't caught her spying.

Not that she meant to be spying. She had been out walking to get some fresh air—until it turned foul.

"How come you ain't got your black ass to town to do the laundry?" Chad asked as he emerged from the brush. She spied his horse appearing behind him as if a dark apparition.

He spat around the wad of tobacco from his mouth. A cowboy hat, dirt brown from years of wear and weather, sat atop hair just as dirty. His horse looked away, embarrassed by his owner's lack of tact.

Zara picked up the scattering of dried tumbleweed around her appropriated hogan, giving her hands something to keep busy. Idle hands became the devil's workshop, and Zara had one devil too many standing in front of her.

"Ya hear me?" Chad shouted. Soon the deep rattling of his cough shook his body and choked off whatever other vile he intended to spew.

Zara stopped and turned to face him. "I hear ya talkin'."

"You ain't been in a week."

Zara took in a breath and released it. "Been down in my spirit."

Chad scowled. "I ain't brought you all the way out here for you to get lazy."

"I brought myself. Earned my own way. Walked on my own two feet. An' I ain't felt too good."

The whole point of coming out to this land and settling was to be free of folks like Chad, men who thought they still owned her and her people.

Chad peered across to her the way folks looked at scorpions scurrying across the road. His dark green eyes narrowed. "I protected ya."

Zara adjusted her headscarf. "Say you."

"So, getcha black ass back to town before I drag you back."

Zara put her chapped hands on her hips. She didn't miss the washing and scrubbing. The harsh lye soap ate into her skin and even now, days later, her hands still bore welts and angry flesh. She looked him up and down before shaking her head. *Some people just don't know how they sound.*

"I go to town when I'm good an' ready. I ain't yo slave no more."

Chad spat out another wad of tobacco. It sounded like coughing out a hairball—wet and dark. It landed near her skirt. He wiped his mouth with the back of his hand and shrugged like her words didn't matter.

They did.

And she knew it.

"You see, *girl*, just 'cause we living in the new frontier don't mean we like being dirty. We're civilized, not savages."

Zara peered harder against the glint of the sinking

New Mexico sun. The wide-brimmed cowboy hat cast his face all in shadow, except the slash of anger on his lips. This close to dusk, the leaving light revealed the slivers of smoke escaping from Chad's back, smoke that the ordinary folk wouldn't see. Could be trick of the light. Could be trick of the devil.

"No point in being clean when your soul's stained black," Zara said.

"You know all about being black, don't you? How many good people died 'cause of your kind? And for what?" Chad scratched at the beard crawling along his jawline.

Zara didn't give a direct answer. She'd traveled far, across hard, unyielding earth, to get to what some called the Promised Land. She wouldn't waste time on the likes of him. With a sigh, she turned to go inside her home.

The cocking of a gun caught her attention, and she turned back to him.

"You don't turn your back to me." Chad pointed his pistol in anger. "That's enough damn disrespect, you filthy n—"

On instinct, Zara lifted her hands and, with palms out, swept them upward, toward the heavens. A huge gust of wind rushed over Chad. The language of her forefathers and foremommas rushed in a stream of verbal magic. She commanded the winds, and they readily obeyed.

The blood in her connected to all that came before. They took their payment from her, payment for her calling them out and waking them. They always left her tired. So tired.

Sometimes, it was worth it.

Like now.

"Come, great winds!" She commanded the wind to whirl around him. The roaring of the blood in her body spoke to her fury, and it called to theirs. Pent up anger from years of enslavement, cruelty, and torment had unfurled.

Chad's lips puckered. Eyes bulging, he clawed at his neck trying to ease the pressure on his windpipe. The winds stole his breath. His face became a dark purple, and he'd drawn blood in thin rivulets along his neck before Zara lowered her fists.

"You a nasty person, Chad Wilkins." Zara coughed out blood, thick and wet like the tobacco wad now drying on the parched earth. Zara wiped her mouth. She didn't like using it, the magic. Not because of the damage to her own spiritual core, but because it frightened folks.

And frightened folks did foolish things.

She peered at him, the roar of power burning in her palms' centers. The skin along Chad's temple bulged outward and crawled down to his mouth. He opened it and a spew of black smoke shot out. Zara raised her hand and wind rose up to whisk it away.

Chad cackled, but behind his eyes, Zara saw something *other*.

With her chest burning in agony, she waved her hand, and a whispered, "Thank you," to her ancestors. To Chad, as he mounted his horse, she said, "Go on now, Chad. Y'all leave me be."

Chad gasped, his inhales rattling in a wet, sickening manner. He coughed out some words in her direction, before yanking on the reins and leaving, just as she had wanted. The red-purple hue had started to fade, but the damage to his windpipe would take days, maybe weeks, to heal.

As he left, he wheezed out three words. "You. Gonna. Pay."

Zara sighed. Now she'd done it. The wickedness would come for her. The movement behind Chad's eyes and rippling beneath his skin didn't belong there. The very thing she had hoped to avoid by relocating to this desolate place, she had angered.

The devil would have his due.

And clean laundry.

Trouble arrived first thing in the morning.

Throughout the previous evening, the wind's howling had warned of approaching evil. Despite the pain and soreness in her muscles, she'd risen early, heeding her ancestors' wisdom, and found Sheriff Hicks waiting outside her door, his fist raised to knock. He didn't have his usual smile.

Sheriff Hicks tipped his hat, but didn't enter. He hesitated, then said, "Understand me fully, Zara. Chad Wilkins come to see me last night. Now, I dunno what happened. You can't just go around attacking folks. This ain't some juju village in Africa. We might be living 'round in a wilderness, but we observe the social graces of life. I won't stand for base savagery out here . . ."

Zara listened, allowing Hicks to say his piece. He was the law, after all.

Men like Chad looked strong, but that strength didn't go all the way through. Just on the surface. She suspected

Chad had taken it bad, but it went deeper than hurting his feelings. The *other* inside him, housed up in his body, recognized her power, and that of her ancestors. It wanted it, craved it.

But Sheriff Hicks didn't wanna hear 'bout all that.

So, she crossed her arms. "He drew on me."

Sheriff Hicks climbed back onto his horse and leaned over his saddle. "What did you do to make him do that, Zara?"

She sighed. "Sheriff, I done lived a bunch of places, and the land always changes. Sumthin' that don't always change—*hate*. Whether it be here or in the deepest hell of Mississippi, the wickedness don't care. It feeds on the hate."

Sheriff Hicks's breath shuddered. "Look here, Zara. I'm a Christian, so I don't believe in that mojo stuff. All I got was a battered cowpoke crying foul. Dunno how you did it, or even if you did it. Just stay away from him. Okay?"

"I'm a freed person. No more master. No more followin' orders."

"You still gotta follow the law."

"What about him? What about the pistol he drew on me? Threatened my life! He didn't even tell you that."

"You sayin' it's self-defense?"

"I'm sayin' he's the lowest value of a coward, drawin' on me when my back's turned. If he come out here again and tries to take my life, he won't be comin' to talk to you about it."

As she stood just outside the threshold of her residence, she studied the broad-shouldered lawman. He rode a dark horse. The tan cowboy hat kept the sun from his face. His gun belt slung low over his hips contained his guns, and his badge shone from his chest. Wiry and red-haired with spectacles, he didn't look like danger. A mistake that many numbered dead had made.

"I see. You like getting your own way, don't you, Zara?" Hicks rubbed his chin. Then, his usual smile emerged on his lips.

She shrugged. "Don't ever'body?"

"Indeed." He laughed.

"Changes are shiftin' things, Sheriff. The wickedness ain't gonna lie still. It be comin'. Sum folks better be gettin' used to that."

He studied her for a moment, before shaking his head. "What you goin' on about? More of that juju?"

She fixed her gaze on him. "Sumthin's here and that little pistol ain't gonna help."

"Ain't no problem these guns can't solve, Zara." He patted the butt of a gun, but his smile sagged a little. "Now, will you just come into town and wash? The unmarried men folk like going to church with clean clothes. Might find 'em a good God-fearin' woman."

The sound of wagons and galloping horses couldn't drown out the saloon's music next door from filtering into the laundry. She could smell the alcohol and unwashed bodies sweating off their drunk over the scent of the lye. Despite being early in the day, laughter and howls emitted in concert with the music of frontier life. Inside the store, she sat perched on the stool as the water-filled caldrons warmed over the fire. Beyond the buildings, the blistering and scorched landscape stretched out across the New Mexico territory.

That morning Zara ate her breakfast and walked back into town with the morning sun accompanying her as it rose higher in the heavens. Some townspeople called the land enchanted. Spirits rose from the ground and inhabited the trees, the animals, and the stars. The sky birthed humans and all living things. Here, the line between reality and mystery blurred. How else did you describe the towering mesas, the deep canyons, and magical terrain? One thing was certain. Living in this wilderness wore down lives. She saw it in the eyes of customers who came to get their clothes washed. All men. Single. Widowers.

It'd been three days since Chad Wilkins's visit. Recovered, Zara stood on the storefront's porch, attempting to catch the breeze. Already, the New Mexico sun wrought high heat and little relief. The mile trek into town had been slow, but she got there.

"Ah, you finally drag your sorry ass into town!" Chad leered as he stumbled out of the saloon. The inky smoke drifted from him and his shadow shimmered as if unable to hold the shape.

Zara tried to ignore him, well *it*. She shifted her eyes instead to the beautiful mesa beyond him, but the smoke skewed her view. No one else on the street—those strolling past, those standing around talking—seemed to be able to see the wickedness that had claimed Chad Wilkins.

"You hear me?" Chad roared.

"Yeah. Ever'body can hear you." Zara turned to go back inside her shop. Maybe he'd knock off and go back to the abandoned hogan, back to his demonic master, or he'd follow her in, which would at least take him away from those on the street.

His bellowing drew a crowd from the saloon. Several people paused as they strolled along to observe the antics of the town idiot.

Darn it! That's what she didn't want—a group of folks in danger of getting hurt if Chad's *other* decided to engage her.

"That's 'cause I got somethin' to say to you! Witch!"

Zara paused inside her store. The wind whistled as it slipped in. Yes, she heard the warning. Chad and the others moved down the short porch toward her.

"Sheriff Hicks let you off. You should be in a jail, woman." Chad spat out the word *woman* as if it had been a curse. "I betcha bewitched him too. I can see it in ya even if they don't." Tendrils of dark smoke spiraled from the corners of his mouth as he leered at her.

The crowd, now gathered at her door, shuddered in unison. Hot and fast whispers whipped about them, chasing after Chad's words. Zara put her hands on her hips, but held her peace.

"You deny you did this?" Chad pointed at his neck, the contusion still visible, but fading.

"Quit your bellyaching. You got your ass kicked by a woman," Bud chided from just behind Chad, before elbowing his way to the front. He tipped back his cowboy hat. "Belly back up to the bar and drink your sorrow like ever'body else."

"She's a filthy witch! I tell you," Chad repeated. His face flushed.

Zara watched as the flush deepened to black blotches blossoming along his cheeks, across his forehead, and down into his beard. The hard green of his eyes turned dark. His hands sprawled long, beastlike claws.

No one else noticed.

Right before her, the wickedness consumed the rest of Chad's humanity.

"Eh, yeah! She's made the dirt on my Sunday shirt disappear!" shouted Rancher John.

Laughter.

From the rear someone added, "Aye, ain't that magic!"

More laughter.

It ripped through the group, cresting in volume before tapering off as members tired of the fun and turned back toward the saloon. The noonday sun made one thirsty.

Zara suppressed her smile but glowed inside at their kind words about her washing skills. It failed to eclipse the mounting fear inside her. Already her hands tingled in anticipation. The being inside Chad might attack now, or wait. Most of the time, devils did things in the dark, under the cover of night, when man's defenses were lowest.

Chad shoved Bud away, still fixing Zara with a glare. There, the hot gaze of the *other* inside him, the wickedness that puppeted him. She'd seen that look on many a frustrated white man's face. He'd meant to cause her strife, but that had failed.

The man wanted to make her pay for that. The demon wanted to feast on what remained.

She shuddered at the thought and the deep knowing of truth in that thought.

With the words of her ancestors in her ear and her

heart, the voice of her grandmamma spoke of their strength. *Do not fear. We are one.*

"Leave. I have work to do." Zara nodded toward the saloon.

Chad grunted, made a rude gesture, and stormed off. The angry dark wickedness flowing behind him like a cape.

Dusk. Few people remained on the road. Most had retired to their homes and families. Even the saloon next door had intermittent periods of silence. Shoulders singing in fatigue, hands raw from the lye, and back throbbing from lifting and bending, Zara longed for a hot cup of coffee and a comfortable bed.

She'd just closed the door when Chad Wilkins appeared in the road.

"You whore! Witch!" he yelled. He clutched two lanterns, one in each hand. The flames inside each held an eerie and otherworldly green flame.

"Go home, Chad. Just walk on back to where you came from," Zara warned. The hair on the back of her neck stood up.

"You know what they used to do with witches?" Chad bellowed, spittle flying.

He raised the lanterns high in the air.

Chad hurled the first one at her.

She fell backward against the door. With swift hands, she turned the knob and raced inside. The lantern missed her but slammed into the store's wall, bursting and sending the green fire and oil all over.

"You fool!" Zara screamed as the second one shot past into the laundry.

Fire latched onto the wooden structure as fast as lightning. It chewed, not just her store, but soon the saloon next door, too. Dry air and even drier wood burned, encouraging the flames. Growing every second, the flames spread—greedy and propelled by the desert's high winds. Billows of smoke wafted into the sky and back into Zara's store.

"Fire! Fire!" Screams rose into a chorus.

Blinded by smoke, Zara crouched down to get air. On her knees, she crawled out the door and off the porch. Fear spread as fast as the fire itself to the few who remained in town.

Chad disappeared into the smoke and falling light.

"What happened?" Sheriff Hicks met Zara in the center of the road.

"Chad," Zara coughed out.

"Water! Get water! Form a line from the arroyo!" Sheriff Hicks shouted at a group of men racing from the smoking saloon.

Horrible wickedness ravaged one building, skipping in delight from one wooden area to the other, greedily consuming all in its path.

That's what the Devil came to do. Kill. Steal. Destroy.

The harshness of ignorance and hate may have come to the West, but Zara and her ancestors wouldn't let this Promised Land be destroyed by it.

No.

What to do? She'd just recovered from her last attempt to fight off Chad Wilkins. That had been in anger, and the fury rolled forward in her even now.

The Indians could call down the rain, but it was her

African ancestors who controlled the wind. Even as she pulled from her inner strength, the fire began to fan back toward the already charred sections, lowering the heat. The magic pulled on her life force, and she coughed, bloody spittle dark and wet against the dirt road. She got to her feet, her lungs burning. Her ancestors had blessed her. The winds had calmed the flames. The townspeople raced to put out what remained of the blaze.

"Thank God the whole damn town didn't burn." Sheriff Hicks clapped a hand on her shoulder. "You all right?"

"That's twice Chad tried to kill me." The burning lessened as the wind calmed around her.

"You sure it was him?"

"I got two eyes, Sheriff."

"All right. All right." He put his hands on his guns. "I'll bring him in."

"No. Imma gonna talk to him. Alone." Zara started toward the west. Toward the wicked Chad Wilkins. He wouldn't get a third try.

"Zara! Get back here. Don't do anything foolish!"

She paused, looked back over her shoulder, and said, "I'm not the one that tried to burn down the town."

Sheriff Hicks hung his head and reached for her arm. "I'll go. You're angry, Zara, and you're being reckless."

She searched his face and saw the concern shining in his eyes. She had to be the one to settle the issue with Chad. Sherriff Hicks's bullets wouldn't exorcise the demon inside Chad. Only she had the power to do that, because, well, it wanted her magic, her power. White men always did.

That demon ought to be careful what he asked for.

"So was movin' out to this desert." Zara removed his hand and resumed her trek.

Chad had presented his wickedness.

Now, she'd show him what she had.

As she walked down the path toward the outskirts of town, Zara called upon her ancestors, and one by one, they appeared beside her, dropping out of the sky like falling stars. Each apparition wore his traditional dress of her ancestral homeland.

Amari

Bwana

Henry

George

Kwame

Soon, the noise of town faded. In the distance coyotes howled, and the light faded. Once she reached Chad's cabin, her ancestors stood with her as watery silhouettes against the velvet night, casting an eerie glow. The two-room home sat on a stretch of barren land. A few feet away, a barn sheltered the beasts, but not the one locked in Chad Wilkins's heart. The light in the window flickered and the sky above sparkled. Zara stood at the end of the walk. The wickedness she'd hoped to avoid had provoked this confrontation. Evil. Sinful, the Christians called it.

"I'm callin' you out, Chad Wilkins!"

The door creaked open. A shirtless Chad walked out onto the porch. His bare feet moved silently across the wood. When he saw her, he frowned.

"You survived?"

Her presence answered that, so she didn't reply. She raised her hands as she came closer.

"You always looked lived in, Chad." Zara spied the possessing entity as it hissed out of his mouth, a spiral of buzzing darkness pouring out between his lips toward her. She pulled the wind down and spun her hands to push the attacking evil away and out of sight.

"You oughta died in the fire. Then we'd feast on your power!" Chad screamed, but the voice no longer sounded like him.

"Is Chad still in there?" She'd seen so much death and just plain wickedness. Despite the hard pit of anger in her gut, she wanted Chad to live.

The glowing red eyes narrowed, suspecting she meant to trick it. Blisters lined the soles and sides of Chad's feet. He walked as if he felt nothing. The round pus-filled sacks burst with each step, leaving wet tracks behind.

The demon no longer cared for his host.

"Well, is he?"

No reply.

"There's some emptiness that can't be filled, huh?" Zara asked.

Every inch of her hurt. Almost all of her spiritual energy was being syphoned into holding her ancestors here. They helped guide the wind.

"We want you dead!" Chad answered, leaping at her, claws out.

Zara willed the wind once more. Arms heavy with fatigue, she knocked him backward.

"Power is acquired by taking it," Chad breathed. His

descent spiraled down into the absolute wickedness that continued.

"You can't just take what you need. Round here that's called stealin'."

"Not if you're dead," he screamed, stepping down the porch's two flat steps.

"Who'd do the laundry?" Zara wheezed and collapsed to her knees.

So. Weak.

He came at her once more, claws stretched out toward her neck. She pivoted to avoid his right hand, but his sharp nails caught in her left side. They shredded her thin blouse, flesh, and muscle. Chad whirled to face her, licking the blood from his fingers.

Gritting her teeth against the searing agony, Zara pushed herself to stand.

He rushed her again, but as he swung, Zara dropped to the dirt. Standing took too much physical strength, of which she had little left. Zara fought to keep her eyes open. She wouldn't cower from death.

"Wait. Who them with you?" Chad squinted, peering with red eyes into the distance.

Zara's ancestors moved to intercept him, and once he spied them up close, he screamed. Turning to run, he tripped and fell, his legs tangled up in each other. Scrambling to his feet, he tried to flee.

Zara's ancestors stepped into her, each one adding their strength of spirit into her body. One after the other, until Zara could stand on her own, full of strong magic and powerful, they joined her. Pain vanished beneath the strength of her ancestors. With them came the iron will to survive the Middle Passage, long lashes of whips, war, and torture.

"No! More!" Zara shouted in the voice of many. With fingers splayed, she called the winds, and they readily obeyed. They rushed Chad Wilkins, pinning him to the ground. She shortened the distance between them. Once she reached him, she demanded, "Leave Chad. Leave him, now! Get out!"

"No!" the demon spat back, laughing in glee. "Kill him. We will still live."

Anger pushed forward, but Zara's ancestors soothed her. *Be calm. We will force him out.*

She pushed the wind, faster. If the demon wanted to stay, it would have to stay in a wind-swept and battered host. Chad screamed until he became unconscious. Before her, the orange glow spiraled out of Chad's body. His mouth split from the entity's mass.

Exhausted, Zara stumbled as her ancestors took their leave, as did her magic. She'd emptied it all.

"Until next time . . ." the thing promised before slithering into the ground and disappearing from sight.

With her entire being singing in misery, she watched the spot for a moment to make sure it didn't crawl back into Chad. With her power temporarily spent, she couldn't protect him.

After a few minutes, Chad stirred awake, his face ripped raw by the wind, his clothes tattered. He glared at her with confusion that melted away to anger.

"You did this to me!"

She nodded, too tired and too hurt to say much more.

"We ain't even, bitch." He coughed and tried to push

himself to a sitting position. He collapsed backward with a *thud.*

Zara studied him for a moment, before turning back to the walk. Slowly, she headed down the long path to her home.

"Come." Zara sat in front of her fire, a pipe stuck between her teeth, gazing out across the dawn of a new day.

Sheriff Hicks stood in the doorway. "Mornin', Zara. I'm here about Chad Wilkins. I went over to arrest him this morning, and well, he's in a bad way. Had to call out for the doctor from Tohatchi to come and take a look at 'im."

Zara nodded. Puffed.

Sheriff Hicks shifted his weight to his other foot. "It's lookin' like a heart attack."

"Too much wickedness ain't good for you." Zara met the sheriff's gaze before turning back to the view.

"Yeah?"

"Yeah."

She puffed.

"Funny thing. You went tarrin' after him," Sherriff Hicks said.

Zara puffed. "Imma uneducated person, Sheriff, but I didn't think talkin' to a person could cause them to have a heart attack."

Sherriff Hicks nodded. "It can't."

"All I did was talk to 'im."

He studied her for a few long seconds, before asking, "You comin' in to do the laundry? John said you can set you up in one of them back rooms until repairs are done."

"Sure. Ever'body deserves clean laundry."

CHANCE CORRIGAN AND THE LORD OF THE UNDERWORLD

Michael A. Stackpole

Chance Corrigan crouched in the tall prairie grasses. *So that's what she'd meant by a Black Bart.*

The Grand Hotel in Chimney Springs, Wyoming, offered its guests a hearty breakfast with coffee "strong enough to melt a Black Bart." He'd assumed the reference had something to do with the Dominion Brimstone Mine #1—most likely a small steam engine that hauled ore cars up from the mine's dark depths. He'd not asked for clarification because he hadn't wanted to alert anyone to his interest in the mine's operations.

Clearly my mistake. Chance clicked his mechanical left eye in, the lenses shifting to bring the dark figure closer. At the first it looked almost human, serenely patrolling with a measured pace. The figure's stiffness— its arms didn't swing and it walked without too much bend to the knees—planted the idea of it being a living creature firmly in the grave.

If the coffee will *melt it, I'll order up a couple gallons.*

The automaton had been clothed as if a man, entirely

in black, from boots and jeans, to gloves and even hat. Only its neckerchief broke that pattern—this one wore red. Chance guessed it was meant as a way to identify the individual automatons at a distance. The mechanical man also wore a pair of six-shooters, one on each hip. It had no face *per se*, just a narrow slit where eyes should have been, and a round opening for a mouth.

It marched along a line of fence posts fitted with iron balls on top. As it approached the nearest fence post, the Black Bart paused for a moment. It looked down at the ball, then its head came up and it continued on along the path its endless trudging had worn into the ground. The pace remained steady, and the thing focused on its forward path. Its hands hung inches from the pistols, primed to draw.

Chance remained low, letting the automaton amble past. No one had bothered to string a single strand of wire between the posts, which suggested the automatons patrolled without any rest. He figured that if he watched any longer, another would come along the same route, regular as the clockwork which drove them. *All in all, wire would be cheaper, but not nearly as intimidating.*

Chance assumed that the automaton's barrel chest concealed a small engine which drew power from the Tesla generator set up in the middle of the mine's buildings. The engine powered the limbs through wires and gears. The torso also had to contain a couple of gyroscopes to provide balance, and a gyrocompass to aid with directions.

That realization led to a cascade of other conclusions, prompting a smile. The iron balls had to likewise draw power from the generator, and pushed it back out in the form of Marconi's wireless telegraphy. The automaton, in reaching a waypost, logged its arrival and likely received directions on to the next post. Somewhere inside it, through a series of gears and registers, the automaton could receive and then proceed to execute instructions. It didn't appear to Chance that the instructions were terribly complex, but to successfully patrol the mine's perimeter didn't require much thinking.

Chance waited for the automaton to reach the next waypost, then followed in its wake toward the mine facility entrance. He'd seen automatons before, but never anything quite this mobile. From the depth of the footprints, he guessed it weighed half-again as much as an equivalently sized man would. This suggested limbs made mostly of wood, with a thick armor plating on the torso— presumably to protect its operational machinery. And while its gait wasn't that fast, he knew better than to assume the same would be true of its ability to draw and fire a gun.

The automaton continued past the mine's buildings. The mine's opening—a grand earthen ramp descending to shadows—stood to the south. A tiny office building occupied the center of the compound, with the Tesla generator behind it, and a coal storage warehouse west of that. Another coal storage building stood to the north of the office, and a rail spur led away from it, to connect with the main rail line further north of the town.

Chance knocked on the ramshackle office's door.

A small bespectacled man answered, smiling weakly. "How may I help you?"

"I was hoping I could see the managing partner, Mr. Van Sloos?" Chance had to step back to read the name from the sign beside the door. "Would that be you?"

"I am his secretary." The man pushed his glasses back up on his nose. "What would this be concerning?"

Chance smiled. "I'm Alfred St. James. You recently ordered some special power-coupling equipment from Hyperion Electrical in St. Louis. I was on my way to Seattle, but decided to stop in and see how those devices were working for you. You did get my wire, didn't you?"

The little man blinked, then glanced back at a tiny desk with a telephone receiver perched on it. "Western Union delivered no wire." He attempted to close the door.

Chance's foot stopped him. "Perhaps Mr. Van Sloos has a moment for me."

The secretary sighed, resigned, it appeared, to the fact that he'd never get the door closed. He crossed to his desk, ran the phone's crank around several times, then picked up the earphone and spoke into the mouthpiece in hushed tones. Because the man raised a hand to hide his mouth, Chance didn't bother to click the telephoto lens into place in his eye and read the man's lips.

The secretary nodded once, then replaced the receiver. "Mr. Van Sloos has deigned to see you."

The man opened a door in the cabin's far wall, and waved Chance on through. Chance smiled and entered a very small, featureless box—barely suited to being a line shack on the range, much less the office of the mine's managing director. As he spun around, the secretary slammed the door. Bells sounded, then the entire room descended.

Chance took the elementary precaution of stepping out of line with the hidden lift's door, but stopped short of filling his hand with the derringer in his jacket pocket. Assuming hostility where eccentricity could suffice as an explanation wasn't going to get him what he wanted. *It's best if it's a* peaceful *negotiation.*

The lift came to a rest with a creak and a groan. Chance opened the door onto a subterranean office that had been gouged from the rock and built out with tall shelves. Books filled them, walnut paneling upon which hung oil paintings of hellish landscapes stood between them, and a parquet floor—fitting since the room was big enough to host a ball—united all. The furnishing ran to the baroque, with lots of gilding and embroidery. Red velvet curtains covered what bare rock had escaped paneling, and blood-red satin sashes did the same for the ceiling. *And behind at least one of those drapes there's a door into the mine itself.*

He turned toward the slender-legged desk, which held an electric lamp at both forward corners. Instead of seeing a man seated in the high-backed chair, he saw the chair's back. Van Sloos, it appeared, had a flare for the dramatic.

"Thank you for seeing me, Mr. Van Sloos. I am—"

"A liar."

Chance blinked his good eye. "I beg your pardon."

"A liar." The chair slowly turned around, revealing a scarecrow-thin man, with straw-colored hair and a scar over his left cheekbone. "I would recognize your voice anywhere, Chance Corrigan, even after all these years."

Chance's left eye clicked in for a closer view. The man's emaciated state, and the way his hair had thinned, would have denied Chance vital clues to his identity. But the scar, that triggered memories. It began as a straight line along the man's cheekbone then, under the eye, it curved down and around in a distinctly sickle shape. "As I recall, you were always a more accomplished liar than I was."

The man rose. His dark suit suggested the prosperity his cadaverous body belied. "I was told you'd come. I know you killed Alex Gavrilis. I told the Brotherhood I wasn't afraid of you."

Chance shook his head. "You haven't changed at all, have you, Bertie? You'd never have called Gavrilis 'Alex' while he was alive—at least not in earshot of your brother and his cronies."

Bertie Palmerstone slowly smiled. "Oh, how they used to laugh at you, Corrigan. Smart boy from a tradesman's family, thinking he was worthy of our company simply because a benefactor bought you a place at college. We shared many a chuckle over you—especially after the accident and your apparently illusory death."

Chance laughed sharply. "You're not fooling me, Bertie. You were never part of it. Randolf couldn't tolerate your presence. Likewise his friends. When you were off scheming, they laughed at you, too. They loved telling stories of your misadventures."

"Liar!"

"They roared at the story of your burglary of that convent in England and your being driven out by eighty-year-old nuns wielding brooms." Chance's smile sharpened. "Or, especially, the unfortunate affair of you bursting out of that confessional, ready to conduct a Black

Mass. On Easter. At Notre Dame. In front of the Archbishop."

The room's pallid light reduced the flush of Bertie's cheeks to a grey smudge. "They would never . . ."

"They *did*. Happily. Your occult dabbling provided endless entertainment." Chance's chin came up. "In fact, you've got no more reason to love the Brotherhood than I do."

"No, no, we have nothing in common." Bertie punched his desk, then did his best to cover the pain. "I am a Palmerstone! I am one of them."

The indignation in Bertie's voice prompted Chance to laugh harshly, but he caught himself. "You weren't one of them. Yes, you are a Palmerstone, but Randolf was the heir. You were the spare. You have never had an original idea in your life; and you never fully think through the ones you've stolen. The Brotherhood tolerated you simply to fend off boredom."

Bertie's head came up. He stared at Chance, naked hatred blazing his eyes. And stared past him. Clearly the words had penetrated—not opening a wound, but *reopening* one. "You're wrong, Corrigan, incredibly wrong. On all counts. But none of that matters. I'll show you. I'll show them."

Chance opened his arms. "Here, with this? A coal mine? Your brother and his friends are becoming the masters of the world. Even if you supply them every speck of coal they need, you'll be nothing more to them than a servant."

Bertie laughed low and cold, in tones Chance had heard many times before and always associated with irredeemable insanity. "Oh, I understand them and their desires, Corrigan. I understand yours as well."

"What is it you think I want?"

"Me, dead, of course. To hurt my brother."

Chance shook his head. "As always, wrong."

"I know better than to believe you." Bertie sucked at a knuckle. "But, let's pretend. Why are you here?"

"You ordered things from Hyperion Electric. I'd used the same equipment to improve the spider constructs that Gavrilis was using to build his dam at Aswan." Chance shrugged. "I assume you've converted one into a burrowing device. I need it. How much?"

Bertie snorted. "Is that it?"

"I don't see much more on offer, here, though I find the Black Barts interesting."

"Thank you."

"Who did you steal the plans from?"

The man's nostrils flared. "How dare you!"

"There aren't that many people who can do that sort of work, and you're not one of them." Chance smiled. "No matter. Now, about the burrower . . ."

"No! No! Absolutely not!" Bertie thrust a quivering finger toward the surface. "Be happy I let you live, Chance Corrigan. And I advise you to leave Chimney Springs as fast as you can. I'll spare your life now, but not always. Run while you can!"

Chance stepped back toward the elevator, but paused in the doorway. "I hope you know what you're doing."

"I doubt you are sincere in your concern."

"Oh, I am, Bertie, I am." Chance sighed. "Your follies always ended badly. At school, someone could always cover it up for you. Here, people might react less kindly if you hurt them."

"The locals know that to vex me is dangerous." Bertie's brown eyes became slits. "And, soon, I become yet more dangerous."

"I'm sure you believe that." Chance nodded a brief salute in his direction. "I don't. And based on past experience, I'm thinking no one will get a laugh out of it this time."

Chance made it back to the surface unmolested. The secretary saw him out of the office, and the patrolling Black Barts ignored him as he headed back to town. For his part, he noted their presence and that passing automatons tipped their hats at each other, but paid them little attention other than that. That they could acknowledge each other made sense, and was proof that Bertie clearly *had* stolen the technology.

He only thinks of himself. No reason he'd think to put that into his creations.

Bertie Palmerstone's residence in Chimney Springs had come as a surprise, and forced Chance to recall things he'd gladly, long since forgotten. At university, Randolf Palmerstone, Alexander Gavrilis and others had formed their own secret society: the Pharaonic Brotherhood. Sons of politicians and industrialists all, they'd planned for world domination via a return to feudalism. They somehow considered this plan *enlightened*.

They'd never formally invited Chance to join, but were happy to use his genius at invention to further their plans. And while they'd never had any intention of letting him into their club, they were quite free in telling him that they'd make him rich enough to be their equal, provided his experiments bore fruit. The promise of wealth, and other inducements, had blinded him to their true nature.

And I paid the price for that blindness.

Bertie had entered university two years after Chance, despite being a year older than him. Bertie tried too hard to join his brother's circle of friends. They gladly tormented him, making Bertie look for new and different ways to garner power and prove himself both worthy of their company and of use to their group. Whether a mad scheme to marry into European royalty, or somehow track down the Templar treasure that had gone missing in Paris centuries before, Bertie's desperation had driven him further and further from reality.

Chance couldn't recall much in the way of specific detail on the host of schemes Bertie had hatched. The fact was that he'd been too busy working to ingratiate himself with the Brotherhood to concern himself with a failing rival. Despite that, however, he had a vague sense that Bertie's plans had become increasingly unsavory, and could only imagine the occult depths to which the man had sunk in the decade since Chance had last seen Palmerstone.

Chance made it back to Main Street, then turned south past the Golden Fortune Saloon and Gambling Emporium. The smoke drifting out was as foul as the piano was out of tune. A bit further on he walked by the Western Union office. He glanced quickly up through the alley between it and the Grand Hotel. Even knowing what to look for, he couldn't see the wires he'd spliced into the telegraph lines the night before.

Chance paused in the lobby to ask for his key. The small, wizened woman who'd previously warned him about the coffee, plucked the brass key from the mailbox, but didn't hand it to him.

"I wouldn't be telling a man his business."

Chance smiled. "But."

"Seems a few people saw you go out to the mine this morning." She put the key down on the counter, but covered it with a liver-spotted hand. "No business of mine, but the Finns, they are a suspicious lot."

"Finns?"

"Most of the miners, they live to the west, they is all miners from Finland." She jerked a thumb at a folded copy of the *Chimney Springs Gazette*. "Front half is English, back is Finnish. They is always a bit close, but since Van Sloos closed the mine to them, they's been getting angry. Talk is you might be working for him."

Chance raised both hands. "Just from St. Louis checking on something he ordered. If it helps, he kicked me out."

She nodded once and extended the key to him.

"I have to ask." Chance accepted the key. "Why did he lay the miners off?"

"They was fixing to stage a strike. Back wages."

Chance frowned. "If they weren't getting paid, shutting down doesn't make any sense."

"Welcome to Chimney Springs." She cackled. "Passenger train from Denver be up this afternoon. Likely you'll want to be on it. I'll prepare your bill."

Before Chance could respond, a tinny voice sounded loudly from Chimney Spring's main street. "Kaveli Nieminen, your time of reckoning has come."

The old woman closed her eyes. "It's Azrael!"

She offered no further explanation, so Chance stepped to the boardwalk in front of his hotel. He looked south, toward what appeared to be an abandoned church. *That Black Bart is special.*

He instantly catalogued differences between Azrael and the other Black Barts. This one wore a black neckerchief and a higher hat. The boots featured silver spurs, which looked great, but were little more than ostentation on a machine that would never sit a horse. The most notable difference between Azrael and its peers was that Azrael moved fluidly. Instead of its arms hanging stiffly, they swung with its steps. The automaton's knees bent. The fingers flexed and Chance imagined a very quick and smooth draw with either of the two pistols it wore.

The automaton stopped in the center of the street and looked north. "Kaveli Nieminen, face your doom as would a man."

Chance couldn't suppress a grin. Azrael looked every inch the hero of Western adventure dime novels, yet spoke with diction and vocabulary born of Palmerstone's Ivy League education. He suspected that the taller hat hid an elongated head, wherein machinery drove the voice and enabled coherent speech. *Always wanting to make yourself superior.*

Further up the street, from the saloon past the Western Union office, a long, lean man strode through the bat's-wing doors. He wore blue jeans and a patched work shirt. He hurriedly fastened the big steel belt buckle securing his gun belt. He carried two Colt Army Revolvers, but in blued steel, not the shiny silver of Azrael's pistols. Yet despite the impressive hardware, he looked utterly unsuited to gunfighting.

He wiped his hands on his jeans. "I am a man. If your master was a man, he would face me himself."

"You are not welcome in Chimney Springs. This town belongs to Dominion Brimstone. Leave off this strike talk, and I will let you and your family leave."

"How? We have no money. You have seen to that."

"You die for nothing."

"I worked for nothing." Nieminen nodded to the other miners who'd ventured out onto the boardwalk. "We all did."

"You barely worked at all. Do you promise to leave?"

Nieminen frowned and, with no further warning, drew as fast as he could. He filled his right hand with a pistol, aimed and fired. His first bullet hit Azrael in the right shoulder. It ricocheted up, ripping a hole in the automaton's hat brim.

And accomplished nothing.

Azrael drew smooth and fast, mocking Nieminen's draw. Azrael's first shot struck the man's drawn pistol. It drove the gun wide, sending the Finn's second shot into a post five feet from Chance. The bullet not only blasted the pistol from the shooter's hand, but a piece of it tore the man's right thumb off.

Azrael's second shot proved a revelation to Chance, and the third confirmed it. Both bullets slammed into the miner's belt buckle, jackknifing him forward and knocking him further down the street. He bounced once in a cloud of dust, then sprawled on his back, leaking from belly and hand. Spectators covered their mouths, or their children's faces with their hands, but none rushed to help him.

Magnetometers! Chance studied Azrael as the automaton holstered its pistol. Hitting the man's Colt revolver seemed like fancy gunplay, but the automaton really targeted the only thing it could sense. One or more magnetometers—one likely located where the eyes ought to be—let Azrael aim at concentrations of metal. A pistol or belt buckle made for great targets. The magnetometers also further explained how the other Black Barts got from iron ball to iron ball on their patrols.

Azrael raised its voice again. "Learn from this fool and cease your dispute with the mine. You can see how it will end." The automaton fell silent and marched up the street toward his fallen foe. He spared him no glance, but continued past, and turned west on Station Street, disappearing toward the mine.

Chance returned to the hotel's lobby.

The woman slid a piece of paper onto the front desk. "Dollar and a quarter is what you owe, Mr. St. James."

"Actually, I'm going to extend my stay."

She gave him a gimlet eye. "Azrael ain't too discriminating about what he's willing to shoot."

"I saw." He grabbed up the copy of the *Gazette*. "You got any influence with the Finns?"

"I hire some of their womenfolk to do cleaning, some cooking."

"Tell them to gather what they can and leave Chimney

Springs, tonight. They have to be gone by morning. Maybe go to Five Oaks, back east of here. It's important."

"I can tell 'em to find them a Moses and light out like the Hebrews out of Egypt."

"Tell them they'll get a wire when they can return: when Van Sloos is gone."

Her eyes tightened. "You're a bit more than a salesman from St. Louis, ain't you?"

"A bit." Chance smiled. "How's the hardware store fixed for copper wire?"

"They have a fair bit left from running a phone line down to Five Oaks."

"Good. Don't be alarmed if you hear some hammering."

"I'm half-deaf anyway." She smiled. "And if you're getting rid of Van Sloos, I ain't to be minding losing the rest of my hearing, not at all."

Chance started on his fourth cup of coffee despite his confidence that the first three had seriously begun to melt his teeth. Unfortunately they'd done little to lift the fog resulting from his lack of sleep. One minor benefit of the coffee was that it had killed enough of his taste buds that he didn't have to endure the sensual experience that had arrived at his table for breakfast. *Times it's better just not to know.*

"Chance, there you are." Hubert Palmerstone sat at the table without invitation, as if they were old friends. He used a corner of the gingham tablecloth to rub street dust from the shaft of a walking stick. "Just the man I wanted to see."

"That would be one of us."

Palmerstone affected to look hurt, but the half-blind squint ruined the effect. "Come now, old school chums, out here, in the middle of nowhere. We're the only civilized men for hundreds of miles. I was thinking—"

"No you weren't. You were scheming." Chance set his enameled cup down. "What do you think you can convince me to do?"

"Chance, I will offer you a deal that is to our mutual benefit." Palmerstone pushed his glasses back up. "You want the digging spider. I will give it to you, free and clear, in return for some simple work on your part."

"Such as?"

Palmerstone removed a small, leather bound book from his coat pocket. "My automatons. They follow instructions for patrolling and security. I would like to repurpose them to other tasks, more menial tasks, like hauling and loading coal. It's a simple exchange of services."

"Nothing is ever simple with you, Bertie." Chance leafed through the book of cleanly written instructions. *Not his handwriting.* "You have miners to do that hauling and loading for you."

Palmerstone shifted impatiently in his chair. "I'd rather not involve them."

Chance crossed his legs. "You have a labor shortage. That little stunt, that *execution*, yesterday, that frightened them off. You'd already laid them off. Why do you need them now?"

"It's really none . . ."

He tossed the book back on the table. "I guess you don't want me to help you after all."

Palmerstone sighed. "Very well. If you *must* know. I received a cable last evening. A coal mine in Colorado collapsed. I got an emergency order for coal and—"

"And the price had soared, correct? You'll make a killing?"

"There are financial advantages to be had right now, yes."

"What's my cut?"

The man's eyes widened behind the lenses. "I told you, I'll give you the mining spider."

Chance leaned forward, forearm on the book. "You'll have to do better. We split fifty-fifty, *and* I get the spider."

"That, sir, is outrageous!"

"This is more outrageous, then." Chance sat back, crossing his arms over his chest. "I'm not going to help you. Not at all. I am going to stay in Chimney Springs and watch you get your soft white hands all red and rough as you shovel coal into a railroad car. It'll be the first honest work you've ever done in your life. I wouldn't miss it for all the tea in China."

"You're making a mistake. A *big* mistake." Palmerstone shot to his feet. "You'll regret your decision, Chance Corrigan. You have no idea how much." He turned and headed for the door. "Just remember, I might have spared you, but no more. You've brought your doom upon yourself."

Chance gave Palmerstone five minutes, then retreated to his room in the Grand Hotel—the only place in Chimney Springs where he'd be safe. He figured Palmerstone wouldn't actually do anything until the dead of night, but underestimating him would have been a foolish mistake. And while he'd been fairly effective in manipulating Palmerstone so far, there remained one thing he didn't understand, and that made him uneasy.

After he'd visited the mine, Chance's tap on the Western Union line picked up messages going in and out from Dominion Brimstone. Palmerstone's messages had been in cipher and should have been secure. However Palmerstone was using a code which he'd obtained from his older brother. What Bertie hadn't known, or had forgotten, was that Chance had created that cipher at school. Chance had been able to read Palmerstone's messages with no difficulty at all.

Palmerstone had never worked well under pressure, and did even worse when trying to prove himself to old acquaintances. Killing the miner created a situation which Chance exploited easily. Once the miners headed to Five Oaks, Chance sent a cable to the Western Union office about a mine collapse near Denver; then he coded one from Palmerstone's brother, Randolf, demanding coal. Greed had always motivated Bertie, so offering him a fortune, then having him realize he no longer had a workforce to help him deliver, really tightened the screws.

Chance anticipated Palmerstone's appeal for help. Chance knew his refusal would further frustrate him, and would make Bertie feel humiliated. Bertie, in turn, would see only one way to redeem his honor.

He'd send Azrael to murder Chance, which was exactly what Chance had wanted.

And prepared for.

The only loose end that caused a bit of concern was

figuring out how Bertie had come to be in Chimney Springs in the first place. The man had avoided anything even approaching work the way a drunkard avoided temperance meetings. Bertie wanted something from the mine, and the demand for coal did make such ventures profitable; but certainly not on the scale that Bertie had always desired.

But what?

Bertie always had his secrets. His schemes, shared with the Brotherhood, had grown more and more outlandish. Chance found it hard to imagine that one of Hubert's schemes might have borne fruit—especially in the middle of nowhere. He caught himself before he dismissed Bertie out of hand however, because even if he'd failed at everything else, he might have finally succeeded. *Even a blind squirrel finds an acorn now and again.*

That thought sent a shiver down Chance's spine. *Whatever it is, it won't be as benign as an acorn.* He drew in a deep breath and double-checked his preparations. He might not be able to imagine what Hubert had gotten up to; but he was equally confident that Hubert believed he couldn't be stopped. *And that belief, quite literally, could be the death of him.*

Then Chance heard the first of Azrael's heavy footfalls on the Grand Hotel's staircase.

Smiling, Chance tucked himself down behind the room's cast iron stove. *Here goes nothing.*

In the depths of Dominion Brimstone Mine #1, Chance walked up a short incline, following the mining cart rails directly into what appeared to be a shadowed wall. He played the light from his electric torch on the wall, but the shadow just swallowed the light. Not sure what to expect, Chance reached a hand out, but it passed through the shadow as if passing through mist.

He pulled his hand back and studied it in the torch's glow. It tingled a bit, but he didn't see anything amiss. A heartbeat later he exhaled sharply and stepped through the shadow. Beyond it lay a massive cavern at least thirty feet high and twice that in diameter. Off to the right lay the spider-digger machine, on its back, legs pulled in as if a true spider that had died.

The chamber's illumination came from the far side of the opening. A lintel, threshold and doorposts made of obsidian defined a doorway in the far wall. Letters of a language Chance had never seen before glowed gold and wavered as if being viewed through great heat—yet he felt no warmth. Flames filled the open doorway, leaping, twisting and writhing, yet in silence. No snapping, no roar from the inferno, and no heat. The opening stood twenty feet tall and half that wide.

That shouldn't be here.

Bertie thumbed back the hammer on a Colt revolver. "I don't believe it."

Chance ignored him in favor of the other figure in the room—his eyes involuntarily drawn in that direction. Well dressed in a mourning coat, with matching black trousers, vest and cravat, the only hint of color on the figure was the incarnadine shirt that remained all but hidden by the outer clothes. Black also described his flesh—not the color of an African, but the color of coal. *Or darker.*

He looked hauntingly familiar, but Chance couldn't place him.

The man held up a hand. "I told you, Hubert Palmerstone, it was not yet his time."

Chance gave the dark man a frown. "Who are you, and what is that portal?"

"I go by many names." The man smiled indulgently. "You may call me Mr. Scratch, if that pleases you."

"And I'm in Hell?"

Bertie's snarl filled the chamber. "Should have been there sooner, Corrigan. I sent Azrael to deal with you. How did he fail me?"

"The telegrams about the mine collapse, and then the order for coal? I sent those—you forgot I created your cipher. I also got the miners to leave. I knew you'd come to me." Chance smiled despite staring down the bore of a .44-caliber revolver. "And, after I turned you down, I knew you'd send Azrael to murder me. So, I visited the hardware store, got a lot of copper wire. I turned half the room into a Faraday cage. Azrael stepped in and the Tesla generator's power couldn't get to him. He became a statue."

Bertie's jaw dropped open. "That's not possible."

Chance fished in his vest pocket and tossed Bertie a plum-sized iron ball. "I pulled that out of his skull. I liked how you had one of those in each Black Bart, so they could identify each other through Marconi telegraphony and know not to shoot each other."

Bertie caught the ball and his shoulders sagged a hair. "Azrael, you were so perfect." He tucked the ball into his pants pocket. "Very clever, Corrigan, but all your cunning won't get you out of this. I warned you."

Mr. Scratch chuckled. "Your restraint, Hubert, is admirable. I would have thought a bit of gloating justified."

Chance snorted. "Gloating just leads to disaster. That's his history."

"Not this time, Chance." Bertie tipped the pistol toward the ceiling. "You dismissed my studies as frippery. They were anything but. Did you know the Koran says there are Seven Gates to Hell in the world? The Greeks and Romans believed Mount Etna was one. Scholars fight over where the others are, but I learned a truth. Seven gates *do* exist, but not in a fixed place. They move. They locate themselves where they need to be."

"And this is one, here, at the bottom of this mine?"

"You see it. Could it be anything else? It's here because I *willed* it to be here." Hubert's voice rose in triumph. "I found this place, Chimney Springs, to be like so many of the other fabled locations. I made the sacrifices. I performed the incantations. I even tricked my brother into exiling me here, to keep me out of his plans—all the while knowing he was sending me to my victory."

Chance wanted to think Bertie madder than any hatter, but he couldn't dismiss what he saw as hallucinations caused by breathing mine gas. "What do you get for your victory?"

Bertie glanced at Scratch. "For opening the doorway, I get what I desire, yes?"

"As we agreed, yes." Scratch opened his hands. "However, your desires are, well, rather plebeian." The man covered a yawn with his hand. "Why give you mansions and concubines and even an empire, when I can give you the power to take all of those things? And so much more."

Bertie blinked. "I, ah, I . . ."

Chance laughed. "Of course you don't know, Bertie. You've only ever wanted what others have. You've never earned anything. Never worked for anything. Mr. Scratch, he can never appreciate what you offer him."

Hubert snarled. "Give me power. Give me all the power!"

The dark man gestured casually, as if a rich man sowing pennies in a crowd of beggars. A series of sparks leaped from his fingertips. They swirled as if fireflies, changing colors quickly, growing angrily intense. They flew up toward the roof, then dove upon Hubert. They swarmed him and stung him, hitting every joint. Hubert jerked with each sting.

Violent muscle spasms shook Hubert, flinging the gun from his hand. The sparks landed on his flesh, then burrowed their way into his body. Light shot through him, tracing veins and arteries. His head jerked back, his spine bowed, his mouth opened, yet no screams sounded. The light shifted colors, running down his body in green, then racing back up in a molten red. It shook Hubert so mightily that when the light blazed up his neck, Chance expected the top of his head to explode and brains to geyser out.

Then the light died, and Hubert slumped, yet avoided completely collapsing. He looked like a scarecrow half-fallen from his watch post. Chance clicked his eye in for a closer look. Fire, swirling as had the sparks, played through Hubert's eyes. *He lives?*

Hubert's head snapped up, then slowly turned toward Mr. Scratch. "What power is this?" He raised his left arm, hand limp at the wrist, as if a marionette in the hands of an apprentice puppeteer.

"The greatest power. Men are now to you as puppets are to the puppeteer. Your will is their will."

Hubert turned to look at Chance. "Dance for me."

Power burned through Chance's body. His electric torch fell from his open grasp. His arms came up as if to embrace an invisible partner. He began stepping through a waltz, spinning about in time to music he could not hear. He danced with a woman he could not see, yet he remembered the essence of her. His fingers tingled with distant memories—things he'd long since shut away.

"No!" Chance balled his hands into fists. His feet stopped. "I don't dance for you."

Hubert's nostrils flared as he looked at the dark man. "You have lied."

"Have you forgotten that I am the Prince of Lies?" The obsidian figure shrugged. "But I have not lied to you, Hubert. Mr. Corrigan is a man of strong will. He will not be able to defy you once you have mastered your skills. Your ability to bend men to your will grants you access to everything you desire."

Hubert threw his head back and laughed. "The people of Chimney Springs shall be a whetstone for my skill."

Chance's dancing had taken him close to where Hubert had dropped the Colt. He turned, but Hubert frowned.

"Stay!"

Chance froze, the vehemence in Hubert's voice locking his limbs in stone. "You can't do this, Bertie."

"Do what? Claim what you and others have denied me?" Hubert snorted, then sketched a brief bow in Scratch's direction. "Thank you, my Lord. And you, Chance, you'll remain here until I have determined what I will do with you."

Chance struggled against that command, but might as well have been trying to shift the whole planet without benefit of a lever. "You don't have to do this. It will not end well."

Hubert chuckled coldly. "This is what I was born to do." He turned and walked off into the darkness, slowly regaining control of his body as he went.

The Prince of Darkness walked over to Chance and studied him. "Many people will suffer at his hands."

"You've read my mind."

Mr. Scratch shook his head, but before he spoke, he completed a transformation into a feminine avatar. She wore the same clothes, clearly outsized for her, but somehow suddenly more alluring. "I do not read minds. *That* is the purview of my adversary." She brushed a taloned figure over Chance's chest, picking at his vest's buttons. "It is given to me to read the hearts of men. In you, so much emotion. Hatred, the desire for vengeance, hints of love, all that wickedness. Better, there's regret, remorse. Those last, so wonderful. So rare."

She twirled away as if she'd been his partner, long hair flying. "If people die because of Hubert and you've done nothing to stop him, you will feel true pain. Someone like Hubert, there's never any remorse. Sadness, yes, and frustration, but those are too common to be interesting."

"If he bores you, why let him destroy the lives above?"

"It's not for me to stop him. I do not care." Her eyes became red slits. "But I would let you do it."

"In return for . . . ?"

"Mr. Corrigan, you may have long since abandoned belief in my adversary, but you certainly have heard the stories." Her lips twisted ever so slightly. "All that you are. All that you will ever be."

"Not interested."

She cocked her head. "You *would* be able to stop him. No deception there. No lie. As I did with Hubert, I keep my bargains."

A ripple of gunshots, a dozen or more, echoed from beyond the shadow curtain.

Chance, having regained the use of his limbs, straightened up. "I don't think I will need to test the truth of that claim."

Her brows arrowed down. "How . . . ?"

"The ball I gave him. The one in his pocket." Chance rotated his wrists, stretching his forearm muscles. "I altered the message it sent out. It broadcast a shoot on sight order to the Black Barts patrolling the mine. If I had to guess, Hubert saw them, used his power to order them to stand aside . . ."

". . . and discovered the power only worked on *people*." She raised an eyebrow. "You intended him to die from the beginning."

"I warned him."

"Barely. You set him up to be murdered." She pressed her hand over his heart. "And you are not sorry in the least."

"I don't believe I am." Chance shook his head. "And I don't believe you offer anything that interests me."

"Here and now, perhaps not." She ran a black talon lightly down his right cheek. "But you are not so far from being my plaything that you should sleep easily."

"I haven't in years."

The obsidian woman smiled, white teeth a bright contrast with her dark lips. "Then I look forward to our next meeting." She snapped her fingers. The chamber immediately fell to darkness. The portal vanished, and she along with it.

Chance dropped to his hands and knees, suppressing a shudder, and searched for his electric torch. *It appears I have a new quest*. Altering part of Azrael to get the Black Barts to kill Bertie had been the work of moments. To alter Azrael to be able to drop a god; that wouldn't be so quickly done.

He found the torch and smiled. "Time, not really a problem." After all, no rest for the wicked, and he had it on the best authority that he was quite wicked indeed.

THE GREATEST GUNS IN THE GALAXY

Bryan Thomas Schmidt & Ken Scholes

John Selman had shot John Wesley Hardin, the deadliest gunman in the West, in the back, you're damn right. He'd done what had to be done to take down a monster. To some, including Selman himself, that made him a hero. To others, it made him a target.

So when the two odd-looking strangers with distended eye sockets and peculiar orange-tinted skin walked into the Acme Saloon and called his name, Selman knew they had come for one reason: to challenge him. He downed his latest shot in one gulp and left his cane resting against the bar as he whirled to face them. "You two must be the ugliest strangers to walk in here in months," Selman said with a cocky smile.

The saloon's swinging doors let through dust and sand from the desert outside. The usual scents of El Paso—cow town, dry heat, mixed with human and animal waste from the sewers just below the streets. Selman was almost used to it by now. But tonight, the winds seemed to bring it out.

"Is that the sewers or you?" Selman asked, sniffing the

151

air, and the bartender and a few locals chuckled around him. But the strangers showed no reaction.

"They say you killed the greatest lawman in the West," one of them said, its overly large beady eyes scanning back and forth as it took in the room.

Who was this—a male or a female? It ain't no human. Its limbs looked stretched out, overly long, hands resting just below the bumpy knees. Its companion looked just as strange, only slightly chubbier, and both of 'em stank worse than Mexicans from across the border in Juarez. *Just more foreign scum wandered into another Western town.* Well, Constable John Selman was intent on cleaning up El Paso, and he'd damn sure clean this mess up.

Selman's adrenaline spiked, his heartbeat racing, as his hand hovered over his Colt .45, flexing and ready. "Yeah, I shot him. Three times. Son of a bitch threatened my son." Selman's eyes narrowed.

"That makes you the champion," the other stranger said, flashing sharp teeth in what might be a smile.

"Champion of what?" Selman scoffed. The way the two strangers looked at him made him feel cold all of a sudden and he hesitated, fear rising for the first time.

"We are the best in the universe," the first stranger said.

Selman laughed. "Not the humble sort, are ya?"

In an instant, Selman had drawn and the two strangers did, too, pointing oddly long, wide-barreled pistols of a sort at him while the bartender shouted for them to "Take it outside!"

They all fired simultaneously, Selman's hand so used

to the Colt, it barely bucked at the recoil. His stare locked on the strangers, cold, hard, and sure.

Selman felt the wind sucked out of his lungs as a searing hole opened in his chest. There was a burning pain as an invisible force caused his body to buck.

"Son of a bitch!" he cursed as he fell. They'd shot him. Suddenly, he couldn't move. His hands were clammy, and sweat dripped down off his forehead to sting his eyes.

"That was too easy," the first stranger said, shaking its oddly shaped head. "Maybe it's true he shot John Wesley Hardin in the back like a coward."

"I ain't no coward," Selman whispered, choking on blood. He spat and tried again, but the strangers paid him no mind.

"Shot him in the back? Too afraid to face him. This is no great gunman," agreed the other.

Selman's anger rose at the insults, but they were the last words he heard before he slipped into darkness, the bartender calling for someone to get his son and the town doctor.

Everyone in the Acme stared at Jailak and Mairej as the two Andromedans holstered their blasters. They stood over Selman's body lying on the floor in a widening pool of blood.

"He was supposed to be good," Jailak said. "We traveled back in time for this?"

"He was not," agreed Mairej. The man who shot the greatest gunman in the Old West had been a pure disappointment. John Wesley Hardin was legendary. John Selman had become famous for shooting him. Mairej saw no other reason why such an unexceptional human being should be remembered. The man was skinny, almost like he'd barely eaten, a bushy mustache over his lip, gray streaks in his blondish hair.

They turned to the bartender. "Is this not the man who killed the great John Wesley Hardin?" Mairej asked.

The bartender nodded. "Shot him in the back right over there." He motioned down the bar a few feet. Mairej could still see the stain on the floor where the great gunman must have fallen.

The two aliens exchanged a look and headed for the front door.

"Wait! The sheriff'll be coming!" the bartender called.

"We are done here," Jailak said, ignoring the man, and followed Mairej through the swinging doors, dodging blowing tumbleweeds—some of them bigger than the aliens themselves—as they stepped onto the smelly, dusty Old West street. Sand clouded their eyes and made them water a bit as the sounds of saloon music and laughter resumed, filling the night air.

The Andromedans returned to the chrono tag and ported back to their ship, leaving 1895 behind them like the dust of that El Paso street. The familiar warmth and clean smell of home greeted them, and once they were orbiting Earth again, they took lunch in the observation deck cafeteria and watched the demolition of the Eastern Seaboard. The various time crews wrapping up their exploitation of the planet's past would witness the treat of its demolition prior to the development fleet's impending arrival.

"That," Jailak said, "was a waste of time and budget."

Mairej nodded. "It was...unsatisfying. And not nearly enough footage."

Raiding the timelines of inferior species for entertainment purposes was considered the bottom of the *duggha* trough in the new Andromedan economy. Anyone with CNS mapping could capture the experiences. And then the recordings of them could be resold in small rapidly consumable experiences—even several at a time. The sample (in a neat handful) that Jailak fed him after the first interview had Mairej under the moons of Garglex killing Charlobundix III, their greatest warrior, with a blowgun. Only he'd done it while sampling the finest Dambril wines and having sex with three of the four poet sisters of Telpaz Prime. It was four minutes and thirty-seven seconds (Andromedan Standard) that boggled his mind and convinced him to join Jailak's small company on the brief break between Garglex and Earth's assimilations.

Jailak's eyebrows went up, and he nodded at the glass wall and the burning planet below. A bright light flared and then collapsed upon itself. "That was Boston I think."

"New York," Mairej said. "So what is our plan?"

Jailak took a bite of his Glomboli sky bat salad. "Well, we have to go back. I think maybe we need to kill John Wesley Hardin ourselves."

Mairej nodded. "Kill him before Selman does?"

Jailak thought about it some, then clapped and pointed. The cafeteria waitstaff saw and started moving their direction. "That is New Jersey; I'm sure of it."

"Miami," the waiter said as he rearranged a bat wing.

Andromedan cafeterias were known intergalactically for their fine dining and apt help.

"No," Jailak said.

"I'm pretty sure it is," Mairej said.

Jailak waved at the screen. "Not that. No, we don't do it before Selman. Can't. It violates all kinds of rules." Jailak took another stab at the bat on his plate. "For starters, Hardin wasn't killed by aliens in the original timeline. He was killed by Selman."

Mairej blinked, his partner was talking in circles. "But Selman wasn't killed by aliens in the original timeline either. So haven't we already violated all kinds of rules?"

Jailak shook his head. "No, not really. Just one rule. But if we do it to Hardin, too, then it's *all kinds of rules.*"

"Or two," Mairej said. But he was fairly certain that it didn't matter what he told his new boss. "Then what are you thinking we do?"

Jailak leaned forward and smiled. "I think we go back, bring John Wesley Hardin back from the dead, and kill him all over again ourselves." He waved his hands around like they were six shooters in a flurry of bad pantomiming.

Mairej pointed. "That was D.C. there."

Jailak laughed. "No. Seattle."

"Seattle is on the West Coast." And that was when Mairej experienced the first inkling that things might not work out.

The dust and stink of the nineteenth century was a shock after the cool green mist of the restaurant when they slipped back to work. Mairej noted that El Paso had changed during lunch and it baffled him.

"Where are the horses?"

Jailak shrugged. "I'm not sure."

"The buildings are different, too."

"We're in a different part of town," he said. He pointed. "There's the cemetery there."

The night air was hot and quiet other than the sound of automobiles slipping past beneath the gray light of buzzing streetlamps. Mairej took it all in. "We are not in 1895 El Paso. This isn't the Wild West."

"No," Jailak said, already moving toward the gates of the Concordia Cemetery. "Just a bit later."

Another internally combusted engine rumbled past. This metal beast had a 1968: NIXON'S THE ONE sticker on its bumper.

"But our license is for 1895," Mairej said.

"A brief stop. Then 1895." Jailak was over the gate now and moving off into the dark. As he counted paces, Mairej followed at a distance and kept an eye out.

The Concordia Cemetery was in the center of the city near several busy roads and an interstate highway that rose above it on stone pillars—dust, exhaust, and debris raining down from passing vehicles above. Stone grave markers of various colors, shapes, and sizes were lined up in neat rows. A couple had buildings or shelters around them. The cemetery's owners seemed to have made an effort at grass and flowers, but most were dead or dying from being beat down by the desert. The place was open with a nice breeze and so smelled no different than most of El Paso.

Mairej thought humans had odd burial rituals. The stones were rather plain, no valuable minerals had been used. What kind of respect did they have for their dead?

Jailak stopped at a flat marker and fished a tube from his coveralls. "This is it."

"What are we doing?"

Jailak had the look on his face that said he hated working with amateurs just before he rolled his eyes. "We're resurrecting John Wesley Hardin so you can gun him down on the streets of El Paso."

"So much for the rules."

Jailak sighed, then squeezed the contents of the tube onto the grave. "A minor violation at best. We're not going to gun him down here. We'll take him back to 1895."

"1895," Mairej said raising his eyebrows as he watched a puddle of black goo twist itself into a slender worm and squeeze itself into a crack near the marker. "And why aren't we just bringing him back in 1895?"

"We're not licensed to perform resurrections in 1895."

Mairej decided against pointing out that they didn't even have a license to be whenever they were now. Instead, he watched the ground. Something was happening. He heard a distant hum as the ground vibrated beneath their feet. He'd not seen a resurrection before. "So it's bringing him back to life underground?"

Jailak shook his head. "Just watch."

The goo was back, only it was a mottled gray instead of black. First a slim tendril, then another. And then another. Until there was a gray puddle growing large enough to make them step back.

Mairej glanced up at Jailak and saw concern on his face. "What is it?"

He shrugged. "Usually it's pink, not gray. But see? It's working!"

The goo was spreading out in the form of a human body there on the ground above the grave. Mairej took another step back. "It smells."

Jailak wrinkled his nose. "That's not normal either." The smell was something akin to *gundar* carcasses left in the sun too long before cooking, only much, much stronger.

The body was taking on more definition now but it looked decayed and unhealthy, as rotten and barely hung together as the suit it wore. They both jumped when the eyes popped open, black and full of nothing. A pale worm crawled from one socket and disappeared back into another.

"Good evening, Mister Hardin," Jailak said as he offered the man a hand. "Time is short, so if you'll come with us."

John Wesley Hardin took the hand and stood, growling as he did.

Mairej finally found a question that he suspected he could handle the answer to. "How many times have you resurrected humans?"

"Oh this is my first human," Jailak said. "But it was pink on Orthon V."

Their new traveling companion seemed bewildered but willingly led. He said nothing, groaning and growling instead. As he walked, the top of one ear flopped up and down, hanging off his head.

When they slipped into the time pod, the bio screen filter paid John Wesley Hardin no notice at all as Jailak dipped them back in 1895.

★ ★ ★

It was approaching High Noon on Main Street when they gave John Wesley Hardin a pair of loaded Colts and a gun belt. He wouldn't take them and strap them on so Jailak had finally buckled them around the man's moldering waist himself.

Mairej moved upwind of the gunslinger. In brighter light, the man looked even worse for wear. Whatever the goo had done, it didn't look like any kind of healthy. And Hardin didn't like the sunlight or the people who stopped and stared. It wasn't clear which he was growling at but he sniffed at the growing crowd of horrified onlookers.

"Is that John Wesley Hardin?" Mairej looked and realized it was Jailak who had said it. "Get ready," he said in a lower voice. "Are you rolling?"

The sensory capture bug clicked in his ear as Mairej checked his blasters. "We are."

"Me too," Jailak said, tapping his own ear. "Go."

Mairej checked his distance from Hardin, spread his legs, and held a hand over the butt of his pistol. "John Wesley Hardin, you are the most notorious gunslinger in the *Homo sapiens* American Wild West, and I aim to gun you down, you murderous son of a bitch."

He reached for his gun and when John Wesley Hardin did nothing, Mairej paused.

"Say that last part again," Jailak said.

"I said, 'I aim to gun you down, you murderous son of a bitch.'"

Still nothing.

"Shoot him, then."

Mairej drew, convinced that any moment the rotting hand would slap leather and beat him to it.

Hardin sniffed at a woman near the edge of the crowd.

Mairej took aim and fired, watching the shot tear into Hardin's side. The resurrected gunslinger howled but it wasn't pain or fear—it was something else—and then immediately he leapt at the crowd.

Jailak pulled Hardin kicking and flailing off the woman. Her leg was bleeding and a huge lump of flesh tore off, clamped between Hardin's teeth. The stinky bastard chomped it down as quick as he could, whimpering and whining the whole time. The crowd screamed and hollered as they scattered in panic, some fleeing as fast as they could down the street, others backing away, but still watching and chattering.

"Well, as Dylan said, 'He ain't no friend of the people.' This is a mess." Jailak looked around. "We're going to need a different plan."

Suddenly, every implant in Mairej's body went off in instant alarm. "What is that?"

"It's a chronoalert," Jailak said. "Some idiot has damaged the timeline. We're being recalled." Hardin was struggling even more now and his howls sounded hungrier than Mairej wanted to allow. Jailak pulled him away from the crowd. "This isn't working anyway. Shoot him again so we can get out of here."

"Don't we need to take him back to where we got him?"

Jailak rolled his eyes again. "No. He was dead there, remember? And with whatever else is going on, we don't need to add to the problem."

Mairej shrugged, shot John Wesley Hardin once

through the head, and helped Jailak move the body off the dusty street.

Back in the cafeteria, it was more of the same but this time, Europe. They were detonating Paris, London, and Rome simultaneously as part of the early dinner show. And by tomorrow, Earth and all of its resources along with its rich history would be safely tucked into the Andromedan Expansion Plan.

They found themselves at the same table with a waiter who looked unexcited to see them again so soon. This time, Mairej tried the bat. It was dry but adequate. "So what do you think happened?"

"Hard to say. I'm just glad we wrapped up before anything else could go wrong."

Speaking of things going wrong, Earth below was dark now and that seemed odd. They'd left the lights on, after all, so it could be seen. And the show should've started but didn't.

There was whispering.

A waiter slipped by and Jailak grabbed his sleeve. "What's happening?"

"I'm certain it will be resolved shortly."

Mairej leaned in. "Is it serious?"

When the waiter spoke, it was with a low voice. "There was a timeline disruption in the late nineteenth century."

Jailak met Mairej's eyes. "Really? Somewhere in Europe or Asia, I'm guessing?"

"American West, actually," a new voice said. This Andromedan didn't wear gray like the rest. This one wore black. And there were only three black uniforms in this particular Expansion fleet. "But I think you know that already, Jailak."

"Chronogeneral Terflex," Jailak said, his face turning red, "I didn't realize you were with this fleet."

"No," he said, "but I knew *you* were. And I knew just whose license to pull when I saw humanity wink out of existence. The origin point of the disruption is El Paso, Texas, 1895. Sound familiar?" Andromedans weren't particularly tall or intimidating but Terflex pulled off both. "So come along. If you're lucky, you only have some questions to answer."

"What if I'm unlucky?" Jailak asked.

"Then you get to help fix the mess you've made before it costs us our work here."

Mairej kept his eyes on his plate and worked on finishing the bat as Jailak stood.

"You too," Terflex said, looming over him.

Sighing, Mairej left another unfinished meal, having no idea just how grateful he would be for his empty stomach when he smelled what the late nineteenth century had become.

El Paso stank before, but now it was out of this galaxy. Mairej and Jailak wore masks to cover their faces, and the stench was still almost unbearable.

"Son of a Taglothomri *gundar*," Mairej hurled a classic Andromedan epithet at the ground as he spit, "don't worry about the rules, you said. Minor violation. Does that smell minor to you?"

"It smells dead," Jailak said as they looked around. The creatures were everywhere—formerly human but like rotting flesh, falling apart, worm infested, and moaning and growling instead of speech. "This is odd. We killed Hardin."

"Maybe we just wounded him," Mairej suggested.

"I keep telling you, take your time and aim first," Jailak complained.

"Your mother mated with three Orthonians," Mairej snapped. "This is not my fault. The whole thing was your plan."

"Well then you come up with a plan to fix it!" Jailak said, ducking and jumping aside as one of the creatures grabbed at his arm, chomping its teeth in a clumsy attempt to bite him.

Howling, another grabbed Mairej from behind, nibbling at his neck.

Mairej felt a sharp pain and stiffened his skin, a protective instinct, then loosened his joints, bowed, and flipped the creature up over his back, slamming it down onto the dirt street. Gooey, stinky flesh rubbed his back as it slid, moaning and chomping the whole way. The thing smelled even worse up close, which was almost hard to imagine.

Jailak turned and shot it with his blaster. "You're welcome," he said.

"Terflex said 'it's all your fault,'" Mairej repeated. "He can't mean this?"

"We're gonna have to do a lotta killing, if it is."

With that, they began aiming and shooting at every formerly human creature they could see, one after another, but more showed up as quick as they dispatched them. They quickly discovered that shots through the foreheads worked most effectively. Creatures shot there fell to the ground and didn't get back up. Those shot anywhere else just kept on coming, even if they lost a limb or huge wads of flesh. One creature crawled across the ground with one arm and no legs, chomping and moaning at them the whole time. It almost made Mairej feel guilty, then he looked at Jailak and got pissed all over again. His partner had caused this and was enjoying the carnage far too much.

"What?" Jailak asked, seeing Mairej's glare.

"You're enjoying yourself."

Jailak grinned. "We're hunters and the greatest shooters in the galaxy. This is what we do."

"My mother warned me throwing my lot in with you was dumber than a *gundar*, but I didn't listen," Mairej said, shaking his head.

"This street's clear," Jailak said. "Let's go find another."

It turned out no street stayed clear for long, and it took them hours and hours to kill all the hundreds of creatures wandering around El Paso. But when they went back to their ship, Terflex's angry face filled their comm screen.

"You're not done. There are creatures like this all over the planet. You've got a lot more work to do. Get busy!"

Mairej scoffed. "He's got to be kidding."

"You know the policy. Our mess, our problem."

"Your mess, my problem," Mairej muttered.

Jailak rolled his beady eyes. "Just stop complaining. I got an idea."

"It's your ideas got us into this in the first place," Mairej pointed out.

Jailak punched a code into the communicator, ignoring him.

"Who are you calling?"

"Jonnapit, my cousin," Jailak said.

"For the love of the stars, don't involve anyone else!" Mairej warned.

"Meh, he has lots of friends in his hunting club," Jailak said. "They'll get a kick out of this. Besides, we're stuck here until we're done."

Mairej sighed and stopped complaining. Despite his anger at Jailak for getting them into this, help would be welcome and sounded like a good idea. Mairej was already exhausted.

Jonnapit did more than bring his club. Word spread to every flesh-hungry, gun-thirsty Andromedan on the planet, and soon, hundreds showed up with blasters to lend their aid.

"These creatures are too damn easy, like insects or Orthonian *remars*," Jonnapit complained. "I thought you offered us a challenge."

Jailak shot another and rolled his eyes at his cousin. "Cleaning up an accident. Good target practice. Stop complaining. It's the most shooting you've done in months."

Jonnapit blasted three creatures with one bolt of his rifle and cackled. "Yippeee kayay, motherfucker! You're right about that, and it's still fun."

"What the hell does that mean?" Jailak asked.

"Something I heard on a human broadcast once," Jonnapit said, smiling.

Then the two cousins opened fire again together, looking delighted as they sliced down more creatures.

Mairej left the two cousins by themselves and wandered off on his own to clear another street. They'd finished El Paso and Las Cruces long ago and were now across the border in Mexico, clearing the streets of Juarez which made El Paso look like a rich man's paradise by comparison.

"How do these humans live like this?" Raijah asked. She was one of the better shooters and far less annoying than most, so Mairej hadn't hurried off when she'd joined him.

"Well, this is how they lived a couple centuries back, but you're right," Mairej agreed. "Very primitive, not very intelligent."

"That thing they call tequila is delicious, though," Raijah said, taking another sip from a flask that hung around her shoulder on a strap and belching. "I'd like more of this."

"Once we wipe them out, maybe you can search the planet," Mairej reminded her.

She bounced and twirled, taking down five more creatures with a stream of laser fire as she did. "If we bring enough back, we might get rich."

"It's all yours," Mairej said, shaking his head. "I want to forget this place ever existed." His body tensed at the thought of ever returning to El Paso or Juarez again, especially with Jailak. It was time for him to find a new pastime.

Raijah shrugged. "There's a reason the Andromedan Expansion Plan is so successful. We are far superior to most of the galaxy. I almost feel sorry for them. But mother of a bat do they stink!"

It took two weeks to clear the rest of the planet, but between the hundreds of hunters, spread out, they managed it. The bigger chore was burning the bodies, which Chronogeneral Terflex insisted they do before they returned home. Raijah even managed to find a beverage she enjoyed more than tequila—vodka, made by some creatures in a very cold, rugged land to the northeast. Raijah brought back an entire ship just to transport it, and in the end, she did grow quite wealthy. She even found an Andromedan chemist who could replicate the formulas.

Terflex was waiting for them both in decontamination when they finished, taking no risks with the nineteenth-century *Homo sapiens* undead. "I suppose you've seen the value of correcting your work?"

Jailak and Mairej both nodded. "We did."

"Good," he said. "You'll be needing to trade in your grays then."

Mairej wasn't surprised. Purple was the color he expected. Penitentiary purple. He was surprised when Terflex nodded to two black uniforms hung up in their lockers. "Raijah's uncle is a highly placed colonel, and she's recently lauded your economic development strategy in facilitating the introduction of a new beverage that may indeed be an intergalactic hit. Further, Andromedan scientists concur that ending the human industrial revolution in 1895 has increased the property's current value due to less wear and tear upon the planet. There is even talk of establishing a theme park here around this new drink." He smiled wryly but his eyes showed clearly that he knew they didn't deserve it. Still, he managed to say the words. "So you've both been promoted to special ops." The smile widened. "Under my command, of course."

Mairej looked to Jailak then to the uniform and the chronogeneral. They both managed to say, "Yes, sir!" in unison and he furrowed his brow at them.

"First things first," he said. "Uniform up and meet me in my office. You've one last thing to do."

John Selman had shot John Wesley Hardin, the deadliest gunman in the West, in the back, you're damn right. He'd done what had to be done to take down a monster. To some, including Selman himself, that made him a hero. To others, it made him a target.

So when the two odd-looking strangers with distended eye sockets and peculiar orange-tinted skin walked into the Acme Saloon and called his name, Selman knew they had come for one reason: to challenge him. He downed his latest shot in one gulp and left his cane resting against the bar as he whirled to face them. "You two must be the ugliest strangers to walk in here in months," Selman said with a cocky smile.

One of them looked at the other and then at Selman. "Actually, Mr. Selman, I think we look rather resplendent in our new uniforms."

He squinted at them, certain they were Canadians or maybe French now that he'd pegged their accents. Still, his hands itched for trouble almost as much as his throat itched for a drink. "What exactly are you?"

One of the strangers stepped up to the bar and plunked down a stack of shiny new silver dollars. The stranger looked uncomfortable with the words that came next. "I'm someone who is terribly sorry to have inconvenienced you with my poor choices, Mr. Selman, and I am sincerely hoping this round of drinks will make amends."

Selman looked down at the dollars and licked his lips. Then he looked back up to discover the strangers were gone.

In the end, he decided they must have been French. And there was a fancy French word for thinking you'd been in the same shitter before, after all. Only he'd been certain when those ugly fellers came into the bar that they were gunning for him. The drink—and everything else he could buy with the small fortune they'd left—was a nice surprise after a long, thirsty August.

"Viva la France," Selman said as he knocked his whisky back.

DANCE OF BONES

Maurice Broaddus

By the time Bose Roberds spied the lone, empty wagon, he got the nagging suspicion that he was meant to follow the stranger's trail easily. The noon sun beat on him like a whip in a heavy hand. He'd followed the tracks across the plains for quite some time. Whoever he tracked could've traveled through thickets so dense that neither man nor horse could see for more than a few yards at a time. More than once, Bose feared that the man might lurk in the brush, hiding in the draws and canyons.

The other cowhands lingered a few lengths behind him, more than a mite cranky—fueled by their rumbling stomachs—but Bose couldn't be both cook and tracker at the same time. He ignored their grumblings until he found the wagon they were meant to find. It slumped to one side, wheels busted, like a hobbled steer. The covering still appeared new, but there were no signs of any of their horses.

"The Ninth marched out with splendid cheer," Bose sang to himself, a bit of a nervous habit. *"The Bad Lands to explore."*

"What's that?" Dirk Ramey loosed a stream of tobacco juice. A big man with cruel, thin lips stained with brown spittle, an unshaven face and hard eyes, Dirk proved a difficult man to like.

"A ditty I used to know from when I marched with the 9th." Bose never referred to the 9th as Buffalo Soldiers. He had joined the 9th Cavalry at his first opportunity. The Cheyenne nicknamed the 9th and 10th Cavalry the Buffalo Soldiers after the noble, sacred animals they respected. If only the Army held the soldiers in similar regard. Instead, they were given old and worn saddles, blankets, and tents. Their horses often went lame. To his shame, he won a Congressional Medal of Honor for leading an attack on the Cheyenne despite he and his men being severely outnumbered. Protecting whites from Indians, forcing the Indians to move because the government found some new resource of theirs to exploit, filled him with disgust. Rather than huddle close to stoves during another winter, he deserted the Army.

Bose adjusted the gun in his holster, loosening the leather thongs for easy draw. These Circle T boys were one step above useless, carrying only one Colt, usually wrapped in their bedrolls. Mighty handy if they had intentions on dying in their sleep. Bose swung off his horse, studying the wagon for any clue to what happened. The legs of the driver remained in his seat, the rest of his body hidden by the wagon's canopy. Bose pulled back the tarp. Sprawled out on the seat, a man still clutched his pistol. His wife rotted behind him. Both were dressed in their best Sunday-gone-to-meeting clothes. Too dried out to be done recent. Their empty skulls screamed

wordlessly at the noon sky, their dreams of a new life for
themselves cut brutally short in the harshness of the West.
The presentation of the bodies, so carefully staged, tickled
something in the recesses of his memory.

Bose's mother feared such a fate for him when he first
told her that he planned to venture to Los Angeles, where
the laws against holding blacks as slaves were strongly
enforced.

"Why?" she asked.

"Because I've got to find my own way."

Funny how memories had a way of sneaking up on a
feller at the oddest times. Bose knelt beside the wagon
and picked up an arrow. Scattered here and there, too
carefully staged, he thought.

"Could be Utes," Dirk said. "This here's Ute country."

"They been killing a lot of folks," another hand
echoed. He scanned their surroundings nervously as if
Utes might jump out from the shadows.

"Pile their graves high with rocks. We don't want the
coyotes to get them." Bose turned his back to them.

"Why?" Dirk challenged him for their benefit. They
bristled at being ordered about by a Negro.

This scene played out on occasion as if they needed
reminding. Over six feet tall, with bulging muscles like
thick metal cords and skin like smoked leather, no man
ever struck fear into Bose. If there was an attack, he led
the charge. When in doubt, he spoiled for a good fight just
for its own sake. He turned to let them see the seriousness
in his eyes before returning to his study of the trail. In the
end, Bose Roberds was not a man to be trifled with.

"Because I said to. Then we can get back to camp."

Bose returned his attentions to the ground. The tracks disconcerted him. The other hands thought cattle rustlers worked the trail. If that were the case, the cold thing stirring in his stomach wouldn't bother him so. No, what disturbed him was that they had been led so far astray from the Goodnight-Loving Trail and whether or not they admitted it, no one knew much about what lay in the wilderness.

"What'll we say about him?" Dirk gestured at the waiting trail of the stranger for Bose's benefit.

"Don't worry about him." Bose stared at the puff of dust that rose in the distance. "We'll catch him sooner or late. He ain't trying to cover his trail none."

Things hadn't been right since they left Abaddon three days earlier.

Taking one gander at the string of makeshift buildings that dared call itself a town, Bose had decided against going in. Abaddon was still as a corpse's whisper. He'd been in this kind of place before: a town deceptively dead, yet the wrong word to the wrong person could cause the place to explode. A cemetery set the boundary on the west. Cow custom made the more respectable north side of town off limits to cattle herders. The seven buildings on the south side included a general store and a bank that begrudgingly catered to them. The saloon and gambling house that thrived on them. The building at the end of the row—the one that all the decent folk seemed to take special pains to avoid—housed girls who waited for the trail herds.

That night, preparing to go off gal hooting, the Circle T boys cleaned their guns, washed their necks, and dusted their hats. All duded up, they hollered and carried on like young bucks in need of wrangling. When they returned, though, they avoided Bose's eyes. He didn't press them. Whiskey-loosened tongues allowed him to piece together a general picture of what had happened. A mean argument had erupted at the brothel, ending with the Circle T boys hightailing it out of Abaddon.

Soon after, Bose noticed that they were being followed. Hunted.

The Circle T bunch was a simple contingent who took Bose on without much complaint or question. Theirs was a pretty salty outfit, reduced to a sullen, hard-bitten crew. Bose rose earliest to prepare coffee and biscuits. Years of privation at the Army's hands trained him to go without much sleep. Most nights he stretched out on an old horse blanket when he wasn't off stalking about in the night. Bose preferred the honesty of the range. Cow custom, the common law of the range, defined people. The trail crew needed a marksman, a handy trait in the cook. He liked the work so he settled into it first thing. It was hard, hard work, but Bose could settle into the illusion that competence, not skin color, mattered on a drive. It paid a solid $125 per month, second only to the trail boss. He didn't mind the work, but every job had its bosses and its problem children.

Henry McCormick, the first to arrive for chow, handled their herd of horses. Other than that, the wrangler spent too much time in a bottle, always ailing when there was work to be done. He was good with the men, though. Like a gruff mother hen.

The relief hands ate next before relieving the night

guard. Not a spine among the lot of them. A pack of wild dogs ready to piss all over everything, always in search of someone to follow.

The son of the cattle owner, Will Grimes fancied himself the trail boss, but was more of an arrogant windbag who couldn't stomach men who wouldn't kowtow to him. Under the tutelage of his father, Will insured that the trail was passable for the wagon and the herd, acting as a buffer between theirs and other cattle drives. His deep-set coal eyes often peered right at Bose. He believed that the men turned to Bose when trouble arose and resented it. Bose didn't cotton to him right away. He wasn't much by way of good judgment. Rash the way the young and privileged could be.

"Hand me the coffee," Will said. Bose didn't move or acknowledge him. "What?"

"If you want me to do something for you, you say 'please.'"

"My 'please' is implicit," Will said, self-impressed with what book learning he had.

"I'm an explicit sort of cuss." Used to all manner of gun trouble, Bose didn't bat an eye.

"You got a lot of sand in you, boy."

"Sand has a way of toughening you up." Bose handed him a cup of strong, black, cowpuncher coffee. He waited for the boy to take a swig. Will gagged and spat, throwing the rest of the cup on to the fire. He stormed off in a snit, his back to the snorts at his expense.

"Seems he right can't handle the coffee," Henry said between sobs of laughter. He tipped the contents of his metal flask into his coffee mug.

"You tell him that you mix chili juice in it?" Dirk asked.

"He didn't ask." Bose tucked away a wry smile.

"Don't mind my boy." Wiry, with rust-colored hair and eyes like steel, Bradford Grimes ambled toward the camp in his wide-brimmed planter's hat and his black, broadcloth suit.

"I don't." Bose beat the dust from his chaps.

"He means well, just comes on a little strong trying to earn the men's respect," Mr. Grimes said.

"Respect comes to a man if he does his job well." Collecting the cups and plates, Bose washed and stored away dishes.

"Well, he can check the herd. I heard tell that one or two might've taken sick. Let's see how he handles that before anyone thinks too harsh on him."

Mr. Grimes spoiled his boy, Bose guessed, not having anything to measure it against since he had no children of his own. Mr. Grimes gave Bose a measure of latitude since Bose saved the man's life once. The hands were cutting cattle when a steer charged after Mr. Grimes. Without hesitation, Bose tossed the bridle over his horse's head, and jumped in the saddle. When the steer tucked its head to hook himself a white man, Bose roped it, bringing it down with the flourish of a holler. Mr. Grimes promoted him on the spot, on the condition that he never talk about it. After all, it "didn't look good to owe your life to a nigger."

A mood settled over the men. They gathered in clusters. They whispered but kept a nervous eye on each other, like watchmen waiting for a crack in a dam. By nine a.m. the Circle T boys coaxed the cattle into a moving column about a mile long. The elder and junior Grimes rode point with four others at swing and flank. The cattle moved, bawling and frisking, making the occasional stop to crop with disinterest at some grass. Skittish and more jumpy than usual, Dirk and Henry lingered at the drag to prod the sluggish, footsore, or weak cattle. Riding ahead of the herd in the chuck wagon, Bose followed the tracks of the lone rider who dogged their trail, but stayed just out of reach.

Henry rode to catch up to him, stale whisky heavy on his breath. "Y' don't strike me as much of a talkin' man."

"Reckon not, lessen I got something to say," Bose said.

"Y' don't take much guff, even from Mr. Grimes. Or his no-good son."

Bose recognized a man fishing for information when he smelled one and, right then, Henry stank of the Mississippi at low flow. He kept silent, his eyes fixed on the horizon. Like men, terrain had to be seen in more than one light. Shadows distorted the silhouette of the land and the early morning or late evening showed things sun-blurred by day.

"Don't mind Will," Henry continued, "he's still fumin' cause he had to ask his pappy to make him trail boss. He couldn't stand starting at the lowest cow ranch job: cuttin' wood for the cook."

"Not just any cook, but a drifting Negro cowhand riding the grub line," Bose said with deliberate caution. He didn't want his tongue wagging too much.

"Probably got used t' his pappy bein' the sole power 'round these parts. Used t' be that . . ." Henry coughed like a hound baying at a possum. At first Bose took it as a holdover from his time as a miner, but there was something else. A nervousness, the weight of no sleep, crept about his eyes. He had the look of a man haunted by a secret, a burden he wished to share. Henry reached into his vest for his metal flask.

"Henry!" Mr. Grimes barked.

Henry cursed under his breath.

"Come back here. A couple of these steer look sick."

The men made camp in the lee of the cliff while Bose studied the terrain searching for any sign of the rider. Maybe that was what troubled him so much. After he informed Mr. Grimes that someone had been hounding their trail since Abaddon, he'd been ordered to track the stranger. Fear of rustlers was one thing, but it struck Bose that only men with secrets or guilty consciences feared a single man following them.

The rider's path hadn't crossed his back trail. The route became dusty. Like a man on the dodge, Bose held to the grassy side to raise no dust. Watching Will ride up reminded him of his theory about horses and partners. Both had to have staying power such that they could ride all day and all night and still be with him at sun up. Both needed to be scrappy, savvy, and, most of all, loyal. Showy was a distraction, a trap to cover a poor horse. Will Grimes was showy.

"We got a problem with the steers," Will said.

"That's too bad, but them animals are your business."

"The men ain't feeling none too good either."

"You blaming me?" Bose sat up straighter in his saddle.

"We'd all just feel more comfortable if you stayed in camp with us from now on." Will smiled, a painful and pitiful thing, not disguising the insinuation that the situation was somehow Bose's fault. The tacit implication that Bose must've purposely sought out a sick steer to serve for dinner.

The pall of a funeral settled on the camp. Mr. Grimes stalked the corral a pale ghost of himself. By the best counts, some four hundred head of whiteface cattle had been struck with disease. Out of a nearly three thousand count herd, the cattle run was closing in on becoming a bust. The disease had the flesh rotting from their bones. The cows lumbered about, languidly chewing cud with half of the flesh from their mouths falling off in gangrenous chunks. The herd smelled of rancid meat. The men decided to camp upwind. Henry and Dirk stood at the edge of camp as if on guard duty. Dirk slipped a clump of chaw into his mouth.

"Drift over here a minute," Henry waved Bose over. "How's it going?"

Bose walked with the easy step of a woodsman. "Mostly quiet night. Except . . ."

"'Ceptin' what?" Henry perked up with renewed interest.

"Except for the rider," Bose said. "I can't tell if we're following him or if he's following us."

"I ain't even convinced there's even a rider out there." Dirk spat a yellow stream at Bose's feet. "Just a rumor some folks started to spook the boys."

"Seems like all our trouble started after leaving Abaddon," Bose said to Henry, not bothering to acknowledge Dirk.

"You buttin' your nose into things that don't concern you none," Dirk said.

"And you sound like a man who needs to clear his conscience." The men seemed ready to bolt, distrust made them turn on one another. On him. Bose leveled his steady gaze on Henry. "Now I'm not a holy man or nothing, but I'm the best you got if you need to confess something."

"You having the dreams?" Henry asked Dirk.

"I got t' thinkin' it was only me." Dirk's tobacco juice sizzled in the campfire.

"What dreams?" Bose asked. Neither of them met his eyes. "What dreams?"

"It . . ." Henry's voice trailed. He wasn't going to be able to tell it, perhaps too embarrassed at the telling, at least not under Bose's steady gaze. Understanding this, Bose moved closer toward the fire, stoking its gentle flames, and giving him a measure of privacy. "Nightmares not fit for a man t' rightly have. She comes t' me every night, naked as a sunrise. We start t' know each other, in the Biblical sense, then, while we're still . . ."

"Knowing?" Bose offered. Henry turned away, but nodded.

"She starts t' rot underneath me. Her skin just slides off like she was wearing a costume of flesh, becomin' little more than a skeleton. Worms winding their way through the fleshy bits of what remained of her ribs and such. When I wake up, I can still smell her perfume. An' I have a few additions to my collection."

Before Bose could ask, Henry turned around and raised his shirt. Scratches crisscrossed his back, many scars not quite healed over.

"Damn," Bose said.

Dirk trembled in the reflected amber light of the

campfire, tugging his shirt tighter as if afraid the wind might catch it just right and reveal his own nail-scarred back.

Henry seemed to weigh his options for a minute. He coughed up a wad of blood onto the ground. Sweat beaded along his forehead, making him look even more pale and haggard. "You ever hear of a soiled dove?"

"A prostitute that gets . . . hurt in the line of duty," Bose said.

"Henry . . ." Dirk cautioned.

"It's alright, Dirk, he might as well know. We were heading into Abaddon, t' have a few to cut the dust. Well, soon as we got there, we knew something was right peculiar. All eyes were on us, the people not saying a word. When we approached the end building, people made themselves scarce, steppin' inside or shutterin' their windows. Made us no nevermind. Didn't want a bunch of pryin' noses in our business no way. The bartender lined up a few without meetin' our eyes, but the women . . . the women were angels. The most fetchin' collection o' gals I ever did see."

"Been my experience that the prettier the gal, the bigger the passel of trouble that follows," Bose said.

"You ain't lyin'. It was all we could do t' keep our tongues from fallin' out o' our fool mouths. Each o' the women picked a man an' made a bee line right for him. This gal saunters up t' me askin' what brings us to town.

"'Jest an old cowhand, ma'am. Lookin' t' take a break from the trail,' I tell her.

"'You must be very good at your job,' she said." Henry affected a female voice. He wasn't very convincing.

"'Ain't much on which t' court a woman.'

"'You are very handsome.' Now I'm used t' women lyin' about such things when business was at hand. Heck, that's what I paid 'em for. Still, to hear her say it, I near got t' believin' it myself. What did I know? I was no hand with women. Never could read their signs.

"She led me t' one o' the upstairs rooms. She put her hands on me, wantin' me to draw her near. Something in the way her hands reached along my back made me uneasy, but . . ."

"But what?" Bose asked.

"But she was so pretty. An' it had been so long. I ignored that little voice in the back o' my head, the one that says y' oughten not be doin' something. I kissed her, hard an' long. She was as soft an' as pretty smellin' as any woman I've been with."

"Then what happened?" Bose wanted him to skip ahead before Henry got too caught up in details he didn't want to picture.

"We kept kissin'. I started feeling along her back t' try an' get her out o' her outfit when I ketched a glimpse o' her mirror. I thought something was out o' place about the room. I may not know much about women, but I know that their mirrors are the center o' their rooms. This one was in the corner, out o' the way. I reckon it would have been too odd t' not have one in the room at all. Maybe I was meant t' see her, jest not right away. Anyway, I ketched her reflection in the mirror an' what I saw didn't match what I was holdin'. She looked like she stepped right from a grave, all rotted an' foul."

"Like the cattle?" Bose studied Dirk to see if he was

being put on, but Dirk turned from him and spit into the fire.

"Kinda. 'Ceptin' worse, cause her skin was black as pitch, an' her flesh peeled back straight t' the bone in spots. I ain't ashamed to tell y' that I screamed an' pushed her away from me. I reckon whatever it was that kept her lookin' pretty may have tricked my eyes, but mirrors couldn't hold illusions.

"'What's the matter?' she had the nerve t' ask. I would've chalked it up t' bein' in the sun too long, iffen she hadn't smiled at me. Smiled. A knowin' grin, even as a maggot crawled out o' her arm in the reflection. Like it was some grand joke. That was when I heard the gun shot."

"Will," Bose said with the certainty of him having been there.

"I reckon it didn't take too much figurin' on who had the itchy trigger finger. He was never one for jokes."

"I didn't think anyone took their guns into town."

"He carried a derringer with him. Blew a hole clean through her face, breakin' whatever spell kept them all pretty. Or leastways not looking like a grave spit them out. A howl came from downstairs. All the men had the same thought, skedaddlin' out the windows an' out o' that God-forsaken place."

"You thinking that it might be the . . . proprietor that's trailing us?" Bose asked.

"Reckon so. Makes sense anyway, what sense there is t' be had."

Bose studied the sickly face of the men. He found himself prejudiced in favor of Henry, realizing the dilemma of not wanting to go against the man who paid his salary. Dirk stared at the fire, caught up in his own shame. Lips set in a grim line, Bose stood, ready to quit. He wanted no part of the vendetta, or whatever was after them. And he damn sure wasn't gearing up to defend Will Grimes. He needed some time to get his thoughts together.

During his time as a soldier, he'd been in some horrible places and seen some awful things, and heard tales of a strange brand of magicians. The stories sounded too much like something he'd hear at his mother's knee to scare him into good behavior, never believing them because he knew how tales got exaggerated around a campfire.

A desert judge.

The cold feeling coiled in his belly again.

With the creeping of night, talk died down. Still putting the pieces into place, the first shift of night duty allowed him the peace to gather his wandering thoughts. The second shift was the least desirable since the cattle often stretched and were prone to wandering. Bose watched the desert. A coyote yipped in the distance, complaining about the sudden cool. Dirk and another of the Circle T boys relieved him.

"Don't stray too far from camp. The moon will be full and things happen out here that no white people have seen."

"Since when does a nigger talk so uppity to whites?" Dirk turned back to his fellow hand, wanting to save face.

Slow and deliberate, Bose turned to him, allowing the

drape of his shirt to reveal his undulating muscles with each movement. "Since your lives depend on it."

Dirk took a step backward like a small dog determined to bark louder in retreat. "We'll do as we please, without any say from you."

"Makes me no nevermind. I'm paid to bring in cattle, not men determined to die."

"Go to the devil. I worry more about Indians scalping us in our sleep than I do any bedtime monsters."

Bose wasn't too worried about Indians. No, something else was definitely at work here. Rumor had it that desert judges sold their souls to become well versed in dark rituals. Some of the rituals supposedly involved eating human flesh, the younger the better, to be granted great power. The evil they communed with had a way of changing a body, transforming a person.

Bose pressed his head into his bedroll for the fitful thing that he called sleep.

Though he didn't remember drawing it, Bose snapped awake with his gun in hand. His trouble reflex stirred him to wakefulness. A horseshoe clicked against stone. Soft-footing it toward the source of the sound, he had to catch himself from humming.

A frail, gaunt figure leaned over the body of a dead coyote. With quick, fluid movements, his body obscured his actions. When the figure stood up, he held a tin cup overflowing with a dark liquid. He turned toward Bose with the truculent stare of hollowed eyes that had stared too long into the sun. Or the darkness of men's souls. Yellow, broken teeth spread in full reveal approximating a smile. His roan, a black beast that snorted in a fit as the man approached, had the wild bearing of a horse used to long miles of hard riding. His hand patted a small sack which hung from about his neck.

"Only the guilty." He raised his cup in toast.

Bose took aim, not taking his eyes off the man for an instant, but the man and his horse disappeared, swallowed whole by the night.

"Damn it!" Dirk yelled.

The whole camp scrambled.

"What's the matter?" Bradford Grimes stormed from his tent, Winchester in hand. Will ran up to settle in at his father's side.

"The cattle. I went down to check the herd." Dirk held his hands up like he didn't want to be splashed with blame. "They all dead. Some look like they've been rotting for some weeks even though they were fresh this morning."

"There nothing for us here." Bose spoke not from cowardice, but from his pragmatic self. "We should cut our losses and get as far from this country as possible. Skins intact. Because he'll be back."

"Who?" Mr. Grimes demanded.

"Go ahead and tell him," Dirk chided. "Your boy here's been going on about a fairy tale."

"A desert judge," Bose said. The light of recognition flickered in Mr. Grimes's eyes. "You've heard of them, too."

"Don't rightly know what you mean," Mr. Grimes said.

"Your lies will soon find their end," a voice of an open grave rang out. The men turned to see the gaunt figure step into their midst. If the man had ever been one of those everyday, weather-worn faces Bose had come to expect in frontier life, those days were long behind him. His face a skein of dark scars. He flexed long, gnarled fingers in anticipation.

"Who are you? What do you want?" His Winchester held at his side, Mr. Grimes took a tentative step toward the man. Bose wondered if the rifle might be more useful trained on the man's heart.

"Revenge. You took my daughter, my life from me at Abaddon. Now I've come for yours. You will know the measure of a father's grief," the man said. "Bit by bit, I will take away everything you hold dear. Your livelihood. Your men. Your son. Until all you have left is grief enough to turn a man's soul. And only then might I trouble myself to take what remains of you."

"She was already dead," Will protested. All eyes turned to him.

"Not to me. None of them were. We all make our homes in our corners of hell. Abaddon was ours. We had dreams once, of settling the West, until an Apache raid cut them short. Only my power saved me. I couldn't let the dream die."

"So you what? Raised them from the dead?" Bose slowly pieced the story together. The man glanced at him with only a fraction of his intense scorn. Hatred emanated from him like waves of heat from desert sands. The death of a child could drive any man insane, twisting him so that any straw to stem the pain was grasped.

"Her death broke my spell that held us together. No matter where they were. All my friends, my family, returned to the grave." The desert judge spoke softly, with an almost defeated tone.

"You'll know my torment." Almost unconsciously, the wizened creature touched the small pouch dangling from his neck. "You'll watch all you love die."

Mr. Grimes aimed his Winchester at the man, but before he could fire, the man let loose a soul-piercing scream. The men covered their ears, not that it helped. Bose caught sight of movement from the corner of his eye.

The steers.

The stink of flesh rotting from their bones rose to a near physical pitch. Most of the bodies huddled near one another, as if knowing that death approached, seeking the comfort of one another in their last moments. The corpses of the fallen steers formed a burial mound of sorts, yet something stirred in the pile. Bones drew to one another like magnetized bits, not caring how they lined up. Flesh knitted together, bits stitched from each steer melting into one another, forming a patchwork quilt of rotted skin over the skeletal creature. A looming longhorn head, larger than the skull of any single steer, topped the monstrosity. It opened its maw, echoing the ear-bleeding shriek of its master.

Moving with terrifying speed, it attacked the Circle T boys. Mr. Grimes stepped between the creature and Will, leaving his men to fend for themselves. It tore into them, trampling some, scattering the rest with its thunderous hooves. Lowering its head, the beast looked on to Henry, who stood his ground. Henry fumbled with his metal flask, downing a quick swig before welcoming the steer's gouging horns with a grimace of near relief. The horns pierced him in his belly and with a sharp upthrust, ripped him to the top of his ribcage. His insides spilled out while he still stood.

"Dear God," Mr. Grimes muttered, watching the scene.

"There is no God. Not for you. Not for me." Fine lines radiated from the desert judge's dark eyes, a filigree of sun, wind, and hard living. Hate convoluted his brain so deep, his eyes seemed to withdraw in shame. Cruelty etched around his mouth when he turned toward Will Grimes. "Your boy. Such enormous vitality he possesses. It will be a pleasure to drain him."

"Pa?" Will suddenly looked every bit of his teenage years.

Bradford Grimes stared at his son, the word "no" formed on his lips.

"You've had your fill of blood." Bose loosened the thong holding his gun in place. "Why not leave them with what they've seen. They've paid enough."

The desert judge turned to him. "True, this won't relieve my soul. The burdens that scar it aren't so easily erased, but it will make them, make her, rest a mite easier."

"Can't say that what either of them did was right," Bose said. "But Mr. Grimes here still owes me for a few days."

The man waved his broken-nailed hands, summoning the creature. The monster turned, chewing the broken body of Dirk with languid disinterest. Dirk's shirt exploded in red, slickening the creatures flank. It spat him out with a snort and charged toward Bose. Like a boxer, he moved easy on his feet and let his hand swing to the gun butt, cocking the gun as he grasped it. The tip of his finger squeezed the trigger, a tuneless hum on his lips. Bullets snarled and snapped, chipping rocks like jagged teeth.

The bullets met something solid in the swirling shadows that formed the chest of the desert judge. The man dropped to his knees and collapsed forward. Bose moved in to examine him. The man's legs spasmed. His arms jerked, regaining life by inches. Beginning to push himself up, the tiny sack dangled by leather thongs from his neck. On instinct, Bose snatched the bag. The desert judge wailed as Bose poured out its contents. Bits of burnt bone, far too small to be an adult, fell to the earth. A glint of metal landed in the ash. A locket fell open, revealing the picture of a young girl. Not quite on his knees, the judge reached toward the locket. All strength fled him and he collapsed.

"Looks like I owe you my life again." Mr. Grimes nudged the body with the tip of his boots.

"You're many things, but you're no welsher." Bose turned to Mr. Grimes and held out his hand. Without any words, Mr. Grimes counted out Bose's owed pay. Bose envied the heroes of dime novels, how their exaggerated exploits tickled the fancy of the public. Knowing that no one would tell his tale, his restless heart grew ready to hit the trail. He'd heard that some Exodusters traveled toward Cascade, Kansas. That sounded like it might be a fine town to spend some money.

So he rode.

DRY GULCH DRAGON

Sarah A. Hoyt

Would you let your sister marry a dragon? The words ran through Jack Hemming's mind, over and over. As the train rocked beneath him, left and right, clackety clack, the question echoed as though the sounds of the train itself were asking it, *Would you let your sister marry a dragon?*

He'd never heard the words spoken. He had read it in half a dozen letters from Dry Gulch. It was amazing, he reflected as he looked out a window made amber by the smoke from the coal-fired engine, at an endless expanse of prairie flecked with the occasional herd of buffalo. It could knock you dead with surprise how many people with no interest in either words, or his own private life, had found they needed to write to him, as he was in Chicago, winding up his late uncle's estate, to tell him that Maisie was walking out with Deep Mine Pete.

The stable keeper had written him, and Ted who ran the saloon, and Jim who kept cattle in the scrubby lands over the river.

And the thing was, Jack didn't know what to answer.

He knew Deep Mine Pete and liked him, in the way he could be said to like anyone he'd never had much dealing with. Deep Mine Pete was a good man, or would be if he were a man. In his human form he was taller than most and thinner than most, and was none too bad with a gun, but nothing out of the way. In his dragon form—well, he hauled mine cars from the Silver Dollar mine. Which was, Jack reminded himself, an honorable job, if menial. And he took gold shipments on over to Denver, on the wing, avoiding bandits. None of it paid a lot, but he lived decently, in a tidy little cabin.

People said that Pete scoured the hills and the prairies at night and ate buffalo raw or perhaps alive, and if he was not nearby and they felt brave, they would add to the tale that he also ate miners, raw, if he could catch them.

And if a damn fool disappeared while panning for gold, or fell down some gorge while looking for nuggets, people in town whispered that Pete looked well fed and gave Pete the glare.

Jack couldn't hold with that. There was no proof, and no reason to suspect Pete of anything untoward. He had treated Pete as he treated everyone else. Pete behaved like a man of honor, and he got treated like a man of honor. And that was why people had taken such delight in writing to Jack about Maisie. Because they thought he'd been too soft on Pete and was now reaping what he'd sowed.

But to Jack the question wasn't "Would you let your sister marry a dragon?" The question was "What kind of man takes advantage of another man's absence to court his sister without chaperonage?" And "Had anything else gone on than walking out together?" Maisie was out there, day in, day out in that log cabin on the mountain, and Jack had been away for a month.

A lot of things went on in a month.

Would he let his sister marry a dragon? Well, he might at that, if he didn't have to shoot him for a faithless varmint first.

Jack arrived at Dry Gulch late, and was grateful for the silent streets, the dark houses. All he needed was to have to dodge a committee of concerned citizens, each one informing him of goings-on in his absence, each one demanding to know what he was going to do about it.

Part of it, he thought, was that they were bored. Most people who moved to Dry Gulch were looking to escape and maybe for adventure. People didn't live on the edge of the magical lands, pushing humans into territory that had been held, time out of mind, by the tribes of magic workers who had escaped from Europe as humans took it over, without having a taste for the unexpected. And there hadn't been a robbery or a riot or even a duel since Six-Shooter Malcolm had taken out the water wizard three years ago.

So he was glad of the silence and the darkness, as he walked, carrying his valise, past rows of houses where everything was shuttered and the only noise was the occasional barking of a dog or whinney of a horse.

The saloon was open and well lit, but even there the noise of conversations and arguments was so muted you could hear the forlorn tinkling of the piano playing "Clementine."

And further on, as he walked past Madame Madeleine's Maison of Mechanical Pleasures, that was lit too, and he could hear the sound of a girl being wound up for yet another customer.

Nothing disturbed him as he took the path up the cliff and around the sacred grove—where fairy lights shone and there was a weird sound like a harp played so high the ear could barely catch it—and then on, past the turn in the mountain road, to his cabin.

And right there, he knew something was wrong, because the cabin was dark, and it shouldn't be dark. Maisie didn't even like to have the oil lamp unlit while she slept. It wasn't so much that she was afraid of the dark, as that she said it felt lonesome. Like she was the last person left on Earth. He'd had to remonstrate with her about the danger of fire often and again, before she'd snuff off the wick.

Getting closer to the cabin, he found more causes for worry. Before he witnessed the door beating forlornly in the wind, he heard it, and when he entered the cabin, he heard things scurrying out—wild creatures who must have come in while the cabin was opened and untenanted. Maisie would never leave the cabin open.

"Maisie," he called to the cold dark, knowing full well there would be no answer. And then again "Maisie!"

Wind blew through the windows, too, where no one had bothered to fasten the shutters, and he had to find his way to the fireplace by touch, tripping over things on the floor, which told him that the whole inside of the cabin had been overturned, as though by a small, vicious, indoor tornado. He couldn't find the oil lamp, at first, and since the fireplace mantel was curiously denuded, he feared it had been overturned, but then his hand grasped its rounded metallic belly, and he felt upward for the hurricane glass. He set it aside, by touch, and felt around for the box of matches, which he found on the point of falling from the mantel.

Striking a match against the rough brick seemed to produce almost too bright a light after the total darkness. Jack struck it to the wick of the oil lamp, and as that flared up, it was bright as a mini-sun to his unaccustomed eyes. He blinked until he could see more clearly, then put the hurricane glass back on and looked around.

The cabin had been turned upside down, just as he'd expected.

In the corner, near the Franklin stove, which Maisie called the kitchen, though it was just part of the same great room, the table had been overturned, the flour bin had been burst as though by a powerful kick. There was a frying pan on the floor in a puddle of oil and what looked like the remains of eggs and bacon.

On the other side of the room, the bed that Jack used at night had also been inverted. He blinked at it, because it hadn't been turned wrong side up as though someone were searching for something, but more like someone had clutched the mattresses trying to hold on to them and had been dragged nonetheless. The mattress was half-off the box springs, and the bed clothes formed a trail toward the door. Part of the headboard was missing. It was an iron headboard, and the decorative finial that screwed into the pole was there on the right side but not on the left.

Jack picked up the oil lamp and carried it with him to

the inner room. Maisie's room. It was curiously neat, clean, as she kept it normally, her bed made with the multicolored quilt which was their only legacy from their mother, and her clothes hanging on the pegs on the wall. He squinted at them: night shift, and Sunday-go-to-meeting dress, which left Maisie in her everyday skirt and blouse. The final peg was taken up by her winter coat and her bonnet, which meant wherever she'd gone, it hadn't been willingly because she'd never go out willingly without her bonnet.

"Oh hell," said a male voice from the door. And then a wavering call, "Maisie?"

Jack jumped. Before he had himself in hand, he was by the fireplace, setting down his oil lamp, and it was a good thing his revolvers were in his valise, and that his Remington shotgun didn't hang where it normally did, over the fireplace, because otherwise it would have been out and he would have—

He would have put a bullet in Deep Mine Pete's head, as the dragon, in his human form, stood at the entrance, pale and disheveled, and looking like he'd been dragged through hell backward by his hair.

He had the time to say, "Hi, Jack, is Maisie—" before Jack was on him.

Now the truth is at that moment Jack would have taken on anyone, man, dragon or demon without the least bit of thought. He had his hand around Pete's neck and was trying to lift him off his feet, against the frame of the door. He couldn't, of course, because dragons even in their human form weighed as much as, well . . . a dragon, and dragons were heavy creatures which could only lift up and fly because they were magical creatures, too.

But what woke Jack from his fury, more than the fact that he couldn't lift a full grown dragon, was that Deep Mine Pete wasn't fighting. He wasn't even defending himself. Instead, when Jack barked at him, "Where is my sister you son of a snake?" all the dragon did was blink his oddly amber-colored eyes, swallow hard—his Adam's apple bobbing under Jack's clutching hand—and say, "Oh no. You don't know where she is either?"

It could have been dissembling, of course, but it didn't feel like dissembling. It felt like the genuine thing, honest shock at Maisie's absence.

Without taking his hand from around the dragon's neck, though Jack was starting to suspect it really made no difference to the dragon, Jack swept the room with a grand gesture of his other hand. "As you see," he said. "And she didn't go willingly. I'm going to guess around breakfast this morning, from the spilled eggs and bacon."

Pete shook his head. "No," he said. "Couldn't be this morning. They don't come out while there's sunlight."

So Jack hadn't shot Pete's face off, mostly because he couldn't get to his guns in time, but also because like everyone else he knew that normal bullets did nothing to shapeshifters, and he didn't have any silver ones on hand since there had never been any trouble with lycanthropes in Colorado, not since the Kidd gang had been captured. But he had growled, "They? Who are they?" and if Pete had been a normal man would have bounced his head off the doorframe a time or two. Instead, his hand met the resistance of that more-than-mortal weight, and then Pete was removing his fingers from Pete's neck, gently, and grasping him by the shoulders, not gently, and frog-marching him to the one chair still upright in the mess that had been the kitchen. He pushed Jack down on the chair and said, "Sit, and I'll tell you what's happening."

Perhaps Jack was in shock, but it seemed to him no time at all before Pete had the table and the other chair upright too, and sat down on the other chair, facing him across the table.

"You thought that I wouldn't let my sister marry a dragon," Jack said. "So you kidnapped her and—" He heard the words leave his mouth before he realized how idiotic he sounded, even as Pete shook his head and said, "No, come on now, you are better than that. Why would I come looking for her and be shocked not to find her if I'd taken her?"

"To . . . throw me off the scent?" Jack asked, but it sounded as flat as he felt.

"Why would I have a need to do that, if I had taken Maisie away? I could simply have flown her somewhere like Denver."

"How do I know? How do I know how a dragon's head works?" Jack asked, as the entire day in the train caught up with him, the bouncing and jostling of the third-class carriage, with its hard wood seats, the heat of the sun, and the cold as night descended and they climbed toward Denver.

Pete made a sound that in any other circumstances could be called a chuckle. "Oh, hell," he said. "I don't know how dragons think, either, only how I think, and though Maisie is the best gal I've met in centuries, I did not kidnap her. If time should come for . . . well, I can do things in the mode of the time like any other civilized creature."

Before Jack could digest that *in centuries,* Pete said, "No, Maisie and I weren't walking out together that way, or maybe we were, too, and just lying to ourselves, but what I've tried to do this last month is prepare her for . . . for the attack at summer solstice."

"The what?"

"When the days are at their longest, before the year turns from waxing towards summer to waning towards winter," Pete said, as though talking to a child. "You know, the longest day of the year. Today. The night when the dark elves dance in the sacred grove." He looked at Jack, very earnestly, and it seemed to Jack his amber eyes flicked, like the moon changing aspect. "Every year for five years now, they take someone at the solstice. I know I usually get blamed for eating them, but I do not eat humans. And this year, I knew there weren't any isolated trappers or prospectors around, but Maisie was here all alone, in this cabin. I knew they'd get her. I tried to prepare her. I thought I could defend her—"

Jack was on his feet, still blurry with fatigue and confusion, but as ready as he was going to be. "What do they do to the people they take at the solstice? Kill them?"

"Devour them," Pete said. "At midnight."

Jack remembered the shuttered town, his silent walk. He didn't know how far off it was, but midnight could not be far. "What are we waiting for?"

"What kills an elf?" Jack asked, raising an eyebrow.

"Does a normal gun do it, or do they need something special?"

Pete smiled as Jack rummaged through the wreckage in the cabin, casting about for usefuls. "Oh, a gun will do the job just fine. It's the bullet that's the trick—for an elf, you need cold iron. Works for knives and swords and things too—the more cold iron the better."

"Cold Iron? As in, not red hot?"

"No, iron that has been beaten, not forged. The more it's been heated, the less effective it is—never did figure out why." Pete explained. "As it happens, during the late war, I ran across the LeMat revolver—a good gun, though a bit puny, with nine rounds of forty-five and an extra barrel of sixteen-gauge shotgun slung underneath. After it all ended, I had a couple made up custom that fit me a little better."

Pete unslung the satchel that'd been over his back, all four feet of it, and laid it on the ground before opening it up and pulling forth a pair of huge revolvers and a gun belt that looked unusually sturdy. "They're a bit heavy, especially with two of them, but they fit my hand. I kept the forty-five idea, but went with a ten-gauge for those times you really want to get your message across. Bullets in the forty-five cylinder are a little special—lead poured around a cold iron spike. The shot in the ten-gauge is all cold iron."

"That'll kill elves?"

"It'll kill everything but vampires and werewolves, one way or another. And it'll give *them* a very bad day."

"One of those for me?" said Jack, eyebrow still raised at the newly impressive hardware as he stumbled across his shotgun, a bit beat up but still functional amidst the rubble.

Pete laughed again, a dry laugh with no humor behind it. "No. It would break your wrist. Might break it clean off. What do you pack?"

"Remington forty-fives and a Winchester 1887 ten-gauge shotgun. Why?"

Pete grinned, handing him several boxes of forty-five ammo and ten-gauge shells. "Welcome to the elf-killing league. Ammo I can share. The forty-five is a little stiff, but a Remington should handle it and it'll be just fine for you. The ten-gauge is fine, as long as you're not stupid enough to run it through a pistol."

Jack returned the grin with a nod, and then noticed Pete still rummaging through his satchel. He pulled out a long wooden box that looked like walnut that had been varnished till it seemed to glow. It glittered like a jewel against the roughhewn floor where Pete had set it.

"What's that?" Jack asked.

"Well, you carry a shotgun, right? Well . . . so do I, sort of—just built for my size and strength. You ever hear of those market hunters up north? I stole the idea from them and their punt guns and made a couple of improvements."

Pete opened the box and drew forth a bandolier holding what looked like long soup cans hanging in the loops before reaching back into the box and drawing forth something that resembled a double-barreled shotgun the Wells Fargo coach drivers liked to carry. Only this one was the big brother of the Wells Fargo drivers' gun. The big, big brother. The one who could pick up the other gun and carry it around like a baby.

Jack's jaw dropped as he looked at maybe thirty pounds of wood and steel with muzzles nearly two and a half inches wide and all of three feet long. His eyes bulged. "Um, Pete? What in God's name is that thing?"

"It's my kind of coach gun. Two shots, about a pound and a half of cold iron I chopped into tiny little squares myself, quick to reload using these newfangled cartridges *and*, with this bandolier-thing, I can carry a *lot* of cartridges. After the war, I was a little worried about unfriendly visitors. Now, let's load up." Pete pointed at the boxes of newfangled ammo he had cooked up before shrugging into the bandolier and shoving what could only be *God's Own Shotgun* into a scabbard slung over his back and strapping on the monstrous gun belt with the two mighty overgrown LeMats.

Jack shrugged, still a little boggled by the dragon's armament, and began putting on his own gunbelt and—looking at the dragon's rig—grabbing a saddle scabbard and some string, slung his shotgun across his back much like the dragon had.

Moments later, they were on the road under the moonlight, back to the sacred grove.

"Fairyland is lousy with elves," Pete said. "Dark and light and everything in between. They are the Lords and Ladies, and the rest of us serve their needs." They walked under the moonlight toward the sacred grove, or rather, in the sacred grove. The weird thing was, though Jack had walked from his claim to the cabin and past the sacred grove every day, he'd never known how big it was.

From the outside, one was tempted to wonder why it

was called a grove at all, since no tree could be seen, just an odd lot of standing stones and glittering sand. And he'd never stepped in it before, because it gave him a funny feeling in the pit of the stomach just passing by. But it turned out that once you stepped past the perimeter, the feeling got worse, and the land changed.

He and Pete walked through a forest under the moonlight. "Will we get there in time?" he asked.

"Yes," Pete said very assuredly. "Time is different here, but I can feel it. I know enough of fairyland time. I lived in it for centuries. But a body, man or dragon, gets tired of being commanded and ordered about by capricious beings who have no other interest but their own pleasure and power. And they said the world of men was so bad, and they hated it so much, I thought I'd like a try." He was silent a while until they crested a hill. From its top, Jack could see a winding road to the valley and, at the end of it, what seemed like a melee of tall, well formed men and . . .

"Maisie!"

"So it is," Pete said. "And she's holding them at bay. I wonder how." He put out a hand and restrained Jack from running. "Not down this road, or they'll be on you. They have bows and elf shot. They'll bring you down in no time."

"Why haven't they shot Maisie with elfshot, then?" Jack whispered.

"They haven't, because they need her alive for the ceremony. We'll take the woods, and ambush them around the back and lend Maisie aid. But never mind the whispering. I have . . . a silence spell around us. That's not what it is, but close enough. At any rate, the elves won't hear us."

"So you threw in with humans," Jack said. "Could you always shift into human form?" He wasn't really interested, but the talk, and concentrating on it, kept him from throwing all caution to the winds and running down the road toward Maisie.

"All of us dragons can shift to human form. But the thing is," he said. "I shifted and started finding jobs among humans and living like a human. And I was in Philadelphia when the Declaration of Independence was read. I fell in love with it, and America, right then. That all sentient creatures were created equal. Those words I carry in my breast, like the *chem* on a golem."

Jack nodded. He wasn't absolutely sure what that meant, except that best he could figure this dragon was American. "You've lived a long time," he said.

"Yes. Though I can't expect to do so much longer. Once in the world of men, we only live two or three times the normal human span. It is enough. While I live, I'll defend the world of men from the elves that have kept elfland in tyranny. After I die—" He shrugged. "No one can control the world after they die. And now we should be quiet, because they might have listening magic that counters my silencing. But listen, before we go in, you must remember, lead off with the shotgun first, and take out as many of the bastards as you can. We'll pick off the survivors with the handgun after."

"Huh . . . what if we hit Maisie with the scatter shot?" Jack asked, uneasily eyeing God's Own Gun.

"Aim away from her, first. At the distant elves. There

will be dozens of them at this. We have to outthink them first."

As they drew near, they could see that Maisie was surrounded by fifty elves, all of them glitteringly beautiful and blond, wearing buckskins of the finest, palest color, and with bows and arrows upon their back. Maisie held something like a lance in her hand, and every time one of them tried to grab her, she flourished it in his direction. The thing was that it was only one against many, and she had to keep retreating down the road.

Down the road, that way, were those standing stones that Jack had seen from outside the perimeter, and he had a feeling that the elves were herding Maisie exactly the way they wanted her to go.

Deep Mine Pete made gestures, indicating that they should split, so the shots didn't all come from the same direction. Not being an idiot, Jack understood, too, that they should move right after taking a shot. His guess was that those deadly elf shots could find them, no matter whether the elves could see them clearly or not. It wouldn't make the shots less deadly if they were just flung blindly among the trees. There were so many elves even blind shooting would kill them, and dead is dead.

So they split, and before Jack had spied out a place to lie down, behind a protective trunk, he heard the crack-boom, as God's Own Gun barked up ahead.

A dozen or more elves disappeared in screams and smoke, and the rest were too confused to fire back. Jack fired his shotgun and took out another eight or nine. Who was counting anyway? All he knew was that half the enemies were gone. God's Own Gun boomed again, and there were only a dozen elves left or so, and they were all around Maisie, which meant they had to be careful about shooting.

The other elves had recovered from the surprise, at least enough to react. They turned, from fighting Maisie, and in the blink of an eye, three archers were letting arrows fly in the general direction where the shots had come from.

Which was when Jack hit them, crack, crack with two shots from his own revolvers. Two more elves fell down, and before they hit the ground, Jack rolled away from his position, then ran to hide behind a thick oak tree. While he took deep breaths, he thought this was magical land indeed, as he didn't think there were oaks this thick in Colorado.

He heard arrows fly, striking the log that had protected him earlier. And then Pete fired again. And then Jack. And both times, they moved fast away from their former positions.

Down below—in a glimpse caught between rolling and shooting—Maisie was taking advantage of the elves' distraction to touch them with her lance, which made them writhe and fall, too, if properly applied.

After a while, there was only one elf standing. He was trying to hide behind Maisie, and he pulled his bow off his back and—

Maisie struck backward, her lance penetrating his eye. There was a sound like thunder, and his head exploded.

"Maisie!" Jack said, running towards her, at the same time as Pete.

She removed her apron, and was wiping elf-bits off her face and hair. "About time you boys got here," she said. "But don't let your guard down. I think there are more of them around."

Pete sniffed the air, which to Jack smelled mostly of exploded elf, and shook his head. "No," he said. "But others felt their comrades' deaths, and they'll be here soon. Unless—"

"Unless?" Maisie said.

"Unless we destroy the sacrifice grove."

"And how do we do that?"

"We put a cold iron spike into the center of the circle," Pete said. "If we had a cold iron spike."

"You mean like this?" Maisie asked, flourishing her lance.

It was a broomstick, with the missing finial of the daybed tied to the end, with a portion of Maisie's apron strings. "They still herded me here," she said. "But they couldn't carry me." She looked at Pete. "You were supposed to be there to protect me."

"I know, I know," he said. "But the people from the town came to talk to me when I left the mine. They said I was shredding your reputation. By the time I got rid of them—"

"There're fools everywhere," she said, and Jack made a note to talk to her about her reputation. Later. After this was through.

It turned out putting the iron spike in the center of the circle made the entire grove implode. One moment there had been trees and a forest, and vast distances inside the circle as had never been seen from outside. And the next there was nothing but some rocks on the cracked, red clay of Colorado.

Even so, Pete must be a distrustful bastard, as he spread one-inch iron caltrops on his way out of the sacred grove. "If they rebuild the circle," he said. "They won't be able to come out. Nor will they be able to ride their fairy horses out."

Jack felt he appreciated distrustful bastards. The walk back to his cabin was far more than the mile and a half or so that it had always taken. He realized the battle had taken far longer than he expected, and taken far more out of him than he'd hoped.

When they were back at the cabin, and Maisie was fussing and cleaning and making clucking sounds over the destruction, he watched as Pete humbly helped her. And he took note of the looks he gave her. Oh, sure. Maybe he'd only been trying to protect her from the dark elves. But unless dragons were completely different from human men, he was half gone on her, too. Or more.

Would I let my sister marry a dragon? Jack thought. *Well, truth is, she could do worse.*

THE TREEFOLD PROBLEM
A Mad Amos Malone story

Alan Dean Foster

The children were wailing, his wife was sobbing, and that pitiless sliver of scum that walked like a man and called himself Potter Scunsthorpe (the individual with whom Owen was arguing fruitlessly) remained as merciless as a bull fixated on chewing three days' worth of unmasticated cud. To add to the human cacophony at the forest's edge, a pair of ravens flew past overhead, cackling like a pair of perambulating witches intent solely on taunting Owen Hargrave in his present misery.

Scunsthorpe let the farmer stem-wind for several minutes longer before raising a commanding hand for silence. He had the look of a successful undertaker, did Scunsthorpe, coupled to the unctuous mannerisms of a banker who could squeeze an orange in one hand, a nickel in the other, and get juice out of both. Slender as a reed, his skin the color of wild rice, he was clad in a finely tailored black suit entirely out of keeping with the present woodland surroundings. A black top hat one size too small clung to his white-fringed scalp with grim determination. The single red silk ribbon that protruded from the hatband was the color of blood. From the front of his immaculate white shirt, a gold watch chain dribbled into a bulging pocket. Only his scuffed and dirty boots marked him as a citizen of far Wisconsin and not more civilized New York or Philadelphia. His two troll-like lackeys flanked him, disinterested and anxious to be away.

The subject of the animated and decidedly inequitable discussion between the two men was an inundation of unbroken verdure, a veritable mantle of virgin forest that stretched as far to the west as one could see. White and red pine stabbed at the heavens, interspersed with stout woodland guardians of northern and red oak, red and sugar maple. Here and there a solitary basswood made an appearance, and where sunlight was sufficient, dense thickets of blueberry, wintergreen, and partridgeberry burst forth in energetic tangles.

All this green glory the Hargrave family owned, as part and parcel of their deeded land. It was coveted in turn by Scunsthorpe. The paper he now held out before Owen Hargrave might as well have been signed and stamped by the Devil himself. It was the mortgage to the Hargrave property. As is the way of those who lurk, wormlike, just below the surface of decent society, Scunsthorpe had bought it up on the sly. Now the final, balloon payment was due. Based on their existing equity, a Milwaukee banker would likely have extended credit to the family. Scunsthorpe was no banker. He was brother to the ravens who had just cawed past overhead, and like them, a soulless scavenger.

"The timber is mine by rights of this deed." It was an evident struggle for Scunsthorpe to speak the words while masking his enjoyment of them. He kissed each vowel with a perverse joy. "That, and the land upon which it stands, and the adjoining farm, as well. Together with any buildings, wells, fences, barns, and other physical improvements you may have made thereon." Unable to restrain himself any longer, he nodded toward the untouched forest. His prominent Adam's apple bobbed as he spoke. "The law says it is so if you have not cleared this land. I see no evidence of it."

Hargrave glanced over at his wife, who was trying to ease the crying of their youngest, held in her arms, before once more confronting his tormentor.

"I have explained and explained, sir. It was a difficult winter. I meant fully to hire a crew to at least commence the requisite clearing of the timber, but all our efforts had to be bent to preserving our livestock and thence getting in the spring planting. I had no time left for tree felling."

Scunsthorpe straightened, which made him loom even higher over the stocky farmer. "My concern is not with the vagaries of the local climate, sir, nor with your petty domestic matters. The law is the law, fixed and immutable." He swept a scythe-like arm to the west. "You have not, as specified, made use of the forest. Therefore, it and all else included in this deed, is now mine by right."

Unable to contain herself any longer, Hargrave's wife spoke up, her pleading carrying above the sobs of the children. Only ten-year-old Eli, who gazed at Scunsthorpe with undying hatred, was not bawling uncontrollably.

"But sir, I beseech you, what are we to do? I would

take a job and work myself to pay you something of the cash money you are owed, but with the farm and the four children I have little enough time to sleep."

Scunsthorpe's mouth drew tight in a line as closed as that of his purse. "Then at least, Madame, you will very soon have time to sleep, as the arduous burden of caring for a farm will be lifted from you."

Greatly pleased with himself, he turned to depart . . . only to pause and frown as a singular shape caught his attention. It interrupted the horizon most notably. The Hargraves saw it, too.

Considering the present circumstances, all of them would have ignored the newcomer save that he could not be ignored. He appeared on the trail that led over the slight rise that hid the farmstead from the discussion, his mount ambling along at a leisurely pace along the barely foot-wide pathway. Scunsthorpe certainly would have ignored him had not Hargrave turned to stare, but one cannot continue to denigrate a suddenly indifferent subject. Louisa Hargrave went silent, as well, and even the children stifled their sniffling. Ten-year-old Eli simply gaped.

Not a great deal smaller than Forge, the Hargrave's breeding bull, and considerably hairier, the traveler emitted an odor not altogether different. Attired in abraded buckskins crossed by a double bandolier of huge cartridges, he wore a wolf's-head cap that gleamed as gray as the cloudy Wisconsin sky. His beard, long hair, and wooly eyebrows were jet black flecked with white, and his equally black eyes peered out from beneath brows that appeared to have been chiseled from granite instead of bone. His mount, an equally enormous beast, was likewise black as night save for flashes of ivory at tail, fetlocks, and one circle that surrounded a squinting eye. A patch on its forehead concealed an odd bulge. It pawed once at the ground and snorted derisively as its rider brought it to a stop.

"With all this 'ere yellin'," the mountain man opined, "a feller can't hardly 'ear the forest think."

"With all good will let it be said that this is a private matter, sir, and it be none of your business. It is advised that you continue on your chosen path, whereupon the silence of the woods will soon once more envelop you." Irritated at having his pleasure of taking possession thus interrupted, Scunsthorpe was in no mood for digression, especially when it was propounded by a total stranger.

Making no move to secure the reins, the giant slid with surprising litheness off his mount and came forward. His approach woke Scunsthorpe's minions from their torpor. Both tensed. The one on Scunsthorpe's left, a thickly constructed gentleman of the Negro persuasion who looked as if he had been run over by one of the Wisconsin Central's trains and then backed over again to finish the job, commenced a slow slide of his right hand toward the holstered pistol at his waist. As he did so, the visitor met his gaze. Not a word passed between the two men, but the descending fingers stopped advancing and their owner found sudden reason to look elsewhere.

The other scalawag was bigger and stronger, with the face of a dyspeptic baby. Turning his head to his right, he elevated a copious glob of spittle toward an inoffensive stand of broomweed. The stranger promptly matched the prodigious expectoration, with somewhat different results. The weed upon which he chose to spit swiftly shriveled and curled in upon itself, in the process venting a slight but perceptible twist of smoke. Eyes widened on the underling's baby face and his lips parted in surprise.

This did-you-see-it-or-did-you-not moment in time was sufficient to persuade Scunsthorpe, at least for the moment, to caution restraint on the part of both himself and his suddenly wary associates . . .

"I repeat myself, sir." Despite his own not inconsiderable height, Scunsthorpe found himself having to tilt back his head in order to meet the newcomer's gaze. "With all good will—"

"One can't offer what one don't possess," the stranger interrupted him. "Leavin' aside fer the nonce the matter o' what limited quantity of good will you might or might not enjoy, I do now find myself takin' a sudden interest in the proceedin's."

Bold as the suspenders that held up his pants, Eli Hargrave stepped forward. "He's trying to take our timber, sir! Our timber and our farm!"

"Hush now, Eli!" Cradling the baby in one arm, an alarmed Louisa Hargrave hastily drew her son away from the menfolk. "Get back here and be quiet!"

From within the depths of the stranger's mighty face mattress, a smile surfaced, as unexpectedly white among the black curls as a beluga in a lake of coal slurry. Its unanticipated brilliance dimmed as its owner regarded the boy's father.

"Is what the boy says true, Mr. . . . ?"

"Hargrave. Owen Hargrave."

The stranger extended a hand. At first glance Hargrave thought it similarly clad in buckskin, but closer inspection revealed it to be ungloved, if extraordinarily weathered. The fingers completely enveloped his own.

"Malone. Amos Malone."

As he guardedly shook the newcomer's paw, Hargrave reflected that he'd heard locomotives whose voices were higher pitched.

"And I," the gangly ringmaster of the discussion declaimed, not to be left out of this sudden fraternity, "am Potter Scunsthorpe. Investor, speculator, developer, and now rightful owner of this land."

Malone turned to him. Between the mountain man's unblinking stare and his personal aroma, Scunsthorpe was tempted to retreat. But he held his ground.

"By what right d'you claim this family's land?" the giant asked him.

Though it was nothing more than a piece of paper, Scunsthorpe held the deed out before him as if it was made of steel. "By right of this, as attested to under the laws of the great state of Wisconsin and the United States of America!"

"With your permission?" Without waiting for it, the mountain man took it from a startled Scunsthorpe's hand as deftly as if plucking a petal from a daisy.

"If you damage that," the scavenger warned the giant, "I can have you arrested! Not that it would be of any consequence anyway. There are copies on file with the county clerk."

The mountain man chuckled once. "Last time anyone tried t'arrest me were the Maharaja of Jaipur. Claimed I'd stolen one o' his fancy aigrettes right off his turban. Tried t'feed me to his pet tigers, he did."

Nearly oblivious now to the adults around him, Eli Hargrave stared wide-eyed at the visitor. "Tigers! What happened?"

His beard preceding his smile, Malone peered down at the boy. "Why, we ended up sharin' a meal instead."

"You and the Maharaja?" Eli murmured wonderingly.

"Nope. Me an' the tigers."

Holding the document up to the light, Malone studied it carefully. Looking on in silence, Owen Hargrave was plainly puzzled, his wife suddenly afflicted with an unreasoning hope, while Scunsthorpe quietly marveled that the excessively hirsute creature who had appeared among them could actually read.

When the giant finally lowered the deed and turned to the farmer, his tone was solemn. "I'm afeared this 'ere fella has you legally dead to rights, Mr. Hargrave."

"Ah, you see?" Scunsthorpe relaxed. The wanderer's intrusion was after all to prove nothing more than a momentary, and in its own way entertaining, interruption. "I have told you nothing less than the truth, Hargrave."

"Well, mebbee not entirely all of it, as I sees it." Malone held out the document.

Scunsthorpe frowned. It was an expression he used often and did not have to practice. "I fail to follow your meaning, sir."

A finger that might have come off one of the nearby oaks lightly tapped the deed. "As I read it here, says you can't take possession fer at least five years an' not at all after ten if'n the property in question has been properly cleared an' prepared for farmin'."

A country bumpkin, Scunsthorpe thought to himself.

Verily a great huge one, but a bumpkin nonetheless. "Quite so, sir, quite so. I must commend the accuracy of your swift perusal. Preparation for farming means clearing, by which one must take to mean felling, the obstructing timber. Which of its own accord is most certainly of considerable value. In the case of such clearing, transfer of ownership is indeed denied for a minimum of five years and forbidden, upon full payment, after ten." Struggling not to chortle aloud, he turned to his left and once again gestured at the dense, unbroken forest.

"If Mister Hargrave can, as mentioned, fell all of the timber under discussion, I will most certainly be compelled to withdraw my present claim to the property. All he must do in satisfaction of the terms of the deed is accomplish this by the time specified thereon." He made a show of squinting at the document. "I perceive that to be ten o'clock on the first of October." He smiled humorlessly. "That date falls, I believe, on Tuesday morrow."

Malone nodded at the paper. "Then we're all bein' in agreement, sir."

Scunsthorpe looked baffled. "Once again, I fail to follow your reasoning, sir."

Malone indicated the wall of untouched forest. "If the timber on Mr. Hargrave here's land is felled by ten o'clock tomorrow, you'll take your leave o' him and his family and leave them an' this land in peace."

The colored gentleman broke out in an unrestrained guffaw while his giant baby of an associate looked bemused and, not entirely comprehending the proceedings, commenced to excavate a portion of his soft, undersized nose. Scunsthorpe stared, grunted, and then grinned.

"Verily, Mr. Malone, sir, you are a man who hews to the letter of the law, even if it be for nothing more than one's amusement." He sighed dramatically. "So be it, then. I had hoped to conclude this awkward business today. But on your insistence, I will return tomorrow before the appointed hour." His expression narrowed, sharp as the cleft in a tomahawked skull. "I shall bring along for company and confirmation the sheriff of Newhope, in case any further fine-tuning of legalities shall be required."

"Lookin' forward to it," Malone replied impassively.

Having previously seen to the hitching of their own horses at the Hargrave barn, Scunsthorpe marched off in that direction, trailed by his silent but still intimidating associates. As Malone watched them go, a dubious Owen Hargrave ignored the reek that emanated from the giant and sidled up to him.

"While I appreciate your intervention, Mr. Malone, I fear it to be as futile as it was timely. That viper will return tomorrow, as his promises are as assured as his demeanor is detestable. You have bought us time for a last supper, if nothing else."

"Don't say that, Hargrave." Having started toward his mount, Malone found himself accompanied by the farmer and his wife while their three children attended his long, massive legs. "There still be time to perhaps fulfill the terms o' your deed."

"Now you jest with us, Mr. Malone," declared Louisa Hargrave. "Or do I take it you propose to level a quarter section of woodland in a night? Anyone who put forth such a notion might well be called mad."

"He might indeed, ma'am." Reaching his animal, Malone began to search through one of the oversized backpacks while simultaneously advising Eli's oldest sister. "I'd keep me distance from Worthless's mouth, young missy."

Blonde, precious, and wide-eyed, the girl replied even as she peered up at the wide-lipped equine mouth hovering above her. "Why, mister? Will he bite me?"

"I think not. But Worthless, 'e has a tendency to drool, an' sometimes it burns."

As if to counter this assertion, the huge black head bent low. A tongue emerged to lick the face of the little girl, who hastily backed away, wiping frantically at her cheek while shrieking delightedly. The stallion then turned one jaundiced eye on its master, snorted, and resumed cropping the weeds near its forelegs.

"Hungry. Kin I impose on you fer some feed, Mr. Hargrave?"

"Yes. Yes, of course, Mr. Malone." Turning, the farmer barked at his oldest son. "Eli! Get the wagon. Load it with hay and bring it back here."

"Yes, Pa!" As the boy turned to go, Malone called to him.

"An' barley, boy. If you kin find any barley, Worthless dotes on the stuff. I usually don't feed it t'him because— well, you might have occasion t'see why. But bring it if you kin find some."

"I will do so, sir!" And with that the lad was sprinting over the rise, in the direction of his home.

From the saddlebag the mountain man removed a hinged length of wood. As the farmer looked on with interest Malone snapped it straight, the metal hinge that divided the two lengths locking automatically in place. From the trim and shape it was plain enough to divine its purpose: It was an axe handle. Rummaging deeper in the same saddlebag, the visitor drew forth the matching blade. It was double-bitted and slid tightly onto the business end of the handle.

Hargrave studied the reconstituted tool. "Never seen anything quite like that, Mr. Malone. That wood; looking at it, I'd say black walnut."

"No sir," Malone replied as he made certain the twinned blade was secured to the handle. "This be *m'pinga*, a type of wood from near the coast of East Africa. Some folks calls it ironwood, but there's all manner of wood called that. This kind is too heavy t'float, and too tough to break."

The farmer considered. "And that head; that must be at least a four-pounder. Or is it five?"

"Twenty." Malone held the implement out at arm's length to check the straightness of the handle. Held it out with one hand.

Hargrave laughed. "Begging your pardon, sir, but there's no such thing as a twenty-pound axe head. Double-bitted or otherwise. Isn't no man could swing one."

"Probably you be right, sir. I'm just funnin' you." So saying, Malone lifted the axe without apparent effort and rested it on his right shoulder. Removing his wolf's-head cap he placed it in the same saddlebag from which he had extracted the components of the axe and started off toward the nearby woods. Looking back over his shoulder, he called out.

"Y'kin lend a hand if you wish, Mr. Hargrave, but in any event I aim t'render what service I kin before the designated time of surrender tomorrow."

Halting before the first tree, a noble red pine, the mountain man unlimbered the axe, brought it back, and swung. Entering the tree, the massive steel cutting edge sliced halfway through the thick trunk.

"*Mercy!*" Putting her free hand to her chest, Louisa Hargrave gasped aloud. For his part, her husband uttered a word that was as uncharacteristic of him as it was of considerably greater potency than those he normally employed in the presence of wife and family. Whereupon he whirled and raced in the direction of their simple yet comforting homestead.

"Owen!" his wife called out. "Where are you going, husband?"

He yelled back at her. "To get my axe! And to hurry the boy along!" He looked past her, stumbling as he ran, and raised his voice. "We're going to need the team to move timber!"

All the rest of that morning and on into the cloudy, slightly muggy afternoon, Amos Malone and Owen Hargrave cut and chopped, chopped and cut. According to the terms of the mortgage, as deciphered by the mountain man, it was not necessary for the farmer to clear the timber off his land in order to satisfy the terms of the deed: It was only required that he cut it down to prove that he intended to develop it. Pine after pine, oak after oak, came crashing to the earth as the two men toiled, Malone pausing only once to place a heavy blanket across the back of his energetically feeding steed and secure it tightly in place. Hargrave felled one tree to every ten of the big man's, until finally his aching arms gave out and the blisters on his hands prevented him from wielding the axe any longer.

He nearly broke down when young Eli bravely attempted to take up the slack. Though he struggled manfully, the boy could barely raise the axe, let alone swing it. Taking a break to down a full quart of the cold creek water periodically fetched by Mrs. Hargrave, Malone concluded the imposing draught by wiping the back of a massive hand across his mouth. Then, unbuttoning his buckskin jacket, he slithered out of it and handed it to the boy, who all but collapsed under the load. Shirt followed jacket and lastly, after assuring the boy's mother the deeply stained attire contained nothing likely to imperil her son's life or future mental development, a cotton undershirt from which whiteness had long since fled screaming.

"Here, young feller-me-lad: If 'tis work you want, set yourself to seein' that those there garments get cleaned up a bit, as they ain't been washed in quite a spell now."

Standing nearby holding the water bucket and striving with all her might to look anywhere save directly at the massive spread of hairy chest, shoulders, and arms now revealed before her, Louisa Hargrave had the presence of mind to remark, "Have they truly *ever* been washed, Mr. Malone?"

The mountain man turned thoughtful. "Memory plays

tricks on a man." His expression brightened. "I do recollect on one occasion fallin' in the course of a serious bad storm into the Upper Mississippi one time last year. Came out reasonable clean somewhere near St. Louis." He smiled down at her and at the mound of clothing in whose approximate vicinity her eldest son was presently submerged. "I reckon that this time, a touch o' soap wouldn't be out of line."

"Come, Eli." She turned back toward the homestead. "I'll do what I can for your garments Mr. Malone, but upon initial appraisal I fear I must confess that we may have better luck with prayer."

As soon as Hargrave was able to resume work alongside his towering visitor, his axe handle promptly cracked. This forced a quick trip into town. Unable to keep the amazing story to himself, word quickly spread from the General Store to the general populace. Eventually it settled upon the large, sporadically mobile ears of Potter Scunsthorpe, who determined that despite the unlikelihood of there being any truth to the farmer's tall tale, it would require but little effort to check it out.

Upon arriving at the land that was to be his upon the morrow, he was startled to see the progress that the two men had made. Instead of starting at one end of the property and attempting to clear-cut their way across it, they were taking down the largest trees first. While a wholly sensible stratagem, Scunsthorpe felt that it would in the end avail them nothing. There were simply too many trees for two men to fell by the following day—even if one of them was as strong as a team of oxen. One would have thought that the mountain man would have utilized his heavy horse to help pull down trees that were partially cut through, but that most eccentric steed remained off to one side working its way through an immense pile of hay and feed grain. Scunsthorpe could do no more than shake his head at the futile sight. While he could not fathom the giant's ultimate intent, he had no intention of leaving anything to chance.

Scunsthorpe was not alone that evening in choosing to observe the unprecedented demonstration of lumbering talent. On buckboards and wagons, other townsfolk had come out to watch and marvel at the exhibition, for entertainment of any kind was scarce and much appreciated in that part of the country. Approaching a fine buggy he knew well, the lanky speculator smiled and tipped his hat to its single occupant.

"Afternoon, Miss Pettiview."

"Mr. Scunsthorpe." A parasol of turquoise blue moved aside to reveal a visage of winsome grace, dominated by cornflower-blue eyes, lips brushed carmine, a diminutive and slightly upturned nose, and much speculation. "I am not surprised to find you here. Everyone knows of your interest in and intent to take the Hargrave property for your own."

He pursed his lips. "Does that news displease you?"

"It is nothing to me. My business lies elsewhere."

Scunsthorpe's gaze dropped. "Everyone is aware of where your business lies, Miss Pettiview. It is in knowledge of that estimable topography that I would engage your talents on a matter of some concern."

Teeth white as the chalk their owner employed in her occasional engagement as a schoolteacher flashed in the light of the setting sun. "How then may I be of service to you, Mr. Scunsthorpe?"

The speculator pointed toward the slowly shrinking line of forest off to the west. "Farmer Hargrave has found himself some assistance in his senseless attempt to satisfy the terms of the mortgage that I hold."

Raising a blue-gloved hand to shield her eyes, Pettiview stared in the indicated direction. A slight intake of breath followed hard upon her identification. Scunsthorpe noted it and swallowed his disgust.

"If by 'assistance' you are referring to a most striking Herculean figure who is presently taking down a white pine as if it was a stalk of asparagus, then I follow your meaning quite clearly."

Scunsthorpe tipped his hat to her. "It is of course impossible that any two men should reduce one hundred and sixty acres of forest in a single day and night of effort, but in my profession I have learned to take no chances. To that end it would be useful if the hulking great stranger who calls himself Amos Malone were, for a while, to have his attention diverted from the practice of forestry to—other pursuits."

Reaching into an inner pocket of his fine suit, he removed a couple of heavy coins that glinted gold in the fading light. These promptly vanished into Miss Pettiview's elegantly beaded purse as deftly as if manipulated by a riverboat card shark. Extending a hand, she allowed Scunsthorpe to help her down from the buggy seat, smiling reassuringly at him as his other hand availed itself of the opportunity to clutch fleetingly at the backside of her powder-blue dress.

Parasol in hand, she made her way past murmuring townsfolk and down into the partially cut-over section of forest until she could resume her observations much nearer the two men than either Hargrave or his wife would have liked. But the farmer said nothing, and continued to hack away at the base of a red maple.

"You are quite the specimen, Mr. Amos Malone." Her forwardness would have surprised none who knew her.

Bare-chested and perspiring like a Bornean rainforest, Malone paused in mid-swing to set the head of his massive axe on the ground. He responded with a nod.

"And if m'lady will pardon an old reprobate such as myself, you are as trim a vessel as these watery eyes have set upon since a distant week spent in San Francisco."

"Oohhh . . . 'm'lady,' he says! 'Tis quite the gentleman you are, Amos Malone. And you have been to San Francisco, too."

"San Francisco, yes." Malone swung the axe. Wood chips flew, from which assault Pettiview had to defend herself with her parasol. "And—elsewhere."

"I know one place you haven't been," she said coquettishly.

"An' where might that be, m'lady?"

"*Melissa* will do for you, if you will do for me."

He paused once again. "I don't follow you, m'la— Melissa."

"Such strenuous exertions on the part of such excessive musculature must engender a healthy appetite. I would be pleased to satisfy such, if you would but extend me the courtesy."

"I *am* tendin' a mite to the famished," he murmured.

"What would a good meal cost me?" He looked past her. "I would ask it of the wife Hargrave, but she already has five mouths t'feed."

"Whereas I have naught to occupy me save to stand ready to prepare your supper." Pettiview pivoted, the parasol twirling over her shoulder as she looked back, eyelids fluttering. "Come with me then, Mr. Malone, and I will see to it that you find rest, food, and succor for as much of this evening as should be necessary to satisfy your needs."

"A most temptin' offer, an' one I fear it would be impolite t'refuse." So saying, he leaned the colossal axe against a nearby solitary ash. "I should recover the rest of my clothes, if they be dry enough."

"No need to bother, sir." She led him out of the woods and toward the waiting buggy. "I am quite comfortable with dining informally, as you shall see." Whereupon she turned briefly to him and inhaled, thereby stretching the top of her dress to such an extent that anyone within range of some half-dozen forthright buttons might not unreasonably be expected to have to dodge them, as if by breathing any deeper she might effortlessly turn them into weapons imbued with lethal velocity.

When Hargrave saw his possible savior leaving in the company of the notorious Pettiview, he all but surrendered to despair. Only the mountain man's encouraging shout of, "I'll be back in time, Hargrave!" offered the most forlorn hope. But that was now forlorn indeed. Not that they'd had much of a chance of felling the entire quarter section of forest before morning anyway, but it had been something to work for, something to work *toward*. Now, the despondent Hargrave felt he had nothing.

Slumping down on a stump, he would not allow himself to weep. Only then did it occur to him that he too was starved for nourishment. With a heavy sigh he left behind his newly bought axe and staggered exhaustedly toward his modest homestead. He would make himself enjoy whatever Mrs. Hargrave had managed to muster for supper.

If for no other reason than it was likely the last one he would ever get to enjoy in the house he had raised up with his own hands.

Sunrise brought renewed hope in the form of the giant mountain man. As good as his word, Malone had returned. Having admired his now spotlessly clean undershirt, shirt, and jacket, upon all three of which Mrs. Hargrave had indeed worked miracles, Malone forbore from filthying them again so soon, carefully removing them and setting them aside before he resumed work in the woods. Hargrave joined him, even though it was plain to see that while they had done an impressive job of thinning the quarter section of forest, within the designated boundary line hundreds of smaller trees still remained rooted and standing. The farmer doubted the ploy would be sufficient to satisfy the avaricious Scunsthorpe. The deed said that all the 160 acres had to be cleared. Despite their yeoman efforts, this he and Malone had plainly failed to do.

So it was that at precisely nine-forty-five, the wicked Scunsthorpe made his presence known. He was accompanied this time not only by his two hulking underlings of dubious ancestry but also by Hander Cogsworth, sheriff of the town of Newhope. All was patently lost, an exhausted Hargrave realized. Malone might fast talk even Scunsthorpe, but with the law at his side, the insatiable speculator would not hesitate to take immediate possession.

Malone joined the exhausted farmer in confronting the officious arrivals, glancing at the nearby hillside as he did so. "Where at the moment might be your family, Hargrave?"

The farmer was inconsolable. "Back at the house—for the last time. Saying their goodbyes. Making their peace with the sorrowful inevitable." He gazed mournfully toward the crest of the low rise. "Louisa will be directing the children to gather up their things, and has no doubt commenced the packing of her own humble body of possessions." He looked up at the mountain man. "Of myself, I have but little beyond wife and children that any longer holds meaning for me. My sole concern now is to see them safely on the train to Milwaukee, and thence to Chicago, where she at least may throw herself on the sympathy of family members. As for myself,"—he swallowed hard—"I, too, shall go to the city, there to look for whatever work I may be so fortunate as to obtain."

"Are you not bein' a mite premature, Hargrave?" Malone looked skyward. "I make it t'be not quite ten o'clock. Y'all are still rightful owner of this land."

"For another fifteen minutes." Hargrave let out a disgusted snort. "Years of work, of dreaming, of what might one day be: lost now because of a lack of time and a bad winter." A sudden thought made him blink. "What of the schoolteacher Pettiview? Did she not beguile you sufficiently?"

"Beguilin' be a knack that works both ways, friend Hargrave." Raising his gaze, Malone peered in the direction of distant Newhope. "Her cookin' weren't much to my likin', but I fear she may have treated herself to overmuch dessert. Last I saw her she were takin' herself to the town doctor. To treat a condition recently acquired, I believe she said." He looked down. "Anyway, I am here. Now let us greet this itch that persists in troublin' you. A mite further to the eastward, I calculate."

"To the east? But why?" Hargrave eyed him uncom-prehendingly.

Malone turned a fixed gaze in the opposite direction. The farmer followed the mountain man's stare, but saw only forest and brush, cloud and sky. That, and the mountain man's idiosyncratic steed. Unbelievably, it was still feeding. Insofar as Hargrave could recall, it had not stopped eating all night, having availed itself of a veritable mountain of silage. It was, if truth be told, looking more than a little bloated. Hargrave did not begrudge the animal or its owner the fodder; only marveled at an equine appetite the likes of which could scarce be imagined.

With sheriff and minions in tow, a triumphant Scunsthorpe presented himself, deed in hand, before mountain man and farmer. Eying the moderately thinned forest, the speculator pronounced himself well satisfied.

"The time is at hand, gentlemen." A snake could not smirk, but Scunsthorpe came close as he looked up at the silent Malone. "The precise time, as you wished it, sir. I can even say, with all honesty, that I am thankful for having met you and for your noteworthy presence." With a wave of one hand he took in the thinned woods. "As you have by your remarkable yet pointless labors saved me a good deal of money by felling such a quantity of valuable timber."

"And I can even say," Malone replied, "with all honesty, that it were no pleasure whatsoever to havin' made your acquaintance, though yours is a type I know well, Scunsthorpe."

The investor shrugged. "Insult me as you wish. I have no time to take offense, for I must perforce take full possession of my new lands."

Malone nodded, checked the sun, and said, "Five minutes remain, Scunsthorpe. I would advise strongly they be used to move over this way." Indicating the crest of the nearby hill, he began to move in the other direction, toward his waiting mount. Uncomprehending and uncaring, a devastated and benumbed Owen Hargrave moved slowly toward the hill and the homestead that was no longer his. So too did the sheriff, a heavily mustachioed man who was pleased beyond measure that his intercession would apparently not be required with so formidable a force as the mountain man.

Uncertain, Scunsthorpe's minions started to follow the disconsolate farmer. Their master, however, betook himself in the other direction, his long legs allowing him to catch up to Malone.

"And get this disgusting excuse for an animal off my property immediately!" Scunsthorpe said loudly as he stomped toward Malone's placidly munching mount.

Having reached the stallion, Malone unfastened the stays that secured the heavy horse blanket and flipped it up over his saddle and saddlebags. This small chore accomplished, he unexpectedly took off at the run in Hargrave's wake.

"This way, Scunsthorpe! Follow me while time remains!"

"Pfagh! You try to toy with me, Malone, but Potter Scunsthorpe is not a man to be played with! If you won't move your cow pile of an animal, I'll move it for you!" He continued toward Worthless, one arm raised preparatory to delivering a sound slap on the horse's rump.

"Try if you must, Scunsthorpe!" Malone yelled back as he quickened his pace, "but fer your own sake, move to his front now!"

Scunsthorpe scoffed as he continued his approach. "What's he going to do, Malone? Kick me? Do you think me so immersed in the law of the land that I am ignorant of horses?"

"Then y'all will note," shouted Malone as he hastily ducked down behind the top of the rise, "the consequences of his interminable consumption, proceeding without interruption from yesterday morning until this moment, which are presently about to deliver themselves not as a bout of colic, but in the form of . . . !"

Worthless's tail rose, perhaps semaphoring a warning. That, more so than any of the mountain man's admonitions, drew Scunsthorpe's attention. He hesitated, his eyes widening, and turned abruptly away from the gravely bloated animal. Whereupon the noble if unclassifiable creature did not so much break wind as shatter it, destroy it, and biblically obliterate the entire atmosphere directly astern.

A fart of tectonic dimensions lifted the stunned Scunsthorpe off the ground. It blew him backward through the forest in company with the hundreds of trees—pine and ash, maple and oak—that the unquantifiable expression of equine flatulence summarily flattened. It blew him over the horizon and clear out of sight.

Great was the chanting among the local Indians at this brief if invisible manifestation of the sacred Thunderbird. Frantic were the cries of bewildered townsfolk as far away as Eau Claire, whose eau remained claire even if the air they breathed did not. Pike dove deeper into Lake Winnebago, crowding the catfish for space. It is said that ten thousand dead frogs washed ashore that day on the beaches of Green Bay.

Though they were both protected and upwind, the sheriff, Scunsthorpe's underlings, and Owen Hargrave were not entirely spared. The Negro gentleman commenced crying and could not stop, while his putty-faced counterpart began retching and did not cease so doing for a good thirty minutes. Blessedly, the sheriff had simply passed out, while Hargrave had the foresight to cover his face with a bandana. As for Malone, being used as he was to the occasional hindgut disquisitions of his mount, he simply rose and brushed at something sensed but unseen in front of his face. It dissipated with thankful rapidity.

Having summarily and volcanically relieved himself of a truly astonishing buildup of gas subsequent to his owner granting permission through the raising of the uniquely restrictive blanket, and apparently none the worse for the episode, Worthless astoundingly resumed his feeding on what little remained of farmer Hargrave's reserves.

"What . . . ?" It was all Hargrave, being the only one of the group presently capable of coherent speech due to the fact that his lungs remained relatively untrammeled, could muster.

"Normally Worthless eats—normally," Malone explained as he topped the rise to scrutinize the completely flattened quarter section—and more —of forest. "But if'n I let him, the stupid sack of silly soak will just continue t'eat, an' eat, an' eat. Until his internal mechanisms, which are as abnormal in their way as the rest o' him, kin no longer appropriately process their contents. They therefore release at one go all the ignoble effluvia they have unaccountably accumulated, in a volume and at a velocity that would stun any zoologist an' cause the most sober veterinarian to forswear his chosen profession. 'Tis a regrettable social imperfection that he and I usually have no difficulty avoidin', as I have a care to regulate his feeding carefully. In this instance, however, I considered that lettin' his appetite run free might prove useful, and relatively harmless bein' as we are in a relatively unpopulated region.

"And now, if'n y'all please, I think it both safe and pleasant for you t'see to your fine family and wife, and for me t'have the distinct pleasure of donning, for the first time in some while, clothing that has been properly cleaned an' disinfected."

A dazed Hargrave surveyed his 160 acres: felled and,

if not stacked, at least neatly aligned all in one direction. Why, he mused wonderingly, the force of the equine eruption had even cleanly topped the fallen trees. He had lumber aplenty for his own use, good timber to sell, and cleared forest land sufficient to satisfy the demands of the unrelentingly greedy Scuns—

He looked around.

Where was the unpleasant speculator, anyway?

Scunsthorpe was found several days later, wandering the western shore of Lake Winnebago, a glazed look upon his eye. Save for a broken right arm, a sprained left knee, and a lack of intact clothing, he was apparently unharmed. Wrinkling their collective noses and keeping their distance, his rescuers proceeded to burn his surviving attire while offering the speechless survivor food and drink. For the latter, he was most volubly grateful, but for the former somewhat uncertain.

It appeared most strange to his rescuers, and while a cause could not immediately be determined, it was clear to one and all in attendance that the man's olfactory senses had been irrevocably damaged, for Scunsthorpe could not smell so much as one of his own farts.

FOUNTAINS OF BLOOD

David Lee Summers

Billy McCarty sensed an ambush, but if he had known its true nature, he would have gone to his room, locked the door and slept in the next day. Instead, he spent the night playing faro, smoking cheroots and occasionally taking a sip of whiskey. When the saloon owner chased the last drunks out into the street, Billy ambled over to the livery stable, and hitched the horses to the old buckboard. Once done, he returned to the hotel and knocked on his employer's door.

Mr. Fountain answered a moment later, already dressed. Even in the early morning hours, the white-haired man with a handlebar mustache cut a distinguished figure. Without lighting a lamp, he reached over and jostled a form buried under blankets. A boy emerged and sat up, rubbing sleep-crusted eyes.

A respected attorney, Fountain had been in Lincoln County investigating a messy affair involving ranchers, feed store owners, and murder which shook territorial politics right up to the governor's office in Santa Fe. Most called the fifteen-year feud an outright war.

Near the beginning of the whole mess, Billy worked for one of the ranchers. One day, armed men ambushed the rancher. Billy gunned them down, saving his boss, but he faced murder charges. Fountain defended Billy and the two became friends. Billy left Lincoln County, but Fountain continued investigating the murders and rustlings in the area. After fifteen years, Fountain almost had enough evidence to bring indictments against those responsible. He'd just spent a few days in Lincoln conducting interviews and collecting affidavits.

Fountain hired Billy to be his bodyguard for the trip. That part made sense. Billy was good with a gun and knew all the players. What Billy didn't understand was what possessed the man to bring his eight-year-old son into such a dangerous situation.

The boy pulled on his boots, Fountain grabbed a duffel bag and Billy closed the door behind them as they made their way out to the buckboard waiting in front of the hotel. Soon they rolled out of Tularosa where they'd stopped for the night and began the trek through the barren dune field known as White Sands on the way home to Las Cruces.

A full moon hung low to the west—a mixed blessing. It provided plenty of light, but the tall dunes cast long shadows. Billy held a rifle in his lap while Fountain drove the horses.

"Look at that! A white rabbit!"

The sudden exclamation startled Billy and he lifted his rifle by instinct. A white jack rabbit hopped away, startled by the squeaking, rattling buckboard.

"Those rabbits have lived here so long they've turned

white to match the sands," explained Mr. Fountain.

Billy never knew his own pa, and he shook off a brief pang of jealousy as he lowered the rifle and held his finger to his lips. "Let's stay quiet right now and let ol' Billy concentrate, all right, pardner?"

The boy wilted as though whipped.

"If you stay quiet until the sun comes up, I promise I'll let you hold my six-gun when we get to Aguirre Springs."

"Really!" The boy perked up.

"Really." Billy winked.

Henry settled back and wrapped himself in one of his mother's quilts.

"Thank you," said Mr. Fountain. "I appreciate the attention you give him. It's not easy being a father so late in life."

"You're a busy man, Mr. Fountain. You have a lot of demands on your time."

"Still . . ."

Whatever Fountain intended to say was never spoken. He pulled back on the reins. A stranger stood in their path, arms folded, a wild shock of red hair blowing in the wind. Billy lifted his rifle and aimed right between the stranger's eyes. "Whoever you are, step aside. We don't want no—"

Before Billy finished the sentence, the stranger dashed forward. The rifle flew from Billy's hands and he sailed through the air. He had just enough time to hear Henry scream and notice the stars above before his head hit the ground and everything went black.

★ ★ ★

Billy awoke lying in the sand, looking up at a blue sky, his neck in pain. He reached up and winced as he touched ragged, wet tissue. His fingers came away covered in blood. Struggling to his feet, he looked around. The buckboard stood before him but there was no sign of Mr. Fountain or Henry, just reddened sand on the far side of the wagon. One of the horses pawed the ground, bored, while the other munched on a tuft of grass. Billy found his rifle undamaged near where he fell. The wind blew as he walked around the buckboard. Sand already covered the wagon's tracks and any footprints were long gone.

He opened the water barrel mounted to the buckboard's side, dipped his hand in, and gently patted his neck, cleaning the grit and blood from the wound as best he could. Once done, he unfolded a bandana and tied it around his neck. Had some varmint taken a bite out of him? If so, what scared it off?

He took a drink from the barrel and considered what to do next. With no trail, he only had two options, return to Tularosa and talk to the sheriff or continue on into Las Cruces and contact the U.S. Marshal. He worried about the boy, but couldn't imagine those behind the ambush would hurt a kid. The sheriff in Tularosa sided with the faction Fountain investigated, so going forward seemed the better plan. Billy climbed onto the seat and continued on his way.

As he traveled, Billy tried to piece together what happened. The stranger had no weapon drawn and his own rifle suffered no damage. No bullet holes punctured the buckboard. The blood on the ground seemed to indicate Fountain, the boy, or both were dead, or at least seriously wounded, but where had they gone? He worried he was abandoning Henry, but he had no clue where to start looking.

By the time Billy reached Las Cruces, the sun had already dropped below the horizon. Billy was exhausted and didn't think the marshal would appreciate him banging on the door this late. His pockets bulged with money Fountain paid him in advance, so he rode to Mesquite Street. After stabling the horses, he ambled down to the Long Dobé, hoping no one had purchased an evening with Marcella. Only she could help him forget such a terrible day.

Marcella was the Dobé's most beautiful dove, hardly soiled at all, or so it seemed. The Cajun woman from Louisiana had lustrous black hair and porcelain-smooth skin that showed no more age than when he first met her over a decade before.

As he stepped through the door into the Dobé's smoke-filled lobby, Marcella emerged from the back, leading a dazed farmhand. Billy held up a wad of cash and she motioned for him to come on back. Once they were alone in her immaculate room, decorated in shades of dusty rose, she penetrated him with her fierce blue eyes. "It's been a long time, Billy. What brings you to Marcella?"

"This has been a rotten day." He sat on Marcella's pristine bed, hardly rumpled even though she'd apparently finished with a client. He was sure sand fell out of his britches onto the white coverlet.

"Let's see if Marcella can make it better." She untied his bandana and eyed the wound with almost clinical interest. She leaned over and brushed the wound with her lips and tongue. The pain dimmed to a dull throb, but she sat back, eyes wide. "Who did this to you?"

Billy blinked. "I didn't exactly get a good look."

Marcella stood and strode to a dresser. Opening it, she retrieved a dime novel and tossed it onto the bed next to Billy. "Have you read that?"

He picked up the book called *Carmilla* by some dude named Sheridan Le Fanu. "Sounds like some Frenchy book." He idly thumbed through the pages.

"Actually, he's Irish," said Marcella. "It's a story about a creature called a vampire who looks like a human, but never ages and subsists on human blood."

"Sounds like a fairy story if you ask me." Billy tossed the book on the bed. He hadn't stopped at the Dobé to solve the mystery of what happened that morning. He wanted to take his mind off the mystery before he went looking for more trouble.

"It's no fairy tale." Marcella shook her head and sat down next to Billy. "I think the man that attacked you was kindred."

Billy narrowed his gaze. "Kindred? You mean he's kinfolk to you?"

"You could say that," she said. "Take the book when you go. It may help. In the meantime, let Marcella help you feel better." She leaned in and licked the wound again. It went numb. A moment later, needle-sharp pain made him sit up, but before he could protest, the room spun and went black.

A rude shove sent Billy tumbling out of the perfumed

sheets to the hardwood floor. He reached for his six-gun on the end table, but a voice stopped him.

"If I were here to kill you, Billy, you'd be dead already."

Larissa Seaton was the only woman marshal he knew. The president himself appointed the former bounty hunter to the job after she used newfangled gadgets to bring some bad hombres to justice over in Arizona. He reached for the sheets to cover himself only to realize he still wore his britches.

"Why, Marshal, I was hoping to see you today." Billy flashed a smile he thought charming.

"Is that so?" Larissa took out a pocket watch and eyed it critically. Unlike most ladies, she didn't wear a dress. Instead, she wore black trousers and a matching jacket. Except for the Army cap she affected, she could almost pass for a sister of those Earps over in Tombstone. "It's almost ten in the morning. You sure ain't in much of a hurry."

"I've had a rough couple of days." Billy looked for his shirt.

"You were hired to protect Albert Fountain, but his wife Mariana says he's late returning from a meeting up in Lincoln. And here, I happen to be walking by, and I see his buckboard stabled just a few doors down from the Long Dobé. I know Mr. Fountain well enough to know he ain't the philanderin' type. So what's going on?"

Billy buttoned his shirt. "We got ambushed."

Larissa reached out to the wound on Billy's neck and he flinched away. "That ain't no bullet graze. More like some animal gotcha."

"It's all a blur," admitted Billy. "We were out on the White Sands when some red-headed stranger confronted us. He musta had friends. All I know is that I got knocked out cold. When I woke both Mr. Fountain and his son were gone. The wind already blew the tracks clear. I really did mean to get up early and come find you."

Larissa pursed her lips. "Word is, Mr. Fountain was investigating some of your old buddies up there in Lincoln. Sure you weren't doin' someone a favor?"

"No, ma'am. Albert Fountain saved my life when he defended me. Nothin' could get me to betray him." He clenched his teeth. "And you can bet I'd never do anything to hurt his son, Henry."

Larissa folded her arms and nodded. "All right, but I want you to show me where this ambush happened. Maybe I can find some clues."

"Just give me a little bit to get my horse ready."

"Daylight's burnin' fast. We'll take the wolf." She referred to one of those gadgets that brought her to the president's attention.

Calling the wolf a motorized bicycle did it a disservice, especially now that she'd tinkered and worked on it for several years. Billy had seen pictures of motorcars they'd been developing back East. They weren't as powerful as Larissa's so-called wolf. She turned to leave. "It'll take me about an hour to get everything ready for the trip. Meet me at my office." She pulled out the pocket watch again. "And don't be late!" With that, she strode out the door.

Billy finished dressing. As he did, he wondered where Marcella went. He tried to remember what happened after she nuzzled his neck. It was all a blur, but as usual he had the giddy sensation that he'd just spent the best night ever with a woman. As he grabbed his six-gun, he saw the dime novel. He wondered whether there was anything to Marcella's talk of immortal blood drinkers— what did she call them? Vampires.

Larissa didn't seem in the mood to contemplate supernatural creatures, but Billy wanted more information. He knew just the man who would entertain a few wild ideas.

Once cleaned up and dressed, Billy walked a few blocks to a small bungalow just down from a humble two-room schoolhouse with the high-fallutin' name of the New Mexico College of Agriculture and Mechanic Arts. The man living in the bungalow taught both biology and engineering at the new college.

Billy knocked and hoped Professor Maravilla was home and not out in the desert somewhere studying the behavior of some snake or skunk or whatever else caught his interest. He breathed a sigh of relief when the professor opened the door. He wore a white lab coat over a silk waistcoat and striped trousers. "Ah, Billy, what brings you here this fine day?"

Billy held up the book Marcella left on the nightstand. "Have you ever read this?"

"*Carmilla*?" The professor invited Billy inside. "Yes, a rather engaging fantasy, I thought."

"So you've heard of vampires, then."

"Heard of them? Yes. Believe they exist?" He shrugged.

"I need to know what you know, even if it's just hearsay. A little boy's life might be in danger."

"Yes, yes, of course." Maravilla waved hastily at a chair, indicating Billy should sit while he walked over to a shelf and grabbed an old notebook. He passed it to Billy as he took a seat in a leather-bound armchair.

Billy thumbed through the notebook's yellowed pages. It contained scribblings and detailed drawings—an open mouth with fangs, a bat, a cross. "So you do know something about vampires."

Maravilla shook his head. "Just legends and stories, but I find them compelling. Perhaps vampires exist and they are some strange relative of man, but most tales, like your *Carmilla*, are just ghost stories. Wild superstitions to account for plague running rampant. They tell of people who come back from the dead and sustain themselves on the blood of the living."

Billy shuddered. Marcella didn't say anything about creatures coming back from the dead. "We've seen some awful strange things over the years, Professor. If these vampires exist, how would you kill one?"

The professor shrugged again. "If they exist, they're a creature that looks much like a man, but has the teeth of an animal. Such a predator might be very strong and move quite fast. It would be a dangerous adversary. Like most predators, a bullet to the head or heart might suffice." Maravilla stood and began pacing. "Most of the legends say a vampire must be decapitated, staked to the ground or burned. All of those would kill an ordinary living being."

"Would lightning kill a vampire?"

"If a vampire is dead, its heart is already stopped, but the cellular disruption and burns might suffice. Of course you'd have to lure the vampire out into a storm."

"I was thinkin' there might be a way of bringing the storm to the vampire."

The professor's mouth ticked upward. "Ah, you must be thinking of Marshal Seaton's arsenal. That still involves luring the vampire out of the shadows into the open . . ."

As the professor spoke, Billy turned a page in the notebook and gasped. A drawing of Marcella stared back at him, her mouth open, revealing fangs. The caption read "Mircalla."

"You know Marcella over at the Long Dobé?" Billy asked.

The professor laughed. "Hardly. I drew that after reading *Carmilla* a few years ago. The vampire changes names all through the story. One name is Mircalla."

Billy swallowed and closed the notebook. Catching sight of the professor's clock, he leapt to his feet. The book fell to the floor with a thud. "I need to get over to Marshal Seaton's. You've been a big help."

"Billy, be careful. If you do encounter a vampire, it could be quite dangerous. Also be sure to bring me back any observations for my notes." The professor patted Billy indulgently on the back and led him to the door.

Billy ran all the way to the marshal's office. There he found Larissa loading spare fuel cells into the wolf's saddlebags. The wolf was a two-wheeled machine of black anodized steel and shiny brass, propelled by a chemical-reaction steam engine designed by Professor Maravilla. Mounted between the handlebars on a pivot was a strange weapon consisting of a long, narrow cylinder, like a small-caliber rifle barrel. His eyes played along the strange device from the concentric glass disks in the front, to the thick rings of wire hugging the cylinder in the middle, to the wooden handgrip at the end.

Marshal Seaton climbed onto the leather saddle and used a key to bring the fuel cells together, jarring the machine to life in an explosive exhalation. "You ready to go?"

Billy nodded and climbed on the saddle behind Larissa as she lowered a pair of goggles. He cinched the strap on his hat as Larissa turned the throttle, roaring out of town trailing a cloud of smoke and dust.

Larissa and Billy rumbled over the San Augustin Pass and sped across the Tularosa Basin. The wolf sputtered to a stop near the Lucero Ranch, just in sight of White Sands. Billy pointed to a tall snow-capped mountain in the distance. "Just keep your eyes on Sierra Blanca and go straight through the dune field."

Larissa squinted at the distant mountain. "You better be right." She inserted a fresh pair of fuel rods. Billy nearly tumbled off as she turned the throttle and they shot forward.

Half an hour later they reached the dunes and slowed. He looked around, trying to identify some kind of landmark. Soon a dark patch in the sand near a line of rabbit tracks caught his eye. "There! I think that's the place."

Larissa pulled up to an uncharacteristic patch of deep brown sand in the middle of the white gypsum. She killed the wolf's engine, climbed off, and knelt down. "Stained with blood."

Thankful the wind had eased, Billy scanned the area.

A set of footprints led away from the dune's far side. Billy ran ahead to investigate and Larissa followed. Behind the dune, they found three holes, like shallow graves.

"Looks like someone was buried here, then dug up." Larissa removed her hat and wiped sweat from her brow.

The sun rested near the horizon, casting a pink glow across the dune field. Billy shook his head. "There's only one trail, and it leads away from the holes."

Larissa knelt down beside Billy and studied the footprints. "Three people—two adults and a child. They went to Tularosa. Could you have missed these tracks when you woke up?"

Billy scratched his head. "These are plain as day and it looks like they're side by side, like they're all friends." Billy followed the trail a few more yards. "Here, the smaller footprints are further apart. It's like the boy was skipping or running." Billy continued walking. "He skittered to a stop here."

"Maybe the boy tried to run and the gunman ordered him to a halt."

"Or his pa." Billy nodded, but dared to hope Henry might be okay after all. He turned his head and spit. "But what about those graves?"

"Maybe they're not graves after all," suggested Larissa. "Maybe buried treasure. Could be Fountain had something hidden out here and didn't want you to have a cut."

The idea stung, but he preferred it to chasing undead monsters. "Whoever left that trail seems to have gone to Tularosa. I think we'll find our answers there."

"Agreed." Larissa fed the wolf again and they followed the trail into the small town which huddled against the Sacramento Mountains, as though afraid of what would happen next.

Billy and Larissa roared into Tularosa half an hour after the sun set. As they continued through the middle of town, people poured out of a saloon. Instead of stopping to ogle the wolf, they ran past, some screaming. Larissa turned the key, shutting off the wolf's engine and dismounted, drawing her six-gun. Billy followed.

Pushing through the saloon's batwing doors, they took in the sight of overturned chairs and tables. Broken glass reflected the room's gas lamps. In the center of it all, young Henry Fountain held a saloon girl in a frighteningly intimate pose, suckling her neck.

Before they could react, the stranger with red hair appeared on the upstairs landing. He vaulted over the railing. Landing on his feet, he rushed to the child, pulled him from the saloon girl and hurled him toward the bar. Billy cringed, certain the boy would be crippled for life. The girl had a wound on her neck similar to Billy's.

Larissa fired at the red-headed stranger. He spun around and dropped to the floor.

Just as Billy and Larissa moved forward, Henry bolted to his feet, blood dribbling down his chin. "Heya, Billy! Catch me if you can!" He pushed between Billy and Larissa and ran out to the street. The two whirled around to give chase. As they did, the red-headed stranger stirred. Billy hung back as Larissa rushed out the door.

The red-headed stranger sat up, revealing a bloody

hole in his upper chest. He should be dead, bleeding out, but he struggled to his feet. So much for the professor's theory that a vampire could be stopped by bullets. Billy strode over to him. "Who are you? What were you trying to do to Henry?"

"He is dangerous and must be controlled. Unchecked, he could bring doom to the world!" The red-headed stranger seemed to gain strength with each word.

"What is he? Some kind of vampire like in that book *Carmilla*?"

The stranger smiled, revealing a pair of fangs, like a dog's. "Ah, you know *Carmilla*. Then you know what kind of monster we're dealing with."

"We?" Billy narrowed his gaze. "Looks like you're the same kind of monster, maybe worse, hurling little boys around."

"Vampire, yes. Monster, no." The stranger rose to his feet. The hole in his chest closed before Billy's eyes. "Like Carmilla, he is a child turned into a vampire with a child's lack of discipline. He must be used carefully."

Billy grabbed the stranger's arm. "What have you done with his father?"

The stranger shook himself free and sneered. "He's in room two, curled up in a heap, feeling sorry for himself."

Just then, Larissa returned to the saloon. "I can't find him anywhere." She stopped and aimed her six-gun at the stranger. Before she could utter another word, he pushed past her. She followed him back into the street.

Billy walked over to the saloon girl. She moaned and her eyelids fluttered. He thought she'd recover. Henry might be dangerous, but had he actually killed anyone?

The stranger said he lacked discipline. There was only one person who could give that to the boy. Billy ran up the stairs. He entered the room and sure enough, Albert J. Fountain, former Texas lieutenant governor, attorney-at-law, and newspaperman, sat on the floor, hugging his legs, rocking back and forth.

"Mr. Fountain," said Billy, "you've got to tell me what's happened."

Fountain looked up and blinked. "Billy? You're alive?"

"Yes, sir. What happened to us out in the dunes?"

Fountain laughed and tears streamed down his pallid cheeks. The laugh grew in volume, turning hysterical and revealing fangs. Billy sucked in a breath.

No doubt about it, the red-headed stranger somehow turned both father and son into vampires. Billy smacked the attorney. "Damn it, man. Get a grip!"

Fountain fell silent, his eyes wide and staring.

"What the hell's going on here?" demanded Billy.

Fountain sputtered. "It wasn't supposed to be like this," he managed at last. "Just me. I was the only one who should have been turned. I wanted you to take the boy back home to his ma."

"You wanted to become a monster? I don't get it."

Fountain snuffled, but his eyes cleared. "It doesn't matter how long you live. Death always comes too soon. I wanted to watch Henry grow up."

Billy frowned, remembering how close he came to being hung for murder. He understood all too well. "Who's the red-headed dude?"

"He's called Rosen. He does certain jobs for the governor."

Billy could guess what kinds of jobs. Hired gun—or more like hired fang. "So you didn't mean for Henry to become a vampire?"

Fountain sighed. "Rosen was supposed to knock you out and take me away—make it look like a kidnapping." He held his head. "What happened is a blur. He attacked me, turned me into a vampire right then. I remember insatiable hunger. I turned on my Henry . . . my precious boy." Fountain began rocking again.

Billy grabbed his arm. "Stay with me, Mr. Fountain."

Fountain slammed his eyes shut. "I remember pulling my boy close, grieving. Next thing I remember was seeing my little boy drinking your blood."

Billy reached up and touched the wound at his neck.

"Sunrise approached. We dug graves to hide."

Lightning flashed around the thick velvet curtains despite the cloudless skies outside. Billy ran to the window and pushed the curtain aside. Rosen chased Henry across Tularosa's flat rooftops. On the street below, Larissa followed them on the wolf. She swiveled the strange-looking gun around. Lightning arced, barely missing Rosen, who dove off the building.

Henry turned and looked right at Billy from across the street. "There you are!" he called. "Come and get me!"

Billy turned on his heel. "Mr. Fountain, you've got to do something. If you don't, either that vampire's gonna use Henry for his own purposes or Larissa's gonna vaporize him. I'm not sure which."

"Rosen says Henry will never grow up. He will never know right from wrong."

Billy stepped forward and grabbed Fountain by the

lapels of his jacket and hoisted him to his feet. "Of course, he lacks discipline. He's a little boy. You're his pa! What are you going to do?"

Fountain gaped as though Billy had struck him again. After a moment, he gathered his wits and nodded. They returned to the window together. Outside, Henry ran to the edge of a building and jumped off. Larissa opened the wolf's throttle, rode to the next street and made a sharp turn.

"We've gotta do something, Mr. Fountain."

Fountain nodded. "I'll meet you downstairs." He pushed open the window and leapt to the street below.

Billy ran from the room, down the stairs, and through the wreckage of the saloon. When he pushed through the batwing doors, he found Albert Fountain standing in the middle of the street, illuminated by the moonlight. "Henry Fountain, you come to your father right now!"

A moment later young Henry rushed around the corner of a building and jumped into his father's arms. At the end of the street, Larissa whipped around the corner and stopped, sending up a spray of gravel. She aimed her lightning gun at the father and son.

Rosen appeared at the other end of the street.

Billy leapt from the boardwalk and stood between the Fountains and Larissa.

"Stand aside, Billy," called Larissa. "I don't know what's going on here, but they're not human. Let me finish this."

Billy shook his head. "Marshal Seaton, I was hired to protect the Fountains and I aim to see that job through.

If you want to kill them, you'll have to kill me, too." Billy drew his six-gun, but didn't point it. He turned around. Rosen strolled up to the father and son.

"The boy will go with me," growled the red-headed vampire.

"I imagine an immortal boy would be real handy in your line of work. What do you want him for? Decoy? Innocent-looking accomplice?" Billy turned his head and spat. "He and his father get to leave real peaceable like, or else I'll step away and let Larissa burn you down."

Rosen's mouth ticked upward. "I don't fear the girl's gun."

Larissa's face was unreadable. Her eyes flicked from the Fountains to Rosen.

Billy looked at Fountain, holding his son. "Sir, I'd advise you to get out of here. I don't know how long I can hold Marshal Seaton off."

Fountain nodded and set his son down. He took his hand and the two began walking away. Henry turned. "Billy, will I ever see you again?"

Billy smiled. "Maybe. Learn what you can from your pa."

Rosen snarled and turned to follow.

Billy leapt out of the way and Larissa pulled the trigger. A lightning bolt caught the red-headed vampire, leaving ashes and a greasy smear in the sand. She aimed the gun at Fountain and his son. "You two keep walking until you get to Texas. If I hear about vampires in New Mexico territory, I'll come gunning for you."

Albert Fountain nodded. "Come along, now, Henry." With that, the two continued down the street.

Larissa brought the wolf up next to Billy and glared at him.

"Thank you," he said. "That was right good of you."

"Don't know if it was smart," she said. "Why'd you protect them?"

"Henry Fountain may have attacked me and the saloon girl, but he didn't kill either one of us. Albert Fountain's a good man, I think he can find a way to make this vampire thing work and teach his son to do the same. A boy needs his pa." Billy holstered his six-gun and took a step closer to the wolf.

Larissa shook her finger at Billy. "Oh no you don't. You've made enough trouble. Find your own ride back to Cruces." With that, she opened the wolf's throttle, leaving Billy to cower in a shower of gravel and dust.

HIGH MIDNIGHT
A Dan Shamble, Zombie PI Adventure

Kevin J. Anderson

Gunfire rang out in the Unnatural Quarter—one loud shot, then five more in quick succession.

The audience, both humans and monsters, applauded and whistled. The ghost of the Old West gunslinger, Deadeye One-Eye, had nailed all six target playing cards that hung by clothespins on a wire, right through the Ace of Spades. He shifted his eyepatch in triumph; depth perception did not seem to be necessary for his aim.

"Golly!" said Mild Bill, twirling his spectral handlebar mustache. "And he was only listed as a midrange gunslinger ghost." He stood with a bowlegged stance, putting his hands on his spectral hips as if he imagined holsters there.

"All right, I'm impressed," I said, standing next to him at the edge of the performance area in the fake Western town erected for the show. I couldn't shoot that well with my .38—not when I was alive, and not now that I'm undead. As a zombie detective I might be stiffer, but that didn't mean my aim was steadier.

While the spectators continued to cheer, the ghost of the outlaw gunslinger twirled his pearl-handled ghost Colt revolver and slid it into a shimmering translucent holster. Maybe intangible firearms were easier to twirl than real ones.

Since it was the weekend and late in the evening, I took time off from Chambeaux & Deyer Investigations so we could go see Mild Bill's Wild West Show, an extravagant, if kitschy, affair that the ghost saloon owner had sponsored. And since Robin Deyer, my human lawyer partner, had worked with Mild Bill to take care of all the necessary contracts and waivers, she insisted that attending the show was part of our job. Half the population of the Unnatural Quarter had decided to come out as well.

"It's bound to be a financial success, Beaux," said Sheyenne, my ghost girlfriend, as she intangibly snuggled up to me. "The Wild West Show could become a regular thing in the Quarter."

"Why yes, Miss Sheyenne," I said in a long drawl and tipped my fedora as if it were a cowboy hat, sliding it down to cover the bullet hole in the center of my forehead, from when I'd been killed a few years back.

I'd been a reasonably successful human detective in the Unnatural Quarter, solving the usual run of oddball and mundane cases for the humans and monsters that lived there. After I was killed on a case and then rose from the grave—thereby changing my job title from human detective to zombie detective—business had really picked up.

The Wild West Show continued. Deadeye One-Eye took a break to reload his six-shooter with ghost bullets, and the dance hall girls came out—vampire girls from the Full Moon Brothel. The ladies of the night (but weren't all vampire women ladies of the night?) enjoyed dressing up in flouncy old-fashioned Western dresses. A female werewolf capped each side of the line, and they bounced out kicking and stepping high in an untrained version of the cancan—which I wasn't sure was historically accurate . . . but what do I know? My knowledge of the Old West came from TV reruns, and mid-twentieth-century television programming wasn't known for its veracity.

"Whoo hoo, go dance hall girls!" shouted McGoo—Officer Toby McGoohan, my Best Human Friend. As a beat cop, he had been transferred from a human precinct to the Unnatural Quarter for telling non–politically correct jokes. We helped each other out on cases.

I was surprised by his enthusiastic wolf whistles. "You never showed any interest in the Full Moon ladies before, McGoo."

"Still no interest," he said. "I have enough trouble with human women. I don't need to get involved with Unnaturals."

Robin frowned skeptically at him. "You have trouble with human women? I've never heard you talk about even getting a date."

A flush suffused his freckled face. "And *that* is exactly my trouble."

After the dance hall girls exited the stage, a troop of ghost cowboys galloped out on wild and unruly night-mares—fiery-eyed black horses that looked frightening and difficult to control, yet the ghost riders rode bareback as they twirled lariats over their heads.

Someone had loosed a minotaur into the performance area, and the big bullheaded creature stumbled around with a look of abject confusion. When the ghost cowboys thundered toward the minotaur, he bleated and huffed in alarm. They twirled their ropes and dropped the lassoes around him, cinched him tight, and tied him up, ankles and wrists. The minotaur crashed to the dusty performance ground—again, to much applause.

The minotaur bellowed, "I was just looking for the concession stand."

Next to us, the ghost of Mild Bill let out a belly laugh. "Yesirree, you never can guess what might happen at one of my shows. Lordy!" When he grinned, he showed off bad, brown teeth from chewing ghost tobacco.

Mild Bill owned the New Deadwood Saloon, which had been decorated like an Old West watering hole. He claimed to be the actual ghost of Wild Bill Hickok, but he had mellowed with age, and now he preferred to be called Mild Bill.

Enthusiastic about his Wild West Show, Bill had rented a cursed Indian burial ground for the venue, and hired Robin to work out the real-estate paperwork and the lease. During negotiations, Robin discovered that the owners could not prove that the burial ground had any legitimate curses, and therefore could not charge extra, so Mild Bill had gotten a reduced rate.

Our Robin always insists that Unnaturals are treated fairly under the law.

After the roped-up minotaur was dragged away from the field, Deadeye One-Eye came back into the middle of the wide dirt main street, twirled his Colt again, and started shooting cigars from the mouths of two volunteer mummies, who trembled as the ends of the stogies were blasted into fragments. Sheyenne, Robin, and McGoo joined in the cheers.

The gunslinger fired his pistols into the air. "And that's just a warm-up for tonight's late show, folks." He had a sinister undertone in his voice. "If y'all think I'm good, wait 'til the rest of my gang comes at high midnight. Moondance McClantock and the boys can shoot circles around me—if they're feeling their oats, they can even shoot triangles." The audience applauded as he sauntered away.

Finished with his act, the ghost of Deadeye One-Eye came up to where we were standing at the edge of the performance field. Even with his eye patch, his eyesight couldn't be as bad as his teeth. Despite his unfortunate dental condition, he wasn't shy about showing off his smile. The ghost gunslinger tipped his hat at Sheyenne and Robin, then he fixed his single eye on me. "Dan Chambeaux, Zombie Detective." Somehow, he made my name into a sneer.

I acted professional. "I'm surprised you pronounced my name correctly. Most people call me Shamble."

"I know who you are, Chambeaux—but maybe you don't." He showed off his preposterous teeth in a snaggly snarl rather than a grin. "Are you aware your great-great-umpty-ump grandpappy, Dirk Chambeaux, was the most hated marshal in these parts, give or take a state or two? He was a feared man, made a lot of enemies."

McGoo nudged me with an elbow. "Hey Shamble, law enforcement is in your blood."

"My blood these days is embalming fluid," I said.

Deadeye One-Eye gave me a careful assessment before striding off. "See you later tonight—at high midnight."

"What did he mean by that?" Robin asked.

"No idea."

During the preparations for the Wild West Show, I had watched Robin go through excruciating negotiations and legal convolutions. The ghosts of the McClantock outlaw gang had a ruthless talent representative, and affable Mild Bill was a babe in the woods when it came to making a deal with a cutthroat agent—literally a cutthroat, because he was an accused serial killer, although it was never proven. The agent claimed the gunslinger ghosts were in high demand and tried to extract an outrageous appearance fee. Deadeye One-Eye, though, was a free agent, and he had quickly come to terms for a far lower fee, for which he had been resoundingly criticized by his gang because his concession had affected their collective bargaining power.

Mild Bill wanted to book the McClantock gang for multiple performances, along with roving freelance entertainment—gun tricks and such among the crowd, but the cutthroat agent had tried to triple their fee. At one point, Robin had been so frustrated that I lurched into the negotiating room to ask if she needed any muscle to bring the gunslingers in line. It was a joke (zombies aren't really all that intimidating), but when the agent went back to Moondance McClantock, they promptly agreed to the high midnight show.

I guess I was more scary than I thought.

But Mild Bill could only afford the one designated performance, explicitly defined as a single round of extravagant gun play, nothing else. Any more would be a breach of contract. Despite his disappointment, Mild Bill had promised to make the best of it.

Around the show grounds, the spectral saloon owner put up posters featuring the outlaws, "Wanted: Dead, Undead, or Alive. Moondance McClantock and his gang!" Robin had brought along her executed copy of the contract, just in case McClantock decided to renege on the deal.

Obviously, we all had to stay and see the big performance, which would take place in an hour.

A skeleton played happy piano music in front of the temporary saloon and watering hole, where a potbellied zombie barkeep was pouring beer, whiskey, and shots of blood to cowboy-dressed vampires who looked as if they had just escaped from an undead dude ranch. Albert Gould, the rotting and disheveled proprietor of the Ghoul's Diner, had set up a food stand that served "authentic Western barbecue"—blackened bones (species unknown) covered with sizzling meat. I had heard his special sauce was good.

The Old West must have been a peaceful, nostalgic place.

But then, gunfire rang out—real gunfire, in earnest this time, and Deadeye One-Eye was not just aiming at targets. Over by the rickety corral, he had untied the five angry nightmares, and now he whooped like a Hollywood Indian on the warpath. He fired his pistols again and again, and the noise startled the demon horses. Even though they were supernatural creatures, they certainly spooked easily.

The ghost gunslinger laughed maniacally, something he did quite well, and the snorting black horses thundered out in a violent panic, racing into the crowd of naturals and unnaturals along the main street.

"Shoot, that's not part of the show!" Mild Bill flashed a glance at Robin. "You said we couldn't afford the insurance for a full stampede."

"We better get these people out of here," I shouted. "And bring the horses under control."

As I lurched into motion, McGoo kept up with me. "Great idea, Shamble. Throw ourselves in front of a bunch of demonic stallions?"

"Don't make it worse than it is, McGoo—these are mares, not stallions."

The horses stormed forward, their hooves striking improbable sparks on the dusty ground. Flames chuffed from their nostrils.

McGoo drew his two service revolvers, one loaded with normal bullets, the other with silver bullets, but I didn't think these wild horses would be cowed, regardless the type of ammunition.

As the crowd of mummies, vampires, werewolves, mad scientists and their assistants fled to the boardwalk and the store fronts, the horses stormed toward us. McGoo opened fire, shooting into the air. If the demonic horses could be spooked once, they could be spooked again.

The resounding gunfire scared the nightmares enough that instead of charging into the crowd, they split up and galloped toward the concession stands. The skeleton piano player and Albert the ghoul fled. The rampaging nightmares crashed into the barbecue display, knocking the tent down and spilling meat-covered bones in all directions, along with a bucket of smoking sauce. The "secret ingredient" burned craters in the sawdust-strewn ground.

Two of the black horses still came toward us, and I drew my .38, also firing into the night sky, but my gun wasn't as loud as McGoo's heavier-caliber weapons. I added some harsh language, and that did the trick. The snorting nightmares wheeled about and stampeded back toward their corral.

Then amidst the gunfire and whinnying, I heard something that made my artificial blood run cold—a scream. Sheyenne's scream.

"McGoo, come on," I yelled.

The ghost of the evil gunslinger stood front of Sheyenne, Robin, and Mild Bill. Deadeye One-Eye had both of his Colts out, and he opened fire. Sheyenne spun, crying out in pain—pain!—as a ghost bullet grazed her upper arm, and I saw a splash of ectoplasmic blood.

Robin was in the line of fire too, but she dove out of the way. Somehow, the bullets missed her.

McGoo and I put on a surge of speed.

The one-eyed ghost gunslinger turned the firepower on his real target, Mild Bill. The avuncular saloon owner raised his hands in surrender. "Don't shoot!"

"Why not?" Deadeye One-Eye emptied his pistols.

Ectoplasmic blood sprayed out from deadly wounds in the ghost saloon owner's chest, like the sauce from a

Spaghetti Western. The ghost gunslinger laughed at what he had done.

McGoo and I ran up, our guns drawn. I had eyes only for Sheyenne, who was wounded, and Mild Bill, who was mortally wounded—for a second time.

In a rage, McGoo snarled, "You are under arrest, Deadeye One-Eye!"

"You'll never take me alive, lawman—it's already too late." The gunslinger sneered at the dying ghost of Mild Bill, then looked up at me. "Now there's no way he can rescind the contract. When Moondance gets here, Chambeaux, you're a dead man."

"I'm pretty sure that's how I started out the day," I said.

The gunslinger's ghost vanished into thin air while he was still laughing.

McGoo and Robin went to Mild Bill. I raced to Sheyenne. She had clamped a hand against the ghost bullet wound in her shoulder, and red ectoplasmic blood seeped around her fingers.

"How could you get hurt?" I asked. "You're not even corporeal."

"That gunslinger has ghost bullets," Sheyenne said. "And I'm a ghost."

She lifted up her hand, stared at the ectoplasmic blood, and shook her head. She looked beautiful with her blond hair and her startling blue eyes. "I'll be fine Beaux—it's just a flesh wound . . . figuratively speaking of course."

McGoo checked over Robin quickly. "You're not hurt?"

"Just lucky, I guess." She looked shocked.

The ghost of Mild Bill lay on the ground, moaning, his

blood evaporating into the spirit world. "Never thought they'd shoot me!" With his dying gaze, he looked up at me and uttered a final sentence. "Shamble . . . beware, high midnight." He gasped, let out a death rattle, and his ghost dissipated before our eyes, along with all the bloodstains.

After his ghost vanished, the air continued to shimmer, like the image from a faulty projector at a drive-in movie theater, and we watched a vision from the past.

All right, I know that drive-in movie theaters are also things of the past, but this went back much further. A bonus for the Wild West Show, at no extra charge.

In the vision, we saw a lawman wearing a gold marshal's star on his leather vest, and his thumbs hooked in his wide belt that held a holstered revolver on each hip. He had a stern, satisfied smile on his face.

"He looks like you, Beaux," Sheyenne said.

Upon closer inspection, I saw that the lawman's face was indeed square-jawed and handsome, though he wore a tan cowboy hat instead of a fedora.

"Poor guy," McGoo said.

The vision was like a grainy old cowboy movie, only drier and dirtier. I didn't expect to see the words "In Technicolor" splashed across the screen.

The lawman stepped up, spurs jingling from the heels of his boots, and he faced a gallows, where six seedy-looking men were lined up at the rickety wooden steps, hands cuffed behind their backs, shackles around their ankles. The first man—it was Deadeye One-Eye, looking no better and no fresher in life than after a century and a half being a corpse—was nudged up to the dangling rope in the middle of the platform.

"Sorry we could only afford one noose," said the lawman. "You'll have to take turns, one at a time."

"We've got all day, Marshal," said the man in the back, apparently the leader. He had a round face and long sideburns.

"Yeah, but I have other things to do, McClantock. Let's move it along. Come on, Deadeye—you've seen hangings before. You know what to do."

Annoyed at being rushed, Deadeye One-Eye ducked his head as a prissy hangman looped the noose over his neck and then pulled it snug with more fastidiousness than I would have expected from an executioner.

The trapdoor dropped, and we could hear an audible *crack* as Deadeye One-Eye's neck snapped.

"Ewww," said Robin.

The speed of the vision increased, like a historical documentary on fast forward, probably for pacing. One after another, the six outlaws took their turn swinging on the noose, and when they had stopped kicking, they were pulled up again, disentangled from the rope, and placed in the undertaker's wagon, which was conveniently parked in a spot close to the gallows. He must have had a special permit from the town.

Finally, when only the leader—Moondance McClantock, I presumed—remained, the lawman looked at his pocket watch, snapped it shut, and nodded impatiently. "Let's get a move on, McClantock. It's almost over." He tucked his thumbs in his leather belt again, watching as the hangman slid the well-used noose over the last outlaw's neck.

"Oh, it's not over, Marshal Chambeaux," McClantock

said. "Not by a long shot." He looked at the lawman, but then he turned and seemed to be looking right out of the vision. Right at *me*.

When the trapdoor dropped for the last time, the vision vanished, as if the spectral film had snapped in perfect synch with the outlaw leader's neck.

"Well, no wonder he looked familiar, Shamble," McGoo said.

"I didn't really have time for a family history lesson," I said.

"It's always good to learn your roots," Sheyenne pointed out.

I felt angry and sickened. "Not right now. You could have been hurt. Now I know that Deadeye One-Eye caused the stampede as a diversion. We should've stayed with you three."

"Beaux, you couldn't have known," Sheyenne said.

The nightmares had wandered back to the corral and now munched contentedly on thistles. Several werewolves and zombies had darted into the wreckage of Albert the ghoul's barbecue tent and slunk off with dripping bones, leaving a trail of barbecue sauce that exuded curls of green acidic smoke.

McGoo wiped sweat from his brow. "What did Mild Bill mean about high midnight?"

"That's when the ghosts of the McClantock gang are coming, per the contract," Robin said. "Deadeye One-Eye didn't want Mild Bill to rescind the agreement. He's the only one with a legal signature on it."

Sheyenne tore a strip of gingham from her ectoplasmic dress and tied it around her wound. "It all changed when

Dan found out his ancestor was a ruthless Old West lawman. And that vision told us the whole story."

"But I never heard of Dirk Chambeaux before today," I said. "What difference would that make to me?"

Then, on the ground before us where Mild Bill's ghost had died, the air shimmered, flickered, and a second even wispier form of the spectral saloon owner rose up. He seemed even less substantial than before.

"Mild Bill, you're alive!" McGoo said.

"Golly . . . not hardly. I'm a ghost. But this time I'm a ghost of a ghost."

"What are the chances of that happening?" I asked.

"Pretty damn slim. I wish I'd had this kind of luck when I was alive, yesirree." Mild Bill stroked his handlebar mustache, as if he was particularly pleased with his renewed existence.

Robin asked, "What's going to happen at high midnight? Why should we beware?"

The doubly spectral cowboy blinked at her. "Haven't you been paying attention, Ms. Deyer? Moondance McClantock and his gang are coming back—we arranged for it, you and me. It was all part of their plan. What they really want is to get revenge. I went to all that trouble to show you the vision after I died again. Don't you get it? Dan's great-great-umpty-ump ancestor was Marshal Dirk Chambeaux, the lawman who sent McClantock and his gang to the gallows. They're not just here to perform in my Wild West Show, they're coming to get revenge on you." As he pointed at me, the wispy ghost's mouth drooped in a sincere frown. "And you're going to have to face them at high midnight, Marshal."

"Private investigator," I corrected him. "McGoo's closer to being a marshal."

"Hell, I haven't even made detective yet," McGoo said.

A crowd had begun to gather, listening to the conversation, but when they learned that the murderous gunslingers were riding into town soon, they fled, not wanting to be anywhere close to the line of fire. A full-furred werewolf muttered that he had left the bathtub running and quickly retreated. The rest of the crowd eased away with similar, or more outrageous, excuses.

I looked at them all, seeing fear in their eyes. Many of these were clients of mine, past clients and future clients. I stood my ground, turning to face them. "What time is it now?"

The ghost of the ghost of Mild Bill flipped open a pocket watch that hung from a chain in his vest. "Eleven forty-five—fifteen minutes 'til doomsday."

"Fifteen minutes?" McGoo cried. "Shouldn't there be more time to build up suspense?"

"It's a faster-paced society nowadays, McGoo," I said.

He lifted his chin. "Well, I'm standing with you, Shamble. Something doesn't smell right around here, and it's not just you."

"Thanks, McGoo," I said sarcastically.

Sheyenne looked weak and dizzy from the ghost gunshot, as if she'd lost some of her spirit, literally. "We'll stay here to help you, Beaux."

"Not you, Spooky—you've already been hurt," I said as firmly as I could. "If the ghost bullets are flying, I couldn't bear to lose you again. We've got plenty of people around here to help stand against those gunslingers."

I turned to the crowd that McGoo and I had just saved from stampeding demonic horses. Oddly, the spectators that had previously been so numerous now muttered excuses and began to melt away like vampires on a hot summer day.

Even the ghost of Mild Bill's ghost muttered, "I better go check on my saloon. All these frightened people are going to need drinks."

I felt discouraged. "You too?"

"I have already been shot to death once today." He vanished.

I couldn't hold it against him.

McGoo calmly reloaded both of his service revolvers, regular bullets and silver bullets. "I know you would've taken a bullet for me, Shamble."

"As I recall, I already have. What are friends for?" I stood next to him in the middle of the dirt main street, which was bounded on either side by the colorful, but thin, facades of a movie-set cowboy town.

The town clock tower, which had been erected for the Wild West Show, rang out, sounding 11:55.

"That's an odd time for the hour to chime."

"I think it's to give people time to prepare for the midnight festivities," Sheyenne said.

When the loud bells ceased chiming, the dirt main street on the old cursed burial ground was deserted, dust blowing in the night wind. On either side, the windows were dark in the tall clapboard storefronts, the buildings seemingly abandoned. Back in the corral, the nightmares neighed. The dude ranch vampires had fled, but not too far. I could see them behind the display window of the general store, watching me.

Sheyenne, looking weak and ghostly, drifted to the safety of the boardwalk at my insistence. "Be careful, Beaux—I love you."

"I love you too, Spooky," I said.

Clearly angry, Robin refused to leave us. "This is not the way one should solve problems. We have a legal system, courts, and judges."

"It was the courts and the marshal that ticked off these gunslingers in the first place, Robin," I said.

At precisely 11:57, Moondance McClantock and his gang of murderous gunslinger ghosts appeared, including Deadeye One-Eye, who had joined the party, even though he was a free agent.

McGoo and I faced the six gunslingers in the middle of the main street. The ghost outlaws were a surly, rumpled-looking lot, greasy with sweat and prickly with razor stubble—apparently, none of the spectral gunslingers had found time to bathe or shave in the century and a half since their demise.

"We're here for Chambeaux." Moondance McClantock was a round-faced man with long sideburns, a ten-gallon hat, and enough turquoise and silver to fill an entire roadside souvenir stand. I remembered seeing him in the vision. He had a gleaming gold front tooth, which clashed with all the silver and turquoise. "I've waited a long time for this, and finally with the Big Uneasy, us vengeful ghosts have our chance."

"We haven't even met," I said, "and I've only had fifteen minutes to build up my anticipation."

The gang leader shrugged. "Sorry about that. Back in 1856, Marshal Dirk Chambeaux sentenced us all to hang, which wasn't fair."

In unison, the gunslingers all lifted their chins to show off their necks. McClantock shifted a gaudy bolo tie of turquoise and silver to reveal a long rope burn across his throat. The other outlaws had similar noose burns. One man with a full beard and huge eyebrows had a crooked neck as if even his ghost hadn't been able to realign the snapped vertebra.

"A miscarriage of justice," said Deadeye One-Eye.

"Weren't you guilty?" I asked.

"Absolutely," McClantock said. "But my crimes were far worse than any of my boys, here, yet I got the same treatment. I would have gone down in history if he had skinned me alive or burned me over hot coals, but your ancestor lacked imagination, Chambeaux."

"But what does that have to do with me?" I asked.

"We've come here to get our revenge on the last living descendant of Marshal Dirk Chambeaux. You'll pay for his crimes."

I looked at McGoo, then back at the outlaws. "Sorry to point this out, boys, but you missed your chance." I slid back my fedora to reveal the bullet hole in the center of my forehead. "I'm already dead—I'm a zombie. You can't kill me."

I tugged down my sport jacket to show the prominent stitched-up bullet holes across the chest from yet another time I had been gunned down in the street.

"It'll have to do," McClantock said, and his gunslinger gang members nodded vigorously. "You being dead actually works to our advantage."

"How do you figure?" McGoo asked, fidgeting with his grip on the service revolvers.

"Because we're all ghost gunslingers," Deadeye One-Eye explained. He pulled out both of his Colt pistols; Moondance McClantock did the same, as did all of his boys. "All we have are ghost bullets—and as you saw with Mild Bill, ghost bullets do just fine against the undead."

"I'm a zombie, not a ghost," I said. "There's a difference."

Moondance McClantock frowned, as if he hadn't considered that. I glanced over at Sheyenne, who waited at the boardwalk. She spread her hands, clearly not knowing the answer. The ghost gunslingers didn't know either.

Robin marched over to stand close to me, her expression stern. "You all have to stop this, right now. It's against the law."

Seeing that all of the vengeful ghost gunslingers had drawn their weapons, I urgently pushed her out of the way. "McGoo, get her out of here. I don't want either of you in the line of fire. Robin's been lucky enough once today."

She tried to argue, but McGoo didn't. Though she resisted, he escorted her toward the boardwalk.

As soon as they were three steps away, Moondance McClantock and his gang lifted their revolvers, ready to gun me down. The ghost gunslingers aimed their weapons at me, and the staccato sound of twelve hammers being cocked back sounded like a high-caliber rattlesnake.

I was standing there all by myself in the middle of the

street, arms loose at my sides—or as loose as a zombie's arms could be. I held my .38 in my right hand, but how could that stand against six pairs of six-shooters full of ghost bullets? Besides, my real bullets would just pass through the outlaw apparitions, but the ghost bullets were not likely to pass harmlessly through me.

As the tension ratcheted up, the town clock started bonging again—apparently the previous bells had just been a warm-up for high midnight. It all happened very quickly.

Just as they all opened fire at their target of a lone, and hopefully brave, zombie detective standing in the middle of the main street, McGoo let out a shout and threw himself in front of me like a human shield, flailing his arms. The twelve ghostly Colts roared with the sound of thunder.

From the boardwalk, Sheyenne and Robin both screamed.

In instant reaction, I managed *not* to fire my .38—a good thing, or I would have shot my Best Human Friend in the back, and he was already facing a storm of bullets from Moondance McClantock and his gang. The gunfire went on and on until the outlaws emptied their revolvers into my friend.

I expected McGoo to drop lifeless to the ground. Instead, he stood there and turned to look at me in astonishment. "Well, that was one of the stupidest things I've ever done."

Robin bounded into the street, grabbing McGoo's shirt, patting him down, looking for the dozens of bullet holes. But there were none.

He showed me a nervous, relieved grin while the ghost gunslingers gaped at him, surprised and annoyed. "I guess I'm smarter than I thought I was," McGoo said. "I figured it out, Shamble. Robin wasn't just lucky earlier, and she didn't dodge the bullets when Deadeye One-Eye gunned down Mild Bill. Ghost bullets can kill ghosts, but they don't harm normal people, in the same way that normal bullets don't harm ghosts."

I still couldn't believe he was intact. "That was an awfully idiotic way to test a theory, McGoo."

"You wanted me to think it through for a day or two? I didn't really have the time to do my due diligence. I had to act right away." He patted his chest again, just in case he had missed a few dozen bullet holes.

I felt a lump in my throat, and it wasn't from anything nasty I had swallowed. "Thanks, McGoo. You saved me."

Moondance McClantock shouted, "Reload, boys! Time for round two."

Now Robin stormed forward, striding down the main street toward the ghost gunslingers. I could tell by That Look on her face that she was angry now, really angry—and no one got in Robin Deyer's way when she was angry. "Oh, no you don't!" She faced the twelve six-guns, and even if she hadn't already seen proof that ghost bullets couldn't harm her, I think she would have walked right up to the surly gunslingers regardless. "You are not allowed."

Robin's handbag was actually more of a satchel for legal documents, and she had been working with Mild Bill's ghost nonstop until the day of the Wild West Show. Now she reached into her satchel and yanked out a folded document, waving it in the faces of the ghost gunslingers. "Holster your guns. You are not allowed—it says right here."

McClantock guffawed. "Oh, little lady! So now you're the lawman?"

"Not the lawman," Robin said with a sniff. "I am *the law*. Legal contracts. You signed this yourself."

"Not me." McClantock adjusted his turquoise bracelets and straightened his bolo tie. "That was our agent."

"And he has power of attorney. It's signed in blood."

"Not our blood, borrowed blood."

"It's still legally binding. The terms specifically state 'a limited engagement, one and only one exhibition of gunplay.' Your agent was very specific, and a ruthless negotiator. You all insisted on the terms." She jabbed her fingers at the contract. "You emptied your guns. You shot at your target. Therefore your legal obligations have been satisfied. You are no longer allowed to fire any bullets at Mr. Chambeaux, whether for vengeance or for entertainment purposes. You cannot rescind the contract."

"That's ridiculous," said McClantock. "That wasn't the spirit of the contract."

"It's the letter of the law," Robin said.

The gunslinger with the big beard and big eyebrows said, "Better be careful, boss—we don't want our agent to dump us."

Deadeye One-Eye groaned in disgust. "Why do you think I went freelance? I've told you guys over and over that you have to read your contracts! It's your own damn fault."

Sensing there was more fun to be had at the Wild West Show even after the gunfire, the skittish crowd began to reappear. Apparently they had shut off the water in their bathtubs, checked on their pets, stirred the burning casserole on the stove, and whatever other excuses they had made to get out of the danger zone.

The unkempt gunslinger ghosts stood, grumbling. They gathered around Robin's copy of the contract, scrutinizing the clauses again and again to find some loophole—which was difficult, as many of them were illiterate.

The ghost of Mild Bill's ghost shimmered in the air before them. He clapped his hands and grinned at the spectators. "Show's not over yet, folks! Lots more fun all through the night."

Albert the ghoul began picking up dust-encrusted remnants of his barbecued bones scattered over the ground. He inspected them with a drooping, milky eye, painted more sauce over the dirt, and offered them for sale again.

Still muttering, Moondance McClantock tucked the folded copy of the contract in his vest, and then all the ghost gunslingers vanished into the darkness.

Sheyenne ran forward from the boardwalk, looking restored now. The ectoplasmic blood in her makeshift bandage had faded. I cocked my fedora and said in a completely unconvincing drawl. "You look pretty as a picture, Miss Sheyenne." Then I turned to Mild Bill's ghost. "Show's over for us. We've had enough of this sort of entertainment. I prefer something a little more noir."

McGoo was already telling tall tales to the enthusiastic

audience members, and I let him have his day in the moonlight. His selfless bravery had certainly touched me.

But when the crowd congratulated me on my victory over the ghost outlaws, insisting that they'd really wanted to help, if it weren't for so many other obligations—I didn't want to hear the excuses. I wondered how great-great-umpty-ump grandpappy Marshal Dirk Chambeaux had felt in the Old West facing outlaws and bank robbers.

"Too bad we can't just ride off into the sunset," Sheyenne said. I felt a tingle as she slipped a ghostly arm through mine.

I shook my head. "No way—sunset is when things start hopping in the Unnatural Quarter."

"Then let's get hopping," she said.

Together, we all left the cursed Indian burial ground, looking for a good time on our own.

COYOTE

Naomi Brett Rourke

The wrinkled face of the hills surrounded the little town. Patchwork light and dark rolled its way across the hills and the valleys like good and evil crawling across the earth. Wispy clouds shaded the baking sun but never for long. The ground was dry, parched, and dusty. The old man shaded his eyes from the strong glare. It was after midday and the heat of the sun was boiling down in waves—in pulses a man could feel in his face, chest, and hands.

"Granddaughter," he said in a querulous voice, "get me a drink of water."

"Yes, Grandfather," the girl answered. She was tall and slim, with a river of blue-black hair streaming down her back. She was young, only sixteen, but she was already beautiful and would make a good wife for a strong Apache man, if only she didn't have the dark circles under her eyes. Dark circles that spoke of nightmares and long nights of remembrance. She wore a white calico shirt and a faded blue-and-white skirt, moccasins, and many necklaces of beadwork and shell. She came back with a dipper of water and gave it to her grandfather, watching as he tipped the cup and slowly drank it. She accepted it, replaced it, and came to sit beside the old man.

The day was sweltering and the old man had the last bit of shade under the roof of the local store. Dewdrops of sweat started on the girl's hairline but she made no move to wipe them off. Her grandfather, even with his long-sleeve cotton shirt, ancient vest, pants, kilt, and long moccasin boots, looked cool and remote. His white hair was tied with a headband and his kerchief, red faded to coral by constant washings, was tied around his neck. He also wore long necklaces of shell, and on his vest, odd designs worked in beads livened the rusty brown of the old garment.

The street was busy although most of the townsfolk were inside trying to escape from the Arizona sun. The old man and his granddaughter could not enter a store. They were Apache, and the Apache were not welcome in most of the stores and saloons in the white town. Apache still fought outside the town in the high hills and valleys, killing the pale interlopers as often as they could, but they did not dare come into the town. The grandfather's village had been destroyed in one of the many skirmishes against the white government and they went home to poverty every night on the reservation, but every day the old man insisted on sitting in the town.

A cowboy on a horse went by, both filthy with red dust, and the man looked at the girl with brief interest. Then he saw the old man and his face changed. He spat.

"Damn Apache." And he was gone, his horse trotting slowly down the dirt road, kicking up tufts of dust with every step.

The girl's hands clawed and her eyes darted to her grandfather and back. He never even blinked.

The old man hadn't always sat in the town. When his village was several miles from the town, he hadn't cared what went on with the whites and with their village. The great leader Cochise had made a treaty, and his people, the Chiricahua Apache, remained at peace with the whites until his death, even though other Apache tribes still marauded elsewhere. Then the treaty was broken, and the old man's village was destroyed, the young men killed or driven off and the women and babes killed. The old man's wife died with their village, her heart breaking while the bullet pierced her brain. The whites couldn't tell the Apache tribes from one another. They had no way of knowing that the old man's tribe, which had remained at peace, and the other tribe, the tribe that was still killing and pillaging in the many hills and valleys, were two entirely different entities. To the whites, the name Apache was a name to fear and mistrust. The old man and his granddaughter lived on the reservation, with meager stores, boredom, and disease, but still the old man and the girl came into the town every day on two mules and sat and looked at the white town.

A shadow fell over the two. The old man looked up and saw a tall dandy—black velvet coat, embroidered waistcoat, glittering watch-chain and ring, and highly shined red boots, blood red boots, even in the dust of the road.

"Old Man," he said. "You're in my way."

The girl looked up in anger and down at his boots. The fine gentleman with the shiny red boots, blood red, dark red. Her eyes widened with recognition, and then narrowed with hate. So many years waiting and here he was. Did the city slicker recognize her? It did not matter.

"Itza-chu."

"What?" The dandy's eyes saw her, saw her fury.

"Itza-chu. It's his name. It means Great Hawk. You should address him by his name."

"I should, should I?" The man threw back his head and laughed. His sandy blond hair under his expensive hat caught the light, looking like gold, or dread. "He doesn't look too much like a great hawk to me. More like a little chicken." He threw out his foot and kicked the old man. He swayed. The girl's eyes snapped and she gathered her legs under her to rise. *He was the subject of her dreams. Recurring dreams. Pointing fingers. Yelling of the crowd. The sheriff tying her father's hands behind him. Escorting him to the jail.*

"No, *jeeken*," the Apache murmured. Other than regaining his balance after the kick, he had not moved.

"'No, jee-ken,'" the fop said, "stay where you are and let the great hawk fight his own battles. Or little chicken." His voice took on a higher tone, one of mocking distain. "Here, chickie, chickie."

Itza-chu did not look at the man but continued looking out across the dirt street.

"There is more than enough space for you to get by me. I am not in your way," he commented softly.

"Not in my way! You damn Apache . . ."

The girl shot to her feet. *His lie had killed her father. The dandy had stood with the sheriff, pointing at her father. He did it. That Injun. He killed him. And they believed him. Believed him because he was a white man and not Apache. Nothing she could say would change the sheriff's mind. He didn't do it. That man's lying. Just a little bit of a girl, a little Apache girl in beads and braids. He didn't do it. The sheriff shook his head slowly, sadly.*

"Leave him alone!"

"*Jeeken!* Sit down."

The girl stood glaring at the dandy, who smirked at her, and she slowly sank back down, to sit cross-legged by the old man.

"Perhaps, *jeeken*," Itza-chu murmured, "you should tell the man a story." The girl looked up in surprise at her grandfather, and then, examined the ground, trembling.

"A story," the man jeered. "What makes you think I want to hear a damn Apache tale?" He looked at the girl and his expression changed with the speed of horses across the desert. "Maybe I'll just take this little girl and teach her a thing or two." He grabbed the girl's brown arm and yanked her to her feet. One of her necklaces burst, spilling shells that went dancing over the wooden walkway in front of the store. Their *plink, plink, plink* sounded loud in the hot air.

"No," the old man insisted in the same calm tone. "You must hear the story first. You might hear something that you like. That you value. You might learn."

"Learn? Learn? Learn from an Injun? From an Apache? Now, that's funny." He looked at the old man, who still hadn't moved and who still hadn't raised his voice. The old man was silent. The white man looked at the girl; her eyes still looked at the ground, but suddenly the dandy thought they looked sly, like a thieving cat or a horse just before she bites. He hesitated, thinking.

The slicker nodded. "All right. All right. You tell me a story and if I like it, I won't beat the Injun out of your sorry hide." He threw the girl down in the dirt and leaned against a post, putting his hands in his pockets and bringing up one leg nonchalantly to rest on the post. "Go on. I'm waiting."

"She will tell you the story," the old man said, watching as the girl righted herself and brushed off the dirt, "but you must swear to go and leave us if you learn from it."

The man nodded, smirking, and waved his arm.

"Cocheta," the old man smiled, his first smile in many years, "tell the story of Coyote and Yellow Jacket. Begin."

"Cocheta," the dandy snickered, "that your name?"

Cocheta glanced at him and looked down again. She put a hand in her pocket and took out a small drawstring bag. Putting her hand in the bag, she pulled out vials of yellow, blue, red, and black powder. Singing quietly to herself, she drew a circle, and within it she drew designs in the four colors, East, South, West, and North, red for blood, black for strength, white for purity, and blue for wisdom. The dandy sighed noisily, bored. She ignored him and continued to sing, passing her hands over the powder. She was silent for a while, and then began.

"This tale was given to me by our brothers the Jicarilla Apache, was given to me by Lolotea, daughter of—"

"Do you really think I want to hear this stuff?" the dandy cried. "What's wrong with you? Can't you tell a damn story? Get on with it."

"This is the way we tell our stories," the girl muttered. To the dandy, she said, "I will tell you the way a white man will understand."

"Good," said the white man.

You know Coyote was a trickster and was always trying to get things other people had—their wives, their food, their homes. One day Coyote was walking and came upon Yellow Jacket walking with a bag. Coyote addressed him, "Yellow Jacket, what is in your bag?" Coyote thought that Yellow Jacket must have good food in the bag and Coyote wanted some.

Yellow Jacket explained, "Coyote, I am carrying my children in my bag."

Coyote didn't believe him.

"No, Yellow Jacket. I don't carry my children that way. You must have something good to eat in there."

"No, Coyote, I carry my children in the bag. Come close. You can hear them."

"Yellow Jacket, do you think I am stupid? You must have good food in the bag if you are trying to get me to believe that you are carrying your children in there."

"No, Coyote, no. I carry my children in the bag. Believe me."

Coyote would not believe him so finally Yellow Jacket, tired of arguing, conceded,

"Coyote, you are too clever for me. The people had a feast and they gave me some fruit, all kinds of fruit to take home to give to my wife and children."

"I knew it. Yellow Jacket, why would you try to deceive me? Let me help you carry your fruit."

"No, Coyote, I can carry the fruit." Yellow Jacket knew Coyote wanted the fruit for himself.

"Yellow Jacket, I can carry your fruit for you. You look tired. Why don't you rest and I'll carry your fruit and when you are rested you can catch up with me."

So, Coyote took the bag from Yellow Jacket and started ahead while Yellow Jacket sat down to rest.

Coyote walked until he couldn't see Yellow Jacket anymore and then ran to his house. He was greedy and wanted all the fruit for himself. He placed the bag on a chair and eagerly opened it and thrust a hand in.

"Oye!" he yelled. A wasp had stung him from inside the bag.

"I must have put this bag on a thorn," he muttered and reached into the bag again. A wasp stung him harder. He jerked his hand out of the bag and the bag ripped. All of Yellow Jacket's children flew out and began stinging Coyote. Coyote waved his arms around and started running but the children of Yellow Jacket flew faster than Coyote could run. They were caught in Coyote's fur and stung him and stung him and stung him. By the time the children flew back to Yellow Jacket, Coyote's face and body was swollen and every part of him hurt. Coyote didn't dare to show his face for a long, long time.

The dandy was silent, looking at the girl. She and the old man also were quiet.

"What, exactly, am I supposed to learn from that little tale?" The dandy came forward and stood over the girl. The heat must have been affecting him because he looked red-faced and sweaty. "What," he barked, "am I supposed to learn from that?!"

The girl stood up and faced the dandy.

"What did you learn?"

The dandy's hand shot out and struck the girl, whose head snapped to the left.

"Maybe *you* learned not to sass white folks. Maybe *you* learned not to tell your damn Injun tales to people who have better things to do than to waste time listening to them."

The girl slowly turned her head and stared at the man. The dandy stood in silence, suddenly uncertain, suddenly unsure.

"Can't believe I spent time listening to you two yeehaws." He spat at the girl and it landed on her cheek, running slowly down to her jaw. The dandy turned on his heel and stomped down the dusty street. Cocheta wiped it off of her cheek, squatted, and carefully added the fluid to her powder design and stirred it. She cautiously added it to her bag and returned it to her pocket. Then she sat down near her grandfather, and closed her eyes. *Her wailing, pleading, he's innocent! The crowd cheering at the hanging. She, screaming; screaming and wailing, collapsing on the dusty ground as her father fell and the life was choked out of him. Later, her grandfather lifted her up from the ground and carried her home, one bright tear suspended on his wrinkled cheek. Her father—his only son. He walked all the way to their village and into*

the wickiup where they stayed for days, mourning her
father, his son.

When dusk came, a woman came out of the store with
a bag. She approached Itza-chu and Cocheta and handed
it to the girl. Then she faced Itza-chu.

"*Da goTe*, Itza-chu."

"*Da goTe*, Hetty." he responded. "Thank you for the
supplies."

The woman looked abashed. "Don't think nothing of
it. I had extra." She looked around to see if anyone could
hear her and said in a quieter voice, "I wish I could ask
you to come into the store to, you know, get out of the
heat during the day. It'd hurt my business, though."

Cocheta gave her a glare out of blazing eyes, but the
old man understood.

"We must all do what we can to survive. Thank you for
your kindness to me and my granddaughter."

Hetty dipped her head and watched them walk into
the street, sighing. Passersby side-stepped to avoid them,
to avoid their dark skin and strange ways. The girl's hands
curled into fists but Itza-chu just chuckled and they
walked off into the darkening night.

The dandy stepped out of the saloon into the shadowy
night. He was aggravated. All that money he had lost on
the faro game and he had lost it to that damn cowboy with
the blue bandanna. The dandy was convinced blue
neckerchief was cheating but try as he might, he could not
see how the man was doing it. He was doubly angered
because *he* wanted to cheat but he spent all night

watching that dad-blame bandanna man. *Damn.* He stumbled. *Too much whiskey, too.* He hiccoughed sour breath. *Pay for it tomorrow.*

He meandered slowly down the street, not quite in a straight line, headed for the hotel. *Maybe that pretty little Annie was still around.* The dandy was cheered by this thought and picked up his pace a bit more. Pretty little Annie with the pert nose and the soft shoulders. As he walked down the street he thought he heard a buzzing sound. The dandy looked around and saw nothing. The buzzing stopped. *Huh. I must be more drunk than I thought, hearing things.* He entered the hotel and informed Mrs. Hope that he would like to see pretty little Annie in his room as soon as she was available. Mrs. Hope was pleased and agreed that Annie was a charmer and she would come to his room as soon as she was free. The dandy went to his room content.

Itza-chu and Cocheta had finished their meager dinner and were sitting in their drafty wooden house. Itza-chu missed the warm, domed wickiup of his vanished village, but the white government had built the wooden houses hastily and they were ill-made, cold, and depressing.

Cocheta took the bag from her skirt pocket, kneeling on the dusty floor, and began to recreate the design that she drew earlier that day, before her story with the dandy, this time mixing the powder with his spit and loathing. She sang and chanted over it. The fire gave its reddish light and the shadows jumped and danced over the girl and her work, climbing higher and higher on the walls.

The silhouettes leaped and growled and at times they looked like the old spirits coming together—Ganhs, the mountain spirits; White Painted Woman; Child of the Water; Naiyenesgani, the Creator God; and, most importantly, the god of war, Tobadzistsini. Cocheta sang with eyes closed and with a power that would have surprised the white man. She sang of loss, of love, of sorrow. She sang of the injustice and the loss of balance, and finally, she sang of revenge. Itza-chu watched her as the black night passed. *The sheriff shook his head slowly, sadly.* After several hours, a wind entered the hovel spinning and spinning—a wind when there was none outside.

The dandy came outside when the moon had passed and the night was still and dark. Pretty little Annie had exceeded his every expectation and he no longer felt the hurt of loss and drink. He stretched his arms to the sky and breathed in the silent night air. Taking a leisurely stroll up the still street would do him well and then he would sleep. He loved the night and its possibilities. A wind skittered the dust on the street and gave the dandy a chill. He rubbed his arms as the gooseflesh raised, and then the breeze was gone.

He walked to the end of the street and, turning around, he felt a nip on his neck. Slapping it with his hand, he thought, "Damned 'squito." He turned to return to the hotel but he felt another sting, this time harder, on his outstretched hand.

"Damn!" he cried. Another one—was it a bite or a sting—on his face and suddenly he didn't want to be in the dark and lonely night any longer. He quickened his pace but almost immediately he was set upon by many *things*, they felt like insects, stinging, biting. The pain was enormous and he waved his arms wildly, trying to cover his head and face, but to no avail. They were everywhere. They stung through pants and jacket. They found their way inside his shirt. Some even managed to get inside his nice, shiny boots. He jumped, he danced, he jigged trying to avoid the swarm. He was in agony. His eyes were so swollen he could barely see. His nose was a mist of pain. He grabbed handfuls of his hair and pulled it out, trying to dislodge the hoard that had burrowed in and were stinging his scalp. His knees buckled and still they hounded him. One entered his ear, and when he tried to yell, two more found his mouth, and then his throat. He could not breathe! He collapsed on the ground, gasping for breath, clawing at his throat, legs thrashing, until slowly, so slowly, he stopped moving at all and the only movement were the lights and shadows playing on his nice, shiny boots, blood red boots, now covered with dust.

Several miles away, the old man watched his granddaughter as she slept.

Hetty came out to give Itza-chu his supplies and she was replete with news of the horrible death of the dandy from the hotel. It seemed he had come outside in the late night and been attacked by something.

"It was horrible," Hetty said. "You should have seen him. All swoled up like he'd been dead for a week. Doctor said it was wasp stings or yellow jackets or some such thing. Awful." Her voice lowered. "They said he'd just been with one of Mrs. Hope's girls and she just started screamin' and carryin' on and just fainted right there on the street. Horrible. I could hardly even look at him."

"Wasp stings," the old man disagreed, taking his bag, "wasp stings. Wasps do not fly at night."

"Oh," wondered Hetty, "well, what else could it be? Poor man. Poor, poor man. Imagine what he went through before he died."

Itza-chu stood silent.

"Oh, I've got one more thing; just hold on." She ran into the store, hiking up her skirts.

The old man looked at his granddaughter but she just looked at the dirt under her feet.

Hetty came back out with some calico in her hands. "Look, Cocheta, I have a new skirt for you. Look, pretty colors." She handed it to the girl. The girl stood mute.

Itza-chu said, "Granddaughter."

Cocheta raised her head. "Thank you." She passed her hand over the crisp material. "Thank you."

"Doesn't say much, does she?" Hetty remarked. "Cocheta. Real pretty name," she chatted, trying to get a smile out of the girl. "Cocheta. What does that mean, anyhow?"

The girl raised her head and smiled mirthlessly, her eyes glittering. Hetty felt suddenly that the girl was old, older than her years, older than her grandfather and the hills and valleys surrounding the town. She shivered. *She's just a little girl.*

"Your name," she stammered. "What's it mean, darlin'?"

"The Unknown," the girl replied.

THE KEY

Peter J. Wacks

Yuma, Arizona; The New West.
Tuesday midday.

The saloon doors swung open, dust blowing in on the wind from the street. Noonlight framed a young Chinese woman, dressed in a Stetson, a Chinese frog button shirt, and wearing chaps over her pants. Her nose was buried in the new H. G. Wells novel, *The Time Machine*. A pistol sat holstered on each hip, pearl inlaid dragons on the grips. Despite her slight stature and youth she seemed to fill the entryway.

The room was packed with furniture that had aged poorly, and people that had aged worse. They tried to ignore both the woman and the off-tune notes sadly floating out of the player piano. The young woman tipped her Stetson to the room in general, never taking her nose out of the book, then walked to the long wood bar. Every step was a swagger. She knew something no one else did, and it was obvious in the confidence of her stride.

She hooked a stool with her foot, sliding it out and

sitting down, then rapped her knuckles once on the bar top, signaling the barkeep. Glancing quickly at the bottles and dirty mirror behind the bar, she shifted slightly, positioning to be able to see the room as she slid the novel into a pocket.

The barkeep, a tall lanky man whose sun-wrinkled skin told of a life never lived in comfort outside of the territories, raised an eyebrow and spat. He walked over to the stranger and leaned on the bar, hands placed wide. "Get ya a drink?" he asked lazily.

The stranger pulled some coins from the lower pocket of her shirt, then stared at them for a moment. "Pretty sure you don't take wen here, as calculating a rate of exchange then delivering the coinage for a spendable medium would be tedious at best . . . What about pesos? High silver content, imminently spendable." Her clipped accent was Chinese, but still had a hint of the local lilt to it.

The bartender jerked back as though he had been slapped. "Pesos? You obviously just crossed from Mexico, as your kind ain't allowed immigration, and I wouldn't be offering those around. Ain't ya heard we ain't none too friendly with Mexico?"

The stranger shrugged and dumped the coins back into her pocket. "Well then. Since my silver isn't any good here, perhaps I can trade a tale for a glass of whiskey?"

The barkeep frowned. A Chinese gunfighting woman was a rarity, but this was Yuma, where every week some new mysterious stranger wandered into town with a tale of adventure. "Stranger, this is Yuma. Stories are cheap and whiskey's expensive. You ain't the first, not by a long shot, to try that."

The stranger nodded, then spoke loudly enough for the whole room to hear, over the warbly piano. "I am here to tell you a tale of a man named Hummingbird, and his best friend Inazuma. Some of you may have heard of them. They are my godparents."

The barkeep's eyebrows raised. He had indeed heard of them. Who was this girl, making claims like that? He grunted, and grabbed a bottle of whiskey. "Perhaps you is a bit more mysterious than most as comes in here. Go ahead."

She smiled, a quick twitch of her lips, then inclined her head and spoke to the room. "I will share a tale with you all, about some really big fellows. If you decide it's worth a drink when I'm done, buy away. If you don't, fair enough. I'll tell you this though, it is true. Every word. Believe those words or not, it's up to you. Now listen carefully. For I'll tell you in the order they experienced it, which isn't the order it happened, and if you don't listen carefully—you'll likely miss what actually transpired. It started fifteen years ago . . ."

22:17 Thursday;
British Consulate Warehouse at Canton Docks

Lightning cascaded across the copper dome of the rooftop. An energetic maelstrom, from the thirty-foot-tall Tesla coil shielded in a massive Faraday cage and the thunderstorm overhead ejecting its rage across the city of Guangzhou, made the very air sizzle and hum.

Outside the cage, Hummingbird fought for purchase along the slippery roof, his clockwork arm dangling, wrecked and useless, barely attached to the acupressure plates on his chest and back. One of the tradeoffs of being five foot two and less than a hundred and thirty pounds was being quick, not solid. He looked around warily; most of his enemies seemed dead. All but one, in fact.

One.

His foot slipped, dropping him to one knee, an actinic glare and ozone smell presaging a crackling doom. He leapt wildly as a lightning bolt tried to kill him.

Gnashing his teeth at the storm, he shouted. "Inazuma! Watch out!"

The six-foot samurai caught the warning in time to see a massive bolt of raw power rip through the sky and arc off the coil's cage toward him. Inazuma threw himself forward, instinctively protecting the young crying girl by his side, and buried his katana into the copper roof on the far side of the small ventilation platform she huddled on. Heaven's cruel arc struck home. Ina formed a perfect shield—and circuit—around the girl, protecting her from the deadly voltage.

He was far less fortunate. Bright light struck the katana, traveling to the copper roof and up the sword to Inazuma's hand. The samurai was thrown, lifeless, across the dome, slipping down the side and plummeting to the street so far below. Hummingbird watched, frozen in disbelief. Rage threatened to overwhelm him as he crawled forward to the limp form of another of his companions.

He crouched over the man and slapped his face furiously. The thin, well-dressed man didn't move. "Dammit, Tesla. Wake up! Fix this, you bastard! You promised the storm would power the Key with no problems and then we could get it the hell out of here!"

Hummingbird's ministrations halted abruptly as a blade emerged from his chest, blood quickly washed away by the storm. He looked down. *What?*

A man spoke behind him. "She is mine, little American," he said in a thick Russian accent. "Dosveydanya."

Hummingbird looked to the eleven-year-old crying on the platform. "I'm . . . sorry . . ." he said, fighting a losing battle to not collapse atop the senseless Tesla.

As he fell forward, his vision blurred, but he saw the girl stand up and throw her arms wide. Energy arced off the coil, met by a bolt from the sky, and the girl vanished in a blinding light as the Faraday cage exploded.

Time slowed down for Hummingbird, raindrops creeping to a halt as they tried to fall to the roof. The tableau was frozen, Tesla just inches below him, gears flying from the explosion all frozen in amber, suspended in midair.

Hummingbird blinked, pulling his pistol in the space of that motion, and spun, pulling the trigger. The scraggly Russian impaler's hand erupted and his blade went spinning into the night. Hummingbird finished his fall onto Tesla, pistol falling from his fingers, and closed his eyes.

09:32 Thursday; Guangzhou Central Constabulary

"I say, old chap, been in the wars?" Biggleton snapped his fingers, the sharp noise bringing Hummingbird back to the conversation.

"Sorry, what?" The small man, a gunfighter from the American West, was normally sharp-eyed and inquisitive. He had been drifting off, watching something in his own mind.

Biggleton frowned. "Winston here will be accompanying you on the mission." He waved his hand toward the dark-haired young man lounging in the corner, maybe twenty, but already wearing the regalia of a second lieutenant. He was a stark contrast to Biggleton, who sported an unruly mop of blond hair atop his pale, thin frame. He seemed almost frail, especially against the hale and muscular, if baby-faced, Churchill. The officer's ruddy cheeks and unfocused gaze bespoke, however, of someone already in his cups. "Forgive his demeanor, he is one of our bravest. He is familiar with the delicate nature of the transport. Isn't that so, Second Lieutenant Churchill?"

Winston made a wry face. "Delicate indeed, sir. Yes, I am more than familiar with the Key."

Hummingbird shook his head, trying to dislodge the scraps of vision. "So, the goal here is to transport this Key across the city? That's it?" His western drawl, obviously from the States, isolated him as the only one of the four present who was not from Britain. "Why don't you mili'try boys take care of it?" he added. "We usually work bounties for the Chinamen, not mili'try transports."

Inazuma pulled his hands from the sleeves of his kimono, placing a placating palm on Hummingbird's back. The large man was generally unflappable, but Hummingbird could feel his hand shaking, at which point he realized Inazuma had shared the same vision.

The samurai interjected, "What my colleague is trying to say, albeit in a highly uncouth fashion, is that we have a highly specialized skill set. Normally Constable Baojia hires us to catch the more slippery criminals, ones that evade capture by physical strength alone. In short, we specialize in tracking and manipulation of the mind, not in guarding or force of arms."

Biggleton nodded. "I understand. I am not military either. Scientist, in fact. Regrettably, our fine lads in uniform have failed to get the Key to the appointed destination. I asked the provincial government of Canton to recommend alternatives based on a need for sharpness of wit, rather than strength of muscle. I was shown your rather remarkable track record. Combining that with the fact that your adopted father is an ambassador for Her Majesty, Mister Inazuma, you two were the natural pick." He smiled wanly and arched an eyebrow. "The Key must be moved safely. More than you can ever know depends upon this."

Hummingbird and Inazuma looked at each other, their thoughts echoing in unison. *"He said* must, *and that means more money."*

Inazuma spoke up. "We can handle it, but I have three questions. If you aren't military, who are you? And what is so important about this Key?"

Biggleton replied with a well-practiced speech. "I have been charged by the Crown to oversee the Ministry of Extraordinary Weapons. The Key is one of these weapons. What the Key is ties directly to the reason we have failed to move it to the high-voltage laboratory. As amazing as it may sound, we believe the Key to be a device of ancient design which can alter time by predicting outcomes. Every time we attempt to complete the mission, our forces die, and then they wake up the previous morning remembering having died the next day. It's frankly giving me a headache reading the reports."

He paused for a second, framing his next words carefully as he shifted in his chair. "The Key was activated by accident twenty-four hours ago by the Russian scientist Nikola Tesla. He was working with a group of savant children, trying to unlock the Key's secrets. Unfortunately, he brought the Key too close to one of his brilliant coils and the electricity being emitted activated it before we could run tests. Too many of the other powers in this world are on the verge of technological superiority. We cannot allow the Key into their hands. What I have told you is only the tip of the iceberg, gentlemen, but it is all I can offer. The Crown needs you."

Hummingbird shrugged. "Inazuma?"

The samurai thought for a moment, then nodded. "We accept the assignment."

"Excellent!" Biggleton slid a folder across his desk, motioning for the two bounty hunters to take it. "Here are the accounts of the soldiers who have failed; I hope they will help you learn your enemy. As I said you have young Winston's help, he will take you to the Key now. Godspeed and best of luck, gentlemen."

Hummingbird and Inazuma, accompanied by Churchill, left the constable's office. The sun shone down brightly over the bustling streets of Canton. Hummingbird looked to the horizon, scanning for coming storm clouds, while the three negotiated the busy foot traffic. The skies couldn't be clearer.

Inazuma flipped through the folder while Winston flagged down a rickshaw, all three men brooding in their own thoughts. They piled into the cart, giving the driver directions to their destination well across town in the martial district. The driver cranked the engine lever, triggered the gear assembly, and began jogging in place on the rickshaw's treadmill. The gear assembly was far more efficient than a bicycle, and the rickshaw quickly moved off. They rode in silence to the bounce of the street's uneven cobblestones.

Hummingbird broke the silence first by asking, "Y'all have visions?"

"Indeed I did," Churchill replied. "Most days, I manage the rather remarkable feat of sobriety in the face of idiocy until the sun is at least starting to dip below the horizon. Before the sun goes down, I must live the life of an officer, befitting my rank. Not today, though. Not today." He held up a finger, pulled a flask out of his pocket and took a deep swig. "After what I've seen, I fear that while I will wake up starkly sober tomorrow, the world shall still be quite insane."

Both of the bounty hunters chuckled, warming up to the young man. The three conversed over the course of the ride across Canton. Hummingbird's western drawl stood out next to the proper British tones of Churchill and Inazuma.

The trip took forty minutes, and by the time they arrived the three were engrossed in a deep conversation. The building they pulled up in front of was more of a complex housing a dojo. Gray ten-foot walls, topped by red clay shingling, flanked a pair of massive oak doors. The doors currently stood open to the public, and students could be seen practicing the movements of their forms in the courtyard. Churchill paid the rickshaw operator and the three walked into the dojo.

Carefully skirting the courtyard so as to not interrupt the students, the trio spoke quietly amongst themselves, while a chorus of *hai*s echoed from the students with each punch and kick. Winston led them to the back of the dojo. As the back room door opened all three stumbled, and their vision went white. As one, they collapsed.

21:43 Thursday, British Consulate Warehouse at Canton Docks

Rain poured down, a waterfall from heaven like the tears of Quan Yin. In front of a warehouse, along the city's docks, a dozen dead Wuyi fighters lay in the streets intermixed with equally lifeless Kazakh warriors. A rickshaw, its motorized treadmill torn apart and gears scattered across the cobblestones, stood at the center of the tableau. The rain washed blood past the feet of the survivors, who were squared off in combat against each other.

Inazuma and Hummingbird crouched back to back, surrounded by the ring of burly Russians. Lightning flashed across the sky, a web of light ripping through the darkness.

Hummingbird grinned, gripping his twin Colt Peacemakers tightly. "Ina, they only sent twelve of them. Apparently they haven't heard of us."

Inazuma shifted his right foot slightly forward, letting

the blade of his katana dip. "It does seem slightly unfair to them."

The Russians, bearded, wrapped in fur to a man, made space in their ranks. A giant stepped through the gap. The man was almost two meters tall, with a long, scraggly beard and hair: the glint of madness in his eyes. The collar of a priest's cassock poked up from below his furs.

"What have we here?" The man spoke with a heavy Russian accent. "Two little men who oppose the will of God? Stand aside. Let us have the Key and you shall be spared."

Hummingbird rotated slightly to his left, bringing one of his Colts to bear on the giant. He recognized the madness in the man's eyes, the madness of a zealot. "Who the hell are you, big fella?"

"My name is Grigori Rasputin, the prophet of God. Now stand aside, little man." The Russian pulled two swords, barely larger than knives in his meaty hands, from under his fur-lined coat.

Hummingbird nudged Inazuma's calf with his heel. "Looks like the big guy is yours. I'll get the rest." He sprang forward, slipping under the first man's arm. "Come on y'all, time to play." Hummingbird thrust the butt of his pistol upward, slamming the Russian's chin with a meaty *thunk*.

As the storm raged overhead, Hummingbird sped up, dispatching attackers with ease. He was small, but deadly. Arguably the fastest gunslinger in the West, he had also mastered the Eastern arts because of his clockwork arm. It was a high-end Cantonese-designed arm relying on over fourteen hundred acupuncture needles, each with a steel thread running into the arm and joint assemblies, layered perfectly to mimic human muscle fibers. The needles in his torso were protected by a steel plate covering both his chest and his back. Gaining proficiency with the arm had required years of Tai Chi training, making the small man a deadly hand-to-hand opponent.

He spun through the larger Russian group, using their force against them, never even pulling the triggers of his Colts. Burly men went cartwheeling through the air every time they touched the small tornado that was Hummingbird.

Inazuma's fight was not so quick or clean. As Hummingbird intercepted his opponents, Inazuma locked blades with Rasputin. The young Russian titan whirled his two blades in front of him, daring the samurai to attack. Inazuma saw the implied invitation and accepted.

Sliding his left foot forward to a dominant position, Inazuma struck. He thrust his katana forward at the two swords, forcing Rasputin to cross them in defense. With a quick roll of the wrist, Inazuma twisted the katana past Rasputin's blades, cutting deeply into the knuckles of the mad monk's left hand.

The mad Russian let out a terrific basso roar and launched himself forward. Dropping the blade from his bleeding hand, he grabbed at the katana and slapped it aside, smashing the pommel of his sword knife down on Inazuma's left arm with a sickening crunch.

Inazuma kicked Rasputin's knee and backed up. Hummingbird dashed between the two men, a tiny blur, headed to intercept the Russians on the other side of their fight. The left sleeve of Inazuma's kimono was torn open, exposing wrecked gears beneath a dented exoskeletal framework that lay over his skin. The kimono had hidden the whole rig perfectly.

The samurai grinned, taunting his opponent. "Something I picked up in the Philippines. The assembly boosts strength and speed, using counter pressures. Doesn't even need an engine. It'll take an hour to fix. So, how's your hand feeling, Grigori?"

Rain matted Rasputin's hair and beard to his face. "Little man. You're Japanese, but speak British. Either way, you are a tea-drinking woman" He charged, answered in kind by Inazuma.

Luck saved Inazuma. Hummingbird charged by the two last standing Kazakhs, ducked the grasp of one, caught the punch thrown by the other, and spun him through the air directly at Rasputin. The Kazakh collided with the wild-eyed zealot, and both fell to the ground. Rasputin swore, a deluge of Russian cursing, and struggled to get his heavy henchman untangled and off him.

The bounty hunters glanced at each other, then back to the ruined rickshaw. Inazuma nodded once while sheathing his blade. Hummingbird holstered his pistols and called out. "Mister Tesla, y'all can come out now." He ran to the building and hammered on the door. "You ready, Winston?"

The second lieutenant poked his head out of the warehouse door. "My word. I guess you really didn't need me helping out here. Come along, everything is ready. Did you manage to switch the blades?"

Hummingbird patted both of Rasputin's blades, tucked into his belt. "Yup. I'm so small, he never even saw me. He has the replacements."

Churchill nodded, then beckoned to the two frightened people in the rickshaw's remains.

The passengers exited the ruined vehicle. A rail-thin mustached man chaperoned a young Cantonese girl of eleven, wearing a pink-and-white outfit with her hair done up in pigtails. Both ran to the building.

The man spoke with a mild Eastern European accent. "You are sure this is safe?"

Inazuma watched the sky, silently counting, leaving Hummingbird to answer. "As sure as we can be. Every other way . . . let's just leave it at 'this is the best chance we have.'"

Tesla nodded, putting his arm around the scared child. "On your word then." They quickly walked over to the open door of the warehouse, Churchill ushering them inside.

Inazuma said ten aloud as a bolt of lightning ripped the sky in half. "That was it. Come on, Hummingbird, let's get to the roof."

The smaller man nodded, and joined his friend in the doorway. As they vanished inside, several more Russians approached. Grigori's cavalry had arrived. They all gathered around the groggy Rasputin as he sat up, rubbing his head. He pointed at the building. "*Vnutri.*"

They helped him up and charged the building.

11:47 Thursday, Shoa Dojo, Guangzhou

Hummingbird leaned by the room's doorway, thumb hooked behind his belt in a casual way, positioning his hand near his pistol. There was no danger nearby, but he liked to be careful, and everyone else was engrossed in watching his partner and the child.

Inazuma held the young girl by the hand, crouching down so he could look her in the eye. She tried to retreat behind her own pigtails, bashfully looking up at the imposing, but friendly samurai.

He patted her hand. "*Nĭ hăo.* Do you speak English, little one?"

The girl nodded.

"Well, good! You are very smart, aren't you?"

The girl nodded again.

"Good. You are going to be safe now. My name is Mister Inazuma and this is my friend Mister Hummingbird. We are here to protect you." He touched her cheek gently, then released her hand and stood up. As he turned to face his comrades, the girl lunged forward to hug Inazuma's waist.

"Thank you, Mister Inazuma. You're the best." Her effusive words surprised him, but he hugged her back. Orphaned himself until he was ten, there was a bond between the two.

He warmly patted her back. "You go have a snack. We are going to work out a plan, okay?"

The girl, Qi, nodded seriously. Turning on her heel, she marched out of the room toward the dojo's kitchens. She stopped on the way out, turning around to look to Inazuma. "The necklace showed me, Mister Inazuma. You are the only one who can save me, so I trust you."

Inazuma watched her leave as Hummingbird spoke up. "Okay, fellas. I think it's time y'all explained things a bit for us. Let's start with you, mister scientist." He could see Inazuma's mind working, and he knew his partner well enough to know what was troubling him. The tall samurai wouldn't want to turn the kid over to a life of being studied by a government. Inazuma's sword was hard but his heart was soft.

A thin man, seated a few paces to the left of the wall Winston leaned against, nodded solemnly. The scientist sported an extremely well-groomed moustache and was dressed in a conservative suit, his accent faintly redolent of the sounds of his Serbian homeland. "It is a complex tale, scientifically, though simple in execution. I was experimenting with one of my coils, attempting to see if I could solve a logic problem I discovered. A series of interlocked logic . . . gates, I suppose you could call them. The series would take the inputs and use it to make decisions."

Hummingbird held up a hand. "Now, forgive me here, Mister Tesla?" he drawled thickly, "but what all is a logic gate?"

The scientist nodded. "In this case it is a . . . gate composed of two inputs and one output, which, by virtue of the units, is a binary logic system."

"A what . . . ?" asked Hummingbird. He knew he was hearing English words, but it sounded like Greek to his ears.

"Two units!" Churchill answered, ever quick of wit. "A system of two units, like yes or no."

"On or off, true or false, one or zero," added Tesla. "The logic gate will output one of those two binary units, depending on which combination of the two binary units is fed into each input."

He held up a medallion. It was round, about five inches in diameter, and layered in its design. At a casual glance, it seemed to house a dozen moving pieces arranged in various layers.

Tesla twisted one of the layers, showing off the leveled rotations of the device. "This medallion is a curious artifact unlike anything I have seen in modern science. This is like the logic gate of the gods! With over two hundred settings per layer, it is capable of changing in, quite literally, billions of different ways, if properly activated."

Churchill scoffed. "Proper. Yes, and by a long chalk, too."

The other three, all understanding the second lieutenant's frustration, let him be. Inazuma, still holding back his opinions, asked. "How is it properly activated?"

Tesla nodded to himself again. "It requires two things. One was a known factor, which is Qi. She is a savant, a mathematical mind capable of calculations greater even than those I can solve. Those calculations power this medallion. However, without the second activator, she accomplishes nothing, which is why most thought the legend of the Key was a myth. That is where I come into this tale. Electricity is the second ingredient. It was only when the Key, and Qi, were brought into the presence of one of my coils that the medallion was activated."

Churchill took a swig off his flask again, staring off toward the kitchens, and then offered it to Hummingbird. He shrugged and accepted it. Taking a sip, he asked Tesla. "Okay. Truth time. We've all been having weird visions. What, exactly, happens when you activate it?"

Tesla shifted uncomfortably in his seat. "That is a question worth asking. Mark this occasion well, gentlemen, for you will rarely hear these words from me." Churchill chuffed as the scientist went on. "I do not know. What is happening should not be physically possible, yet it is happening, which leads me to believe it is simply beyond the scope of my current understanding. I believe that it is some form of travel to the future by the conscious mind, as evidenced by the echoes we have been seeing."

Inazuma scowled. "Echoes?"

"Yes." Tesla confirmed. "Echoes. I know not why we are seeing them, but it is the best word to describe it. An echo of another time, not too distant. A time in which we all die."

The four men sat quietly, each mulling over his own vision.

It was Hummingbird that broke the silence. "Things aren't always what they seem to be, Mister Tesla. Allow my colleague and I to confer, and I think we might have a solution which allows for Qi, as well as the rest of us, to survive."

Churchill sighed. "All well and good gentlemen, but it seems a shame to save the child only to sentence her to a life of being studied in a lab." He stared at Tesla. Hummingbird noticed Inazuma smiling slightly at the officer's sentiment.

The scientist raised his hands. "I study the medallion, sir, not the child. Please do not take offense with me. The alternative, the Russian zealots, would be far worse for her."

Inazuma coughed quietly. "Winston. I may be able to give everyone what they need. Including Qi."

The soldier's back stiffened. "Now, hold on there . . ."

Inazuma looked Churchill in the eye. "Let's get the job done first, then we can discuss the rest. We will not endanger the mission, you have my word."

Winston nodded, mollified.

Nikola looked between the three of them. He thought for a moment then carefully spoke. "I believe that I can work on the medallion while you three sort out the physical side of this. Perhaps if I designed a machine which could calculate the computations for me . . ." He stood, walking toward the side door. "I need to grab my sketchbooks. I shall be back in an hour, after compiling my thoughts."

The remaining three gathered to plan.

22:19 Thursday,
British Consulate Warehouse at Canton Docks

Grigori rubbed his eyes, careful of his badly wounded hands, trying to clear the temporary blindness of the lightning flash. Finally, he looked around. The American and the Japanese bounty hunters were both dead, and Tesla was either unconscious or dead.

Either way, it didn't matter. The scientist had never been important to him. The Key was gone, along with the child, both destroyed by the lightning strike. He shook his soaked hair out of his eyes, then worked his way across the slippery rooftop.

The storm had started to clear with the final lightning strike, almost as though it had been building up to a precise moment and now, spent, it was slinking away into the night. Grigori bent down near the impact site and found what he was seeking. Shards of the medallion littered the area near the Tesla Coil. He gathered them up. Useless though the shards were, he wouldn't risk his enemies gathering them.

Staring at the shards in his palm he shook his head. "Such a waste. Perhaps they will make good mementos for my men." He shoved them into a pocket of his fur-lined coat.

Surveying the silent rooftop one last time, he walked back to the entrance shaft and started to lower himself down. "*Boze moj*," he sighed, "The Almighty has shown me this moment in a vision. Had you but listened to the true seer, you might have lived. May God have mercy on your souls." With that, he climbed back down into the building.

For several minutes, nothing moved on the rooftop. Once the sound of Rasputin taking leave floated away, Tesla pushed Hummingbird's still form off his chest. "I can't believe that worked."

Hummingbird shifted, a quiet laugh escaping his lips as he also sat up. "Tell me about it. That was crazy." He fumbled with his shirt, only able to use his left hand, until he was able to pull off the rig attached to his chest. The clunky assembly fell out from under his jacket to the rooftop, the fake blade popping back out with another squirt of pig's blood. Several gears rolled off the spent contraption, runaways from the spectacular effect the trick had produced.

Tesla helped him up then walked to the edge of the roof, fiddling with something tied there. Once he was done releasing the rope ladder hidden on the side of the roof, he walked over to the platform. Glancing back, he saw Hummingbird, one handed, helping Inazuma up the ladder back onto the roof. The scientist smiled then kicked the platform, producing a hollow sounding clunk. The platform popped up, revealing Winston, protectively curled around Qi under the trap door. He looked up. "It worked then."

Tesla nodded. "It did. Even the fake medallion pieces I crafted."

Winston unfolded himself and the two crawled out of the small secret compartment. "Well done, chaps. Well done. Now let's get the Key to Biggleton and be quit of this mess."

"No!" The child fought against Winston's grasp and, breaking free, ran to Inazuma clinging to him tightly.

He placed his arm around her. "I'm afraid I can't let that happen, Winston."

Churchill's eyes narrowed. "I'll not let you harm the Crown. It is true that you have succeeded where we have failed, but the girl must go to Biggleton." His hand hovered over the service revolver holstered on his belt.

Hummingbird held up his hand. "We were hired ta get the Key to safety, not Qi . . . Ina isn't trying to rob you of anything, Winston. We don't need to be in conflict here. There is another way . . ."

A light went on in Churchill's eyes. "You . . . cunning men. You are absolutely right. That is exactly the letter of my orders." His hand, still hovering near his revolver, did relax a bit. "I will hear you out, at the least. What is your plan?"

03:00 Friday,
Guangzhou Central Constabulary

Biggleton stared at the pieces of the medallion on his desk. It was beautifully complex, obviously ancient, with layers upon layers of tiny wheels interlocking on the artifact's face. Even with the missing layers, it was awe inspiring. "So let me see if I understand this properly. I hired you to transport the Key, and all you bring me is the medallion; where's the girl? Isn't she needed to use the Key? Where is the rest of it? Rasputin's men have it?"

Churchill, hands grasping his own wrists behind his back while standing stiffly at attention, spoke. "It was all they could do, sir. Grigori Rasputin is a force to be reckoned with, sir. I highly recommend the Crown keeps a close eye on him, sir. Bloody miracle we made it out alive." Winston watched the wall behind Biggleton's head. "The exact orders were to transport the Key, which is the medallion, sir, which Tesla called a probability matrix. And Tesla thinks he can eventually get it working without the child, sir. He says even with the missing pieces, it's just a matter of numbers."

Inazuma leaned forward, supporting his weight on the edge of the desk, looking their employer dead in the eye. "You have the Key. Exactly as you asked. Should the Crown ever have dire need of it, I am sure Tesla will rise to the occasion."

Biggleton held up his hands, placating the room. "I'm just trying to get the facts clear here. Now, you used the term probability matrix. Please explain."

Churchill launched into the explanation Tesla had given them as to the Key's true purpose. "It isn't a device to move to the future at all, sir. Rather, it's some sort of complex calculating machine that can sort out what might happen in the future. In fact, what most likely will happen. It is rather limited, however, in that it only delivers visions of those futures which lead to making sure it doesn't get destroyed, sir."

Biggleton nodded, thinking. "And how exactly does it do that? The delivery of visions?"

Churchill continued to stare at the wall, parroting what Tesla had trained him to say. "No clue. Mister Tesla had some ideas about it. Said it linked to the electricity in the brains of those that will be present at a future in which it will be destroyed in order to avoid it. Said that the gearing system is just like the engine on an airship for lifting the bladder, only smaller than we could craft it. Said it is a miracle of invention, sir."

Biggleton thought for a moment. He knew he was getting the runaround. He also had an artifact that was extremely powerful, yet extremely limited. He made his decision. "And you are sure that there is no way on this Earth that the medallion can be reactivated now that the little girl was incinerated in the lightning strike?"

Churchill nodded briskly. "Correct, sir. Not until Mister Tesla comes up with a new way to make machines that make decisions."

Biggleton slid the medallion into a parcel and jotted the name Herbert on it. "Back to the isles with this and off with you then. I have a report to write. Gentlemen, you will find Constable Baojia is holding your pay come morning. The job has been serviceably done, if not precisely in the fashion I had in mind. A good day to you both. You too, Winston. I'll favor you in my report, and perhaps you can get that posting to the Khyber Pass you have been requesting."

12:15 Friday,
streets of Guangzhou

Inazuma had left his partner at the clockwork engineer. His arm was getting repaired, which would eat up his days for the next week. This wasn't the first time the arm had been destroyed. Both men knew the drill.

Ina whistled softly to himself as he strolled down the street, carefully watching to make sure he wasn't followed. His destination was a small house located on a side street off of one of the nicer districts on the edge of Canton. He knocked on the door.

Churchill answered. The officer smiled. "She loves it here! Such a great choice. But where are my manners? Come in, come in!"

Inazuma followed him to a small courtyard.

Qi was sitting in the courtyard, playing with a little boy a couple years younger than her, being watched fondly by Constable Baojia and his wife Ling. Baojia spied Inazuma and walked over to him, openly smiling. The men hugged and Baojia clapped Inazuma on the shoulder. "Seven years, we have made do, knowing we could never have a second child. Then you and Hummingbird bring this miracle into our lives. Forever I will be indebted to you, my friend."

Inazuma nodded once, returning his friend's smile.

Qi looked around, spying them talking, and clapped in delight. She got up and ran to Inazuma, throwing herself into a hug from him. "Thank you, Uncle Ina. I knew you were the one who would find me a family! The Key did, too. Thank you so much! Here! The Key wanted me to give these to you to help you and Mister Hummingbird!" She held up several folded slips of paper, still hugging him with her other arm.

Inazuma took the papers then hugged her back, and he smiled to himself. As far as he was concerned, Biggleton had hired him to deliver Qi to safety, and that was just what he had done.

Yuma, Arizona; The New West. Tuesday midday.

Qi scanned the room as she finished the story. The room applauded, appreciating the tall tale she had shared, and several people signaled the barkeep to get her a drink on them. She lifted the shot glass with her left hand but paused with the drink at her lips.

Her eye lit upon a bearded man, wrapped in furs despite the desert climate. He dwarfed everyone else in the room. The man noticed Qi watching him and stood, reaching for the two pistols under his thick jacket.

Qi drew a pistol in the space of a blink, pulling the trigger a single time. She was almost as fast as Hummingbird. One of the burly Russian's pistols flew out of his hand and he bellowed in pain as Qi's bullet found its home. Before he could react and draw the second pistol she darted forward, jumping on the table between them scattering chips and cards.

"So sorry," she apologized as the stunned poker players watched her dart through their game.

The Russian grabbed the table he was at with his good hand and jerked it up, lobbing the whole thing at her. Qi dropped to her ass on the edge of the poker game bouncing off the table and rolling under the second, airborne, piece of furniture. She popped up inside his guard, still somehow holding the unspilled shot of whiskey upright, with her pistol in the other hand. Flashing a pearly white smile she tossed the drink in his eyes. "Hi there, big fella!"

"You little . . ." The burly giant pawed at his eyes with his bad hand while pulling his second pistol with his good. Qi hooked her Colt under the trigger guard of his shooter and spun to the side while pushing up. His gun fired harmlessly into the ceiling.

He pulled his hand back trying to line up another shot. Qi slid her Colt along the barrel of his pistol then jabbed her other hand over her own arm, locking the empty shot glass between his hammer and firing pin.

Hopping back she pulled the trigger twice and shot him in each foot.

The giant went down howling in pain. As his scream quieted into sobs, she bent over the downed Russian and jerked a cord from around his neck.

"I am so sorry about the damages, sir." Pocketing the tiny gear attached to the necklace, she glanced back to the room at large. Qi patted her pockets and pulled out a folded piece of paper. She unfolded a wanted poster and held it up to show the saloon keeper. "If you get the sheriff, you'll find he has a reward on him. Please accept that to repair your establishment."

The bartender furrowed his brow, reading the name. "Dim . . . Dim-eye-tr-eye. Whatever. He's one of that Rasputin's men? And you ain't gonna kill him?"

Qi blinked in surprise. "Well, no. He may be a murderer who tried to kill me and my godparents, but I was taught better than that. I have what I need from him, and I don't needlessly hurt people."

Her tale told, she winked at the room then walked out of the saloon. The barkeep wasn't done with his questions though. Did she know where the legendary gunfighter Hummingbird was? Why was the Russian here in Yuma? Was the Key thing going to start working again? He leapt over the counter and ran out to the street to ask her to continue her story, but the street was empty of all but a lone tumbleweed drifting lazily through the afternoon sun.

He shook his head and muttered to himself. As he stepped back in from the street he rang a steel triangle to summon the sheriff. It was time to get back to business and this was Yuma, after all—tomorrow there would be a new mysterious stranger, a new tale, and a new glass of whiskey.

A FISTFUL OF WARLOCKS

Jim Butcher

The American West was not the most miserable land I had ever traveled, but it came quite near to it. It was the scenery, more than anything, that drove the spirit out of the body—endless, empty plains that did not so much roll as slump with varying degrees of hopelessness, with barely a proper tree to be seen. The late summer sun beat the ground into something like the bottom of an oven.

"I grow weary of Kansas," said my not-horse. "The rivers here are scarcely enough to keep me alive."

"Hush, Karl," I said to the *näcken*. "We are near to town, and to the warlock. I would prefer if we did not announce our presence."

The *näcken* sighed with a great, exaggerated motion that set the saddle to creaking, and stomped one hoof on the ground. With a pure white coat and standing at a lean and powerful seventeen hands, he made a magnificent mount—as fast as the swiftest mortal horse and far more tireless. "As you wish, Anastasia."

"Warden Luccio," I reprimanded him tartly. "And the

sooner we catch this creature and his master, the sooner you will have served your probation, and the sooner you may return to your homeland."

The *näcken* flattened his ears at this reminder of his servitude.

"Do not you become angry with me," I told him. "You promised to serve as my loyal mount if I could ride you for the space of an hour without being thrown. It is hardly my fault if you assumed I could not survive such a ride under the surface of the water."

"Hmph," said the *näcken*, and he gave me an evil glare. "Wizards." But he subsided. Murderous monsters, the *näcken*, but they were good to their word.

It was then that we crested what could only quite generously be called a "rise" and I found myself staring down at a long shallow valley that positively swarmed with life. Powdery dust covered the entire thing in a vast cloud, revealing a hive of tarred wooden buildings that looked as if they'd been slapped together over the course of an evening by drunken teamsters. Then there was a set of gleaming railroad tracks, used so often that they shone even through the dust. Upon the northern side of the tracks stood a whitewashed mirror image of those buildings, neat streets and rows of solidly built homes and businesses. Corrals that could have girdled the feet of some mountains were filled with a small sea of cattle, being herded and driven by men that could scarcely be distinguished from their horses beneath their mutual coating of dust. To one side of the town, a lonely little hill was crowned with a small collection of grave markers.

And the people. The sheer number of people bustling

about this gathering of buildings in the middle of nothing was enough to boggle the mind. I sat for a moment, stunned at the energetic enormity of the place that looked like some obscure passage from Dante, perhaps a circle of hell that had been edited from the original text.

The warlock I pursued could take full advantage of a crowd like that, making my job many times more difficult than it had been a moment before.

"So," said the *näcken*, sourly. "That is Dodge City."

The warlock would hide in the rough part of town—his kind could rarely find sanctuary amongst stolid, sober townsfolk. The unease they created around them, combined with the frequent occurrence of the bizarre as a result of their talents made them stand out like mounds of manure in a field of flowers. But the same talents that made them pariahs in normal mortal society benefited them in its shadows.

I rode for the south side of the tracks and stopped at the first sizeable building.

"Do not allow yourself to be stolen," I advised Karl as I dismounted.

The *näcken* flattened his ears and snorted.

I smiled at him, patted his neck, and tossed his reins over a post and beam set up for the purpose outside of the first building that looked likely to support human beings in better condition than vermin. I removed the light duster that had done as best as it could to protect my dress from the elements, draped it neatly over the saddle, and belted on my sword and gun.

I went into the building, and found it to be a

bathhouse and brothel. A few moments of conversation with the woman in charge of it resulted in a job offer, which I declined politely, a bath, which I could not enjoy nearly thoroughly enough to satisfy me, and directions to the seediest dens of ruffians in town.

The warlock wasn't in the first location, or the second, but by the time I reached the Long Branch Dance Hall and Saloon near sundown, I was fairly sure I'd found my man.

I entered the place to the sound of only moderately rhythmic stomping as a dozen women performed something like a dance together on a wooden stage, to the music of several nimble-fingered violinists playing in the style of folk music. The bar was already beginning to fill with a crowd of raucous men. Some of them were freshly bathed, but more were still wearing more dust than cloth, their purses heavy with new coin.

But more importantly, the air of the place practically thrummed with tension. It was hardly noticeable at first glance—but eyes glanced toward the doors a little too quickly when I came in, and at least half of the men in the place were standing far too stiffly and warily to be drunkenly celebrating their payday and their lives.

"Pardon me, ma'am," said a voice to my right as I came in.

I turned to find a very tall, lean fellow whose wrists stuck out from the bottom of his coat's sleeves. He had a thick, drooping moustache, a flat-brimmed hat, a deputy's star pinned to his coat, and wore his gun as if it had been given to him upon the occasion of his birth.

His demeanor was calm, his voice polite and

friendly—and he had the eyes of a raptor, sharp and clear and ready to deliver sudden violence at a moment's notice.

"Yes?" I asked.

"City ordinance against carrying sidearms, ma'am," he said. His voice was deep and musically resonant in his lean chest. I liked it immediately. "If you're not a peace officer, you'll need to turn in your gun for as long as you're in town."

"I find this ordinance irksome," I said.

The corners of his eyes wrinkled and his cheeks tightened slightly. The moustache made it difficult to see his mouth. "If I was a woman as good looking as you in a place like this, I'd find it powerful irksome too," he said, "but the law is the law."

"And what does the ordinance say about swords?" I asked.

"Can't recall that it says anything 'bout that," the deputy said.

I unfastened my belt and slid the gun from it, still in its holster. I offered it to him. "I assume I can turn it over to you, Deputy?"

He touched the brim of his hat, and took the gun. "Thank you, ma'am. Might I know your name so I can be sure your weapon gets safe back to you?"

I smiled at him. "Anastasia Luccio."

"Charmed, Anastasia," said the deputy. He squinted at my sidearm and said, "Webley. Lot of gun."

He was not so very much taller than me. I arched an eyebrow at him and smiled. "I am a lot of woman. I assure you, Deputy, that I am more than capable of handling it."

His eyes glinted, relaxed and amused. "Well. People say a lot of things, ma'am."

"When my business here is done, perhaps we shall go outside the town limits and wager twenty dollars on which of us is the better marksman."

He let his head fall back and barked out a quick laugh. "Ma'am, losing that bet would be a singular pleasure."

I looked around the saloon again. "It seems that tensions are running high at the moment," I said. "Might I ask why that is?"

The lawman pursed his lips thoughtfully, and then said, "Well, there's some fellas on one side of the tracks upset at some other fellas on the other, ma'am, is the short of it." He smiled as he said it, as if enjoying some private jest. "Shouldn't be of much concern to you, ma'am. This is a rough place, but we don't much take kindly to a man who'd lift his hand to a woman." A pair of cowboys entered the saloon, laughing loudly and clearly already drunk. His calm eyes tracked them. He slid my holstered gun around beneath his stool and touched his finger to the brim of his hat again. "You have a good time now."

"Thank you, Deputy," I said. Then I walked to the exact center of the room.

As a Warden of the White Council of Wizards, I traveled a great deal, and dealt with dangerous men. I was comfortable in places like this one, and worse, though I had noted that they rarely seemed to be comfortable with me. The only women in sight were those working behind the bar, in the kitchen, and on the stage, so I rather stuck out. There was little sense in attempting anything like subtlety, so I donned my little bottle-green spectacles, focused upon my supernatural senses and began a slow survey of the entire place.

The energy known as magic exists on a broad spectrum, much like light. Just as light can be split into its colors by a sufficient prism, magical energy can be more clearly distinguished by using the proper tools. The spectacles gave me a chance to view the energy swirling around the crowded room. It was strongly influenced by the presence of human emotion, and various colors had gathered around individuals according to their current humor.

Angry red tension tinted many auras, while lighter shades of pink surrounded the more merrily inebriated. Workers, including the dancers and dealers at the tables evinced a steady green of those focused on task, while the deputy and a shotgun-wielding man seated on a tall stool at the end of the bar pulsed with the steady, protective azure of guardians.

The warlock sat in the little balcony overlooking the stage, at a table with three other men, playing cards. Through the spectacles, shadows had gathered so thickly over their game that it almost seemed they had doused their lanterns and were playing in the dark.

I drew a breath. One warlock was typically not a threat to a cautious, well-trained, and properly equipped Warden. Two could be a serious challenge. The current Captain of the Wardens, a man named McCoy, a man with a great deal more power and experience than me, had once brought down three.

But as I watched through the spectacles I realized that the warlock hadn't simply been running. He'd been running to more of his kind.

There were four of them.

I took off the spectacles and moved into an open space at the bar, where I would hopefully be overlooked for a few moments longer and thought furiously.

My options had just become much more limited. In a direct confrontation with that many opponents, I would have little chance of victory. Which was not to say that I could not attack them. They were involved in their card game, and I had seen no evidence of magical defenses. An overwhelming strike might take them all at once.

Of course, fire magic was the only thing that would do for that kind of work—and it would leave the crowded building aflame. Tarred wood exposed to a blast of supernatural fire would become an inferno in seconds. Not only that, but such an action would violate one of the Council's unspoken laws—wizards were expected to minimize the use of their abilities in the presence of magic-ignorant mortals. It had not been so long since our kind had been burned at stakes by frightened mobs.

While I could not simply attack them, neither could I remain here, waiting. A warlock would have fewer compunctions about exposing his abilities in public. The wisest option would have been to report in to the captain, send for reinforcements, veil myself, and follow them.

I had never been a particularly cautious person. Even the extended life of a wizard was too brief a time, and the world full of too much pleasure and joy to waste that life by hiding safely away.

I was not, however, stupid.

I turned to begin walking decisively toward the door and practically slammed my nose into that of a handsome man in his midforties, beard neatly shaved, dressed in an impeccable suit. His eyes were green and hard, his teeth far too white for his age.

And he was pressing a tiny derringer pistol to my chest, just beneath my left breast.

"Timely," he said to me, in a fine German accent. "We knew a Warden would arrive, but we thought you would be another week at least."

"I don't know what you're talking about," I said.

"Please," he said, his eyes shading over with something ugly. "If you attempt to resist me, I will kill you here and now." He moved smoothly, stepping beside me and tucking my left arm into the crook of his right, positioning the tiny gun in his left hand atop my arm, keeping it artfully concealed while trained steadily on my heart. He nodded once at the balcony, and the four men in it immediately put their cards down and descended, heading out the door without so much as glancing back.

"You're making a mistake," I said to him tightly. "To my knowledge, you and your companions are not wanted by the Council. I'm not here for you today. I've only come for Alexander Page."

"Is that a fact?" he asked.

"He is a murderer. By sheltering him, you have become complicit in his crimes," I said. "If you kill me, you will only draw down the full wrath of the Wardens. But if you let me go immediately and disassociate yourself from Page, I will not prosecute a warrant for your capture."

"That is most generous, Warden," said the German. "But I am afraid I have plans. You will accompany me quietly outside."

"And if I do not?"

"Then I will be mildly disappointed, and you will be dead."

"You'll be more than disappointed when my death curse falls upon you," I said.

"Should you live long enough to level it, perhaps," he said. "But I am willing to take that risk."

I flicked my eyes around the room, looking for options, but they seemed few. The fellow in the high stool had his eyes on a man dealing cards at a nearby table. The cowboys were far more interested in drinking and making merry than in what, to them, must have appeared to be a domestic squabble between a wife come to drag her husband from a den of iniquity. Even the deputy at the door was gone, his chair standing empty.

Ah.

I turned to the German and said, "Very well. Let us take this discussion elsewhere."

"I do not think you realize your position, Warden," the German said, as we began walking. "I am not asking for your consent. I am merely informing you of your options."

I flinched slightly at the words and let the fear I was feeling show on my face. "What do you mean to do with me?" I asked.

"Nothing good," he said, and his eyes glinted with something manic and hungry. Then he frowned, noticing that his last words had fallen into a silence absent of music or stomping feat.

Into that silence came what seemed like a singularly significant mechanical click.

"Mister," the lanky deputy said. "You pass over that belly gun, or your next hat is going to be a couple of sizes smaller."

The deputy had moved in silently behind him, and now held his revolver less than a foot from the back of the German's skull.

I let the fear drop off my face and smiled sweetly up at my captor.

The German froze, his eyes suddenly hot with rage as he realized that I had distracted him, just as his fellows had distracted me. The derringer pressed harder against my ribs as he turned his head slightly toward the deputy. "Do you have any idea who I am?"

"Mmmm," the deputy said calmly. "You're the fella who's about to come quietly or have lead on his mind."

The German narrowed his eyes, and ground his teeth.

"He's not asking for your consent," I said. "He's merely informing you of your options."

The German spat an oath in his native tongue. Then he slipped the little pistol away from my side and slowly held it up.

The deputy took the weapon, his own gun steady.

"You will regret this action," said the German. "Who do you think you are?"

"My name is Wyatt Earp," said the deputy. "And I think I'm the law."

Earp took the German to the town marshal's office, which was on the southern side of the tracks and contained a pair of iron jail cells. I led Karl along and the *näcken* was mercifully well behaved for once, playing the role of a horse to perfection when I tied him to the post outside the office.

"Deputy," I said, as we entered the building. "I do not think you understand the threat."

Earp passed me his lantern and nodded toward a hanging hook on the wall. I put it there, as he walked the German into the cell, gun steady on the man all the while. He made the man lean against a wall with both hands, and patted him down for weaponry, removing a small knife— and calmly taking a charm hanging from a leather necklace around his neck.

"What?" he said calmly. "On account of he's a sorcerer? Is that what you mean?"

I felt both of my eyebrows lift. Typically, and increasingly, authority figures had very little truck with the world of the supernatural.

"Yes," I said. "That is precisely what I mean."

Earp walked over to me and held out the necklace, and its simple, round copper charm. A familiar symbol was carved onto its surface—a skull, twisted and horrifically stretched, marked upon its forehead with a single slanted, asymmetric cross.

"Thule Society," I murmured.

"Hngh," he said, as if my recognition of the symbol confirmed his suspicions rather than surprising him. "Guess that makes you White Council."

I tilted my head at him. "A Warden. Goodness, you are well informed. I must ask, how do you know of the Council, sir?"

"Venator," he said simply. "Lost my necklace in a card game. You can take it or leave it that I'm telling the truth."

The Venatori Umbrorum were a secret society of their own, steeped in the occult, quietly working against supernatural forces that threatened humanity. They boasted a few modestly gifted practitioners, but had a great many members, which translated to a great many eyes and ears. The society was a long-time ally, more or less, of the White Council—just as the Thule Society was more or less a long-time foe, using their resources to attempt to use supernatural powers to their own benefit.

I regarded Earp thoughtfully. It was, I suppose, possible that he could be in league with the German, playing some sort of deceitful game. But it seemed improbable. Had he and the German wanted me dead, Earp could simply have watched him walk me out without taking note of it.

"I believe you," I told him, simply.

"That cell's warded," Earp said. "From the inside, he's not going to be doing much." He glanced over at the German and gave him a cold smile. "Makes a lot of noise if you try, though. Figure I'll shoot you five or six times before you get done whipping up enough magic to hurt anybody."

The German stared at Earp through narrowed eyes and then abruptly smiled and appeared to relax. He unbuttoned his collar, removed his tie, and sat down on the cell's lumpy bunk.

"Nnnngh," Earp said, a look of mild disgust on his face. He squinted around the room at the building's windows. Then he looked back at me and said, "Warden, huh. You're a lawm—" He pursed his lips. "You carry a badge."

"Something like that," I said.

"What I mean to say is, you can fight," Earp said.

"I can fight," I said.

He leaned his lanky body back against the wall beside the desk and tilted his chin toward the German. "What do you think?"

"I think he has four friends," I said. "All of them gifted. Do your windows have shutters?"

"Yep."

"Then we should shutter them," I said. "They will come for him."

"Damn," he drawled. "That's what I think, too. Before dawn?"

The hours of darkness were the best time for amateurs to practice the dark arts, for both practical and purely psychological reasons. "Almost certainly."

"What do you think about that?"

I narrowed my eyes and said, "I object."

Earp nodded his head and said, "Only so much I can do about someone bringing spells at me. Can you fight that?"

"I can."

Earp studied me for a moment, those dark eyes assessing. Then he seemed to come to a decision. "How about I'll put up the shutters," he said. "Unless you'd rather me make the coffee, which I don't recommend."

I shuddered at the American notion of coffee. "I'll do that part," I said.

"Good," he said. "We got ourselves a plan."

"Well," Earp said a few hours later. "I don't much care for all the waiting. But this is some damned fine coffee, Miss Anastasia."

I had, of course, used magic to help it. The beans had not been properly roasted, and the grinder they had been through had been considerably too coarse in its work. Some other Wardens thought my coffee-making spells to be a frivolous waste of time in the face of all the darkness in the world—but what good is magic if it cannot be used to make a delicious cup of fine beverage?

"Just be glad you did not ask me to cook," I said. "It is not one of my gifts."

Earp huffed out a breath through his nose. "You ain't got much femaleness to you, ma'am, if you pardon my saying so."

I smiled at him sweetly. "I'm on the job at the moment."

He grunted. "That Page fella you mentioned?"

I nodded.

"What's he wanted for?"

"He murdered three people in Liverpool," I said. "A girl he favored, and her parents."

"Guess she didn't favor him back," Earp said. "He shoot 'em?"

I shook my head and suppressed a shudder at the memory of the crime scene. "He ripped out their eyes and tongues," I said. "While they lay blind and bleeding, he did other things."

Earp's eyes flickered. "I've seen the type before." He glanced at the German.

The German sat in exactly the same place he'd settled hours before. The man had his eyes closed—but he smiled faintly, as if aware of Earp's gaze on him.

Earp turned back to me. "What happens to Mister Page when you catch him?"

"He will be fairly tried, and then, I expect, beheaded for his crimes."

Earp examined the fingernails of his right hand. "A real fair trial?"

"The evidence against him is damning," I said. "But fair enough."

Earp lowered his hand again. It fell very naturally to the grip of his gun. "I'd never want me one of those, if I could avoid it," he said.

I knew what he meant. There were times I didn't care for the sorts of things it had been necessary to do to deal with various monsters, human or otherwise. I expect Earp had faced his own terrors, and the dirty labor required to remove them.

Such deeds left their weight behind.

"I wouldn't care for one myself," I said.

He nodded, and we both sipped coffee for a while. Then he said, "Once this is wrapped up, I think I'd like to buy you a nice dinner. When you aren't on the job."

I found myself smiling at that.

I was an attractive woman, which was simply a statement of truth and not one of ego. I dressed well, kept myself well, and frequently had the attention of men and women who wished to keep my company. That had been a source of great enjoyment and amusement when I was younger, though these days I had little patience for it.

But Earp was interesting, and there was a tremendous appeal in his lean, soft-spoken confidence.

"Perhaps," I said. "If business allows for it."

Earp seemed pleased and sipped his coffee.

★ ★ ★

The town had gone black and silent, even the saloons, as the night stretched to the quiet, cool hours of darkness and stillness that came before the first hint of dawn.

The witching hour.

We both heard the footsteps approaching the front door of the marshal's office. Earp had belted on a second revolver, had a third within easy reach on the desk, and rose from his chair to take up a shotgun in his hands, its barrels cut down to less than a foot long.

My own weapons were just as ready, if less easily observable than Earp's. I'd marked a quick circle in chalk on the floor, ready to be imbued with energy as a bulwark against hostile magic. The sword at my side was tingling with power I'd invested in it over the course of the evening, ready to slice apart the threads binding enemy spells together, and I held ready a shield in my mind to prevent attacks upon my thoughts and emotions.

And, of course, I had a hand upon my revolver. Magic is well and good, but bullets are often swifter.

The footsteps stopped just outside the door. And then there was a polite knock.

Earp's face twisted with distaste. He crossed to the door, and opened a tiny speaking window in it, without actually showing himself to whoever was outside. In addition, he leveled the shotgun at the door, approximately at the midsection of whomever would be standing outside.

"Evening," Earp said.

"Good evening," said a man's voice from outside. This accent was British, quite well-to-do, its tenor pleasant. "Might I speak with Mister Wyatt Earp, please?"

"Speaking," Earp drawled.

"Mister Earp," the Briton said. "I have come to make you a proposal that will avoid any unpleasantness in the immediate future. Are you willing to hear me out?"

Earp looked at me.

I shrugged. On the one hand, it was always worth exploring ways not to fight. On the other, I had no confidence that a member of the Thule Society would negotiate in good faith. In fact, I took a few steps back toward the rear of the building, so that I might hear something if this was some sort of attempt at a distraction.

Earp nodded his approval.

"Tell you what," he said to the Briton. "I'm going to stand in here and count quietly to twenty before I start pulling triggers. You say something interesting before then, could be we can make medicine."

There was a baffled second's silence, and the Briton said, "How quickly are you counting?"

"I done started," Earp said. "And you ain't doing yourself any favors right now."

The Briton hesitated an instant more before speaking in an even, if slightly rushed tone. "With respect, this is not a fight you can win, Mister Earp. If the Warden were not present, this conversation would not be happening. Her presence means we may have to contend with you to get what we want, rather than simply taking it—but it would surely garner a great deal of attention of the sort which her kind prefer to avoid, as well as placing countless innocents in danger."

As the man spoke, Earp listened intently, adjusting the aim of his shotgun by a few precise degrees.

"To avoid this outcome, you will release our companion unharmed. We will depart Dodge City immediately. You and the Warden will remain within the marshal's office until dawn. As an additional incentive, we will arrange for the new ordinances against your friend Mister Short's establishment to be struck from the city's legal code."

At that, Earp grunted.

I lifted an eyebrow at him. He held up a hand and gave his head a slight shake that asked me to wait until later.

"Well, Mister Earp?" asked the Briton. "Can we, as you so pithily put it, make medicine?"

Something hard flickered in Earp's eyes. He glanced at me.

I drew my revolver.

That action engendered a grin big enough to show some of his teeth, even through the moustache. He lifted his head and said, "Eighteen. Nineteen . . ."

The Briton spoke in a hard voice, meant to be menacing, though it was somewhat undermined by the way he hurried away from the door. "Decide in the next half an hour. You will have no second chance."

I waited a moment before arching an eyebrow at Earp. "I take it these terms he offered were good ones?"

Earp lowered and uncocked the shotgun, and squinted thoughtfully. "Well. Maybe and maybe not. But they sound pretty good, and I reckon that's what he was trying for."

"What was he offering, precisely?"

"Bill Short went and got himself into some trouble

with the folks north of the tracks. They want to clean up Dodge City. Make it all respectable. Which, I figure, ain't a bad thing all by itself. They got kids to think about. Well, Bill's partner run for mayor and lost. Fella that won passed some laws against Bill's place, arrested some of his girls, that kind of thing. Bill objected, and some shooting got done, but nobody died or anything. Then a mob rounded up Bill and some other folks the proper folk figured was rapscallions and ran them out of town."

"I see," I said. "How do you come into this?"

"Well, Bill got himself a train to Kansas City, and he rounded up some friends. Me, Bat, Doc, a few others."

I glanced at the lean man and his casually worn guns. "Men like you?"

"Well," Earp said, and a quiet smile flickered at the edges of his moustache. "I'd not care to cross them over a matter of nothing, if you take my meaning, Miss Anastasia."

"I do."

"So, we been coming into town to talk things over with this mayor without a mob deciding how things should go," Earp continued. "Little at a time, so as not to make too much noise." He opened the peephole in the office door and squinted out of it. "Got myself redeputized so I can go heeled. Been over at the Long Branch with Bat."

"The saloon the mayor passed a law against?"

"Well it ain't like it's a state law," Earp said. "More of a misunderstandin'. See, as much as the good folks north of the tracks don't want to admit it, cattle and these cowboys are what keeps this town alive. And those boys don't want to come in at the end of a three-month trail ride and have a nice bath and a cup of tea. Kind of country they're going through can be a little tough. So they drop their money here, blowing off steam." He rubbed at his moustache. "Hell, sin is the currency around this place. Don't take a genius to see that. Those good folk are going to righteous themselves right out of a home." He sighed. "Dammit, Doc. Why ain't you here yet?"

"Friend of yours?" I asked.

"Holliday," Earp confirmed. "Good fella to have with you when it's rough. Plus he's got two of them Venator pendants around his neck. Took one from some fool in a faro game."

"I need to know," I said, "if you mean to take the Thule Society's offer seriously."

"Can't do that, Miss Anastasia," Earp said. "They're only offering me something I can get for myself just as well."

I found myself smiling at that. "You're willing to challenge an entire town to a fight? For the sake of your friend's saloon?"

"It ain't the saloon, ma'am," Earp drawled. "It's the principle of the thing. Man can't let himself get run out of town by a mob, or pretty soon everyone will be doing it."

"If a mob is responsible," I said, smiling, "is not something close to everyone already doing it?"

Earp's eyes wrinkled at that, and he tapped the brim of his cap.

"Idiot," said the German from the cell, contempt in his voice.

"Sometimes," Earp allowed. He shut the peephole

and said, "Those Thule bastards ain't going to wait half an hour. Snakes like that will come early."

"I agree," I said. "But going out shooting seems an unlikely plan."

"Can't disagree," Earp said. "Course, maybe it's just a man's pride talkin', but it seems like it ain't much of an idea for them to try to come in here, either."

It was then that the drum began beating, a slow steady cadence in the darkness.

I felt my breath catch.

The German smiled.

Earp looked at me sharply and asked, "What's that mean?"

"Trouble," I said. I shot a hard glance at the German. "We've made a mistake."

The German's smile widened. His eyes closed beatifically.

"Who are you?" I demanded.

He said nothing.

"What the hell is going on?" Earp said, not in an unpleasant tone.

"This man is no mere member of the Thule Society," I said. I turned my attention toward the outside of the jailhouse, where I could already feel dark, cold, slithering energy beginning to gather. "We are dealing with necromancers. They're calling out the dead. Is there a cemetery nearby?"

"Yep," Earp said. "Boot Hill."

"Deputy," I said. "We need to plan."

"Shoot," Earp said a quarter of an hour later, staring

out the peephole. "I didn't much like these fellas the first time I shot them." He had added another revolver to his belt, and had traded in his shotgun for a repeating rifle. "And time ain't been kind. I make it over thirty."

I stepped up next to Earp and stood on my tiptoes to peer out the peephole. We had dimmed the lights to almost nothing, and there was just enough moon to let me see grim, silent figures limping and shambling down the street toward the jailhouse. They were corpses, mostly gone to bone and gruesome scraps of leathery skin with occasional patches of stringy, brittle hair.

"There's some more, coming up on that side," Earp said. "Forty. Maybe forty-five."

"Properly used, a dozen would be enough to kill us both," I said to him. I took a brief chance, and opened my third eye, examining the flow of energies around the oncoming horrors. "We are fortunate. These are not fully realized undead. Whoever called them up is not yet an adept at doing so. These things are scarcely more than constructs—merely deadly and mostly invulnerable."

He eyed me obliquely. "Miss Anastasia, that ain't what a reasonable man would call comfortin'."

I felt my lips compress into a smile. "After a certain point, the numbers hardly matter. The drum beats for their hearts—it both controls the constructs and animates them. Stop that, and we stop them all, even if there were a thousand."

"And until then?"

"Until then, aim for the head. That should disrupt the spell controlling them."

Earp looked over his shoulder at the German. The

man looked considerably less smug or comfortable than he had throughout the evening. At my direction, Earp had hogtied him to one of the wooden pillars supporting the roof and gagged him thoroughly. I had chalked a circle of power around him and infused it with enough energy to prevent him from reaching outside of it for any magical power. They were crude precautions, but we could not afford to give the German an opportunity to strike at us while we were distracted. Such measures would hinder any particularly dangerous attack—and would not stop Earp's bullet from finding the German's skull should he attempt anything that was not instantly lethal.

I stepped back from the window, closed my eyes, and invoked the communication spell I had established with the *näcken*.

Karl, I murmured, with my thoughts, *Are you ready?*

Obviously, the *näcken* replied.

Have you located the Thule Society?

There was an amused tint to the dark faerie's reply. *On the roof of a building three doors down and across the street. They seem to think that they have warded themselves from sight.*

Excellent, I replied. *Then we will begin shortly.*

Four warlocks, Karl mused. *You realize that your death releases me from our contract?*

I ground my teeth without replying. Then I cocked my revolver, turned to Earp, and nodded.

"Seems like a bad hand, Miss Anastasia," Earp said. "But let's play it out."

And with no more fanfare than that, Wyatt Earp

calmly opened the door to the jailhouse, raised his rifle to his shoulder, and walked out shooting, and I went out behind him.

Earp was a professional. He did not shoot rapidly. He lined the rifle's sights upon the nearest shambling figure and dropped a heavy round through its skull. Before the corpse's knees began to buckle, he had ejected the shell and taken aim at the next nearest. That shot bellowed out, and as the sound of it faded, the crowd of corpses let out a terrifying wave of dry, dusty howls and began launching themselves forward in a frenzied lurch.

I raised my Webley, took aim, and dropped a corpse of my own—though in the time it took me to do it, Earp had felled three more without ever seeming to rush.

"Karl!" I screamed.

There was a thunder of hooves striking the earthen street and the enormous white horse appeared like a specter out of the night. The *näcken* simply ran down half a dozen corpses, shouldered two more out of the way, and kicked another in the chest with such force that it flew backward across the street and exploded into a cloud of spinning, shattered bone.

I swung up onto the *näcken's* back, as summer lightning flickered and showed me the dead moving forward like an inevitable tide. Two more of the things reached for me, bony fingers clawing. I kicked one away, shot the other through the skull with the Webley, and then Karl surged forward.

I shot a glance back over one shoulder to see Earp grip the emptied rifle's barrel and smash a corpse's skull with the stock. That bought him enough time to back toward the jailhouse door, drawing a revolver into each hand. Shots began to ring out in steady, metronomic time.

"To the roof!" I snarled to the *näcken*.

And the dark fae let go of his disguise.

White horseflesh swelled and split as it darkened to a sickly, drowned blue-gray. A hideous stench filled the air, and the *näcken*'s body bloated to nearly impossible dimensions. The smell of fetid water and rotten meat rose up from Karl's body in a smothering miasma, and with a surge of power that threatened to throw me from his back entirely, despite the saddle, the *näcken* leapt from the street to the balcony of a nearby building, bounding to the lower roof of the building next to it, then reversed direction and flung itself onto the roof of the original.

The Thule Society awaited us.

The roof was a flat space, and not overly large. Much of it had been filled with a painted pentacle, the points of its star lapping outside of the binding circle around it—a symbol of chaos and entropy, unbounded by the circle of will and restraint. That same cold and horrible energy I'd felt earlier shuddered thick in the air. Torches burned green at each point of the star—and at the center knelt my quarry, the warlock Alexander Page, a plump, lemon-faced young man, beating steady time on a drum that looked like something of Indian manufacture.

The Briton and the other two Thules stood in a protective triangle around Page, outside the circle. The Briton's eyes widened as the savage *näcken* landed on the roof, shaking the boards beneath everyone's feet with his weight and power.

"Kill the Warden!" the Briton shouted.

He flung out his hand, and a greenish flicker of lightning lashed across the space between us. I stood ready to parry the spell, but it was poorly aimed and flew well wide of me—though it struck Karl along his rear legs.

The *näcken* bucked in agony and screamed in rage. I flew clear, barely controlling my dismount enough to land on the building rather than being flung to the street below. I landed on my feet and rolled to one side, avoiding a cloud of evil-looking spiders marked with a red hourglass, which one of the other Thule sorcerers summoned and flung at me.

I regained my feet and shot twice at him with the Webley—but the first shot was hurried, and the second wavered off course as the third Thule sorcerer called something like a small violet comet out of nowhere and sent it screaming toward my head. I lifted my left hand in a defensive gesture, shouting the word of a warding spell, and the thing shattered against an invisible barrier a foot from my head, exploding into white-hot shards that went hissing in every direction.

Page took one of them in the arm and let out a small shriek of startled agony, dropping the drumstick he held in his hand.

"No!" shrieked the Briton. "The Master is all that matters! Keep the beat!"

Page, his face twisted in agony, reached for the drumstick and resumed the rhythm—just as the *näcken* thundered furiously toward Page.

The three on their feet rushed to interpose themselves—even as the *näcken* crashed into the mordant power of the evil circle they'd infused, as helpless to cross into it as any fae would be.

But in the time it took them to realize that, I had caught my breath and my balance, aimed the Webley, and sent several ounces of lead thundering through the chest and, a heartbeat later, through the skull of the second Thule sorcerer.

Page screamed in terror. The third Thule spun to me and sent multiple comets shrieking toward me, howling curses with each throw. I discarded the emptied revolver and drew my blade. The enchanted silversteel shone brightly even in the dimness of the night, and with several swift cuts I sliced through the energies holding the attack spells together, disrupting them and changing them from dangerous explosives into exploding, dissipating clouds of violet sparks of light.

The Briton, meanwhile, dove out of the circle, spoke a thundering word of power, and sent Karl flying back through the air like a kicked kitten. The *näcken* screamed furiously and vanished into the darkness.

I had no time. I surged forward, striking down one deadly comet after another, and with a long lunge, rammed my slender blade into the third Thule's mouth.

The blade bit deep, back through the palette and into the skull, and I could suddenly feel the man writhing and spasming through my grip on the sword, a sensation oddly like that of a fish hooking itself to an angler's line. I twisted the blade and ripped it back in a swirling S-motion, and as it came free of the sorcerer's mouth it was followed by a fountain of gore.

I whirled, raising a shield with my left hand, and barely

intercepted another strike of sickly green lightning. It exploded into a glowing cobweb pattern just in front of my outstretched hand, little streaks leaping out to scorch and burn the roof, starting half a dozen tiny fires.

"Grevane!" screamed Page.

"Drum!" thundered the Briton, even as he raised his hands above his head, his face twisting into a rictus.

And as swiftly as that, I heard the dry, clicking, rasping sound of the dead beginning to scale the building toward us.

Terror filled me. My allies were gone, and I was outnumbered two to one, even before one counted the coming terrors. Further, I'd felt the power of Grevane the Briton's strike firsthand—and the man was no half-trained warlock, or even a senior sorcerer of the Thule Society. Strength like his could only come from one place.

He was a Wizard of the White Council.

And then, swift on the heels of my fear came another emotion. Rage, pure and undiluted, rage that this man, this *creature*, would spurn his responsibility to humanity and distort the power that created the universe itself into something so obscene, so foul.

He was a *warlock*. A traitor.

I flicked my sword into my left hand, then hurled my right hand forward, and a bolt of searing fire no thicker than my pinky finger lashed out at him, blinding in the night. Grevane parried the blow on a shield of his own, and countered with more lightning. I caught part of it on the sword, but what got through was enough to drive me down to one knee and send agony racing back and forth through my nerve endings.

Even as I fought through the pain, I saw movement in the corner of my eye—the dead, swarming up the building and beginning to haul themselves onto the roof. In seconds, they would tear me apart.

I gritted my teeth, staggered back to my feet and rushed forward, sword leading the way.

Grevane gathered more power, but held his strike until the last second, as I closed on him—and then he bellowed something and smashed down at the roof beneath us with pure kinetic energy, opening an enormous gap just in front of me.

I dove to one side, a bound as light and graceful as any I had ever made, rolled, and felt the horrible, tingling, invasive presence of necromantic energy course over me as I crossed into their summoning circle—and drove my blade straight out to one side and into the heart of Alexander Page.

The warlock let out a short, croaking gasp. The drumstick fell from his suddenly nerveless hands—and, seconds later, silence reigned, marred only by the dry clatter of bones falling two stories down to the streets of Dodge City.

I stared at Grevane, crouched, as Page quivered on my sword. My left hand was lifted, a shield of pale blue energy already glowing, ready for the necromancer's next attack.

But instead, Grevane tilted his head to one side, his eyes distant. He smiled faintly. Then, without a further word, he simply stepped backward and fell over the edge of the building, dropping silently into the darkness below.

I ripped the sword free of Page and sprinted to follow

him—but by the time I got to the edge and looked down, I saw nothing. Nothing at all, but bones in an empty street.

I was so focused on Grevane that I didn't sense the attack coming at my back until it was nearly too late to survive it.

Pain, simple *pain,* suddenly fell upon me as if my entire body had suddenly been thrust into a raging fire. I let out a strangled scream, my back arching, and fought to simply keep from plummeting from the roof myself.

"Bitch," Page panted. He staggered across the roof, one hand desperately trying to stem a steady pulse of blood from what would be, in a few moments, a fatal wound. "Warden bitch. *Dolor igni!*"

Pain wiped everything else from my mind for the space of several seconds. By the time I could see again, I was sprawled back over the edge of the roof, about to fall, and a deathly pale Page stood over me, holding my own sword to my throat.

"You've killed me, bitch," he gasped. "But I won't go to hell alone."

I tried to thrash aside, to push the blade, but my body simply did not respond to me. Pure, frenzied, helpless terror, the kind I had previously only known in terrible dreams of running through quicksand, surged through me.

Page let out a frenzied little giggle and leaned on the sword.

And with a crack of thunder, his head snapped back, into a cloud of misty gore. My sword fell from his fingers, and his body dropped limply down onto his legs, collapsing into an awkward pile.

I turned my head slowly.

Wyatt Earp stood on the street below, a trail of nearly headless dis-animated corpses strewn behind him, along with all but the last of the revolvers he'd been carrying.

He lowered the gun, and touched a finger to the brim of his hat in solemn salute.

"You sure you can't stay, Miss Anastasia?" Earp asked.

I shook my head. Karl, now back in his disguise, stamped an angry hoof onto the dirt of Dodge City's streets as I loaded his saddlebags with fresh supplies. "I'm afraid I can't. Not with those two still out there."

Earp grunted. "I never seen someone so determined to skin himself out of some ropes," he said. "Who was that German?"

I felt my mouth twist with distaste, even as a sour taste of fear touched my tongue. "If our information at the White Council is accurate, his name is Kemmler," I said. "That Briton was one of his apprentices, Grevane."

"Bad men?"

"Some of the most dangerous alive," I said. "I have to get onto their trail while I still can."

He nodded. "I hear you. Shame about that dinner, though."

I winked down at him and said, "Perhaps another time."

He smiled and tipped his hat slightly. Then he offered me his hand.

I shook it.

"Ma'am," he said. "Think maybe I'd have won that twenty dollars off you."

Instead of answering him, I opened my purse, fished out a golden coin and flicked it to him. He caught it, grinning openly. "Have a drink for me, Deputy."

"Think maybe I'll do that," he said. "Good hunting."

"Thank you," I said.

Karl and I headed out of town as the sun began to rise.

"I'm tired," the *näcken* said.

"As am I, Karl," I replied.

"Kemmler," said the *näcken* contemptuously. "You only found him to spite me. To keep me in this horrible place."

"Do not be tiresome," I sighed. I checked the little leather medicine bag dangling from a thong. Earp had been quite right about Kemmler skinning out of ropes with which he'd been bound. The man had left enough skin behind for me to lock onto him with a tracking spell. The bag swung back and forth gently in the direction the greatest necromancer in the history of man had gone. "We only do our duty."

"Duty," Karl said, disgusted. "I hate this land."

"I am not overly fond of it myself," I replied. "Come. Pick up the pace."

Karl broke into a weary jog, and I settled my hat more firmly over my head. The sun began to rise behind us, golden and warm, as we traveled deeper into the West.

BIOGRAPHIES

David Boop—Editor

David Boop is a Denver-based speculative fiction author. He's also an award-winning essayist, and screenwriter. Before turning to fiction, David worked as a DJ, film critic, journalist, and actor. As Editor-in-Chief at *IntraDenver.net*, David's team was on the ground at Columbine making them the first *internet only* newspaper to cover such an event. That year, they won an award for excellence from the Colorado Press Association for their design and coverage.

His debut novel, the sci-fi/noir *She Murdered Me with Science*, is back in print from WordFire Press after a six-year hiatus. Additionally, Dave is prolific in short fiction with over fifty short stories and two short films sold to date. While known for the weird Western series *The Drowned Horse Chronicle*, he's published across several genres including horror, fantasy, and media tie-ins for *The Green Hornet*, *The Black Bat* and *Veronica Mars*. His RPG work includes *Interface Zero*, *Rippers Resurrected* and *Deadlands: Noir* for *Savage Worlds*. David regularly tours the country speaking on writing and publishing at schools, libraries and conventions.

He's a single dad, Summa Cum Laude creative writing graduate, part-time temp worker and believer. His hobbies include film noir, anime, the blues and Mayan history. You can find out more on his fanpage, www.facebook.com/dboop.updates or Twitter @david_boop.

Larry Correia

Larry Correia is the *New York Times* bestselling and award-winning author of the Monster Hunter International series, the Grimnoir Chronicles trilogy, the Dead Six military thrillers, and the epic fantasy series Saga of the Forgotten Warrior.

Jody Lynn Nye

Jody Lynn Nye lists her main career activity as "spoiling cats." When not engaged upon this worthy occupation, she writes fantasy and science fiction books and short stories.

Since 1987 she has published over 45 books and more than 150 short stories, including epic fantasies, contemporary humorous fantasy, and humorous military science fiction, and has edited three anthologies. She collaborated with Anne McCaffrey on a number of books, including the *New York Times* bestseller, *Crisis on Doona*. She also wrote eight books with Robert Asprin, and continues both of Asprin's Myth-Adventures series and Dragons series. Her newest series is the Lord Thomas Kinago adventures, the most recent of which is *Rhythm of the Imperium* (Baen Books), a humorous military SF novel.

Her other recent books are *Myth-Quoted* (Ace Books); *Wishing on a Star* (Arc Manor Press); an e-collection of cat stories, *Cats Triumphant* (Event Horizon); *Dragons Run* (fourth in the Dragons series); and *Launch Pad*, an anthology of science fiction stories coedited with Mike Brotherton (WordFire). Jody runs the two-day intensive writers' workshop at DragonCon, and she and her husband, Bill Fawcett, are the book reviewers for *Galaxy's Edge* magazine.

Sam Knight

A Colorado native, Sam Knight spent ten years in California's wine country before returning to the Rockies. When asked if he misses California, he gets a wistful look in his eyes and replies he misses the green mountains in the winter, but he is glad to be back home.

As well as being Distribution Manager for WordFire Press, he is Senior Editor for Villainous Press and the author of four children's books, three short story collections, two novels, and more than two dozen short stories, including two media tie-ins coauthored with Kevin J. Anderson.

A stay-at-home father, Sam attempts to be a full-time writer, but there are only so many hours left in a day after kids. Once upon a time, he was known to quote books the way some people quote movies, but now he claims having a family has made him forgetful, as a survival adaptation. He can be found at SamKnight.com and contacted at Sam@samknight.com.

Robert E. Vardeman

Robert E. Vardeman is the author of almost a hundred published f&sf novels and scores of short stories. He has written extensively in the Western genre, including many weird Westerns, under the pen name Jackson Lowry. Most recently published is Punished, a weird Western novel trilogy: *Undead, Navajo Witches*, and *Bayou Voodoo*. His work has been nominated for the Scribe Award, Western Fictioneers Peacemaker Award and for numerous NM/AZ Book Awards. In addition to his writing, he has edited anthologies such as Baen Books–published *Golden Reflections* (with Joan Saberhagen) and *Career Guide to Your Job in Hell* (with Scott Phillips). He holds a BS in physics and an MS in materials engineering and worked in solid state physics research at Sandia National Laboratories. He resides in Albuquerque and enjoys the high-tech hobby of geocaching.

Phil Foglio

Phil Foglio is known primarily as a cartoonist, which explains an awful lot about his writing style—as well as his fashion sense, home décor, and the personal interactions he has with his remaining friends.

With his wife, Kaja, he is the cocreator of the multiple Hugo Award–winning webcomic: *Girl Genius* (www.girlgeniusonline.com). He has lived on three of America's four coasts, and is beginning to suspect that he might be addicted to water.

Nicole Givens Kurtz

Nicole Givens Kurtz is the published author of the futuristic thriller series, Cybil Lewis, and she's more than a little bit *weird*. Her novels have been named as finalists in the Fresh Voices in Science Fiction, EPPIE in Science Fiction, and Dream Realm Awards in science fiction.

Nicole's short stories have earned an Honorable Mention in L. Ron Hubbard's Writers of the Future contest, and have appeared in numerous anthologies and other publications.

Michael A. Stackpole

Michael A. Stackpole is the multiple *New York Times* bestselling author of over forty fantasy and science fiction novels, his best known books written in the Star Wars universe, including *I, Jedi* and *Rogue Squadron*, as well as the *X-Wing* graphic novel series. He has also written in the Conan, Pathfinder, BattleTech and World of Warcraft universes, among others.

Currently the Virginia G. Piper Center for Creative Writing at Arizona State University Distinguished Writer-in-Residence, Stackpole's other honors include: Induction into the Academy Gaming Arts and Design Hall of Fame, a Parsec Award for "Best Podcast Short Story," and a Topps's selection as Best Star Wars Comic Book Writer. Stackpole is the first author to sell work in Apple's App Store, and he's been an advocate for authors taking advantage of the digital revolution.

Bryan Thomas Schmidt

Bryan Thomas Schmidt is an author and Hugo-nominated editor of adult and children's speculative fiction. His debut novel, *The Worker Prince* received Honorable Mention on Barnes & Noble Book Club's Year's Best Science Fiction Releases. His short stories have appeared in magazines, anthologies and online and include entries in The X-Files, Predator, and Decipher's WARS, amongst others. As book editor for Kevin J. Anderson and Rebecca Moesta's WordFire Press he edited books by such luminaries as Alan Dean Foster, Tracy Hickman, Frank Herbert, Mike Resnick, Jean Rabe and more. He was also the first editor on Andy Weir's bestseller *The Martian*. His anthologies as editor include *Shattered Shields* with coeditor Jennifer Brozek, *Mission: Tomorrow*, *Galactic Games* and *Little Green Men—Attack!*, all for Baen; as well as *Space Battles: Full Throttle Space Tales #6*, *Beyond the Sun* and *Raygun Chronicles: Space Opera for a New Age*. He is also coediting anthologies with Larry Correia and Jonathan Maberry set in their *New York Times* bestselling Monster Hunter and Joe Ledger universes.

Find him online via his website at www.bryanthomasschmidt.net or as BryanThomasS on both Facebook and Twitter.

Ken Scholes

Ken Scholes is the award-winning, critically acclaimed author of five novels and over fifty short stories. His work has appeared in print for over sixteen years. His series, The Psalms of Isaak, is published by Tor Books and his collected short fiction has been released in three volumes by Fairwood Press.

Ken's eclectic background includes time spent as a label gun repairman, a sailor who never sailed, a soldier who commanded a desk, a preacher (he got better), a nonprofit executive, a musician and a government procurement analyst. He has a degree in History from Western Washington University.

Ken is a native of the Pacific Northwest and makes his

home in Saint Helens, Oregon, where he lives with his twin daughters. You can learn more about Ken by visiting www.kenscholes.com.

Maurice Broaddus

Maurice Broaddus is the author of *Buffalo Soldier* as well as the *Knights of Breton Court* urban fantasy trilogy: *King Maker*, *King's Justice*, and *King's War*. His fiction has been published in numerous magazines and anthologies, including *Asimov's Science Fiction*, *Lightspeed* magazine, *Cemetery Dance*, *Apex Magazine*, and *Weird Tales* magazine. Some of his stories are collected in *The Voices of the Martyrs*. He coedited *Streets of Shadows* and the Dark Faith anthology series.

You can keep up with him at his web site, www.MauriceBroaddus.com.

Sarah A. Hoyt

Sarah A. Hoyt was born (and raised) in Portugal and now lives in Colorado with her husband, two sons, and a variable number of cats, depending on how many show up to beg at the door.

In between lays the sort of resume that used to be de rigueur for writers. She has never actually wrestled alligators, but she did at one point very briefly tie bows on bags of potpourri for a living. She has also washed dishes and ironed clothes for a living. Worst of all she was, for a long time, a multilingual scientific translator.

At some point, though, she got tired of making an honest living and started writing. She has over twenty-three—the number keeps changing—published novels, in science fiction, fantasy, mystery, historical mystery, historical fantasy and historical biography. Her short stories have been published in *Analog*, *Asimov's Science Fiction*, *Amazing Stories* (under a previous management), *Weird Tales*, and a number of anthologies from DAW and Baen. Her space-opera novel *Darkship Thieves* was the 2011 Prometheus Award Winner, and the third novel in the series, *A Few Good Men*, was a finalist for the honor.

She also writes under the names Sarah D'Almeida, Elise Hyatt and Sarah Marques.

Alan Dean Foster

Born in New York City in 1946, Foster was raised in Los Angeles. After receiving a Bachelor's Degree in Political Science and a Master of Fine Arts in Cinema from UCLA (1968, 1969) he spent two years as a copywriter for a small Studio City, Calif. advertising and public relations firm.

His writing career began when August Derleth bought a long Lovecraftian letter of Foster's in 1968 and, much to Foster's surprise, published it as a short story in Derleth's bi-annual magazine *The Arkham Collector*. Sales of short fiction to other magazines followed. His first attempt at a novel, *The Tar-Aiym Krang*, was bought by Betty Ballantine and published by Ballantine Books in 1972. It incorporates a number of suggestions from famed SF editor John W. Campbell.

Foster's work to date includes excursions into hard science fiction, fantasy, horror, detective, Western, historical, and contemporary fiction. He has also written numerous nonfiction articles on film, science, and scuba diving, as well as having produced the novel versions of many films, including such well-known productions as *Star Wars*, the first three *Alien* films, *Alien Nation*, *The Chronicles of Riddick*, *Star Trek*, *Terminator: Salvation*, and two of the *Transformers* films. Other works include scripts for talking records, radio, computer games, and the story for the first *Star Trek* movie. His novel *Shadowkeep* was the first ever book adaptation of an original computer game. In addition to publication in English his work has been translated into more than fifty languages and has won awards in Spain and Russia. His novel *Cyber Way* won the Southwest Book Award for Fiction in 1990, the first work of science fiction ever to do so. He is the recipient of the Faust, the IAMTW lifetime achievement award.

Besides traveling he enjoys listening to both classical music and heavy metal. Other pastimes include basketball, hiking, body surfing, and scuba diving. In his age and weight class he is a current world and Eurasian champion in powerlifting (bench press). He studied karate with Aaron and Chuck Norris before Norris decided to give up teaching for acting. He has taught screenwriting, literature, and film history at UCLA and Los Angeles City College as well as having lectured at universities and conferences around the world. A member of the Science Fiction Writers of America, the Author's Guild of America, and the Writer's Guild of America, West, he also spent two years serving on the Planning and Zoning Commission of his home town of Prescott, Arizona. Foster's correspondence and manuscripts are in the Special Collection of the Hayden Library of Arizona State University, Tempe, Arizona.

The Fosters reside in Prescott in a house built of brick salvaged from a turn-of-the-century miners' brothel, along with assorted dogs, cats, fish, several hundred houseplants, visiting javelina, porcupines, eagles, red-tailed hawks, skunks, coyotes, bobcats, and the ensorceled chair of the nefarious Dr. John Dee. He is presently at work on several new novels and media projects.

David Lee Summers

David Lee Summers is the author of ten novels along with numerous short stories and poems. His writing spans a wide range of the imaginative from science fiction to fantasy to horror. David's novels include *Vampires of the Scarlet Order*, which tells the story of a band of vampire mercenaries who fight evil, and *Owl Dance*, which is a Wild West steampunk adventure. His short stories have appeared in such magazines and anthologies as *Realms of Fantasy*, *Cemetery Dance*, and *Gaslight and Grimm*. He's been twice nominated for the Science Fiction Poetry Association's Rhysling Award. In addition to writing, David has edited such anthologies as *Maximum Velocity: The Best of the Full-Throttle Space Tales* and *A Kepler's Dozen*, along with the magazine *Tales of the Talisman*. When not working with the written word, David operates telescopes at Kitt Peak National Observatory. Learn more about David at davidleesummers.com.

Kevin J. Anderson

Kevin J. Anderson has published 144 books, 55 of which have been national or international bestsellers. He has written numerous novels in the Star Wars, X-Files, and

Dune universes, as well as unique steampunk fantasy novels *Clockwork Angels* and *Clockwork Lives*, written with legendary rock drummer Neil Peart. His original works include the Saga of Seven Suns series, the Terra Incognita fantasy trilogy, and the Saga of Shadows trilogy, but he has the most fun with his humorous horror series featuring Dan Shamble, Zombie PI, as should come across in this story. Dan Shamble has appeared in four novels and a story collection, *Working Stiff*. Anderson and his wife Rebecca Moesta are the publishers of WordFire Press.

Naomi Brett Rourke

Naomi Brett Rourke is a writer and a teacher living in Southern California. She loves the genres of crime, mystery, and horror and spending time with her beloved family and pets. Her short stories can be found in anthologies such as *Life on the Rez* by Tree-Lion Press, *Brewed Awakenings 2* by Caffeinated Press, and *Enter the Apocalypse* by TANSTAAFL Press, and in journals and magazines such as *The Mature Years* by Abingdon Press, London's *Morpheus Tales*, and the Young Adult journal *Refractions* by Golden Fleece Press. Coming out in 2017 are stories in the anthologies *Distressing Damsels* (April) by Fantasia Divinity by and *100 Voices*, *Volume 3* (April) by Centrum Press, *Straight Outta Tombstone* (July 4) by Baen Books. She is currently working on two novels and more short stories. She is a member of the Greater Los Angeles Writer's Society, Horror Writers Association, Mystery Writers of America, and Sisters in Crime. Visit her at www.naomibrettrourke.com, on Facebook at www.facebook.com/naomibrettrourke, on Twitter at NaomiBRourke, and on Instagram at @naomibrettrourke.

Peter J. Wacks

Peter J. Wacks was purportedly born in California sometime during 1976. He has always been amazed and fascinated by both writing and the absurdity of the world in general. Throughout the course of his life, he has hitchhiked across the States and backpacked across Europe on the Eurail. Peter writes a lot, and will continue to do so till the day he dies. Possibly beyond.

He is a bestselling cross-genre writer who has worked in various capacities across the creative fields in gaming, television, film, comics, and most recently, when not busy editing, he spends his time writing novels. He began in the creative fields as a child actor and model, most notably as an extra on *Revenge of the Nerds* and *Thunder Alley*. At age six he began writing short stories, and was first published in high school (1992), a time in which he was also a top ten honorable mention for the NCTE award (1993).

In gaming he was the lead designer and storyline writer of *Cyberpunk CCG*, a consultant for *Allegiance*, and both a writer and editor for multiple books in the Interface Zero line. After the Cyberpunk CCG project he spent a month in L.A. as a consultant for the TV show *Alias*, helping the studio determine the viability of converting the show into a CCG. In the mid 2000s he decided to focus on his original passion, writing stories, once more. His first novel, *Second Paradigm*, was published in 2008.

Peter's first comic, *Behind These Eyes*, garnered a

finalist spot for the Bram Stoker in 2012. Currently, he has published five novels, four novellas, and appeared in sixteen anthologies.

He has been a panelist, guest speaker, and Guest of Honor at a combined total of over 250 conventions, trade shows, organizations, and colleges—including GAMA, Mensa Colorado, and UCLA.

When he isn't working on the next book he can be found practicing martial arts, playing chess, drinking Scotch or IPA, or fighting with swords.

Jim Butcher

Jim Butcher is the author of the Dresden Files, the Codex Alera, and a new steampunk series, the Cinder Spires. His resume includes a laundry list of skills which were useful a couple of centuries ago, and he plays guitar quite badly. An avid gamer, he plays tabletop games in varying systems, a variety of video games on PC and console, and LARPs whenever he can make time for it. Jim currently resides mostly inside his own head, but his head can generally be found in his home town of Independence, Missouri.

Jim goes by the moniker Longshot in a number of online locales. He came by this name in the early 1990s when he decided he would become a published author. Usually only three in a thousand who make such an attempt actually manage to become published; of those, only one in ten make enough money to call it a living. The sale of a second series was the breakthrough that let him beat the long odds against attaining a career as a novelist.

All the same, he refuses to change his nickname.